Julia's Story

BOOK 1
IN THE BELLEVILLE FAMILY SERIES

ABOUT THE AUTHOR

Judith Masters, writing as J Mary Masters, was born in Rockhampton, Queensland, Australia in the 1950s, the youngest of four children. She is married to Peter.

For more than twenty years, she was involved in the magazine publishing industry in Australia as a senior executive while all the time looking to find the time to fulfil her ultimate ambition to be a writer of fiction. Having now given up full time work, writing is her principal activity.

Much of the setting for the story of the Belleville family is fictionalised but knowledgeable readers will recognise real places, particularly in Queensland, and real historical events that have made their way into the background of the story. The characters and storyline are entirely fictional.

You can set up a conversation with the author online
Web	www.jmarymasters.com
Blog	jmarymasters.blog
Facebook	judithmmasters
Instagram	jmarymasters

Julia's Story

J MARY MASTERS

BOOK 1 IN THE BELLEVILLE FAMILY SERIES

FIRST PUBLISHED AS
THE HOUSE OF SECRETS: JULIA'S STORY

WWW.PMABOOKS.COM

Cover design by J D Smith Design
www.jdsmith-design.co.uk

Revised editions 2016, 2019
Updated 2023, 2024

PUBLISHED BY

PMA Books

A division of Peter Masters & Associates, ABN 72 172 119 877

111/1 Halcyon Way, Bli Bli Qld 4560, Australia

www.pmabooks.com

Tel 0488 224 929

Email enquiries@pmabooks.com

To my dear husband Peter,
to my dear brother Marshall,
to my dear sisters Deidre and Beverley
and to those who believed

Cast of characters

AUSTRALIA

BELLEVILLE FAMILY (Prior Park)
Francis Belleville	Father
Elizabeth Belleville	Mother
Richard Belleville	Son
William Belleville	Son
Julia Belleville	Daughter

Jean Dalrymple	Elizabeth's cousin (Melbourne)

Mrs Duffy	Housekeeper, Prior Park
Charles Brockman	Manager, Prior Park
Muriel McGovern	(Brisbane)

FITZROY FAMILY (Mayfield Downs)
Jack Fitzroy	Father
Amelia Fitzroy	Mother
James Fitzroy	Son
Alice Fitzroy	Daughter

Mrs Fry	Housekeeper

WARNER FAMILY (Armoobilla)
Tom Warner	Son
Rebecca Warner	Daughter
Jane Saville	Governess to Rebecca

MANNING FAMILY (Venus Downs)
Stephen Manning	Husband
Margaret Manning	Wife (sister to Jack Fitzroy)

OTHERS
Nathaniel Dodds	Family solicitor
Hospital matron	Maureen Jones

ENGLAND

CAVENDISH FAMILY (Haldon Hall)
Lady Marina Cavendish	Mother, daughter of an Earl
Sir Anthony Cavendish	Father, a Baronet
Catherine Cavendish	Only daughter
John Bertram	nephew to Lady Marina

USA

Captain Philippe Duval	US Army doctor

CHAPTER 1: THE SECRETS BEGIN

TO UNRAVEL THE SECRETS of Prior Park and its inhabitants, we must find a moment in time at which to begin the story. The time to begin is when Elizabeth Belleville's children are reaching adulthood.

The year is 1942. It is a warm day in late March, almost the end of summer in the southern hemisphere, although it hardly seems like it to Elizabeth Belleville who sits at her small, highly polished desk addressing envelopes in her elegant sloping handwriting, her task hampered by the perspiration that trickles down the hollow of her right palm.

She muses almost aloud that the first signs of spring would be appearing in Europe. She imagines a bluebell wood, the tiny fragile flowers merging into a mass of green and blue among sunlit trees. She does not imagine an England fighting for its very survival, where everything is rationed and life is grim and for many, futureless.

At this point in the story, Elizabeth Belleville has no anxiety at all for the fate of the northern hemisphere beyond the most casual interest in the war raging across Europe, which she frets about only because it has thwarted her plans for a grand tour to show her daughter the sophisticated delights of civilised society so lacking, she frequently complains, in their own immediate neighbourhood.

Yet, despite her deep misgivings about her immediate neighbours, Elizabeth Belleville has invited them all, with one exception, to her daughter Julia's eighteenth birthday party. The appointed date for the big event is just two weeks away.

Up until this point, it's true to say that the inhabitants of Prior Park have almost ignored the war in Europe, or so it was thought. It had little direct impact on their lives. It was the menace in the Pacific that drew most of their attention. Of course the men of the household read avidly about the war in Europe in the local newspaper but the reports were already at least a week out of date and the action far away. It was a topic that was hardly discussed at all, unlike the Japanese threat, which seemed real and imminent.

Elizabeth Belleville had been seated at her desk for more than an hour before she finally put down her pen, sealed the last of the envelopes and gathered the invitations together.

She walked briskly downstairs to the front door, just in time to intercept her husband Francis walking across the driveway. Francis was deep in conversation with the Prior Park estate manager, Charles Brockman.

Charles was taller than Francis and she noticed, for the first time, how he outpaced her husband with his long, purposeful stride. Both men were dressed for riding, their horses tethered in the paddock just beyond the garden.

She waved to catch their attention.

'Will anyone be going into town later?' she enquired expectantly. 'The invitations must be posted.'

She held the envelopes aloft to make her point.

The two men stopped but it was Charles Brockman who spoke, first raising his hat in a polite gesture she took for granted.

'I'll call for them later, Mrs Belleville,' he said. 'Before I go, I promise.'

'Thank you, Charles. I'd appreciate it.'

Her husband said nothing but raised his hand in a half salute.

Elizabeth Belleville remained standing at the front door, watching the two men as they strode towards to the horses. She looked critically at her husband.

For the first time, she thought her husband wore all of his fifty-five years on his once handsome face. At that distance she couldn't see the small red spider veins that had sprung a faint web across his cheeks but there was nonetheless a hint of dissolution about his face even observed from afar; she had noticed recently how his fair hair had thinned; his once trim figure had spread so that his middle shirt buttons strained across his stomach, although in reality it was barely discernible. He was, on any day, as on this one, immaculately dressed.

On the little finger of his left hand, although she couldn't see it at a distance but she was sure it was there, he wore a heavy gold signet ring that had once belonged to his father. It bore the Belleville family crest with its intricate mediaeval scrolls and upright sword of honour. The crest had been commissioned by his father but everyone who saw it assumed the distinction went back generations into their European past and she did not dispute the assumption.

For a few minutes, she stood there at the top of steps, thinking how much had been expected of her husband and how little, in reality, he had delivered.

How could she know that the local gossips said much the same as she was thinking, because the gossip did not reach her.

Had she heard the local people speak of him, she would have been surprised at how much he was admired despite his tendency to drink too much and 'reap the fruits' of his father's endeavours and his mother's inheritance, rather than his own efforts, as the idle chatter agreed. There was a resigned acceptance of these facts among those who knew him, well or otherwise.

'Never made a shilling himself' was a popular refrain. But it was from envy that they spoke for they would all have been happy to swap places with him, except, as one or two pointed out, for the necessity of being married to Elizabeth Belleville.

Elizabeth of course knew the Belleville story well. Francis had told her that his father had worked hard and prospered in the gold boom of the nineteenth century, turning gold profits to land acquisition.

New money was all there was in a new country. They both agreed with that sentiment. There were no 'old families' only successful families who laid claim to the same refinements the old families had taken for granted in the old country, and, yes, they harboured the same ambitions through marriage.

Marry one fortune to another and you built a bigger fortune. With a fortune, you could buy power. It was a simple plan that Francis's father Louis had employed in seeking a match for his only son, just as he had done himself by marrying the pretty but insipid heiress Adeline Prior, Francis's mother.

From his mother, Francis had inherited a handsome legacy – Prior Park – to add to the Belleville inheritance but he had inherited too her weaknesses. In her, these weaknesses of character were harmless if somewhat irritating but in him they were devastating.

Where his father's business judgement had been unwavering, Elizabeth mused, his judgement was almost always found wanting. They had argued or rather she had argued and he had humoured her. In the end, she had settled for knowing that his decisions, when he made them, were almost invariably wrong or misguided and that he would always fall prey to the flattery of sharp men for whom she knew he was an easy target. But he would not listen to her so in the end she gave up trying.

All this Elizabeth knew and it regularly played across her mind. How much of the Belleville fortune remained she could only guess at. Money, never once a topic of conversation early in their marriage, had started to become central in their lives, but he would not – or could not – tell her why.

As her daughter approached her eighteenth birthday, Elizabeth began to wonder what lay in store for her only daughter. Would she fall prey to fortune seekers too? Or would she make a better choice than her mother?

Julia doted on her father but did she see his shortcomings? Elizabeth did not know and could not ask. She was not yet ready to disillusion the girl.

She remembered how the chill breeze had caught her veil on her wedding day nearly twenty-five years ago; she had been just twenty years old; Francis ten years older. In a year or two, that could be Julia. It seemed improbable to Elizabeth, who thought of her daughter still as a child.

She sighed quietly and walked back into the house as the two men rode off. The pile of invitations lay neatly stacked on the hall table. She was sure Charles Brockman would not forget. On him, she knew she could depend without question.

Just a few miles from Prior Park, another woman appeared at least to be more satisfied with her life although she commanded much less than Elizabeth Belleville. Jane Saville's only responsibility was her young charge, Rebecca Warner, who was responding well to the lessons she set for her and was doing her study with a dedication that surprised Jane.

The girl had been delighted at the decision to hire a governess, instead of sending her back to boarding school, following the sudden deaths of both parents. Jane in turn responded to the girl's open sunny nature and natural intelligence. She became less teacher and more older sister. The arrangement suited them both.

During this particular week, Jane had driven into the nearby town several times in spite of the petrol rationing. She was in daily anticipation of receiving a parcel of books and materials she had ordered for Rebecca's tuition but it seemed she was to be frustrated on each occasion for there were no parcels waiting for her at the post office.

It was the war, they said. Everything was in short supply. It seemed to be the excuse for every shortage and every failure now.

She was annoyed but there was little she could do. To save her another wasted trip, they promised to telephone when the parcel arrived. With this she had to be satisfied.

Enjoying the break in her daily routine and with an hour or so to spare on her return journey, it was an unaccustomed impulse that made her stop at the river crossing several miles from the Warner property. She was in no particular hurry to get home. She did not look forward to the rest of the drive. It was only a few miles but the road was badly rutted from the summer storms and no one had been along to make repairs.

The war. That was all they said. Can't spare the machinery or the men to do it.

Jane had been sitting out of sight of the road down an embankment on a grassy patch, above the largest of the waterholes, for only a few minutes. A stillness settled about her as she stretched out and enjoyed the luxury of contemplating nothing very much in particular, except the pleasure of indolence in the shade.

With her eyes half closed, she vaguely became aware that she was no longer alone. Momentarily she was startled but she soon regained her composure.

'Richard, what are you doing here? I thought you were away? I didn't hear you pull up.'

Without invitation, Richard Belleville dropped down beside her.

'I haven't been home yet. I just got back. I'd hoped to see you. It's lucky I saw your car. What are you doing here?'

'I've been into town. I'd ordered some books but they haven't arrived yet. They tell me paper is in short supply. I'm tired of this war. Everything is for the war,' she answered, before turning the same question to him.

'It's good to see you,' Richard said, ignoring her question.

But she could tell immediately that he was bursting to impart some important news to her.

They were now sitting very close together. His fingers caressed the side of her cheek, but she pulled away from him, to look at his face, her senses now fully alert.

He almost blurted it out. She could sense his excitement even as he said the words.

'I'm joining up, Jane.'

'What? You can't be serious. You never mentioned you had plans to do this? When did you do this. What does it mean for us?'

She moved further away from him. Her face immediately creased into a frown. Something moved in the grass beside her but she took no notice.

He didn't answer immediately. He was trying to gauge her reaction first.

'When? When are you joining up?'

Finally, knowing that he could delay the answer no longer, he said: 'I leave on Tuesday. I have to get south to Sydney by Saturday.'

There was so little information coming from him. It came in fits and starts because he didn't know how to say it to her.

'Why Sydney? Surely there are training camps hereabouts?'

It was an obvious question which he had known would be asked. Anticipating the question was one thing; it was quite another to give her the answer, an answer he knew she would not want to hear.

'I'm going to Canada.' He almost blurted it out.

He waited for her response. For what seemed like minutes, there was absolute silence between them.

'Canada? Why Canada?' was all she could find to say. It didn't make sense. There was no war in Canada.

She shielded her eyes from the glare with her hand. He'd noticed an almost imperceptible tremor in her voice.

'I've decided I want to be a pilot. They're doing air crew training for the air force in Canada. A lot of our fellows are already flying missions out of England. It takes about nine months of training, then I hope to be posted to a squadron in England.'

In the way he spoke, so matter of fact, it all sounded like a great adventure for spirited young men keen to see the world. She sensed it was a practised speech that attempted to hide the true facts.

He was embarking on perhaps the most dangerous undertaking of the war that raged across Europe and the Pacific: flying missions from England through the Ruhr Valley of Germany to inflict as much damage as possible on the German war effort. That he thought she might not know the danger he would face seemed disingenuous, even to his ears.

'I thought you'd be staying here now you've finished university. You never said anything about leaving.'

Her eyes filled with tears; her accusing words were scarcely audible.

To her, his explanation sounded very matter of fact, with barely a hint of concern for his own safety or the years of separation that could stretch in front of them.

Involuntarily, she stiffened as his hand touched her arm.

This news, he knew, was being received as badly as he feared it might yet it couldn't dampen his enthusiasm for his decision nor could it dampen his need for her.

'I want you to understand; this doesn't change anything between us. I still want to marry you but I must do this. It's my duty, don't you see? And I know I'll be a good pilot.'

For just a moment, she couldn't speak. She couldn't look at him. It was a shock. Worse still, she was angry and confused that he hadn't attempted to soften the news nor to consult her in advance about his decision.

'So that's that, then,' she said. 'No more to be said. There is no point in saying 'don't go' because you are going, regardless of what I say, aren't you?'

She turned her face towards him but he couldn't meet her eyes just then. He couldn't lie outright but he didn't want to disappoint her. He didn't want to make it sound like an either/or choice although he knew it was. He was going and that was that but not because he needed her less but because he felt the demands of loyalty to his country more.

He had tried to soften the blow but he had really only ended up sounding defensive, as if he should apologise for wanting to go.

'There are plenty of couples who are separated by the war. We won't be the first. I have to do my bit, don't you see that? I do love you, you know that, don't you?'

She didn't answer him directly. She wasn't sure of her own feelings now except, in the depths of her being, she felt the return of an aching emptiness that their time together in the past few months had filled.

She was older than him, although not by much. It was the disparity in their circumstances that had caused them to keep their developing relationship secret. Now the hopes and dreams that she had begun to nurture were over. Gone, probably forever, she thought. Just then, as she sat a grass beside, it seemed a hard fact to grasp.

'So that's why you went to Brisbane?' she said, changing tack. 'To join up?'

Her voice was still very quiet but a hint of bitterness was creeping in as she began to realise the extent of his deception. To his mind, he had deceived her because he had wanted to avoid a confrontation. To her, it seemed as if she was less important in his life than he had led her to believe. At the point where there was a big decision to be made, he had done it alone and not considered her at all.

'Yes. And you're the first person I've told, apart from the family lawyer.'

'So your mother doesn't know?'

He shook his head.

For a few seconds they were both silent, each contemplating the likely effect of the news on Elizabeth Belleville. Of her three children, Elizabeth Belleville doted on her first-born, Richard.

Almost all her motherly attentions had been focused on his well-being and his comfort, although she would have hotly disputed any suggestion that she had done so at the expense of the less well favoured William, her second son, or her daughter Julia.

Jane, at least, had some insight into how the news would be received.

'She won't be happy, Richard. I can tell you that for certain. She will be very, very upset.'

He smiled, acknowledging the truth of what she said, but confident that in the end, he could charm his mother into acceptance, as he always done in the past.

'I know. I know. But I have to tell her sooner rather than later. I can't just take off next week and leave a note on my pillow.'

'Will I see you again before you go?'

'I hope so,' was all he would say.

He jumped up quickly from the riverbank and held his hand out to help her up. He tried to take her in his arms but she was still angry with him so he kissed her on the cheek and held the car door open for her.

He raised his hand to wave goodbye but all she could see, through her tears, was a cloud of dust.

A short while later, Elizabeth Belleville heard the familiar sound of a car engine, which was quickly followed by the unmistakeable sound of the gravel of the driveway being scattered beneath the wheels of Richard's hard-driven Buick.

She peered out of the window of her small upstairs sitting room and raised an unseen hand in greeting to her elder son just as he slammed the door of the car, shaking some of the dust from the black bodywork. It would likely settle back just as quickly.

She noticed with satisfaction that he was well dressed although, on a second glance, she thought there was something careless about his appearance today. His light brown hair fell across his forehead giving him a rakish charm that matched his intense blue eyes. He'll break some hearts, she thought, if he hasn't already.

He had been expected by the household since early morning, so the fact that he did not arrive home until three o'clock excited some eager questioning from his mother.

She reached the bottom of the stairs just as he entered the hallway.

'Richard, we expected you earlier. How was your journey?'

'It went well, thank you, Mother.'

He bent to kiss her cheek in the hope that his short almost curt answer would suffice for now.

'How is everything here?' he asked, casually.

It was more a rhetorical question than one to which he expected an answer but she started to answer it any way.

'It's much the same as when you left. I've done the invitations for your sister's birthday party. But more importantly how did you get on in Brisbane? You said you had some business there, but when I asked your father what it could be, he didn't seem to know or at least he wasn't telling me.'

The words hung in the air between mother and son. He could sense his mother's rising curiosity but he was determined to head off her questions.

'You know, I've never seen Brisbane like it. It's really a city at war and likely to be more so before the year is out with the war in the Pacific becoming more intense.'

'Do you think we are likely to be threatened here?' she asked.

There was no panic in her voice, only incredulity. It required a stretch of the imagination she did not possess to visualise Japanese domination of the vast Australian mainland.

'Who knows,' he shrugged.

'I see General MacArthur has arrived in Australia to take charge, so that must be a good thing.'

His mother was silent waiting for him to say more but he remained silent too.

Francis, making a feeble attempt to brush the dust and dirt

from his riding clothes, strode into the hallway and greeted his son enthusiastically.

'So, what did you get up to in Brisbane, son? Come in and tell us all about it.'

There was a hollow falseness to the cheeriness that neither father nor son acknowledged.

That Francis was reluctant to vigorously criticise his elder son's decision to use scarce petrol resources on a trip of unknown purpose was as much a concern for his wife's certain rebuke as for the futility of expressing the opinion.

Francis had long since given up attempting to exert any authority over his twenty-two year old heir. There was never a time he could recall when his wife had sided with him on any issue that had arisen regarding their first son, for Elizabeth Belleville had very early on chosen sides. For Richard's part, he had come to understand that the father he idolised as a boy was not a man he could admire in adulthood.

They stood together awkwardly for a few moments.

Richard knew instinctively that his mother would not be easily sidetracked. He wondered if she suspected something but she gave no hint of it in her reply.

'Come in and tell us about your trip. It's a long drive. You must be tired.'

'A bit,' he conceded. 'It is a long way.'

As the three of them gathered in the drawing room and Elizabeth Belleville ordered tea, Francis Belleville was about to discover to his surprise there were matters on which both he and his wife were in agreement with regard to their elder son.

Under the determined gaze of his parents, Richard had at first faltered but it wasn't long before the whole truth emerged.

Elizabeth Belleville, quite unused to the idea of anyone in the household making a decision that she had not first endorsed, was almost rendered speechless at the prospect of her elder son undertaking such a dangerous mission so needlessly.

She could not understand any reason why someone with a protected occupation would volunteer to put themselves in harm's way half way around the world. That was for other sons to do, not hers, and she said as much.

But that was not his only news. It was the news of his intended marriage that cemented the opposition of both parents but they were to discover that their opposition to his plans were futile.

In the days and months ahead, they would not dare speak the unspeakable but there were to be many times, when days turned to weeks without news of him, that they each began to think the unthinkable.

But as much as she prayed for the safe return of her son, Elizabeth Belleville could not sanction the marriage he proposed for his return. On this subject she was absolutely fixed in her mind. It was, she insisted, a secret they must keep until he returned.

He agreed, reluctantly, that there would be no announcement of an engagement. On that point he was eventually forced to yield but the relationship between son and parents remained tense as the date of his departure approached.

CHAPTER 2: APRIL 1942

IT SEEMED THAT EVERYONE at Prior Park heaved a sigh of relief when Easter Saturday, the day of Julia's birthday party, dawned bright and hot with the expectation that the heat of the day would give way to a perfect warm evening.

As the sun headed towards the distant horizon, a constant stream of cars snaked their way up the Prior Park driveway towards the house, which was already ablaze with lights. It stood out like a beacon against the swiftly encroaching darkness of the surrounding countryside.

Margaret and Stephen Manning were the first to arrive. A small wiry woman with a plain honest face, Margaret Manning was nevertheless careful of her appearance on this particular night. She motioned to her husband to wait while she dabbed with her white lace handkerchief at her black suede shoes in a futile effort to rid them of a fine film of dust before timidly ringing the front door bell. She smoothed down the skirt of her beaded midnight blue dress, new for the occasion, while they waited for the door to be opened.

Stephen Manning looked ill at ease in a suit he rarely wore. His hands were roughened by years of manual labour. The side of his face bore the fading scar of an axe head that had broken away from its handle and hit him a glancing blow. He had taken himself off to the local hospital and been stitched up, so local gossips said, and been back to the hard work of mending fences and building stockyards the next day.

They seemed an ill-matched pair; she, placid but refined by country standards; he, a local stockman made good with his marriage to Margaret Fitzroy. The lack of offspring did not seem to trouble either of them. It had not happened so they went about their daily lives following the familiar patterns of the past twenty years. There were no cross words between them because they rarely exchanged any words at all, apart from the mundane conversation that had become part of their day to day living.

The Prior Park housekeeper Mrs Duffy opened the door to greet them and the orderly queue of people who had fallen in behind them. She knew them all by name, just as they knew her.

'Come in, come in. Mr and Mrs Belleville are in the drawing room. Please go through.'

The sound of music could already be heard coming from the back garden where workmen had laboured most of the day to erect a temporary dance floor.

'They haven't spared any expense,' Margaret whispered to her husband who merely grunted at the revelation.

She could see the brightly coloured lights swaying in the slight breeze as she looked along the hallway towards the open back door.

Quickly, this scene was lost to her view and she found herself being ushered into a beautifully furnished room by Francis Belleville who had kissed her awkwardly on the cheek.

'Welcome, we're so pleased you could come.'

She was pleased Elizabeth Belleville hadn't followed her husband's enthusiastic welcome.

Before she could protest, a delicate glass was thrust into her hands. She didn't know what was in it so she sipped it cautiously. It wasn't a bad taste, she decided. Her husband's eyes lit up at the tall glass of beer which he was about to down in one thirsty gulp before he caught the warning look in his wife's careful eyes.

'I don't see the young lady about,' Stephen Manning said in whispered undertones to his wife.

Margaret said nothing but nodded her agreement.

'I've got lots to tell you, Margaret, I haven't seen you for so long.'

The voice came from behind her and this time she was happy to be embraced. Amelia Fitzroy could have been her sister, the likeness between the two was so often remarked, but in fact, Amelia was her sister-in-law.

The fact that Margaret's brother Jack continued to be annoyed at his parents' decision to give his sister part of the property intended for him in no way troubled the two women, who would seek each other's company on every occasion.

The two men were left to their own devices as the women headed for two comfortable chairs in the corner of the drawing room. With their backs to the wall and cosily seated together, they could observe all the comings and goings and gossip unseen.

'Stephen was just saying that Julia doesn't seem to be down yet,' Margaret ventured.

'No, I noticed that too. You'd think she would be standing alongside her mother. I thought Elizabeth looked a bit annoyed, although she hid it well. Mind you, she could still be brooding over the row they had with Richard. He's gone you know.'

Margaret's eyes widened at this revelation.

'Gone. Gone where?'

'Well, it's a long story,' Amelia said, as if its length meant it would take too long to tell.

Margaret drew closer to her.

'You must tell me all about it. I haven't heard anything at all.'

Amelia needed little encouragement as her eager listener leaned ever closer to the eager storyteller to catch every word.

Twice within half an hour, Julia had stepped out of her bedroom, caught sight of herself in the ornately framed mirror at the top of the stairs and, immediately dissatisfied, returned to her wardrobe to reconsider her choice.

Her first choice had been a black crepe de chine dress which, according to her dressing-table mirror, bestowed a certain sophistication on her appearance. It gave her an air of elegance and maturity. A necklace of pure jet had completed the picture but now she was unsure. Did it make her look too old? Did it make her look like a widow rather than a young woman emerging into society?

She knew she was expected in the drawing room to stand alongside her parents to greet her guests. In fact she was overdue in the drawing room and she knew they would not be pleased at her lack of punctuality but still she found time to retreat to her bedroom and abandon the black dress in a pile on the floor.

She stood in her high heels and underwear surveying the possibilities, hardly mindful of the passing minutes. She scanned the few evening dresses hanging in her wardrobe and despaired that her options were, after all, limited. The war had seen to that. Of the few choices she drew out a figure-hugging bias-cut silk dress in the palest blue. Her mother had yielded to this addition to her wardrobe only after much persuasion. 'It is too risqué for a young girl,' she had said at the time. But Julia stood her ground and the pale blue silk had been acquired.

Late as she was, she found time as she was about to head downstairs, to return to the dressing table and apply her perfume which she had forgotten in the anxiety of choosing the right dress.

Almost as an afterthought, she added a diamond pendant and earrings, a gift for her eighteenth birthday from her parents. This time the mirror at the top of the stairs reflected back a totally different vision, one with which she felt vaguely satisfied.

'Do I really know all these people?' Julia whispered to her mother.

She had already been standing alongside her parents for half an hour, politely thanking each guest in turn for coming and for their good wishes. To her, it seemed quite long enough.

Her mother ignored the question entirely. The rooms set aside for the occasion – the drawing room and the dining room – were filling up and, in spite of herself, Elizabeth felt a quiet sense of satisfaction as she glanced around at her guests. A quick knowing inspection of the assembled throng had reassured her that most of the women wore new frocks for the occasion.

'You should be gratified, child, that so many people have come along,' Elizabeth said to her daughter, who looked as if she was about to relinquish her place in the receiving line.

Julia bristled at the notion she was still a child but said nothing and continued to greet newcomers, until her mother was satisfied that everyone who was coming had, indeed, arrived.

In one corner of the room, Julia noticed Amelia Fitzroy and Margaret Manning deep in animated conversation but she thought little of it. The gossip of middle-aged women had yet to mean anything to her at all, and she thought no more about it.

She certainly did not overhear Amelia declaring that Julia's elder brother Richard had left the household after a terrible argument with his parents.

'I understand there was a frightful row,' said Amelia, who could not hide a small sense of satisfaction that she knew something that was not yet general knowledge, although she supposed it would not be long.

'Really? What about? What have you heard about it, Amelia?'

'Mrs Fry, my housekeeper, is very friendly with Mrs Duffy, the housekeeper here. It seems Richard arrived home from Brisbane two weeks ago and announced he was joining up.'

Margaret absorbed this information but she sensed that Amelia was holding something back.

'Strange. Elizabeth didn't mention it at all at the Red Cross meeting this week,' Margaret mused.

'You weren't there, of course. There was certainly no gossip that I heard there. Everything was much as usual.'

Amelia, uncharacteristically, was enjoying the fleeting pleasure of having information to share that was not widely known. She had not ever known herself to be in such a situation before and she took pleasure in it. She only wished for a wider audience with which to share the news, for there was much more to tell.

'Mrs Fry says that Mrs Duffy told her that the argument was not just about him joining up; it was that he has signed up for air crew training in Canada and will eventually end up in England, flying with the RAF, possibly bombing Germany. His mother was beside herself. According to Mrs Duffy, the raised voices could be heard all over the house. Once they knew they couldn't change his mind, Elizabeth went upstairs to her bedroom in a huff; his father slammed the door of his study and wasn't seen for hours. She said Richard left on the mail train two days afterwards and not a word has been spoken about him since, not that she has heard anyway.'

Margaret sat back in her chair. There was a small smile of satisfaction on Amelia's face. The rumours, she knew, were already spreading like wildfire but the local gossip, not unusually, had been not entirely accurate, which probably accounted for the lack of direct enquiry as to Richard's absence at his sister's party. But Amelia was far from finished. The best, it seemed, was yet to come.

'Mrs Duffy apparently also hinted that he had announced his plans to marry on his return, but she did not know who the girl was that he mentioned. Whoever she is, she isn't part of Elizabeth Belleville's plans, that I can tell you.'

Amelia warmed to her theme, her face flushed with the excitement of revealing such delicious gossip against a woman who regarded them all with an air of disdain.

'According to what I was told, this news inflamed the argument even further. I have really no idea who the girl is. I can't think of anyone around here. I would know if it was Alice.'

The two women sat together in silence to digest the import of this most astonishing of news.

Amelia Fitzroy had for some years nursed the happy but unfulfilled prospect of their proximity to the Belleville house leading to an inevitable joining of their houses. Her daughter Alice she did not claim as a beauty but pretty enough, she thought, to engage the elder son of the house so the news that Richard's heart was engaged elsewhere had been a devastating blow to her plans but there was always William, she thought.

Better the second son than none at all, and perhaps better him altogether if the split between Richard and his parents was irrevocable. She did not say this to Margaret preferring to keep her matchmaking intrigue entirely to herself.

For once in his life, Francis Belleville was cautious about the amount of whisky he was drinking. He recalled, not without embarrassment, the celebrations for his son Richard's twenty-first birthday. The night had gone well, until he rose to propose a toast to his son with words he barely recalled now. The telltale slurring of his words had sent a murmur of disapproval through the crowd of guests.

What he could recall most vividly was the look of contempt in his son's eyes. He would not repeat that performance, he promised himself. So for once the whisky decanter remained largely untouched.

He watched with a mixture of fatherly pride and expectation as James Fitzroy led Julia through the house to the back garden and on to the makeshift dance floor.

'You look beautiful tonight, Julia. The dress really suits you. You look very grown up.'

At twenty-two James Fitzroy was just a month or so younger than Julia's absent brother. The rough edges of his manners had been smoothed by the years away at school. There had been talk of an army career but his father's poor health had demanded he return to help run and then take over Mayfield Downs.

Where his father was known for his quick temper, reports of

the son had been more favourable. He was not conventionally handsome in the way Richard was but his presence turned the heads of young women nonetheless. His dark hair, dark eyes and engaging smile were much in his favour; his easy manners charmed those he took the trouble to impress.

Suddenly, Julia stumbled and found herself more intimately engaged with James Fitzroy than she had expected. He for one was not about to miss the opportunity of holding such an exquisite creature more tightly in his arms.

'I'm sorry,' she said, struggling to regain her footing. 'There must have been a nail left up in the boards.'

'No need to apologise, Julia, this is no hardship, I assure you.'

She blushed at the inference of his words and then more so at his reluctance to release her.

'I'm all right now, I won't fall,' she said, pushing him away.

He had rather hoped that he could go on holding her tightly and feeling her breasts against his chest, but he eased his grip on her slightly as she recovered her balance.

'I don't remember when I last saw you. It might have been two years ago when you were home from school.'

'Probably,' she said, a little ungraciously.

'Are you home for good now?'

'Yes, unfortunately with the war on, mother and I can't take the trip to Europe she had promised me at the end of school. I hate this beastly war. It spoils everything.'

'Yes, it's terrible. So many young men being killed too,' he said, as if to rebuke her for her selfish concerns.

'So you're not joining up?' Julia asked, trying to counter the impression that she was alone in her selfishness.

'No, I'm exempted because of my occupation and my father's ill health. There would be no one to run the property if I left. Is it true that Richard has joined up?'

His statement was matter of fact but he did not express false regret at his inability to join up.

'Yes. He's gone. I'm so disappointed he's not here for my birthday party. Mother and father are furious with him. They feel he could have been exempted too but he said we have enough help with the cattle to be able to spare him. It will be nearly a year before he's in the thick of things but we're all very worried about him.'

He was on the point of asking if there had been an argument about it and was it true that Richard had announced plans to marry but, just then, the music ended and the opportunity was lost.

'We must do this again,' James said, his arm lingering around her waist.

Julia smiled but it was not meant to be the smile of encouragement he took it to be.

His eyes travelled deliberately over her figure. She blushed at the suggestiveness of his look. Had she known his thoughts, she would have blushed all the more at his silent vow to be the first to enjoy the delights of her maturing body. It was a pleasure he promised himself at some future date.

While Julia danced with James Fitzroy, his sister Alice Fitzroy sat alone on a chair, half hidden in the shadows, but with an excellent view of the dancers.

There were eight couples on the dance floor but one couple in particular had attracted her attention.

A slow smile had crept over her face as she watched her brother and Julia Belleville. She had seen her brother's fleeting look of surprise and then pleasure when Julia greeted him earlier in the evening. She hadn't failed to notice his desire to hold Julia more closely to him during their dance than decorum decreed. Not much escaped Alice's attention and this certainly had not. Her brother, she knew, was not used to having his desires thwarted.

Like Richard Belleville, he was the son and heir and the favoured child at home. That a small hint of arrogance had begun to creep into his character was no surprise at all. The surprise in fact was that it had not appeared earlier.

Although not as rich as the Bellevilles, the Fitzroys could lay claim to an ancestry that had its roots in the English aristocracy, a fact that hardly mattered at all to James and Alice, but mattered a great deal to their mother Amelia, although no one had bothered to tell her that the surname had once been reserved for the bastard sons of a king.

Over the years, they had met the Belleville family from time to time, but no real closeness had grown up between them, despite her mother's best efforts and despite their similarity in ages.

Alice was just nine months older than Julia. The boys had attended a different school from James. Alice had had to be satisfied with the local grammar school whereas Julia had been sent away to school in Sydney, so their paths crossed less and less as they grew to adulthood.

Julia's party had been a welcome opportunity for them to renew their tenuous childhood friendships.

Julia's younger brother William Belleville was now also enjoying the night's festivities.

At first, he was surprised by the lack of enquiry about his brother Richard and then later, realising that the rift between his parents and Richard might go deeper and last longer than he had imagined, he felt a warm surge of reassurance that his position in the family was already enhanced by his brother's abrupt departure.

Next month, he would turn twenty and his father had, during the evening, introduced him to quite a number of leading men from the town.

He was quietly pleased with the introductions his father had made, and the warmth of the greetings.

'I'd like you to meet my son William,' his father Francis had said any number of times.

This gratified William more than he cared to admit. He had

never before been introduced first. There had always been the words 'meet my son Richard' preceding any introduction of himself. But not now.

He had not been at home when Richard had returned from Brisbane two weeks earlier but the tension in the house before Richard left two days later was of a kind he could not recall, even on the occasions when his father drank too much, which seemed to be more frequent in recent years.

His mother had never, not in his memory anyway, yielded to sentimental emotion so he was surprised at the animosity that existed between his parents and Richard prior to his departure.

William felt sure he had not been told the full story but he contented himself with the knowledge that now he was the only Belleville son being introduced to the important guests. It was an unexpected but not unwelcome elevation in status.

He did not wish his brother ill. Far from it; he just wished he was the elder son, the first born.

In this rather contented frame of mind, William went in search of a dance partner. He noticed Alice Fitzroy sitting by herself.

She wasn't the prettiest of the girls at the party, he mused, but then his sister was probably the prettiest and he wasn't going to dance with her.

In his current contented mood, he thought Miss Fitzroy would do very well indeed as a dance partner.

'Alice, how are you? You look very pretty tonight. Shall we dance?'

His approach lacked the charm of either her brother James or his brother Richard but she was flattered by William's approach and blushed prettily.

He had not waited for her reply in any case but held out his hand which she took a little awkwardly.

She could not shine in the company of Julia Belleville but in her own way, she was not unappealing.

Her slightly rounded face creased into a genuine smile. Her

light brown hair bobbed around her shoulders. She radiated a wholesomeness that added to her womanly appeal.

William found himself attracted to her, despite his untested expectation that he was immune to the charms of women.

After a short while, Alice, her confidence returning, put the question no one else had been brave enough to ask during the evening.

'Mother said she heard that Richard had left and that there was a family argument about it.'

She hadn't quite meant to blurt it out that way but now that it had been said, she couldn't back away from the question, which seemed to hang in the air between them, even as they made their uncertain way around the dance floor.

'You and your mother shouldn't listen to gossip, Alice. Mother and Dad were obviously upset that he signed up without telling them first. He's on his way to Canada you know. He's going to learn to fly and hopes to join an air force squadron in England. It's brave of him, you know.'

It was his first real defence of his brother's actions. His mother had predicted that the gossip about the row would spread like wildfire among their neighbours but it was the first time he had encountered a direct question about it.

He remembered his mother's words: 'It will be all over the countryside within a week,' she had said. 'I do not like being the subject of gossip. We should not have argued with him. We should have just let him go with our blessing.'

William had been given a brief summary of the argument by Richard before he had left, but his brother had only hinted at there being more than one topic at the centre of the argument and William hadn't pressed him at the time. By nature, he lacked curiosity, but now, curious or not, he was about to find out.

'Yes, William, he is brave, I don't doubt that but Mother doesn't gossip idly. She had a very good account of it from our housekeeper Mrs Fry. Mrs Fry said there was more to the argument than just

Richard signing up to go away. Apparently he said he was going to get married.'

If Alice hadn't quite meant to say as much, she wasn't going to admit it now. She felt that if she was to have any chance with William at all, she had to meet him on equal terms. She wasn't going to be intimidated by him, or by anyone.

William hadn't expected his conversation with Alice to head in this direction and he was tempted to leave her stranded on the dance floor, but his good manners overrode his desire to get away from this line of questioning. There was more to the argument between Richard and his parents, he knew that, but he hadn't been told what it was and he hadn't pressed anyone to find out more. Now it seemed other people knew more than he did and that was intolerable.

He didn't want to admit to Alice that he hadn't known because he felt that this would immediately undermine his new-found confidence in his elevated position in the family. If he wasn't in their confidence, then was he really as valued as he thought he was?

He was beginning to grow angry, but in fairness, he reasoned, it wasn't Alice's fault. She was capable of many things but she wasn't capable of the slyness or the underhand ways he had encountered in other young girls. Alice said pretty much what came into her head.

The fact that he didn't like what she said didn't alter the fact that he didn't know the full story and it appeared other people outside the family did. He was determined to find out.

To Alice, he gave a curt reply: 'I don't think there's much to that, Alice. As I said, you shouldn't listen to gossip. Most of it is made up by people who don't know a dammed thing.'

He was glad that just at that moment the music stopped and his father called everyone inside to propose a toast to his sister. He offered his arm to Alice and he escorted her inside but there was no further opportunity for her to question him.

As the guests gathered in the house, William noticed the youngest of the guests, Rebecca Warner, standing with her brother Tom, near the front of the group.

He knew both of them as neighbours but barely at all as friends. He supposed she was about sixteen. Her long reddish coloured hair, held in place by a childish ribbon, formed a mass of curls half way down her back. Of her governess, Jane Saville, whose appearance in the district had caused so much gossip, there was no sign at all.

He half suspected that his mother had not included her on the invitation.

On this occasion he came close to suspecting the truth as to why his mother had chosen to exclude Rebecca's governess from Julia's birthday party: her invitations did not include hired help, she would have said, if asked, although this ban did not extend to Charles Brockman who stood alongside Tom Warner.

What neither he nor his mother could have foreseen was that, in her decision to exclude Jane Saville, she had achieved far more than she could have ever hoped by this one simple action. Misread as a deliberate snub, the consequences for Richard were to be devastating.

As his father asked the assembled guests to charge their glasses to toast his daughter's eighteenth birthday, William quietly moved away from Alice's side ready to intercept his parents as they made their way from the drawing room to the hallway to begin fare-welling their guests.

He blocked their path at the doorway.

'Alice Fitzroy has just been telling me an interesting little story. She says the row with Richard was more than just about him going away. She says he told you he was going to get married when he came back. You never told me that. He never told me. I want to know the truth,' he demanded.

He was angry now but still he whispered the words taking care to see that no one else was within earshot.

Elizabeth Belleville was the first to recover her composure from the unexpectedly hostile questioning from her second son.

'William, we'll talk about this later, just not *now*.'

Her tone was decisive with such marked emphasis on the word *now* that he backed away, conscious that his interception of his parents had attracted some attention from their guests. He did not want to create another scene to add fuel to the gossip.

Instead, he headed towards the back of the house where the band had already loaded their gear into the van. He was grateful for the night air and the chance to get away from the crowd and think.

If Richard had announced he was going to get married, and none of them knew about it or knew that he was serious about a girl, then it all pointed to one conclusion: it was someone of whom his parents would not approve. That he needed to know more was certain.

Thinking back over his brother's past girlfriends had drawn a total and complete blank. Two of the girls were already married; the third had moved to New York with her parents. He could not recall his brother mentioning anyone recently.

It was no use; he would have to wait until he could talk privately with his parents, for there was no reliable answer that he could deduce himself.

More importantly, he needed to know just how things stood between his parents and Richard. Had this changed anything or was Richard still the favoured son and he the under-study to his older brother? This is what he needed to know most urgently. He would not rest until he knew the whole truth.

CHAPTER 3:

OCTOBER-NOVEMBER 1942

WILLIAM BELLEVILLE WAS PACING the floor and growing exasperated with each passing minute. His mood since his sister's birthday six months earlier had not improved much.

His efforts to get to the heart of the violent disagreement between his parents and his elder brother Richard had proved fruitless. However much he importuned his parents, they would say nothing beyond that which he already knew. Every scrap of gossip he put to them they denied.

He had since written a long letter to his brother but had, as yet, received no reply. He had not asked the direct question about his brother's marriage plans but by what he hoped were subtle means, he thought his brother might take him into his confidence.

So he was left to ponder and speculate, which did not come naturally to a young man of William's temperament. He preferred to deal with certainties. He sensed that his parents did not trust him with the secret and that only made matters worse.

'Finally, you are ready. Let's get going. I never thought you'd come down.'

He barely glanced in the direction of his sister as she came down the main stairs. She did not respond because she was used to his brusque ways. She simply shrugged her shoulders to show that his irritation was of no interest to her at all but he wasn't looking at her anyway, so the small gesture went unnoticed.

Outside in the driveway, the engine of the big Buick had been warming for a full ten minutes, more than strictly necessary, but then William was a much more careful custodian of the prized motor car than his brother had been.

In truth, Julia Belleville expected no gallantry from her brother. She knew he could be pleasant if he chose but he lacked the imagination of the romantic and a turn of phrase that could have pleased a young woman, even his sister, regularly failed to form in his mind.

Looking at him and his lack of charm, she understood why there were times in the past when William had resented his charming older brother. She had seen it. Even through a child's eyes it had been obvious so she could not fail to see it now.

'I think William secretly enjoys Richard not being here,' she had ventured to her mother in one of their rare conversations.

'I think he was tired of being compared unfavourably with him.'

Her mother's response had been predictable. She dismissed the suggestion with a sound that was not quite a word but conveyed her meaning nonetheless.

So Julia had said no more on the topic.

William pressed his foot heavily on the accelerator and the big car responded with a roar of its engine and a spinning of its wheels on the gravel driveway.

'I think we'll be late,' said William testily.

'It's an hour's drive at this time of day to Springfield.'

The poor country road demanded careful and slower driving than he would have liked.

Again, Julia shrugged dismissively.

'So what,' she said, 'I'm sure it's fashionable to be late, isn't it?'

'I hope we don't meet any Yank convoys on the road,' William said.

She hated the use of the slang term to describe Americans but she ignored it.

'Dad said that he'd been told that they've been forcing local drivers dangerously to the edge of the road because their trucks are so big,' he added.

His sister couldn't resist adding another warning as she sat alongside him.

'Never mind the Americans. You should see the lights of their vehicles. You'll need to be careful of kangaroos at this time of day,' she reminded him.

As if on cue, a wallaby bounded across the road several yards in front of them. It was off into the bush before William could react.

'See what I mean,' she said.

'No trouble. I saw it,' he said. 'I'm not like Richard. I'm a very careful driver.'

At the mention of Richard's name, Julia decided to quiz her brother on the reason for the argument between Richard and their parents.

Like her brother William, she too had quizzed her parents but found out nothing more for her trouble.

'I don't know anymore than you do,' he said. 'Mother says that they were angry at him joining up without telling them, but backstairs gossip apparently says there was more to it than that.

'I heard that he announced he was getting married when he came back. That would have been a big surprise to mother and father, I can tell you.'

Julia was secretly pleased at William's frankness and his willingness to discuss the matter with her. As the youngest in the family, she had been routinely excluded from knowing much about the family's business or the cause of the frequent stony silences between her parents.

'Really! He was getting married! Who to?'

He had assumed Julia would have heard the gossip too but apparently she had not.

'Nobody knows except mother and father and they're not

saying. Which leads me to conclude it was someone entirely un-suitable.'

'Unsuitable? What do you mean?' asked Julia, naively.

'Well, not of a good family. No money. Lower class. No property or suitable family,' he ventured. 'You do realise these things are important, don't you?'

He risked a sideways glance at his sister, concerned lest she have other ideas or not understand the expectations placed on them all.

'Does that matter now? In this day and age?'

William could see that she was about to become argumentative, so he didn't respond except to say that he thought his parents would even now be looking out for a suitable husband for her.

William did not hear her response. Just at that moment, he was jerked back to full alertness by a large American army truck being driven on the wrong side of the road.

With almost no time to react, William cursed and swung hard right on the Buick's steering wheel to avoid an almost certain collision. The big car lurched to the right and its wheels left a shower of gravel in their wake as the two vehicles passed with inches to spare.

With the sudden jerking movement, Julia slid sideways across the smooth leather seat towards the driver's side. Instinctively she put out her hand to steady herself, but she was too slow to prevent herself crashing sideways into the steering column.

'Blast it, when will they learn to drive on the left hand side of the road, instead of the right hand side,' was all William said, as he struggled to control the car.

He finally brought the car to a shuddering halt on the wrong side of the road with its wheels in the shallow ditch that ran the length of the roadway. Only then did he become aware that his sister had been hurt.

'Are you all right, Julia?'

His concern was immediate although his first thought had

been for the condition of the car, which on later inspection, had escaped largely unscathed, except for some scratches on the body-work and a slight dent in the front bumper bar.

Before William had a chance to do anything at all to help his sister, there was a tap on the passenger's window followed by the car door being yanked opened with some force.

Captain Philippe Duval did not waste time with introductions. His hands searched for Julia's pulse on her slender wrist and he began checking for vital signs until he was satisfied there were no life-threatening injuries and that she had simply been stunned when her head hit the hard edge of the steering wheel.

'Ma'am, can you hear me? Are you all right? Speak to me.'

He shook her gently, but reassuringly.

Julia groaned and struggled to sit upright. Her silk dress was torn and a small trickle of blood had begun to work its way slowly down the side of her face.

'It's my arm. My arm hurts,' she groaned.

Captain Duval gently eased her into a sitting position to examine her right arm, as best he could in the fading light.

'It could be broken—I'm not sure, I can't really tell here—it will need an x-ray to be sure one way or the other,' he said.

He gently wiped away the blood from her cheek.

Looking at William who was by this stage standing alongside the army medic, he said: 'You'd better get her to hospital.'

'I saw your car run off the side of the road as we passed you,' the American said, by way of explanation.

'I'm sorry. It's so hard for our drivers to get used to driving on the left, especially as the truck is left hand drive. I'm so sorry.'

He apologised again and introduced himself.

William, by this stage, was in no mood for explanations, reasonable or otherwise, or introductions.

'Bloody hell, you could have killed us,' he said. 'A truck that size would make mincemeat of any car. It's lucky I saw you at the last minute.'

'Please, get your wife to hospital. It's only another four or five miles – she needs attention,' Captain Duval said.

'I don't have a full medical kit with me. I can't do anymore here on the roadside,' he said apologetically.

The man's words broke through William's anger.

'Yes, I will. We'll go now. Thank you anyway, and by the way, she's not my wife, she's my sister, Julia. I'm William Belleville from Prior Park. You'll pass our place on this road.'

With that terse response, William slid back into the driver's seat and fired the Buick's big engine back to life. He cautiously eased the car out of the shallow ditch and back onto the roadway.

Captain Duval watched for a few minutes to make certain the car was safely on its way towards the hospital and then turned and walked back to the truck.

'I'm sorry, sir. I forgot about this being a left hand drive place. Are they all right?'

The driver expected to receive a dressing down but it was not forthcoming.

'Don't worry, corporal, so did I, so did I. Hopefully everything will be all right. I think the girl has a broken arm, nothing worse. Let's get going or we won't make camp by dark.'

He did not think it fair to reprimand the driver for he thought the blame was as much his as the driver's but he prayed that the young woman had suffered nothing worse than a broken arm for their lapse of concentration.

'She was a pretty girl from what I could see, sir,' the corporal said.

'Indeed, corporal. Now let's concentrate on the road. We don't want any more mishaps.'

They drove on in silence.

Within fifteen minutes of the accident, William was turning into the emergency entrance of the Springfield General Hospital. It was a large, well-equipped hospital situated high on the hill overlooking the city. In the distance you could see the river winding its way through the city centre.

William stood by helplessly as medical staff eased his sister out of the passenger seat and onto a waiting stretcher. He gave a quick summary of events, for which he received only a cursory acknowledgement. All attention was focused on his sister.

Julia held out her left hand to her brother in a small gesture of reassurance as she was wheeled through the emergency room doors.

'I'll be fine, William, I'm just a bit battered and bruised. They'll look after me but you should telephone mother to let her know what happened.'

And then she disappeared from view. There wasn't much more for him to do except provide his sister's details to the admissions nurse at the front desk and deliver the news to Prior Park.

News of Julia's injuries spread quickly. It was an event that was greatly exaggerated for each retelling such that her wellbeing became the subject of much consternation especially among the guests who had attended her birthday party six months previously.

The fact that she had remained in hospital a mere four days and thereafter bore little visible sign of her trauma, apart from the plaster on her arm and a cut already almost healed on her forehead, was little consolation to those who had heard the wildly exaggerated accounts of the accident and its outcome.

First among her visitors when she returned home was James Fitzroy. Since her birthday party in April, he had become more attentive or as attentive as the demands of Mayfield Downs would allow.

On the Wednesday after the accident, he found her sitting in the back garden at Prior Park, her arm in a sling, but otherwise cheerful and not much the worse for the adventure.

'Julia, how are you feeling? Mother sends her best and Alice will be over tomorrow to see you, but I wanted to see you for myself, to make sure you're fine. We heard you were knocked out completely and all sorts of terrible things.'

She smiled a welcome, pleased to have the diversion of a visitor.

'James, I'm fine. There's been such a fuss, I can't tell you the half of it. But William did very well to avoid the truck. It was on the wrong side of the road you know.'

'I heard that. All those big army trucks on these narrow roads are very dangerous. I'm surprised no one's been killed.'

He pulled a chair close to her and bent down to kiss her on the cheek. She had neither encouraged nor discouraged his attentions since her birthday, but he in turn was not discouraged in his pursuit by her neutral stance.

'Alice and I couldn't understand why you and William weren't at Christina Lowry's engagement party.'

'We found out the next day – I was out riding to look at some of our cattle and came across Charles Brockman on the boundary fence. He told me the whole story. He said you'd likely be home from hospital on Tuesday afternoon. How are you? I've been worried about you since I heard about it all.'

She could see that he was genuinely worried although she guessed that the account he had heard of her injuries was much overdone.

'James. Really I'm fine. Mother sent a note to Christina to explain what happened. It will only be a few weeks before I can use my right arm again, but tennis is out of the question for a few months.'

Tennis parties had become an added feature of life at Prior Park since her birthday party. James and his sister Alice were regular partners now for Julia and William on occasional Sunday afternoons.

'And we will have to get Christina a new engagement present; the crystal vase didn't survive the accident either. Was it a good party?'

James, as she expected, was a poor judge of such things and said she must wait for Alice to tell her the details.

To him it had been unremarkable except that Christina's father had been quite drunk when he proposed the toast to the happy couple.

However there was one piece of news that he was able to tell her that she had not yet heard.

'Oh, did you know the Criterion Hotel is being taken over completely by the Americans for their officers? Can you believe it! Christina's was the last function to be held there for an indefinite period.'

The Criterion Hotel had been built around eighty years earlier as the city itself was being established.

The fine Victorian building occupied a prime corner position overlooking the river but with elevation enough that only the worst floods would ever reach the hotel. Its proportions were graceful and elegant, so its choice as a billet for officers by the American forces would have come as no surprise to the locals.

'Do you mean the whole hotel? Where will people stay now? There aren't many hotels in town.'

She had only been to the hotel twice before with her mother to call on friends from Melbourne who were visiting.

Having satisfied himself that she had come to no real harm, James rose to go, but he hesitated.

'I must go. I haven't told you by the way, that I'll be away for a while. I have to get some cattle on the move to some better pasture. We're leaving the day after tomorrow. I may not be back for a month or two.'

Julia was quite surprised at this news and even more surprised that he had not mentioned it earlier.

The winter had been dry, but that wasn't unexpected. It was the failure of the early summer storms and the early onset of hot weather that had made the situation worse, according to her father.

'I heard Father and William discussing the weather last week.

I know they're concerned about the stock on Prior Park. I could see how dry it was when I went riding last week.

'You won't be riding for a while.'

It was stating the obvious but Julia wasn't pleased to be reminded, so she ignored his words.

'I think Father is preparing to send some cattle to the next sale,' she said.

'I may have to do that too, but there'll be a glut of cattle on the market in the next month I reckon.

'I can hold out if I can get some feed along the road and lighten the load on Mayfield and we get rain by Christmas. I think the prices will improve too with more mouths to feed in the district. I know Americans like their steaks.'

She knew it was a common practice in dry times to take cattle on the road. The long paddock, it was called. Three or four men on horseback would drive a herd of cattle feeding along the roadside for miles in search of better feed.

'Well, I won't be going anywhere that's for sure. Mother and I had planned to go to Sydney for shopping, but we can't go until my arm is out of plaster, and that will be a week or two before Christmas, at the earliest. Good luck with the cattle. I hope it rains soon.'

With the prospect of separation for some months, she did not resist his more passionate kiss good-bye.

'I'll see you when I get back. Perhaps we can talk about us then.'

With that, he was gone.

She was, she acknowledged to herself, confused about her feelings for him; she found him attractive yet she hesitated to respond to him in the way he wanted.

Instinctively, she felt there was a subtle danger in encouraging James Fitzroy, and she was not yet sure enough of herself to feel she could manage his demands.

She was surprised that her mother had not discouraged James

Fitzroy; in fact she was quite open in her encouragement.

Since he would inherit Mayfield Downs, there was no objection from her parents but her own thoughts resisted such a tidy and obvious solution for her future life.

In a country at war, much remained uncertain and such uncertainty permeated every aspect of their lives, even if their everyday lives were largely unaffected.

It was a restless Julia, already more than a week into her recovery, who greeted an unexpected visitor the following Wednesday. She had been ambling along the covered walkway connecting the house to the tennis court, which lay just beyond the back garden of Prior Park.

Lost in her own thoughts, she had not heard her father's voice calling her name until he was almost upon her.

'Julia, there you are - this is the American army doctor who stopped and treated you when you and William had your accident. He's called in to see how you are.'

She did not recognise Captain Philippe Duval because she had no recall of the accident and its aftermath but he recognised her in an instant. His professional interest was immediately drawn by the heavy plaster cast on her right arm.

'Miss Belleville, I came to see how you are and to see if there is anything I can do. I'm glad to see you up and about and clearly on the mend. How is the arm? Is it still painful?'

He smiled at her, encouragingly.

'Uncomfortable. A terrible nuisance, but they tell me I'll mend. But thank you for coming to see me. I believe you diagnosed the broken arm at the time and you were right. It was so kind of you to stop and help us.'

'I'm just so sorry we were responsible for running your car off the road. On a road with no centre markings and little traffic, it's easy to forget about driving on the left hand side. But that's no excuse.'

Until this meeting, Julia had thought nothing further about the American doctor who had come to her aid on the side of the road. She had not remembered him, relying instead on William's accounts of the incident, which in truth were more designed to exonerate him from any blame than applaud the efforts of others.

'I see there is still some swelling,' he said, reverting seamlessly to his professional role.

'It does give me some pain,' she admitted. 'They told me it's quite a bad fracture, but I'll have the plaster off before Christmas.'

Before she could add anything further, her mother appeared at the top of the back stairs, motioning them into the house for refreshments.

'How do you do, Mrs Belleville. I came to make sure your daughter is well on the way to recovery.'

Julia could see how the American charmed her mother with his polished manners.

'Thank you, Captain Duval. We're grateful for your help. It could have been so much worse but she will make a full recovery. I hope you're more careful on our roads in future.'

Elizabeth Belleville was determined to make her point, but it was clear the American was already taking steps to ensure that there was no repeat of the incident.

'Our drivers are much more careful on the roads since that day, I can assure you, Mrs Belleville.

'We have put big signs in all the trucks to remind the drivers to keep to the left and we've held a training workshop for all our drivers about local roads and local conditions.'

'Well that's something at least, although with the number of army trucks on this road now, we wonder what is going on. It's almost like an invasion, Captain,' Elizabeth Belleville said.

He bridled a little at this suggestion. His reply was polite but firm.

'I'm afraid we cannot fight a war without somewhere to train and support our infantry away from the front line, Mrs Belleville.

'I think you'll find army camps right up and down the east

coast of Australia now, but this area in particular is a useful staging point for our joint efforts to defeat the Japanese advance in New Guinea.

'You'll know that General Macarthur has been in Brisbane at his new headquarters for some months now.'

'Yes, we've read about it, Captain,' Francis Belleville interjected.

In truth, Francis Belleville was not entirely happy with the growing American army presence in the district but he did not say as much to their visitor.

If pressed, he would have had to concede that the cause of his displeasure was entirely related to the impact on Prior Park and therefore a very self-centred reason.

Without much notice, the army engineers had fenced off a small but very useful parcel of his land, which adjoined the road, for an army encampment. That he had no say over the matter and that it was only a matter of two miles north of the house at Prior Park was the real cause of his annoyance.

'We're not averse to the activities of the American forces,' he conceded. 'We know Australia cannot stand alone against the Japanese, so we're grateful for the help. It's just seeing so many men in the district, it's a bit of a shock at first.'

He said nothing further on the subject, except to once again express his gratitude for the assistance the medical man had rendered his injured daughter.

'Anyway, thank you again for helping Julia and William. I think my son was worried I would blame him for the accident because I would have immediately assumed that he was driving too fast, but in reality I think he handled the situation well.'

'I can assure you, Mr Belleville, that the fault was all on our side,' Captain Duval insisted.

He stood up ready to take his leave. Francis Belleville warmed to his subject.

'We just hope that our combined forces defeat the Japanese threat sooner rather than later,' he said.

'What they did at Pearl Harbour was quite dreadful. Now they've targeted Darwin too, we feel very vulnerable. And my elder son is currently in Canada for pilot training. This war is worse than we ever could have imagined.'

It was clear the young American shared Francis Belleville's sentiments.

'I agree Mr Belleville. None of us really wants to engage in war. It's just something we have to do and the quicker we win it, the better, as far as I am concerned.'

'I hope we see you again, Captain,' said Mrs Belleville, although under what circumstances she could not imagine.

Julia Belleville watched from the front steps as his Jeep disappeared down the driveway leaving a following trail of fine dust in its wake.

Philippe Duval was the first American she had met. In the short time the American forces had been establishing their camps in the district, there had been no point at which she had crossed paths with any of them. She had certainly seen their vehicles on the road, but until now, she had expressed little curiosity about the strangers in their midst.

It was not that American accents were unfamiliar. In fact they were as familiar to Australians as their own through the wonders of Hollywood but the lingering strength of British culture had meant a marked preference for English and European travel for those who could afford it. America was a destination that was rarely spoken of by those who embarked on the long sea voyages that international travel dictated.

The war, of course, had put an end to all such ambitions, as Julia's mother remarked frequently. She had long expected to spend at least six months with her young daughter on an extended European tour following her graduation from school. Hitler's ambitions, she frequently complained, had put paid to her own ambitions for her only daughter.

As Julia turned to go back into the house, she quizzed her

mother about the young American officer.

'I wonder what part of America he comes from? It sounds like a French name.'

'I don't know, Julia, I've no idea.'

Elizabeth Belleville clearly saw no reason to discuss the matter. For Julia's part, she did not want to pique her mother's interest beyond the casual enquiry, so she let the matter drop.

To ask further questions would have encouraged her mother to pontificate, for that was the only word that suited, on the unsuitability of mixed marriages, as she liked to call them.

'We should be pleased that the American soldiers are here but they should leave and not take Australian girls with them as their wives,' she was heard to say on more than one occasion so Julia knew better than to continue her line of questioning about the American doctor.

For Philippe Duval's part, it would be hard to imagine that the twenty-seven year old American army doctor had not noticed the stunning beauty of his one time patient but he would nevertheless have been surprised at the brief conversation between mother and daughter, had he been around to hear it.

CHAPTER 4:
NOVEMBER-DECEMBER 1942

Prior Park, 20 November 1942

Dear Son

Your letter from Canada reached me only yesterday. I take no news as good news and the delay in getting your letters not unsurprising, although in the dead of the night as I lie awake, such a notion is hardly reassuring.

From what little I know and understand of what you are training to do, I can conjure up the most fearful and awful scenarios of what is ahead of you when you finally get to England. But you will want to know what has been going on here.

Around the very time you were writing to me, we were hosting the Fitzroys to a Sunday afternoon tennis party, although there won't be any tennis for Julia for a while—she has since broken her right arm.

William had to swerve to avoid an American army truck on the wrong side of the road. Julia was with him and she took quite a battering from sliding across the front seat and hitting the steering column, hence the broken arm. The plaster will be off before Christmas and she is, otherwise, none the worse for the accident. The car only sustained very minor damage.

But back to the tennis day. The two Fitzroy offspring, James and Alice, seemed to have turned out better than might have been expected. I had more opportunity to observe them at the tennis day than at Julia's birthday party earlier in the year.

You would hardly recognise Alice now. She is 18 and quite fetching. She has pretty manners, something your own sister would do well to copy at times.

With you away, you can imagine that William is always keen to play the older brother and to assert his authority. He was particularly taken with Alice, I think. It is the first time I have seen him take an interest in a girl.

To see Mrs Fitzroy absolutely itching to know how the land might lie with William's prospects was quite amusing—I suspect she thinks they might improve a good deal because of the gossip she's heard—but, of course, she is too polite to ask.

If you ask 'what gossip?', I'll leave that to your imagination, remembering that our household staff hear most things that are said among us.

I do not judge Mrs Fitzroy too harshly on this point. Any mother with a daughter of marriageable age can be forgiven for needing to gauge the lie of the land, so to speak. It's no good to mark out a 'prospect' and then discover he has nothing to offer. It only leads to heartbreak all round. No doubt I am soon to be led a merry dance by your sister who in every respect outshines the pretty Alice. The Dalrymple legacy may only add to the problem.

Mrs Fitzroy chose not to ask after you at all which only confirmed my suspicions that she believes there is a severe rift between us. But as I said before, it does appear to raise her hopes for William and therefore her ambitions for Alice. I think that will make you smile.

You would not know this place now. During the year, the American Army presence in the district has grown apace. We don't know much about what they are doing here so rumour abounds.

The Criterion Hotel is now a billet for American officers. We frequently pass their vehicles on the road into town (which is where William ran foul of them). For them, I have to say, there seems to be no shortage of petrol.

I do now take Julia with me to the Red Cross committee meetings and working bees, if she feels inclined. I can't blame her for her reluctance though; knitting socks, she says, is something for grandmothers to do. At this point, she and I might well have been heading to England and Europe now that she has finished school but this terrible war has put an end to all the things we might have expected to do.

I do regret, as I have said in previous letters, the bitterness of our parting from you. I can only put it down to the shock of your news on both fronts and our unpreparedness for it.

I don't think life will ever be the same again but I pray that we all come through it safely, especially you, my dear son.

Your loving Mother

Elizabeth Belleville replaced the lid on her fountain pen and sealed the envelope ready for mailing. There was a faint layer of dust on the highly polished top of her writing desk, which she flicked away with her handkerchief.

As events transpired, it was only a matter of a few days before Mrs Belleville was reading something that she knew would be of profound interest to her elder son, but by that time her letter had already begun its long journey.

Under the simple heading *Wedding Bells*, which she could easily have missed in the crowded third page of the local newspaper, she spotted a small news item that turned out to be of far greater importance than that accorded to it by the newspaper, at least as far as Elizabeth Belleville was concerned.

St Andrew's Presbyterian Church provided the setting last Saturday for the marriage of Jane Marie Saville, only daughter of Mrs Irene Baxter and the late Mr John Saville, and Thomas Sidney Warner, only son of the late Mr and Mrs John Warner.

Instead of the traditional wedding gown the bride, who was given away by her stepfather Mr Peter Baxter, wore a dusty pink frock and hat, to which she added navy accessories.

After the ceremony, which was attended by close family members only, twelve guests were entertained at the wedding breakfast at the Leichhardt Hotel. The couple will make their home at Armoobilla station.

It was three small paragraphs in total. But they were three small paragraphs of great interest to Elizabeth Belleville.

If there were more questions than answers that occurred to her as a result of the newspaper's simple report, she did not stop to consider them at all. Her first and overwhelming feeling at the unexpected news was one of relief. Beyond that, she barely considered any other aspects of the announcement.

There was only one person she could tell and that was her husband Francis, for no one else in the household had been privy to the real reason for their heated argument with Richard.

'Francis,' she called over the banister, but there was no immediate reply.

She hurried down the stairs and knocked on his study door, which she opened without waiting for an answer.

On this occasion, she did not rebuke her husband for the half empty glass of whisky in his hand. Instead she brandished the newspaper in his direction.

'Thank goodness we insisted that Richard not announce his marriage plans before he went away. Jane Saville got married. It's here in the paper. Can you believe it?'

Francis picked up his reading glasses from the desk and quickly scanned the few paragraphs that Elizabeth had pointed out to him.

'Well, that's good news, isn't it? It seems she wasn't as in love with him as he thought,' Francis said, as if there was nothing much more to say on the matter now.

But he could see that his wife was keen to say more so he asked the obvious question.

'Have you heard something about Jane Saville since Richard left?'

'Well, only gossip really but I heard that Tom Warner had become quite infatuated with her, but I didn't think anything of it. He must be a year or two younger than her at least so I thought it was just idle gossip,' she said.

She was clearly surprised at the turn of events.

'Perhaps I need not have excluded her from the Warner's invitation to Julia's party after all. I only did it because I don't usually invite governesses and then, with Richard's news, I was pleased I hadn't included her.'

She turned to Francis for reassurance.

'I did think that was a bit harsh, old girl,' he said.

He rarely used any endearments to his wife these days. This was as close as he had come in recent times.

'Richard hasn't even mentioned her in any of his letters. Do you think he knows? Or even knew some time ago and didn't tell us. He says nothing about her at all.'

Francis pondered this question for a time but could not come up with a satisfactory explanation.

'It's hard to say – perhaps he does not write about her because he doesn't want to upset us. Or perhaps he does not write about her because it's in the past and they have both moved on?'

He looked expectantly at his wife who was looking bemused.

'I just don't know,' replied his wife, 'but I won't mention it when I write next time. If he doesn't know and still harbours hope for their marriage, I don't want to be the one to tell him. I don't want his mind on anything but what he is doing.'

Francis nodded his agreement.

'You're right. Leave it alone. Hopefully Jane Saville has had the decency to write to him and break it off, but we can't ask.'

'No, we can't ask. We can't ask anyone,' she said firmly.

With that, she left her husband to the comforts of the whisky decanter.

She read the article again to satisfy herself that she had not misread it.

Whatever the cause of the change of heart on the part of Jane Saville, there was no doubt that the outcome was a particularly pleasing one for Elizabeth.

It was on this same afternoon that Julia Belleville next encountered her saviour Philippe Duval.

Despite the awkwardness of walking with her arm in a sling, she set out across country, her destination Fairy Lagoon, just two miles from the house at Prior Park.

Before the war, Fairy Lagoon had been a popular spot for the local children. Julia had remembered afternoons spent swimming in its clear waters during school holidays. It was true that she could not swim now but she felt a pressing need to escape the boredom that was beginning to overwhelm her. She longed to have the heavy plaster removed from her arm but that was still at least a week away.

She had read the small news item about Jane Saville's marriage but, having no idea of the importance of the news, had not connected this particular revelation with her mother's unusually buoyant mood.

Julia was surprised but it made it easy for her to slip away from the house without her mother's knowledge. She chose her path carefully, following the tree line that ran along the boundary fence heading north.

She had walked almost a mile keeping to the shade of the trees where possible but then she stopped suddenly.

Above the usual bush sounds, she thought she heard footsteps and muffled voices. She had not expected to meet anyone at all so the feeling she was being followed created a deep sense of unease.

She had never before felt the slightest concern in walking or riding alone around her father's property so the sense that she was not alone now began to make her feel slightly alarmed. If they were men her father employed, they would immediately make themselves known to her and greet her openly. The fact that this had not occurred made her feel slightly anxious.

For what seemed like ages, she stood stock still, listening intently, but there was almost complete silence, broken only by the sound of the slight breeze through the treetops and the occasional bird flitting from tree to tree. Had she imagined the sounds? She wasn't sure but she could hear nothing unusual now.

So she walked on, following a path carved out by countless herds of cattle heading from one waterhole to the next. The grass swished against her legs where it had grown long and rank. It was beginning to make her itchy. She waved the flies away from her face with a small branch of leaves that served as a fan.

Before long, she reached a bend in the path where it skirted a stony ridge. The small stones she dislodged as she walked rattled down the short slope. She found it hard even on the gently sloping ground to keep her balance with her right arm making her unbalanced.

She was concentrating so hard on not losing her footing that she did not hear the soldiers until the first one spoke. His voice was mocking and self assured. The accent was unusual, its deep drawl a foreign sound in the Australian bush.

'Well, what have we here boys? A young lady all alone, maybe lost? What do you think eh?'

The man was just in front of her on the track, hands on hips, enjoying her confusion and bewilderment. A leering smile hovered on his lips. Julia stopped dead and swung around to retreat back down the way she had come. Before she could take more than a step or two, two men blocked her return path.

They were all wearing the now familiar khaki uniform of American soldiers.

'Let me pass, please.'

She was trying desperately to keep the alarm out of her voice. In fact it was anger that she felt most of all.

Anger that these men would dare to challenge her on her own father's property, but her anger was quickly replaced by something akin to fear, as she began to realise how isolated she was in this part of the property and that she would be no match for any of them physically.

She realised too late that her mother had been right to insist that she not wander about beyond the house with so many strangers in the district.

'Now, wouldn't it be good if you just stayed awhile and were a little more friendly to me and my friends here. Don't be so hasty. Looks as though you've already met with a little accident,' he said, nodding towards her right arm.

'You don't want to make it worse now. My friends and I just want to be a little friendly now.'

He repeated the words. They sounded anything but friendly to Julia's ears.

There was menace in his voice, a subtle threat that she could not fail to understand.

The big man in front of her moved closer to her to put his arm around her shoulder, avoiding her broken arm but trying to draw her near to him.

She could feel his heavy breath on her face. She could smell his stale tobacco-ridden sweat as his body pressed close to her. She could hear the sniggering and the crude encouragement of the other two soldiers who clearly had high hopes of sharing in the amusement.

'Let me go,' she said. 'Let me go.'

She was frightened now and started to struggle. She was trying to think where her father's stockmen would be working but she had no idea.

She struck out with her left foot as hard as she could but the American stepped back nimbly and avoided it altogether.

It almost unbalanced her.

'That's not very friendly. We're just trying to be friends. Good friends, aren't we fellas?'

He reached out and started to fondle the front of her shirt with his big rough hands. His hand drifted over her left breast.

'Very pretty,' he mumbled almost to himself. 'Very pretty.'

The other two men, sensing that the sport was about to begin in earnest, crowded in around her. She screamed and struggled to free herself from the encircling men.

At that very moment Philippe Duval was about to photograph a kookaburra that had perched very conveniently on a fencepost a short distance further along the track. Julia's scream stunned him into action. He ran along the path towards the group that had previously been obscured from his view.

In one decisive action, he inserted himself between the big American soldier and the terrified girl.

'Corporal, leave that girl alone. What do you think you are doing? Have you taken leave of your senses! For God's sake man, get out of here.'

His anger was barely controlled as he shouted and pushed the soldier.

The self assurance drained quickly from the other man's voice, but he knew he must then and there strike a mitigating tone. Not to do so would go against him, he knew.

'We weren't doing anything, sir. We just wanted to be friendly.'

The excuse sounded lame and Philippe Duval was in no mood to listen to it. He glanced around him and noticed the other two men had melted away into the bush as soon as he approached. Whether he would be able to identify them later was going to be a vexed question but not one that worried him now. They would certainly not give themselves up voluntarily. Getting control of the situation was all that mattered.

His hand drifted to his side arm in a gesture that he hoped would bring some sense to the man in front of him.

'You, Corporal, will be dealt with later. Get back to camp. You'll have your chance to tell your story before your CO. Get out of here! Now!'

It was a direct command but also it was all he could trust himself to say. His anger threatened to overcome his normal measured tone.

He knew he stood little chance in a physical encounter with the bulky corporal but he knew instinctively that his rank would save him, because to strike an officer was an offence for which a corporal would be court martialed. They both knew it. There was no mitigation that would justify such an offence. The soldier, sizing up the situation quickly, turned on his heels and walked away from them without a backward glance.

It was then that Philippe turned his attention to Julia.

She had sunk to the ground and was struggling to get up so he gently put his arm around her and helped her to her feet. He could see that she had been frightened by the encounter.

'Thank you.' It was all she could manage to say.

Her voice betrayed her anxiety although she was trying desperately to recover her composure. Her breath was coming in short sharp bursts as she attempted to suppress her panic.

'You always seem to be coming to my aid. I was so scared. I didn't expect to meet anyone at all here. I didn't know the camp was so close. I didn't know there would be anyone about.'

He could feel her shaking from the shock of the incident and he could hear a tremor in her voice.

'I'm so sorry those men acted like that towards you. It was unforgivable. Are you hurt?'

His voice now was gentle and encouraging, his anger gone, replaced by concern for her.

'I think I'm all right. I just didn't know how to deal with them. I didn't expect to see anyone here.'

She repeated her explanation, tears welling in her eyes, more from relief, he suspected, than any physical injury. His words were softly spoken and encouraging as he continued to half support her.

'Miss Belleville, you don't have to explain. They were at fault. You have a perfect right to walk around your father's property. It's those men who are at fault.

'They'll be dealt with, don't you worry. I'm so sorry for what they did to you. Their behaviour was totally unacceptable. They're just rough bullies and took an opportunity when they saw you were alone.'

Julia's head flicked up nervously, her face creased with a look of alarm.

'I don't want to have to meet them again. You won't need me will you to give any testimony or anything?' she asked, clearly unwilling to have to face her tormentors again.

'No, I saw enough. They'll be disciplined and confined to camp. They'll have privileges withdrawn, but you won't have to be part of it. We wouldn't ask that of you.'

His words were reassuring.

She could see he was concerned about her safety and her well-being, but it hadn't occurred to her that he was also concerned about the reputation of the American forces that relied on the goodwill of the local people.

He knew that there could be unfortunate consequences from making the incident public. At all costs, it must be kept within a tight circle of officers who would mete out the punishment to the perpetrators.

'I'm going to make sure you get home safely. Walk along here with me. I have to go back for my camera. Where were you heading, if I may ask?'

The question was an obvious one. He guessed she was almost two miles from Prior Park. It might have been natural to find her walking to visit the neighbours but there were no neighbouring houses in this direction.

'I was going to Fairy Lagoon. It's only a few hundred yards further along the track. I would normally ride my horse but I can't with my broken arm. We always went there as children to swim. What were you photographing? It would be a good place to photograph.'

Philippe picked up his camera and gave it a cursory glance to ensure nothing had been broken in his haste to pull the strap over his head and drop it on the ground so he could run unhindered.

The kookaburra he'd been hoping to photograph had long since departed the scene. He'd have to hope for similar luck on another day.

'I like photography just as a hobby,' he explained.

'I wanted to take some photos of the Australian bush while I am here, with my new camera. I've joined a camera club in town. Things were quiet this afternoon so I decided to see what might be around here of interest. Just as well as it turned out.'

She smiled at him and nodded, acknowledging the truth of his words.

'I come out here to this camp to supervise the medical unit twice a week. I was on my way back when I decided to stop and walk from the road into the bush to see what there is to photograph.'

'Lucky for me,' she said.

She put extra emphasis on the words and there was a rueful smile hovering on her lips. He was pleased to see that she had almost completely regained her composure with the reassurance of his presence.

'How is the arm, by the way?'

Julia adjusted the sling around her neck with some difficulty.

'I'm really tired of this plaster cast but I expect to get it off next week, if the doctor is happy with the progress. I'll be so relieved. I haven't been able to do anything much at all.'

He smiled, nodding in agreement.

'Yes, awkward things, broken arms, but it will be healed soon. I really think you should be going home now. I'll drive you. We just have to walk back to the road. I don't think you should walk home by yourself.'

'Thanks. I'd appreciate that. Perhaps I can come out with you when you are next going to take some photos? I can show you the best spots.'

It was a naive offer from a young girl that Philippe Duval, older and wiser, knew he should have turned down.

He knew she did not understand the inappropriateness of her suggestion and every instinct within him said that Julia Belleville, young, beautiful and on the brink of womanhood, could lead to trouble, if he did not take the greatest care.

But the offer seemed such an innocent attempt at friendship that he dismissed the inner voice that told him to beware.

Later, he was to remember this particular day with a mixture of regret and remorse that was to bear heavily on his conscience for the rest of his life.

Had he obeyed his first instinct to turn down her offer of assistance, his life and her life would never have become entwined in a way that was to cast a shadow over both their lives.

CHAPTER 5:

DECEMBER 1942-FEBRUARY 1943

AS CHRISTMAS APPROACHED the weather became even hotter and more humid. In every stockyard in the district, restless cattle flicked their tails at the swarms of sticky flies constantly buzzing around them. Tempers were fraying among the stockmen, whose bad-tempered outbursts could be heard all around the countryside.

Tom Warner, however, was in an unusually cheerful mood as he slipped off his horse, a lather of sweat from the morning's exertions, and looped his bridle over the nearest fence post.

The world, he decided, moved in decidedly mysterious ways. It had been less than a month since his marriage and still he could not quite believe that the attractive and elegant woman, who had once been his sister's governess, had agreed to his rather diffident proposal of marriage.

The diffidence was not a reflection of his attraction or his desire for her; it was a reflection of his desire not to be exposed as a silly young fool. At twenty-four, she was two years older than him but there were times when her calm maturity seemed to extend the gulf of years between them.

He remembered the evening just a few months ago when he had slipped his arm around her waist and quietly but persistently declared his love for her and his intention to make her his wife.

It had been his first declaration. He sensed she had been a

little taken aback by the proposal but he persisted quietly. On his part, there had been a declaration of love; that there was none yet on her part did not disturb him unduly, for he believed that she was reserved in such matters and that the love on his side would be enough for both of them.

When he pressed her for information about her life, she had said very little except that her father had died when she was young and that her mother had become preoccupied with her new husband. Not to the extent of neglecting her daughter, she told him, but the family life she had known had been shattered by her father's premature death and nothing was ever going to recapture the warm feeling of security that his presence had meant for the family. That much she did tell him.

So, having become used to Jane Saville, the governess, it was taking a little time for him to adjust to the idea of Jane Warner, the wife, his wife, but the adjustment in no way reflected any disappointment in the changed arrangements. Far from it.

She had surprised and delighted him with her passion. Young and inexperienced himself, he could not recognise in his wife a more experienced partner and he never questioned her about her past, for he did not think there was a past to explore.

Their former circumstances – that of young, unmarried employer and young, unmarried governess – had been, he knew, the source of gossip in the district; he did not know that now the gossips whispered to a different tune, wondering what lay behind the secretive and seemingly hasty marriage.

So, on a day when the hot weather and fractious cattle were testing everyone to their limits, Tom was in a quite joyous and happy mood.

He was delighted to see Jane waiting to greet him as he strode across the back garden to enter the house via the kitchen.

It was what she did in the minutes before he returned to the house that would have disturbed his peace of mind, had he known about it.

She had spent the morning writing and rewriting a letter she knew she should have written at least a month ago, if not more. It was the latest in her many attempts.

Unknown to Tom, she had spent weeks trying to find the right words to break the news of her marriage to a man who expected her to wait until his return from the war that raged across the world.

She turned it over and over in her mind. How could she explain the broken promise to wait for his return? How could she explain that she was now another man's wife and that he must forget her?

How could she explain her decision to him when at times should could not find a satisfactory explanation for it herself.

Every failed attempt at the letter had found its way into the kitchen fire. She thought each stilted effort sounded like justification when in fact she knew she should simply say that she had fallen in love with someone else since he left and decided to get married.

But was that true? Had she really fallen in love with Tom? Or was it just convenient and secure?

With the letter now safely concealed and out of her mind, she smiled as Tom approached.

'Did you get all the cattle you were after?' she said.

With the dry, hot weather and the dim prospects for rain, she knew he was planning to sell down half the stock on the property.

'Yes, we got them. Thank goodness. We'll be loading them on the train tomorrow.

'So what have you been doing this morning? Has Rebecca been helping you?'

His young sister's presence in the house acted as a natural restraint on their intimacy yet Jane was fond of the young girl who had been deprived of first a mother's love and then a father's guiding hand within a few short, cruel months.

'Rebecca is very helpful, Tom, you know we get on well, but she probably should see more girls her own age.'

His response was unexpected.

'You should invite Julia Belleville over sometime. I know she's a bit older but I think she'd be a good influence.'

Jane said nothing because she could think of nothing to say. He had clearly forgotten the deliberate snub in not inviting her to Julia's eighteenth birthday party. She could not risk a further snub by inviting Julia to visit.

She had turned it over and over in her mind but in the end, she could only work out two possible reasons for the snub and both caused her to feel uneasy.

In her rational and considered moments, she convinced herself that the first and most likely cause was that the Bellevilles did not extend their social invitations to governesses. Elizabeth Belleville's local reputation for social condescension rather favoured this explanation and it was one that Tom had advanced at the time.

He had been totally unconcerned by it and suggested she come anyway but she could not happily adopt his cavalier approach to the niceties of social convention. Without an invitation, she insisted, she would not go and she did not go.

The other explanation was more complex but equally pointed.

It was one that had unsettled her and given her a clarity of understanding that nothing else could quite have delivered so tellingly: that Richard had confided his marriage plans to his parents and, by the lack of an invitation, they were sending a clear and very strong message that this was a match of which they certainly did not approve and that she could expect to encounter considerable opposition if she continued with her plans to marry the heir to the Belleville fortune.

She remembered how Richard had dismissed her concerns, sure as he was that such a nonsense idea was not to be taken seriously, but then he had become very accustomed to all his wishes and aspirations being taken seriously by his family.

So infrequently had his wishes been thwarted that he could not easily remember a single occasion when he had not eventually got his way. If there was such an occasion, it was a childish whim and so trivial that it had soon been forgotten.

He had refused to even discuss her fears and concerns.

'They'll get over it,' she remembered him saying.

To those words, she had said nothing, but she knew, deep down, that Richard's marriage to her would be opposed with all Elizabeth Belleville's being. Jane did not want to be something that her mother-in-law would 'get over'. She did not say this either.

So it came as no surprise to Jane when the gossip finally reached her ears weeks after Richard had left that Prior Park had been in uproar. She guessed that emotions had run high between Richard and his parents and she knew that she must have been at the heart of the discussion.

In the end the gossips surmised that Richard's greater sin in the eyes of his mother was announcing his plans to marry a girl his parents clearly believed to be highly unsuitable.

She heard it discussed a number of times but no one had ventured any ideas as to the identity of the girl and it was widely assumed to be someone he had met at university.

When asked her opinion, Jane was relieved to be able to express none at all, claiming little knowledge of the family. She was relieved too that their meetings had been kept secret.

Her response satisfied those who broached the subject because they knew too that she had been excluded from the Warner invitation to Julia Belleville's eighteenth birthday party. Which proved really that she had no information of any use so no one pressed her. For that she was more than grateful.

'You know we'll soon have been married a month. Can you believe it?"

Tom's words cut through her reverie.

She was thankful that the idea of inviting Julia Belleville to Armoobilla did not become the topic of further conversation.

She had not told him about her involvement with Richard

Belleville; now she knew she never could because to do so would raise the inevitable questions: why did she not tell him before they married? How far had the relationship gone? Did she marry him as second best?

She could frame the questions, one after the other, in her own mind and she knew the answers to the questions were ones that Tom Warner had deserved before they married, not after.

Having made the decision not to tell him, she knew she must never ever do so because to do so now, would risk destroying the trust he had so readily given her.

Her face flushed at the knowledge of the letter hidden in her handbag but Tom did not see the slight wave of redness spread across her cheeks.

He was already pulling his chair out from the kitchen table and attacking his midday meal with relish.

Elizabeth Belleville dropped her grey gloves on to the hall table. She did everything deliberately, trying to give consequence to actions that hadn't any.

Despite the heat of summer, she maintained the rigorous dress standard she believed was expected of her. Her gloves, her handbag and her hat all matched perfectly. She might have stepped off a fashionable city street, not off the streets of a provincial city far from the source of any such fashionable considerations.

Elizabeth had not expected to find herself living in a provincial backwater but Francis had insisted that he preferred the life, promising frequent trips to the city to soften her disappointment.

The trips, inevitably, became fewer as time wore on and when she did go, she often went alone.

She had taken to ordering her clothes from an elite city department store preferring to rely on the unreliability of wartime transport rather than patronise the local stores, such was her disdain for what she regarded as the inferior range offered locally.

Wherever she went, her clothes caused envious comment from those less fortunately placed.

Great boxes with their contents carefully swathed in tissue paper arrived regularly for her. The garments she chose were carefully hung in her wardrobe, a cheque was signed to be sent along with the rejected items on their return journey of a thousand miles.

Pride of place in her wardrobe was a fur wrap in the latest fashion. It was this particular item which caused the most whispering behind hands when she appeared in it. If there was any doubt about the source of her other clothes, there was certainly no doubt about the source of this highly desirable item: the local shops most certainly could not supply such a luxury.

'I saw Tom Warner's wife,' she said, almost by way of greeting to her husband, who was far more concerned with other news than the woman who had been the object of his elder son's affection and who now, in his opinion, ceased to matter since her unexpected marriage.

'Oh, really.' Francis could think of nothing more to say.

'To me she looks like a dangerous woman.'

'Dangerous? In what way?'

This statement puzzled Francis, who was unaccustomed to thinking of any woman as dangerous. Beautiful, sly, seductive, attractive, any of these words might easily form in his mind about a woman he'd noticed, but not dangerous.

'I think young Tom Warner will have his hands full, that's all,' she said, by way of explanation.

'I spoke to her for a few minutes. She seemed very nervous. She kept twisting her wedding ring on her finger,' she said.

'I suppose she didn't ask after Richard?'

This question prompted a retort that bordered on contempt.

'Of course she didn't,' Elizabeth said.

'Now that she's married she couldn't possibly ask that question. It's not like they were openly involved.'

Elizabeth realised then that they may have been overhead so

she glanced down her own hallway almost furtively and then up the stairwell leading to the floor above, but all was quiet, so she breathed an audible sigh of relief.

'We mustn't talk about it otherwise someone will hear and then the gossip will start up again.'

'I still wonder why she suddenly opted for young Warner,' Francis said, ignoring his wife's warning.

Elizabeth lowered her voice to almost a whisper.

'Well, there are certain signs.'

'What signs?' asked Francis, bewildered. He had always been bewildered by the subtlety of women's talk and it was no less so this time.

'Wait and see,' was all Elizabeth would say.

With that, she headed upstairs to her bedroom, leaving him to ponder the mysteries of women and their unpredictable ways.

It was only after Elizabeth had gone upstairs that Francis remembered the real reason for her trip to town so he hurried up the stairs in search of her.

He knocked tentatively on her bedroom door. His wife was in the midst of stowing her hat in her hatbox so he came to her aid to replace the ungainly box back on top of her wardrobe.

'Did you see Mr Tucker while you were in town?' he asked, trying to be casual about the enquiry, but failing.

'Yes. I saw him.'

Francis could see that his wife was determined to make him ask the questions because she knew, above all else, that he did not want to ask them.

'What did he say about the trust? Are we able to access some funds?'

'Yes, we can,' was all she said. She then brushed past him and sat down at her dressing table.

Francis walked into the sitting room that adjoined his wife's bedroom. He had not wanted to meet his wife's knowing resigned look. He knew it would be there. It was a look that had imprinted itself on his very soul over the years.

He stared out of the upstairs window across the paddocks, which were quiet this afternoon. The low cloud over the hills had darkened in the past half hour, suggesting that rain might come after all. For all its tranquillity, the scene was momentarily melancholy, as if the disappointments of the years had stifled the life around him.

She called out to him, her voice betraying none of the emotions she felt at his fecklessness.

'It will take a week for the money to reach the bank. That should get the bank off your back.'

Francis turned and walked back into the room. He saw his wife's reflection in the dressing table mirror. She had not bothered to turn around. He felt he had to say something.

'Well, I hope we have better luck now. Thank you.'

That was all he could say.

He had never expected money, which had been in such plentiful supply in his youth, would become such a difficult issue.

He blamed almost everything and everyone but himself for his present predicament, which he regarded as a temporary setback.

The fact that he had been having temporary setbacks for a decade or more had escaped his notice, but not the notice of his wife nor the notice of his elder son, Richard, whose contempt for his father had grown almost in parallel with his own transition from boyhood to manhood.

With the immediate problem resolved, he retreated downstairs. She could hear him whistling for his favourite dog as the front door closed behind him.

'Where's Julia?'

It was an idle question that William directed at his parents across the lunch table the next day.

The doors to the dining room stood ajar to allow as much breeze as possible to enter the room, for the heat of the day was stifling. The breeze frequently failed to materialise and the heat persisted unabated.

'She told me she was riding across to see Alice Fitzroy today; she left just before lunch,' his mother said.

'Are you sure, Mother? Today?'

William's enquiry for his sister's whereabouts had at first been a casual question and he did not expect to have any interest at all in the answer.

'Why do you say *today* like that William? Why shouldn't she visit Alice Fitzroy today?'

Elizabeth Belleville missed nothing and she certainly did not miss the question mark that now hung over her daughter's explanation for her absence from the family's traditional Saturday lunch together.

'Well, I saw Alice yesterday in town with her mother. She told me they were staying in town for a week or more as her father was having some medical tests at the hospital. That's all. He was to get some results on Monday but there could be more tests, so they decided to stay on rather than travel home and then back again. I've offered to take Alice to the Charity Ball.'

This was all news to his mother, but she surmised Alice's absence from Mayfield Downs might also have been news to Julia so William's information did not immediately raise any alarm with Elizabeth.

'Perhaps your sister didn't know, in which case she will return home very soon I would think, unless James is home now? Has he come back yet?'

Francis, who had been silent during the exchange between mother and son, now volunteered his own contribution to the lunch table discussion.

'I don't think so but the family does expect him back in a week or so. After the rain we've had recently, I think he'll want to bring the cattle back.

'Charles Brockman was telling me because we were talking about stock levels, now that we're seeing some pasture improve. He said he'd been talking to Jack Fitzroy about it.'

There was nothing in this new information to raise alarm about Julia's whereabouts for it was generally agreed that she had not known that Alice wasn't at home and that when she found out, she would return home in due course.

For Elizabeth the conversation had revealed more about William than it had about Julia's activities. Was this, she wondered, the first hint that William was more interested in the Fitzroy family's comings and goings than he had ever before revealed?

If he had thought his attentions to Alice Fitzroy had gone unnoticed on the night of his sister's birthday party, then he was much mistaken. There was very little that escaped Elizabeth Belleville's notice and even less still, when it was something involving her children.

'I didn't know you were seeing Alice Fitzroy?'

His mother's direct question brought forward the inevitable direct rebuff.

'I'm not 'seeing' Alice Fitzroy, Mother, I've just offered to take her to the Charity Ball so she will have a partner. With her brother away, it seemed like the polite thing to do.'

His mother nodded.

'Indeed, William, it is the polite thing to do,' his mother concurred.

She refrained from saying that he had not previously been known to place much importance on politeness.

She said no more on the subject but she had begun to think recently that Alice might do very well as a wife for her second son.

However, she had not made her mind up altogether on this point so she resisted the temptation to give consequence to Amelia Fitzroy's ambitions for her daughter by openly acknowledging the possibility that such a match could be countenanced.

As they rose from the lunch table, Francis belatedly announced his plans to travel to Brisbane on business in the very near future, which pushed all further discussion of other matters to the background.

Julia's absence was quickly forgotten in the terse conversation that followed between husband and wife as to what was so important that he felt he must attend to it personally.

'It's just some stuff to do with the other Belleville businesses. Just some boring legal stuff. I'll only be a few days. Quicker if I go by myself,' he said.

With that, Elizabeth had to be satisfied.

William, unwilling to act as family peacemaker, had already made a hasty exit from the dining room. Concern about Julia's whereabouts had clearly been forgotten.

At about the same time as the discussion on Julia's absence was under way across the lunch table at Prior Park, she had reached her destination which was not, as her mother had been led to believe, the Fitzroy's home on Mayfield Downs but Fairy Lagoon on the northern boundary of Prior Park.

It was clear from the familiarity of her greeting of Philippe Duval that this was not the first time her mother had been led astray.

In the months that had elapsed since Philippe had intervened to save her from the American soldiers, their meetings had become more and more frequent and despite his earlier misgivings, he had begun to look forward to them as a respite from the daily grind of his military life.

She dismounted and the two of them walked side by side with her horse trailing behind towards the southern end of the lagoon, which was the more easily accessible. The lagoon was quite broad in places and it was one of a number in the district. These clear freshwater ponds appeared as if from nowhere and disappeared again underground, owing their existence to no visible river or stream.

She tethered her mare safely in the shade and they walked down the gentle slope to the water's edge. For the keen photographer, the vantage point from the southern end was especially favourable. Julia was fulfilling a promise she had made to show him the best spots.

Two large tree branches arched over the clear water, providing an elegant frame for the scene and a convenient perch for the birdlife that abounded around the water.

Today, however, there were no rarities among the birds, just the familiar kookaburra perched above the water like a statue, eagerly seeking its prey in the waters below, a small willie wagtail constantly twitching his tail in ceaseless motion and a group of noisy black crows circling menacingly overhead.

Julia, no longer hampered by an injured arm, helped Philippe set up his equipment. He happily snapped away taking advantage of the light being just right in the mid afternoon.

Most photographers he knew would envy his constant supply of photographic film that was now out of the reach of the civilian photographer, another legacy of wartime shortages.

As he straightened up from his viewfinder, he noticed a serious expression on Julia's face.

'Do you think the war will go on much longer?' she asked unexpectedly.

If he was surprised by her sudden interest in the topic, he did not show it.

He shrugged his shoulders.

'It's hard to say. We are making progress but there is a war on two fronts – here in the Pacific and in Europe. It's not an easy thing to predict. Why do you ask? Any special reason?'

'The newspaper reports are just awful. Just this week there was a report of the desolation in Stalingrad and the bombing of a Japanese base just north of Darwin. But worst of all was the report of a family in Adelaide who had already lost one son, a flight lieutenant, and now their other son is missing, presumed dead. Mother went quite pale. She fears the worst for Richard, I know, but she doesn't say much.'

This was the first time he had known Julia to speak about the war and its effects. She had often asked him about his medical work but this was the first time that he had known her to express a more adult understanding of the events that were shaping the world around them.

He put his arm around her. It was meant as a kindly gesture of reassurance but her head immediately jerked upwards in response to his closeness, seeking an explanation for this sudden intimacy.

Up until this point, he had kept physical contact with her to a minimum, apart from helping her mount her horse or giving her his hand to help her down an embankment. He had felt the responsibility lay with him not to take advantage of her, but his resolve was weakening, as he knew it might.

'I don't want to alarm you but your brother's missions will be dangerous but he hasn't finished his training yet, has he?'

He held her in a loose embrace for only a few moments, then he moved away, putting some distance between them, conscious of the fact that his attentions might have been unwelcome.

'No, it's true he hasn't finished his training yet, but I think he's due to ship out from Canada very soon and I know that's what Mother is afraid of. I think she secretly hoped he would fail the training, but that wasn't likely. Richard has never failed at anything.'

Philippe wanted to offer further reassurance but he valued honesty above all else so he was silent. He did not want to say the soothing and encouraging words he guessed she wanted to hear because to say them was to utter a falsehood and he would not do that, even for Julia.

If there was a scrap of comfort to offer her, he would do it, happily, but not if it raised false hopes that her brother would survive the war unscathed, because he knew it was a false hope. Casualties among aircrew were the highest of any of the operational military roles. This, however, was a piece of information he kept firmly to himself.

They moved further apart as he began to pack his gear. The day's photography session was well and truly over.

She led her horse out on to the path that would take her home and was about to mount. Once more, they were standing close together. He patted the animal's neck running his hand down her glossy coat.

'She's a lovely animal. Just like her owner.'

It was a clumsy thing to say and he hadn't really meant to say it at all but her physical closeness made him uncharacteristically impetuous.

All through his struggle to put himself through his medical studies, he had been single minded and rarely distracted by the girls he had met, first as a medical student and then as a young doctor.

Julia blushed at the unexpected compliment, if compliment it indeed was, for she was unsure. All she knew was that she was beginning to feel an anticipation at the prospect of their meetings that she had not felt before and this unsettled her.

She hoisted herself into the saddle effortlessly, rejecting his offer of help. Philippe stood back clear of her horse but she held the reins tightly for a moment longer.

'I'm staying with Alice Fitzroy in town later this week. We're going to the Charity Ball at the Palais Royal on Friday night. My brother William is going to be our escort. Why don't you come along?'

The invitation surprised him. So far, they had only met under the pretext of his photography and her promise to show him the best places to photograph. To move beyond that, and in a public place, was inviting comment that he wasn't sure would be a good idea, either for him or for her.

He had not asked if her parents knew she was meeting him regularly on his photographic field trips and she had not volunteered the information, but the fact that she rode to meet him and did not insist he call for her at the house suggested that their meetings were not sanctioned by her parents.

This worried him but he let it pass.

'I'll try,' was all he said in response to her suggestion.

With that, she had to be satisfied and urged her horse into a trot.

Just as Julia and Philippe emerged from the edge of the lagoon, Charles Brockman, Prior Park's station manager, rode along the path towards them. A minute later, he reflected, and he could not have avoided them but he was quick to react.

He pulled on the reins of his stock horse and eased the gelding into a clump of trees that hid him from view but afforded him a good view of the pair as they parted.

What he saw disturbed him, not so much for the inappropriateness of their behaviour because there was very little to report on that front, but the meeting itself raised his suspicions that the daughter of his employers was conducting a clandestine assignation of which he was certain neither of her parents knew or would approve.

He could not imagine that her parents would approve of their eighteen year old daughter meeting an American Army officer by herself in the middle of the bush or that they would allow it if they knew. The most likely explanation was that she had simply chosen not to tell them.

Charles, who had worked at Prior Park all his life, found he could draw no other conclusion than that neither Francis nor Elizabeth Belleville knew what their daughter was doing.

Which raised an even bigger question for him: where did his loyalties lie? Should he tell them? Or should he keep out of it, on the basis that it wasn't any of his business?

He remained in the clump of trees for a full twenty minutes before he eased the restive horse back on to the track, sure that both of them were by this time well out of sight.

In that time, he had not come to any satisfactory decision on how he should act and this troubled him. He had rather wished he had been riding in the opposite direction and had never seen the pair whose meeting today was clearly not their first, if their familiarity with each other was any guide.

It was something he would have to mull over further, he decided, for it was far from clear what he should do.

In this frame of mind, he urged his horse into a gallop that startled the birds into flight and alarmed a small mob of cattle heading to the nearest waterhole.

CHAPTER 6: MARCH-JUNE 1943

RICHARD BELLEVILLE WAS a long way removed from the concerns of Prior Park but still home was in his thoughts, even as each day distanced him from the old life he had left behind.

He had learned quickly to roll sideways out of his bunk bed each morning. It was too short to accommodate his athletic frame comfortably, but he knew sleep was essential so he endured the discomfort without complaint however much he longed for the old comforts he had taken so much for granted.

On this particular morning, he took a last look at the letter he had written to his mother the previous evening. It didn't seem much, but he couldn't say much, and the less said the better, he thought.

He had wrestled with just how much detail he should write and in the end had chosen not to refer at all to the most important piece of news he had received.

He knew that his mother would know, in any case. That much was certain, he told himself.

The last thing he wanted to do was engage in writing an explanation for an event that he could not explain himself. Even less did he want to give her the opportunity to ask questions in return and probe for answers he could not give. He chose silence instead.

Dear Mother

I cannot write much, which I know you will understand. I just wanted to let you know that I am well and everything is going according to plan.

As you know our training is coming to an end here in Canada in a month or two. I can't tell you how pleased we will be to be getting stuck into real ops but that is some months off yet. There are lots of other Australian chaps here, although not many from our area, mostly city boys in search of adventure.

It's taken me a while to get used to the cold. The snow is pretty when it settles on the ground but it is a terrible nuisance and needs to be cleared constantly. The countryside, what I've seen of it, is quite pretty, but we're always too preoccupied to take much notice. There is almost nothing to remind me of home, except the familiar accents.

I'll do my best, you can depend on that and I'll try to stay out of trouble, but I hope you are genuinely reconciled to my decision. Please don't worry.

You have William and now Julia is at an age to be a good comfort to you. I hope father's situation has improved. Remember me to him, and to William and Julia. I'll be home before you know it.

Your son

Richard

It seemed a poor effort really but some effort was better than none at all.

How could he write the truth to a mother thousands of miles away in the comfort of the country, whose only real inconvenience of war was having to produce clothing coupons to buy her new dresses and to manage the shortage of petrol?

He couldn't write at all about the operations he would soon be embroiled in nor could he write about the war effort and the terror in the North Atlantic that he now knew so much more about than when he had left Australia.

For a few moments, he sank down on to the edge of his bunk, taking in the orderliness around him. The crews might be training to face danger on a daily basis and to play a vital role in the war but the discipline of the training base was maintained unrelentingly.

He could not have imagined the life he was living now as a young man growing up in the comfort and security of Prior Park.

At 23 he was a year or two older than most of the others he had met. Most wondered if they would make their next birthdays, him included.

It was a real possibility they would face once they climbed aboard their aircraft to undertake actual missions over Germany or to defend Britain from air attack. But that was still a few months off yet.

It was in many ways good to be away from home. He knew that.

It was good to be at a great distance from the event that he now only had recourse to in his imagination. Had he been closer at hand, he would have found it intolerable to remain. It was only the distance that made Jane's news bearable.

He had felt so secure and so happy when she had accepted him; he could not understand how everything had changed for her yet nothing had changed for him.

Her early letters had been full of plans for their life together. Her hopes and her fears she had confided to him without inhibition.

He recalled the softness of her body and then his mind returned to the question: why did she change her mind? Her letters had given no hint at all of her change of mind, until the latest one, which delivered the devastating news.

Writing to his mother was easy compared with the next letter he had written. This too he reviewed in the cold light of day, fighting the temptation to tear it into tiny pieces.

Dear Jane

Your letter was a shock.

I know that we had not known one another for very long before I left for Canada, but I had held fast to the notion that we would meet up again as soon as I was back in Australia and I had plans as to the sort of life I could offer you.

Now you write to say that you are married to Tom Warner. You gave me no satisfactory explanation at all as to why you went against the promise you made me before I left. I feel I am entitled to that small crumb at least.

If you were worried about my parents, I can assure you, they would have reconciled themselves to our marriage in time, of that I have no doubt. I'm only sorry you weren't willing to wait to find out.

It won't be the homecoming I prayed for. To say I am disappointed is merely trite for I cannot express in any satisfactory way the depth of my disappointment. It is a disappointment I will carry with me all my days.

Richard

It was all he could say. What else? For a few short months before he left, they had grown fond of each other and finally declared their love to each other.

He had not planned to tell his family who expected, at the very least, a substantial heiress as his wife, but it had come tumbling out in the midst of his excitement at the news he had been accepted for the Air Force.

The heat of the argument that his news had precipitated was unexpected.

He had known there would be opposition from his parents but he had in no way been able to comprehend the depth of their displeasure at the news of his impromptu betrothal.

He recalled bitterly how his parents had refused to discuss any reasons for their opposition beyond his mother's insistence that she would be an unsuitable wife for him. It was something he could not accept and insisted he would not accept.

With his departure imminent, an uneasy truce had settled among the three of them, his parents having extracted a promise of secrecy about his matrimonial plans until his return.

It wasn't hard to imagine his mother's feelings of triumph on learning the news of the unexpected marriage of Jane Saville, he thought. He knew his mother well enough to know that she would see only triumph in the event.

What had his parents found so objectionable, he wondered?

Jane was attractive, educated and accomplished. He supposed it was her lack of family and, probably, her lack of money.

Richard had not thought her lack of money was important. It would be some years before he came to fully comprehend the impact of his charming but feckless father on the family's fortunes.

'Damn you,' he said to no one in particular.

He screwed Jane's letter into a tight ball and threw it into the charcoal burner. He watched it catch alight and burn to ash.

Her earlier letters, which had been carefully stored in his locker, followed quickly and were consumed by the flames. He poked at the remnants with the blackened fire stoker until nothing of the letters remained.

With that final act, he resolved never to think about her again. It was a resolution that, in the coming months, he would struggle to keep.

He headed out towards the training block for yet more intensive instruction before the afternoon's flying training. That, at least, would keep his mind occupied.

While snow continued to play havoc with Richard's training in Canada, back at Prior Park, the worst of the heat was only just beginning to recede as summer made way for autumn.

The local dancehall, the Palais Royal, its art deco windows crisscrossed by tape and its blackout curtains at the ready, had been decorated with streamers and balloons left over from an earlier and happier time, determinedly defying the gloom of war and the wartime shortages of almost everything.

A large Red Cross banner hung slightly lopsidedly across the stage at the far end of the room, declaring the event to be a fund-raising effort to support the troops in the field.

Elizabeth Belleville had been drawn into the local charity

work quite reluctantly. She was not a favourite on the local Red Cross committee. Where she served on a committee, she expected to be its leader. When she made a suggestion, she expected it to be adopted wholeheartedly.

These traits did not endear her to the other women who shared committee tables with her, but she was nevertheless respected, at least for her ability to exert influence where others could not. The Bellevilles were generally held to be the richest family in the district so no one cared to give offence to such a wealthy patron.

While declining to attend herself, Elizabeth Belleville had volunteered her two offspring, Julia and William, who, on this occasion, were happy to comply with their mother's demands.

There was much whispering among the matrons who occupied the chairs on the circumference of the dance floor when William danced first one dance and then another with Alice Fitzroy.

Julia, on the other hand, had to content herself with a succession of partners whose sweaty hands she did her best to avoid.

Her partners had proved disappointing for they lacked conversation of any wider interest than the weather and the price of cattle.

She observed acidly to Alice, after enduring at least four dances, that her partners' lack of conversation might have been forgiven had their dancing skills exceeded it.

Alice only chided her gently.

'They're nice boys really, Julia. You just need to give them a chance.'

But Alice of course was basking in the glow of success at having been preferred by the most eligible man at the dance.

Alice had never known such triumph so nothing Julia could say was going to spoil it.

The dance had been in full swing for at least two hours when a ripple of whispered comment progressed around the hall.

It wasn't hard to pinpoint the source of everyone's sudden

interest; a small group of American soldiers had gathered near the door before slowly making their way into the dancehall, scanning the room as they went for potential partners.

Julia's eyes immediately searched the new arrivals for Philippe Duval but she could not see him among the group and so returned her attention to her current dance partner, who was expounding at length on the disabilities which had kept him from army service.

Julia's thoughts were miles away when she heard a familiar voice politely but firmly addressing her young partner.

'May I cut in?'

Her dance partner gave way reluctantly to the American, who took over and expertly guided her across the floor without missing a beat.

'Julia, how are you? It's nice to see you. You look so beautiful tonight.'

She smiled.

'Well, I guess I'm not in my riding clothes.'

Philippe smiled.

'I can't think of anything less suitable to go riding in than what you are wearing,' he replied, surveying her at arm's length before continuing with their dance.

A faint colour spread across her face. She was unaccustomed to such elegant flattery.

'Philippe, I didn't see you come in. I thought perhaps you had more important things to do than attend a charity dance?'

There was a query in her voice that only served to highlight the fact that she had been feeling slightly put out that he hadn't made the effort to attend the dance.

'Well, I would have been here much earlier but I had to operate on a soldier who accidentally shot himself in the leg with his rifle. A silly accident really but I couldn't leave the poor fellow to suffer. I think he tripped over it, the rifle that is.'

'Oh, I see. Well, I guess that will have to do as an explanation,' she said, with a smile that hid her relief.

'Will he be all right?'

The question was almost an afterthought.

'Yes, he'll be fine. It was just a flesh wound but he'll be out of action for a month or more.'

Having satisfied herself as to the reasons for his late arrival, she relaxed and resumed her friendly chatter.

'Have you developed any photographs yet from your trips into the bush? I'd love to see some if you have.'

'Not yet, I hope to do some tomorrow if it isn't too busy. I'm billeted at the Criterion Hotel and they've let me set up a dark room in what was once the butler's pantry. I think it will work very well, providing no one opens the door unexpectedly.'

'I'd love to see how the dark room works,' she said, with genuine interest in the outcome of the photographs they had taken together.

'Sure, that would be great. Are you staying in town? I could show you how it is done. It is a bit messy but worth the effort.'

Julia's mood brightened at the prospect of seeing him again so soon. She was still uncertain about his feelings. She had begun to sense a reticence she had not encountered in other young men.

It was a reticence she did not understand now but with more experience, she would come to the knowledge that his early reluctance to go beyond mere friendship had been an act of protection towards her, rather than an act of indifference.

'Yes, the Fitzroys have a house in Victoria Parade now – it's just along from the hotel. It seems Mr Fitzroy may need to be in town for more constant medical treatment although they are not sure as yet. I could come along tomorrow to see how it all works. Alice is expecting me to stay until next week.'

Just then, before she could answer his question as to what was wrong with Jack Fitzroy, the band finished and immediately began a solemn rendition of *God Save the King*, which demanded that all the dancers stop, become silent and stand to attention.

'Come at 4.00. Come to reception at the hotel. I'll leave word that they are to show you to the dark room,' he said, as the anthem ended and the couples on the floor broke apart.

With that he was gone, clearly anxious to check on his latest patient, and she was left to rejoin her brother William and her friend Alice, who was desperate to besiege her with questions but refrained.

William, of course, knew the identity of her partner but was slow to recognise the fact that the few meetings he knew about between his sister and Philippe Duval could not have resulted in the easy friendship the two appeared to enjoy.

Alice, when asked her opinion before Julia rejoined them, said nothing in response to his questions, preferring to keep her own counsel.

She did not want to antagonise William with idle gossip. She'd done that once before and it hadn't worked to her advantage so she was less likely now to share the gossip that was being repeated around the district that Julia had recently made a habit of regular forays into the bush to meet an American officer whose name they did not know.

Alice was determined to keep quiet until such time as she teased out a little more information before she told William anything at all.

So William left the dance dissatisfied with Julia's explanation of a chance meeting with the American and a vague feeling that Alice knew more about it too. But if she did, she wasn't saying.

Alice, after all, was about to become his fiancée he'd decided, a formality that could only be concluded when her father was well enough to consider William's request for his daughter's hand in marriage, so he considered it her duty to report anything to him. He was frustrated that Alice didn't quite see it from his point of view.

William had already been thwarted in one family secret; he wasn't about to let another one get past him.

He walked in silence behind the two girls as they made their way back through the dark streets to the Fitzroy's newly-acquired town house.

The next day, Julia arrived at the hotel reception desk promptly at four o'clock, having declined an invitation to join Alice and her mother at the local church fete.

If the hotel receptionist was surprised at a young lady's request to be shown to the dark room where Captain Duval was developing his photographs, she did not show it.

At nearly fifty and pretending to be forty, the unlikely redhead led Julia through a long narrow hallway to a set of stairs that had clearly been intended for servants and not the prosperous clientele the hotel normally catered for.

'Go down these stairs, lovey, and at the bottom follow the corridor along until you get to the last room on the right before it opens into the kitchen. That's what you're looking for. But knock first, he said, and wait for an answer otherwise you might spoil things.'

Julia thanked her but the receptionist had already retreated to her normal spot, a position which she guarded jealously. It can only be surmised that she had not found the takeover of the establishment by the American Army officers to be an unhappy event, such was her disposition and inclination.

Had she heard it, Julia would not have enjoyed the receptionist's version of her visit, as Violet had recounted it to her room mate later that evening. Violet could imagine only one outcome from an attractive girl visiting a young American officer in a private and darkened room, even if it wasn't the original or stated intention of the visit.

Julia knocked on the door as she had been told. After a second or two, she heard the required answer and opened the door. At first she could see nothing but her eyes adjusted to the only light that was visible, a reddish haze created by a thin strip of red material stretched across the offending white light.

Philippe looked up from his work and motioned her over to the bench.

'I was hoping you'd come. Take a look at this.'

He was clearly excited by the outcome of his work.

'I've just enlarged a print from the day we went to Fairy Lagoon. I think it's one of the best photographs I've ever taken. I'm really pleased with my new camera, and with the subject, of course.'

Julia, still barely able to see, was surprised when she realised that she was the subject of the photograph.

'I didn't know you took a photograph of me,' she exclaimed.

He started to explain the technical aspects of why he was so pleased with the photograph, pointing to parts of the photograph that were particularly artistic.

'I caught the shadow of the tree just right, I think, as it came across your face. It's really hard to get it just right.'

The photograph, taken close up, showed her reclining with her left arm behind her head, acting as a pillow. Her blonde hair billowed out above her head and over her arm. Her eyes were closed.

'Are you telling me I fell asleep and you took my photograph and you never told me!'

He was concerned now that it had been a presumptuous act and that he had offended her. He began to apologise.

'I'm sorry I should have told you at the time what I had done but it was too good an opportunity to pass up and then I wanted to see how it would turn out first before telling you about it. If it had been terrible, I would never have shown it to you and never told you about it.'

He placed his hand on her arm.

'Forgive me?'

He looked at her quizzically, hoping for a sign that she wasn't too upset by the shock of seeing her own image and his taking of the photograph without her permission.

She looked at the photograph intently.

Now that Philippe had switched on another light, she was able to see it more clearly. She was stunned at the maturity of the face he had captured – a far more mature image than she understood herself to be.

She was now nineteen. For Julia, the photograph was the first evidence she had seen of her transition from child to adult.

She was beginning to understand that, in the claustrophobic atmosphere of Prior Park, she would always be the youngest child and the cosseted daughter struggling for recognition and status within the family against her older brothers.

She smiled at him.

'I like it, I really do, it was just the shock at first, because I didn't know you'd taken it and I expected to see a scene of the lagoon or a bird.'

Her shy kiss on his cheek was meant as an act of gratitude and pleasure at his unexpected interest in her, but it became much more than that.

In the absolute privacy of the dark room, there was no chance of prying eyes upon them and for that circumstance, Philippe, even more than Julia, was grateful.

His growing attraction to the young girl had worried him but in the end he found himself absolutely powerless to do anything to stop it. Only he understood the complications that could face them; she, young and naïve, thought herself prepared for anything.

Violet, the hotel receptionist, had been right after all but that knowledge would not have surprised her.

The following Monday, a fierce thunderstorm formed to the west of the city. The big dark clouds were a sure sign that heavy rain was about to descend on the unprotected Julia and her friend Alice. They had been shopping together and had been caught unawares by the approaching storm.

The two young women were still three blocks from the shelter of the Fitzroy's house when a car slowed beside them and Alice's brother James motioned them to get in.

It had been many months since James had left home to graze a herd of Mayfield cattle on the pastures to the north.

He had missed Christmas with his family but the effort had been worth it. The precious cattle had been saved, by moving them to better pasture and he was pleased that this at least was a bright spot amidst the family's concern about his father's health.

James's suntanned face turned to greet Julia as she slid into the back seat leaving Alice to slide in alongside her brother.

It had crossed her mind that James might renew his interest in her when he returned but she had deliberately pushed the thought to the back of her mind.

The events of the previous Saturday afternoon had occupied her mind almost to the exclusion of all else. She did not know when she would see Philippe again but she relived over and over in her mind the events of Saturday afternoon.

In reality, she did not expect to see him often because of his workload—he had warned her that this was possible, in fact, highly probable—but still she held out hope that she would see him again very soon. The idea of not seeing him had suddenly become intolerable to her as she remembered the pleasure of being with him.

She was brought back abruptly to the present by James's warm greeting.

'Hello, Julia, this is fortunate. Mother told me you were with Alice. How are you? I've missed you. There's a lot that has been going on while I've been away. And a little birdie tells me that our families are soon to be united, if we can get your brother to the starting gate.'

Alice started to protest at this presumption from her brother but he ignored her.

'Now that's a good omen, don't you think?'

She was glad he was forced to pay attention to his driving at that particular point.

She managed a nod and murmured her agreement. She was uncertain as to whether he would detect the equivocation in her response. She could not however mistake his meaning.

He did not say anything further until they were back at the Fitzroy's home.

That James had chosen to visit his parents in town so soon after his return to Mayfield Downs did not raise any comment or surprise. The news that his father was having medical treatment had been conveyed to him in hushed tones by the housekeeper, Mrs Fry, immediately on his return.

In the short time he spent at Mayfield, once the main news of his father's ill-health had been delivered, he had been regaled with the latest gossip from the housekeeper. Most of what she said he could not later recall but one piece of news caught his attention, although he did his best not to disclose his interest.

Mrs Fry clearly enjoyed recounting the highly colourful and exaggerated story of Julia's secret assignations with an unknown American officer, unaware that this was a disturbing turn of events for James.

Mrs Fry had added innocently that Julia was staying with Alice and Mr & Mrs Fitzroy in town, almost as an afterthought. This news tipped the scales in favour of a quick trip to the town for James, who would have been expected in any case to visit his father almost immediately upon his return.

Mrs Fitzroy greeted the three young people in the hallway with her usual degree of fussing and tutting, just as the thunderstorm broke over the city. The noise of the rain on the iron roof drowned out her trivialities anyway.

They all headed straight to the kitchen at the back of the house where the slow combustion stove radiated a welcome warmth and the table was set for afternoon tea.

As they sat around the tea table, James talked about his time away from Mayfield and the difficulties he had endured.

He asked Julia what she had been doing in the intervening months but he did not ask her outright about her involvement with the man he now knew to be the very same American medical officer who had treated her at the roadside the previous year.

He was shrewd enough to know that an outright question would bring an outright denial from Julia of any involvement or at least a denial of any involvement that went beyond mere friendship.

He could tell immediately that Julia was certain that the relationship with Philippe was her secret and her secret alone, despite the public display that his mother had spoken about at the charity dance, for she did not mention it at all.

Had she known that her meetings with Philippe were the subject of fevered discussion in the district and that James had already heard it, Julia would have felt less confident.

Earlier, his mother had added another small chapter to the story as she had chatted aimlessly with her recently-returned son.

'Alice says that the American army doctor – you know, the one that helped Julia when William crashed their car - monopolised her at the dance on Friday night,' she had told her son.

'The American wasn't there for the whole night, of course, and he probably didn't know any other girls,' she had added as an afterthought, on seeing her son's concern at the news.

She did not add that she had not been at the dance so was only conveying what she had been told by Alice the next day.

'He's too old for her anyway; he must be nearly 10 years older than she is and he's American and her mother wouldn't approve of it at all,' she said, almost breathlessly, but with considerable emphasis, in a vain attempt to persuade her son that he shouldn't place too much importance on it.

In her opinion, and she expressed it repeatedly and to whomever would listen, although not when Julia was present, Julia Belleville wouldn't be allowed to marry anyone of whom her mother did not wholeheartedly approve and certainly not an American.

Amelia Fitzroy did not add that it was her hope that Elizabeth Belleville's approval would be reserved for James as a suitable husband for the wilful Julia. It was far too early, she decided, to make such expectations public

It had been a week since James Fitzroy's return and in that time the burden of decision-making at Mayfield Downs had shifted, more by deed than by word but he was now acknowledged as the boss, not the boss's son.

There had been very little said between father and son that set out the new arrangements but in the end Jack Fitzroy had yielded up his authority to his son without any argument at all.

That easy and uncontested transition of authority surprised his wife and daughter but reassured them too that he was adhering to his doctor's orders to 'take things easy' and it seemed he would henceforth spend the greater part of his life settled into an easy chair on the front porch of his house in town, and measure the passing of each day with the morning newspaper until lunch time, a restful nap in the early afternoon and the rum decanter which appeared promptly at his elbow at five o'clock.

It was doubtful that his doctor had prescribed such an arrangement for the late afternoon but no one would challenge him on this last point.

The small veranda afforded him a good view of the river, which for all its width and vigour, did not provide a safe passage for vessels of any size at all beyond the city reaches. Rocks barred the way to all but the flimsiest and smallest of craft, but for all the lack of boating activity, there were still things to be seen and the passing traffic to be observed in front of the house.

Jack Fitzroy became familiar with the daily routine of his neighbours and he regaled his wife with a running commentary of their predictable ways when he was awake and rattled the occupants of the house with his snoring when he was asleep.

If his son was satisfied to have the running of Mayfield Downs so smoothly passed to him at the age of twenty-three, he was less satisfied with other aspects of his life.

Somehow he had convinced himself that he had gained enough ground in Julia's affections before he had left more than six months ago to feel confident that she would be happy to resume their tentative courtship on his return.

The fact that this did not appear to be the case became a pre-occupation with him for several days following their first meeting on his return. He detected a coolness towards him, but he was still reluctant to openly challenge her about her new relationship, preferring instead to observe her carefully.

He was, however, to be denied the chance of close observation with her decision to return to Prior Park and his need to return to Mayfield Downs.

So it was by the merest chance that he noticed an American Army jeep parked at the entrance to the Prior Park driveway as he headed up the road towards Mayfield Downs.

The vehicle was parked slightly off the road and partly concealed by the trees, on purpose he thought.

James did not need to slow his car very much to take in the details of the scene. The occupants were unmistakable, Julia's long blond hair caught the late afternoon light and her companion's army uniform was instantly recognisable. In their preoccupation with each other, they did not even notice the passing vehicle.

James Fitzroy felt a surge of disappointment and anger that he had not expected. He swore silently to himself and cursed his luck for having been forced to go away just at the time he might have made his crucial move.

His strongest curses were saved for the American who had usurped him.

CHAPTER 7: JUNE-JULY 1943

IN ENGLAND, WINTER had receded reluctantly. The early summer days were anything but warm although Richard Belleville barely noticed for he had, at last, received his orders. He was beginning to tire of what seemed like endless training but his spirits lifted immediately when he was told he was to receive a commission and be posted as a pilot to 460 Squadron, a Royal Australian Air Force unit, that had only just completed its move from Breighton to Binbrook.

The airfield had been hastily built on Ash Hill in the Lincolnshire Wolds, north-west of the village of Binbrook as part of the pre-war expansion of airfields.

He was pleased with the posting. His initial hopes of flying a fighter aircraft such as a Spitfire had been dashed on being told that he was already too old at twenty-four to be considered. He had to settle for the more cumbersome but newly-acquired bomber aircraft, the Avro Lancaster.

There was nothing sleek or streamlined about the Lancaster. Compared with a Spitfire or even a Hurricane, the Lancaster looked big, awkward and ungainly. Every time it took off it appeared to struggle to gain altitude. In addition to its ungainly appearance, it needed a crew of seven men.

So Richard knew that his first and most difficult task would be to choose his crew.

He had not yet written to his parents since his arrival in England. In fact his letters back home had been sparse and infrequent, whether through guilt at his deception of his family or reluctance to set out the full scope of what he was about to undertake, he could not say.

He only knew that each time he took up a pen to write, the words would not come easily. Australia, so far away, was a part of his life that belonged to another time; it was hard to understand how it fitted with his life in the RAAF. There was no part that overlapped.

He could not of course lay out the detail of what his daily life was about to become. It was easy to fall back on the threat of censorship rather than describe the graphic details of the bombing raids he was about to undertake. Time enough for that when the war was over, he decided, supposing he survived it so he said very little of consequence but enough for his family to be able to understand a little of his life on a busy wartime base.

Dear Mother,

We have finally made it to our ultimate destination, an airfield in Lincolnshire – Binbrook - which has just had its runways strengthened and extended to take the new aircraft, the Lancaster. I'll need to do some familiarisation with the base and the aircraft before I can do any operations.

I have to first meet all the significant people on the base and there are quite a number: the Squadron Adjutant, the commander of the flight to which we (meaning me and my air crew) are assigned and the C.O. of the Squadron, Wing Commander Douglas, who recognised me and greeted me in the Officers' Mess at mealtime on the very first day.

As a commissioned officer, I am billeted in a separate two-storey brick building – it's on the road that leads to what everyone jokingly calls the 'Waafery'. There are a lot of women on the base - WAAFs - the work they do is vital, although of course they are not part of the aircrew. Even their officers are consigned to the Nissan huts, while the aircrew officers get the best of everything (well, that's what they say, anyway).

William wrote me some time ago and you must tell him that I just never got around to replying, and give him my apologies.

I know he wanted to know more about what had happened between us just before I left home. It all seems so long ago now. I don't want to drag it up. Best all left unsaid now, I think.

Tell him I will write separately as soon as I am more settled here.

With any luck, I will get some leave soon. The weather is quite mild now. I didn't enjoy the winter, I have to say.

I must go now. There's a lot to do.

I hope you and father are well. Life at Prior Park seems so far away now.

Your son

Richard

He addressed the envelope and placed it carefully on the writing desk in his room. He was satisfied that he had been careful in his references to William, for he couldn't be sure that William himself might not read the letter.

He knew there was always a risk that the censor would take exception to his references about location and aircraft type, but he thought he would take the risk anyway. The letter might arrive with thick black lines through the offending material but better that than no letter at all.

To Richard, there seemed no point now in laying bare all the facts of his departure to his younger brother. Events had overtaken him in such a way that the fewer people who knew about his involvement with Jane Saville, the better it was.

He thought William could be relied upon. That wasn't the issue, as far as he was concerned. It was simply too painful for him to speak about or write about or even consider the subject for the length of time it would have taken to write a letter to William.

One day, perhaps, he thought, he would explain it but not now.

Yet among his meagre possessions, Richard continued to carry a small, framed photograph of Jane Saville.

Far from keeping the promise to himself to forget all about her, he found himself thinking more and more about her. It had been several months since he had received the news of her sudden marriage and in that time he had found himself no less consumed by jealousy and disappointment than on the day her letter had arrived.

He had regretted almost immediately his actions of burning her letters.

Now he could not even recall exactly what she had said, but still he turned the bitter news over and over in his mind. The one sentence he could be sure of was that she had urged him to forget about her. That was the one thing above all else he found it impossible to do, so he kept the photo by his bedside and maintained the pretence to those around him that the beautiful girl in the photo was patiently waiting for the war to end and for him to return.

His mind stopped short of imagining her in the arms of another man but the image haunted his dreams constantly.

Richard's familiarisation with the new base and its workings took less time than he imagined, but his training, which he had hoped was almost at an end, continued relentlessly.

'She's longer than a cricket pitch you know.'

Richard turned to identify the source of the upper class English accent from among the group of airmen clustered around the stationary Lancaster.

'And she has a cruising speed of 216 miles per hour,' he responded, to demonstrate his own knowledge.

'I see you've done your homework too,' the other airman shot back.

The smaller man thrust out his hand towards Richard in a friendly greeting.

'John Bertram, at your service,' he said formally.

Richard grasped the hand and shook it firmly, offering his name in return.

'Even at 216 miles an hour, it's probably a sitting duck and all of us with it,' Richard said, with a resigned shrug of the shoulders.

'Well, parachute and dinghy drill is next, so I'd take careful note if I were you. Pilot is last out though although the poor bastard at the back can't even wear a parachute, so I wouldn't fancy his chances unless the crate's only ten feet off the ground.'

Nobody mentioned that problem very much but Richard, along with all the other aircrew, knew that the rear gunner's position was the most vulnerable of the entire crew. It didn't do to dwell on such things, although to him it seemed that it was a serious design flaw that had been overlooked in the haste to get the aircraft into service. By the time it was known, it was probably too late to fix it.

As the group was dismissed from the afternoon training session, he found John Bertram by his side once again.

'We're off to the local pub tonight. Want to come along?'

'Sure, why not,' was all Richard could think to say.

It was one of the quirks of being based at an English airfield – being able to lead a nearly normal life in the middle of a war – there had to be some advantages in being in the air force, he reasoned, given the high casualty rate.

The local publican did a roaring trade most days, although the mood was sombre when missions did not go well and the empty stools of the missing crews reminded everyone of what was at stake.

It was the first time Richard had been to the local pub. It was a typically small brick building of indeterminate age. The foundations, he guessed, were probably being laid when Captain Cook sailed up the east coast of what was to become Australia, back in 1770. As far as Richard could see, there hadn't been much done to it since that time.

But it was cheery enough and warm. The beer, as he expected, was lukewarm too, but welcome nonetheless.

The pub was crowded with airmen and the smoke hung over the bar like a fog that would never lift. It made Richard cough and he moved to the door to seek the fresh night air in the pub's overgrown but fragrant garden.

John Bertram followed him out the door, beer in one hand and cigarette in the other.

Richard was curious about him, now knowing that he must be Australian to be in the squadron but the accent was anything but.

'Where did that English accent come from?' he said. He didn't mean it as a jibe. He was simply curious.

John Bertram was used to the question and he didn't mind answering it.

'It's simple really. My folk own big grazing properties in New South Wales – in the Hunter and out from Armidale – but somehow they never threw off their desire to be English,' he said.

'The old man's father was a younger son who came out to Australia in the 1850s. I think he had a bit of money but he managed to get into the good land when it was being carved up and they've held on to it ever since. But the sons get shipped back to Eton and Cambridge without fail.

'That's me and my father before me,' he added.

He was warming to his story. Richard listened in silence.

'My father met my mother when he was at Cambridge, so she's English too.

'Mother spent a good deal of her time as I remember on ships going backwards and forwards, war permitting of course, taking me to school when I was 10 and then visiting afterwards.

'Eton was a big shock after going to a local school at home, I can tell you. I copped a lot in the first months so I soon dropped the Australian accent and said I was from Derbyshire, where my mother's family come from. I'd been there once so I could embroider a few tales.'

He took a long drag on his cigarette before he continued.

'Mother still has family in those parts. I said I'll look them up when we get leave. You're welcome to come along.'

It was a straightforward story told in a straightforward way.

Although he didn't say so, Richard could recognise some parallels with his own family's story. His companion sucked deeply again on his cigarette and then finished his beer in a gulp.

'Can I get you another, mate?'

John Bertram smiled broadly as he saw the reaction on Richard's face, noticeable even in the gloom of the garden, because this time his accent was pure Australian, without the slightest trace of Eton or Cambridge. For all his companion's educated and upper class manner, it was clear that an Australian identity lay just below the surface.

Richard relaxed, now more certain of his new friend's true allegiance.

'Did you go back home between Cambridge and the start of the war?'

'I went back home in '39 and then I'd planned to come back and finish university but the war changed all that,' John said, as he juggled their empty glasses and the heavy door into the bar.

Richard was inclined to follow him but the noise and smoke from the bar was enough to change his mind. It took John only a few minutes to return, the brew from the freshly filled glasses splashing over the side as he negotiated the uneven cobblestones near the doorway.

Richard took a long draught from the glass that John handed to him and then offered up a short history of his own family's life.

'I come from Queensland. Central Queensland. My father has a big cattle property up there. His parents left him that and other properties and business interests too. Father's pretty cagey but I get the feeling that there are money problems looming, so I'm pleased to be out of it at the moment. I've got a younger brother and sister back home too.'

John nodded, taking in the information without comment or question.

'Bloody war, I wonder if we'll ever get back home to take up where we left off. We've got to beat those bloody Nazis quick smart and get the world back into some order.'

They finished their glasses of warm ale in silence, each knowing that the war had thrown everyone's lives off course, not just theirs and that for them, life itself was about to become a day to day proposition.

On the other side of the world, Julia Belleville's life was being equally thrown off course by the war, only no one saw it until it was too late, least of all her.

For the first time in her life, she was less than honest with her family but she saw that as a sign of independence rather than an act of duplicity. Uncertain as to how her parents would react, she continued to maintain a curtain of secrecy around her relationship with Philippe, aided by the lack of suspicion she aroused in them, for they did not credit her with the guile to be under-handed.

The unwillingness of those who knew about the affair to draw it to her mother's attention provided an extra layer of secrecy that she had not expected to enjoy.

So the clandestine meetings went on, unchecked, with the brief and passionate encounters that James Fitzroy had glimpsed becoming more and more frequent.

James had not chosen to mention his sighting of the couple to anyone. While he still held out hope that she would in the end understand that the relationship with the American was doomed, he saw no reason to inflame local gossip by referring to it at all. He preferred to bide his time, patiently, in the hope that she would tire of the American.

And Julia confided in no one. With her best friend now Alice Fitzroy and Alice about to become her sister-in-law, she shied away from such an intimate confidence, knowing that any confidence shared with Alice would soon be a confidence shared with William, and through William, her parents.

She felt slightly envious of Alice whose pleasure at being engaged to be married grew daily. It brought a fresh bloom to her cheeks and a sparkle to her eye that had been missing up until now.

She had come to womanhood with no great expectations, but now she found herself the envy of the single girls she knew who eyed her blue sapphire and diamond ring with mixed pleasure, wishing it was on their own fingers.

Where once her opinion had counted for nothing, she now found that in fact the other girls actively sought her company. She had been pleasantly surprised that her engagement had provided an unexpected boost to her status among the single girls of her acquaintance. She had, they conceded, won a top drawer prize in their eyes. True, William was a second son, but of all the remaining sons in the district, and there were few enough of them, he was the most eligible.

She constantly twirled the ring around her finger, occasionally pausing to hold her arm straight out to examine the exquisitely cut stones adorning her left hand. The feel of the ring on her finger was a new and altogether delightful experience.

Julia lay across Alice's bed, lost in her own world, a world that was not part of Alice's at all. It would have shocked Alice to the core to read Julia's thoughts.

Instead, Alice went on talking about the wedding, although it was still over nine months away. For Alice, there would be almost no other topic of conversation that was going to matter in the months ahead.

'I expect William will ask James to be his best man,' Alice mused.

'That's if Richard isn't back by then,' she added quickly, noticing Julia's querying look.

'Richard, of course, would be the automatic choice if he was available.'

'I don't expect Richard will be back by then,' she said.

'It could be years before we see him.'

No one ever voiced the unthinkable, that they might never see him again. There was very little talk at Prior Park of the danger Richard faced as if to remain silent was the best protection they could offer him.

'Yes, it's so unfortunate Julia,' her friend said, 'I wouldn't think of putting James forward for the role if Richard was here.'

'But you will be my bridesmaid, won't you? There's no one I'd rather have than you.'

She had asked Julia on the day their engagement was announced but she repeated the question now, unsure as to whether Julia had actually given her an answer.

'Yes, of course,' Julia replied. 'Of course I'll be your bridesmaid but I'm not wearing pink or yellow. It doesn't suit me at all.'

Julia rolled over on Alice's bed and tossed the latest copy of the *Women's Weekly* magazine on to the floor. It landed with a thud but Alice didn't mind. Nothing worried or concerned her now. Her future was assured and she wasn't the least taken aback by Julia's direct answer.

'Blue then. Wear blue. Blue will suit you very well,' she said, eyeing Julia's blonde hair and blue eyes.

'Mother says we must go to the dressmaker before Christmas, but how we will get enough material together with the rationing, I don't know, but mother seems to think she can organise it. She told me not to worry.'

The question of material for her bridal gown had been a frequent worry for Alice and her mother, who reassured her daughter, even as she fretted privately, that she would not be forced to compromise and that her wedding gown would be everything she had dreamed of.

Despite this nagging issue, Alice and her mother planned and plotted the wedding day with the same attention to detail that General MacArthur applied to his Pacific campaigns, only to them it was more important.

William's proposal had made Mrs Fitzroy a very happy woman indeed. With her son James now running Mayfield Downs and her invalid husband needing almost her full attention, Amelia Fitzroy had begun to worry that Alice's opportunities to get to know William Belleville better would be reduced.

Instead the opposite had happened.

Alice's friendship with Julia had meant that she was a frequent and welcome visitor to their house in town and William was the one who drove his sister to their house and in turn collected her when she was ready to return to Prior Park.

In this arrangement, Amelia Fitzroy had seen opportunity and she did not waste it.

William, less flamboyant than his older brother and more inclined to an early settled life, had seen the advantages of a union with the Fitzroys, almost before he had found himself attracted to the pretty brown-eyed Alice.

He had expected to encounter some difficulties with his mother for Elizabeth Belleville was known for her disdain of the provincial families and it was widely thought that brides for her sons would be found in the southern cities.

That this proved not to be the case for William was as much on account of the small but respectable dowry that Alice brought with her to the marriage as to his mother's acceptance that, in wartime, there were few options open to her son and rightly or wrongly, she felt that a married man was less likely to be drawn into the war that looked unlikely ever to end.

Back at Prior Park after visiting Alice, Julia walked down the long driveway leading away from the house to the roadway. She had taken this path on numerous occasions so today it did not raise any suspicions in the household.

It was late in the afternoon as the Army jeep pulled off the road and parked under the shade of the trees, a spot now familiar to Philippe and one he hoped would shield them from casual passers-by on the roadway that headed north, not only to Mayfield Downs but to the American camp that was a matter of a few miles further along.

As she approached, Philippe reached across and opened the passenger door of the Jeep. She slid into the seat alongside him.

It had almost become an unwritten rule. They never discussed the future, only the present or sometimes the past.

To discuss the future seemed to tempt fate in a world where many young men, and some young women, ended up with no future at all to look forward to, only a forgotten grave in a foreign country far from home.

But the past was safe territory. It could not be changed and so Philippe had told her of his upbringing on Long Island, where wealthy New Yorkers had holiday homes and their domestic staff lived an altogether different life.

To Julia, his story of a childhood without a father was heart wrenching. It had been his mother's hard work and sacrifice that had helped put him through medical school and for that, he said, he owed her a debt he could never repay. He spoke of his mother with a warmth and affection that she could see would never diminish.

He could see, without even being told, that Julia's childhood had been everything that his wasn't. There had always been money. There had always been privilege. There had always been status and property. She had been denied nothing and he wondered, in future years, how this might show in her character, which was, as yet largely unformed.

But on this particular day, Julia sensed there was something different about him. He did not reach over to pull her into his arms, as she had expected.

Instead he held out a white envelope.

'I'd like you to have this,' he said. 'It's something precious to me.'

There was still enough light for her to see what was in the envelope.

Carefully she opened it and drew out a photograph. She immediately recognised one of the people in the photograph. It was Philippe, proudly showing off his new US Army uniform.

Beside him, a woman, who she guessed was his mother, beamed proudly for the photographer. Even in the black and white photograph, it was possible to see that her hair had turned grey and that she looked tired, but for all that her maternal pride shone from every part of her being.

'It was taken before I embarked for Australia,' he explained.

'I had told you about my mother. I thought you might like to have it and this too.'

A small heart shaped locket strung on a fine gold chain nestled in the open palm of his hand.

He fastened the chain around her neck and showed her how the two tiny compartments opened. The first one was engraved with her initials; the second with his.

'It's lovely, Philippe. It is so lovely. I'll wear it always.'

She fingered the chain for a few moments, uncertain as to why he had chosen now of all days to give her such a gift.

She immediately sensed that he had something more to tell her.

'I have something else to tell you,' he said.

The tone of his voice made her look up quickly.

'What is it?' she demanded.

All day, he had been worried as to how he would break his news to Julia and now that the moment had arrived, there was no easy way other than to come straight out it with.

'I'm being posted,' he said bluntly.

Julia frowned, not quite understanding what he was telling her.

'I didn't expect it. I thought my work here was important but I'm being shipped back to the US, well to Hawaii anyway. It seems they are short of doctors with my specialty, which is neurosurgery.

I haven't really practised it here because of lack of facilities.'

His words stunned her, so much so that she could say nothing. Her reaction was a simple and involuntary gasp, which became a sob, but still she said nothing.

Tears began to trickle down her cheeks, but they went unchecked.

Philippe could think of nothing that would soften the news of his unexpected departure. He knew there was nothing he could do to change the orders he had received.

With the stroke of a pen, Julia's world had fallen apart. It was no consolation to her that it was happening daily to girls all around the country, when Philippe ventured to suggest it.

'Will we see each other again?' was all she could think to ask.

He looked at her steadily. He wanted to answer her honestly.

'Not for a while. I ship out tomorrow and I have a lot to do before then. But I'll write when I get to the next posting. I promise, with all my heart.'

His arms were around her, more in comfort now than in passion.

'I love you, Philippe, I love you.'

Her words were barely audible.

'I love you too,' he whispered.

It was the first time he had said that to her and she believed him. There was an honesty about him that would have prevented him saying the words just to please her.

Julia's sobs grew louder. For the last time, he folded her in an embrace and kissed her tear-stained cheeks.

Minutes later, she stood by the side of the road clutching the photograph and feeling the cold metal of the locket against her skin. She watched his Jeep disappear in a cloud of dust down the road. She watched until long after the dust cloud had settled and the road was silent again.

With no one around to see, she let the tears stream down her cheeks unchecked. In her heart, she knew she would never see him again.

CHAPTER 8:
AUGUST-SEPTEMBER 1943

IT WOULD HAVE SURPRISED and concerned Tom Warner to know that a framed photograph of his wife was one of Richard Belleville's most treasured possessions.

Having decided against telling her husband about her past liaisons, Jane's continued secrecy ensured Tom remained ignorant of his wife's earlier relationship. If asked he would have declared himself an extremely contented man as he settled into the reassuring routine of married life at Armoobilla. But after less than a year of marriage, Jane was making her own discoveries and not all of them were to her liking.

Tom Warner, she discovered, had received a typically provincial upbringing and lived in a much narrower world than she had imagined possible. Having not known his parents, she had nothing by which to understand the man he might become. The man he was likely to become was becoming increasingly apparent as time moved along.

Thrust into running the property on his parents' untimely death, he had missed the opportunity to explore a wider world but it was something he did not acknowledge nor lament, for he was happy and contented in his world.

He expected those around him to be equally happy and contented.

It would have puzzled him to know that someone might want

more in their lives than the routine of rural life as it ebbed and flowed with the seasons year after year.

To him, there was no monotony about the routine at all. The cows calved in the spring. The best of the young steers were sold before the winter. The old cows were culled before the breeding season. The job of clearing the land to create more pasture went on relentlessly. Windmills had to be fixed, stockyards built, horses shod, fences mended and so the daily grind went on, interrupted at the weekend in the summertime by an impromptu game of cricket on Sunday afternoon, if enough men could be found to field two teams.

At Jane's tentative suggestion, they had attended the local theatre to see *Romeo and Juliet* but he had declared it 'nonsense' so she had not suggested such outings again. He did not see that this was his young wife's milieu. He was completely unaware of her quiet distaste at his reaction to the play, which had been performed competently if without the flair that professional actors would have brought to the roles.

They attended local dances occasionally but he had quickly adopted the country man's way of leaving her alone for extended periods while he enjoyed the company of other men outside the dancehall.

Jane, left to the society of the country women inside, found she had little in common with the farmers' wives whose immediate concerns and interests she did not share.

They gossiped relentlessly about their neighbours, talked about their children, of which there were many, and complained about their husbands, who expected such complaints but were happily out of earshot.

So she continued to harbour her secret and to dream of a time when she had pledged her future to another man.

It was in such a state of mind that she received the news of her pregnancy.

'Mrs Warner, you're pregnant, but you probably knew that

already,' the doctor had said, in a very matter of fact way.

Since this was the natural course of events for newly-married young women, the doctor did not pause to remark the deathly pale face that stared back at him across his well-worn but highly polished desk.

'From what you tell me, I think you'll have the baby in March,' he said.

'Come and see me if you feel unwell or anything else appears to be amiss; otherwise I suggest you book into the Hillcrest Hospital. They'll look after you there.'

'Thank you.' She merely mumbled the words.

'Have a rest every afternoon, if you can spare the time,' he said, almost as an afterthought as she stumbled out of his office.

She knew of the Hillcrest Private Hospital. It was where all the local women went to have their babies, at least those who could afford the expense of a private hospital, well equipped for its maternity role.

She drifted out of the doctor's office and was momentarily taken aback by the bright sunshine outside. It had taken the doctor just a few minutes to pronounce the words she had not wanted to hear.

A child tied her to Tom Warner irrevocably. That much she knew. She knew too that he would be delighted and would more than anything want a son to carry on the property in the years to come.

She walked down the main street of the town in a daze. She crossed the road and walked into the nearest café where she sat down in an empty booth.

The waitress was by her side immediately.

'What can I get you, love? You don't look too good.'

The waitress bent towards her but she dismissed her concerns with a wave of the hand.

'I'm fine. Just a pot of tea, thanks, that's all.'

She recoiled at the offer of roast beef and potatoes which the waitress pressed her to have. She could feel a surge of nausea threatening to overwhelm her at the mere suggestion.

In her distressed state, she had walked into the café and simply looked for an empty table. Now she took the time to look around her. It was unusually crowded, mostly with women in twos or threes gossiping over tea and cakes.

It was impossible for her not to see the sole occupant of the padded booth diagonally opposite where she sat.

At the very moment her eyes came to rest on this booth, Elizabeth Belleville looked up. Their eyes met for a moment with the merest nod in each other's direction acknowledging an acquaintanceship that barely existed between the two women.

Elizabeth Belleville made no move towards Jane's table as she got up and collected her shopping. She walked to the counter to pay. She did not glance in Jane's direction again as she left the café.

Yet the encounter occupied her mind off and on for several days. Why had Jane Warner look so unhappy and unwell? What was going on?

It took Elizabeth Belleville only a few days to discover part of the truth, which she took to be the entire story, for want of a more astute informant.

It was shortly after receiving this news that all thoughts of Jane Warner and her situation were forgotten as Elizabeth Belleville instead turned her full attention to her own daughter's alarming news.

At the time Jane Warner was breaking the news of her pregnancy to her delighted husband, Richard Belleville was accompanying his new friend John Bertram on a visit to his relatives, just as he had promised they would do when the two had first met. In truth, Richard was pleased to have found someone of a similar background and the two became close friends in a very short time.

The promised leave came much later than the pair had expected but eventually they were given ten days leave.

On the second of these days, he found himself standing alongside John at the door of an impressive country house not knowing quite what to expect.

An elderly butler opened the door. If he was surprised to see two young airmen on his doorstep, he did not betray it. His face was set permanently to hide any unwanted emotions.

'Yes? Can I help you.'

'My cousin Miss Cavendish asked us to come to dinner.'

John Bertram eased his slight frame past the butler into the grand hall. Richard Belleville followed him with some hesitation.

'It's OK, Myners, I realise you don't remember me. It's been a long time since I visited Haldon Hall.'

'Certainly, sir, of course I remember you, Mr Bertram. May I take your caps?'

Richard Belleville was initially taken aback by the intricately carved oak staircase immediately in front of them and the overall grandeur of the house beyond it. The staircase dominated the entrance to the house.

A bowl of roses sat on a mahogany table at the bottom of the staircase. In the gallery above the stairs, he could just make out some family portraits, probably of distinguished ancestors, he supposed.

Catherine Cavendish walked down the stairs to meet them. Even in the semi-darkness of the stairs, Richard could see that Catherine was every bit as beautiful as his navigator John Bertram had said. She had long dark brown shoulder length hair. Her slender body seemed to float down the stairs.

She smiled a greeting even before she spoke.

'John, I thought you would never come, but here you are, *at last.*'

Richard noticed, but did not comment, on the emphasis.

'Catherine, it is so good to see you. I know it's been ages. May

I introduce my friend and pilot Richard Belleville. He's an Australian, like me.'

Catherine extended a long slender hand.

'How do you do, Mr Belleville. You're a long way from home, like John, although England must feel as much home to him as Australia,' she said in greeting.

He took her hand briefly and bowed slightly.

'Miss Cavendish, it's a pleasure. It's very good of you to invite me.'

He was out of practice at the niceties of polite conversation, which somehow seemed to belong to another world.

In the midst of war, there was little opportunity to socialise beyond the local pub. When the rare chance came, everyone was keen to get away from the grim misery of counting the daily losses and flying operations from which you knew you might never return. But it was hard to get away from the thoughts.

The drone of the aircraft engines, the flash of anti-aircraft guns, the destruction their aircraft left behind and the mental anguish of the daily roll call of dead and injured were constantly replaying in his mind in a continuous loop.

The dream of adventure had quickly soured and become a nightmare of reality. Sleep only came with exhaustion and then fitfully.

Catherine's mother, Lady Marina Cavendish, did not rise to greet them as they entered the drawing room.

The two men stood in front of her and she extended her hand to each of them in turn in a rather languid way.

'John, it's good to see you. It has been a long time. Catherine tells me you are stationed quite close by at Binbrook.'

Richard failed to detect any warmth in the greeting Lady Marina Cavendish extended to her young relative.

'Your mother does not write to me so much any more,' she said. 'Such a pity. I expect she is well.'

It was a simple straightforward statement that revealed a hint of mild reproach, but nothing more.

'Mr Belleville, you are most welcome. Myners will get you a drink.'

There was, Richard thought, a certain abruptness in the greeting. He was pleased he had been forewarned that Lady Marina could be a taciturn hostess

Catherine did not say much but was quick to cover for the coolness of her mother's greeting.

'Come and sit down. We are expecting our neighbours shortly and then we will go into dinner. Father will be along too. He's in his study. Tell me all about what you've been doing.'

Richard was relieved of the necessity of disappointing his young hostess by his friend's eagerness to impress.

He was glad that John took up the conversation. It gave him time to observe and to think.

At much the same time that John Bertram was rashly making sweeping statements to his beautiful cousin about the daring deeds of the RAF in the battle against Hitler, Richard Belleville's family, on the other side of the world, were making unhappy discoveries about one of their own.

It would take years for the full story to emerge. Had Richard been present, it might have all turned out so much better.

For the sixth morning in a row, Julia Belleville had jumped up quickly from the breakfast table and headed straight to the bathroom opposite her bedroom upstairs.

On this particular morning, her left leg dragged the tablecloth completely askew in her speed to get away from the appalling smell of the fried bacon and sausages laid out on the table in front of her.

Her cup of tea shattered on the floor as she fled the kitchen, where she had been eating breakfast with her father and brother.

'Julia, are you all right?'.

Her father called after her, full of consternation that his usually healthy daughter was unwell and her complexion pale.

Her brother William was completely unconcerned by the turn of events, having come to understand less about the female character since his engagement to Alice, rather than more as might have been expected.

He found all the wedding talk such 'nonsense' he had said on more than one occasion, but he had been told to be quiet and to understand that it was a big day in a girl's life.

What other secrets young girls might have completely eluded his unimaginative mind, so he thought nothing more of Julia's early morning bouts of illness and attached no importance at all to its established pattern.

'I'm sorry, Mrs Duffy, but Julia's made a bit of a mess, I'm afraid.'

Francis Belleville's apology on behalf of his daughter mollified the housekeeper who had already dispatched the broken cup and saucer to the kitchen waste bin and wiped the mess from her otherwise clean floor.

'That's OK, Mr Belleville,' she said, 'I can see she's not very well. I know she didn't do it on purpose. No harm done.'

Mrs Duffy said nothing more about the incident to her employer but later confided to the friendly ear of Charles Brockman that there was only one reason why young women got sick morning after morning in her experience and there would be a big 'to do' when her parents found out, as surely they must.

'I should have told Francis,' Charles Brockman muttered to himself after he heard this revelation. 'I should have told him.'

He shook his head at his own shortcomings knowing that he had let his employer down badly for he had made the wrong choice in remaining silent about what he had seen.

Upstairs, Julia lay on her bed, a wet cloth on her forehead, and her pale face framed by her damp hair. If she lay perfectly still, the urge to be sick subsided and if her experience of previous days counted for anything, the urge would subside altogether by mid morning.

She had been caught completely unawares by the suddenness and severity of her morning sickness, although she did not recognise it as such just yet. Only the tiniest seed of doubt at the source of her illness had begun to take hold in her mind.

Elizabeth Belleville had been on the verge of heading downstairs to the kitchen to join her family at breakfast for the first time in a week. She often preferred a tray in her room.

She had been on the point of closing her bedroom door at the opposite end of the hallway when she saw her daughter running for the bathroom.

All thoughts of breakfast were put out of her mind. Her first thought was that Julia had picked up some illness on her most recent visit to town.

'Julia, what's wrong, are you all right?'

Unlike Mrs Duffy, who had seen Julia's discomfort over succeeding mornings, her mother was seeing it for the first time.

Getting no answer from her daughter, she continued downstairs and walked straight into the kitchen.

'Francis, what's wrong with Julia? She ran up the stairs like a madwoman and she won't answer me now. Is she all right? What happened?'

At this point, there was no undue alarm in her mother's questions.

Her father's reply, meant to be just a straightforward recounting of recent events, had the opposite effect on his wife.

'You know, she's done that for the past few mornings. She hasn't been well at all. Comes down and then can't face any breakfast. She seems all right later in the day. I don't know what's got into her.'

He shrugged as if at a loss to understand what was happening.

Elizabeth rounded on her husband. She was about to ask just how many days Julia had been sick but seeing Mrs Duffy in the kitchen, apparently busy with the clearing up but within easy earshot, she turned on her heel and walked out.

'I think we need to discuss this,' was all that she had said as she made a hasty but dignified exit.

Francis knew a command from his wife when he heard one so he followed her, bemused that she should be making so much fuss over something that was probably just a slight illness that would pass in a day or two.

He was equally bewildered when she headed towards his study, a room she almost never entered. It had become an understanding between them that this was his domain whereas her special room was a small sitting room upstairs.

'Close the door, Francis,' she said. 'This is one conversation that we certainly don't want overheard.'

It was perhaps an hour before Francis and Elizabeth emerged grim faced from his study.

In fact his expression was still more bemused than grim as if he still did not believe the hypothesis that his wife had put forward but she was in no mood to be challenged, so he bowed inevitably to her superior knowledge.

It was on this morning that the subterfuge began and Prior Park took to its heart a secret that would take generations to unravel.

From the beginning, Elizabeth Belleville had devised a plan, a fixed and immovable plan, that neither daughter nor father could alter in the smallest way.

The conversation between mother and daughter took place almost immediately following the terse conversation in Francis's study.

In the restrained but tense atmosphere of Julia's bedroom, with the door firmly shut, Elizabeth Belleville did most of the talking and Julia Belleville, between sobs, answered her mother's questions in whispered monosyllables.

'How did you know? How can you be so certain?' Julia at least had gathered her senses together sufficiently to question her mother.

'I know. Your symptoms so closely mirror my own pregnancy with Richard.'

Julia said nothing more but continued to sob.

Despite Julia's muddled and evasive answers, she guessed, as it turned out correctly, that the baby would be delivered in March of the following year.

Of the little information that she could glean from her sobbing daughter, she discovered that the father was, indeed, the American officer and not James Fitzroy, as Elizabeth had secretly hoped.

Had it been James Fitzroy, a quick wedding would have solved all their problems. As it stood, there could be no marriage to an American Army officer who had been posted the previous month and of whom nothing had been heard since, as far as Julia was concerned.

All this Elizabeth Belleville had reasoned out very quickly. Absolute secrecy was now the essential ingredient, but there was one person that would need to be told.

Her earlier experience of keeping a family secret from her second son William had taught her one thing. It was better to trust his silence than his intemperate questioning at being excluded from the family's intimate discussions.

Such a revelation could not be left to Francis, whose silence could be relied on but whose ability to deal with the matter was much less certain.

So it was that brother and sister engaged in a short strained conversation in which he abused the American as a vile seducer and painted an idealistic picture of his sister as the innocent victim who was now left in such a state.

William's concern, however, was as much for himself and the family's reputation as it was for Julia's plight, so he could find no fault in his mother's decision that she and Julia would leave immediately for Melbourne, ostensibly for Elizabeth to receive treatment for a newly-discovered but invisible disease.

Amidst the family uproar which occurred largely in a tense

and quiet way to prevent the indoor staff from reporting all they heard to anyone willing to listen, William was surprised to find himself tasked with an altogether more important duty.

To him fell the task of writing to his brother in England, but only to say that their mother was heading to Melbourne to receive treatment for a mystery disease about which he knew nothing but he expected she would be away from Prior Park for some months in recuperation, and possibly even well into next year.

William accomplished this task which he regarded not so much as a lie to his brother but as a necessity of only telling him that which he felt he needed to know.

In fact, he thought, and his parents agreed, Richard may never come to know that Julia had borne a child out of wedlock – such a disgrace to the family, he offered up in a censorious voice that made him sound twice his age – so if necessary we will tell him but only when he returns.

So they all agreed that Richard would be spared the truth because he had other, more pressing concerns, to contend with.

William was about to seal the letter to his brother when, as an afterthought, he unfolded the two page letter and added a postscript.

P.S (he wrote, in his sloping hand) A bit of local gossip for you. Mother tells me that Jane Warner (you know, Jane Saville, the governess who married Tom Warner) is to have a child. Mother saw her in town and then I saw Tom at the saleyards yesterday and he had a grin from ear to ear. It'll be cigars and rum all round if it's a boy, he said.

To William, this was an innocent piece of news that gave a little local flavour to his otherwise sombre news to his elder brother.

How could he know that Richard, opening and reading the letter some months later, would be cast into a despair that heaped hopelessness on his disappointment, alongside the worry for his mother's health.

*

At Prior Park, arrangements moved at a pace that no one could previously recall. First class sleepers were booked on the mail train south for three days' time, one way, travelling trunks were packed and notes written in explanation.

Julia penned a quick note to Alice in explanation that she must accompany her mother on her journey south and be with her through her forthcoming treatment and that this had been a sudden decision and that she was sorry not to see Alice before she went.

Ever respectful, she asked to be remembered to Alice's parents and to James and that she looked forward to seeing them when she returned, hopefully with good news about her mother.

Elizabeth Belleville was determined that their hurried preparations should not give rise to curious speculation.

There was an air of tension throughout the house, but also a sense of purpose, because arrangements had to be put in place for a lengthy absence by the mistress of the house.

Only one thing remained for further discussion as far as Elizabeth Belleville was concerned and in reality discussion was the wrong word to describe her authoritarian grip on her daughter's life over the next few months.

Just where Julia would be delivered of her child might be something that was yet to be determined, but as far as Elizabeth Belleville was concerned, it had been decided in the first hour of her becoming aware of her daughter's sorry situation that the baby, wherever it was born, would never return with them to Prior Park.

Of that fact alone, Elizabeth Belleville was certain.

CHAPTER 9:
NOVEMBER 1943-FEBRUARY 1944

HAD THE UNEXPECTED VISIT to Melbourne been for any purpose other than to conceal Julia's fall from grace, Elizabeth Belleville would have found great pleasure in it, even allowing for the changes that war had brought to the city, which she complained about almost daily to anyone who would listen.

She noticed how the city's normally staid and dignified pace had given way to an urgency and purpose, the streets thronged with uniforms of all varieties and women, young and old, had taken the place of men in the factories, now producing all sorts of war equipment.

It was approaching Christmas and she and Julia had been settled in the city for just over a month but it was sufficient time for Elizabeth to consider the arrangements for her daughter. Tensions grew between mother and daughter as each day passed as the lines of Julia's slim figure began to blur.

She now brandished on her left hand a plain gold wedding band but she hated the deception and took it off whenever her mother wasn't looking.

In her hour of need, Elizabeth Belleville had turned to the one person who she knew could be relied on. As children they had been the best of friends as well as cousins, and so it was that Jean Dalrymple found herself with two unexpected but wholly welcome house guests.

It was a pleasantly warm afternoon and the two women were sitting on the front veranda of the house, which overlooked extensive but slightly unkempt gardens.

Tea cups beside them, Elizabeth could have almost persuaded herself that she had nothing to worry about but Julia's problem was always the first and almost the only thing on her mind.

'I'm so grateful we could stay with you, Jean. Very grateful. You're so lucky really that you never married and had children. They're nothing but a trouble and a worry.'

It was perhaps a tactless statement but Elizabeth said it anyway. Jean offered up only the gentlest of rebukes.

'You forget, Elizabeth, that I was due to marry Charles White, but he was killed on the Western Front. I never took to anyone else. It was Charles or no one.'

Elizabeth had the good grace to murmur an apology.

'Forgive me, Jean, I'd forgotten about that. It seems all so long ago.'

'So what have you decided about Julia? Where will she have the baby? And what's to become of the baby?'

Elizabeth had told her cousin the details of their predicament but had not as yet confided any of her plans beyond her need to get Julia away from the people she knew to avoid gossip.

'I received a letter this morning from a private hospital in Goulburn so that is confirmed now,' she said.

'I also received a letter from the local orphanage.'

'So you're determined that she won't keep the child? What does Julia say about this?' Jean asked, with a look of real concern directed towards her cousin.

Elizabeth Belleville gave her cousin a straightforward response.

'There is no way she can keep the baby. I'm too old. We can't pass it off as mine. There is no husband, so there is nothing more to be said.'

'It seems such a shame. Your first grandchild.'

Only Jean Dalrymple would have been brave enough to utter those words. It was only their long-standing friendship as equals that gave her the courage to say them.

'Jean, I don't think of the baby as such. I'm thinking only of saving Julia's reputation so that she will eventually make a decent marriage. That is all. I can have nothing more in my mind than that.'

'Well, I hope you're right. I hope this is the right thing for Julia and the baby. I hope you don't regret it in years to come. I hope she doesn't regret it.'

Elizabeth Belleville had no opinion to offer on this point. As far as she was concerned, she was doing the right thing for her daughter and later on, if not now, her daughter would thank her for it. Of that she was absolutely certain.

*

In England, Richard was becoming used to the routine of life at Binbrook, if the daily loss of young lives could ever be regarded as routine. The squadron, having completed the spring campaign of heavy bombing of the Ruhr Valley, turned its attention to more dispersed targets, including the city of Berlin.

The stress of flying and the uncertainty of life had begun to trouble him. He tried to block out of his mind the innocent civilians who he knew would have died as a result of his actions.

He would not allow himself to imagine the families, just like his own, who suffered and would continue to suffer for years. He did not hate the German people but he hated the excesses that Hitler had driven them to.

He could see the impact the bombing missions had on far more experienced flyers than his crew, who were new boys by comparison. He envied John Bertram's eternal cheerfulness but even he was silent at times, no doubt wondering what lay ahead of them all.

The other five crew members joked and laughed a lot to ease

the tension and disguise their fear, to which no one would give voice.

On this particular night, there was no hint of the potential disaster that lay ahead.

As they had done many times before, Richard and his crew, with their aircraft ready, waited on the airfield perimeter for the 'go' signal. The aircraft was heavy, fully loaded with its lethal cargo of incendiaries and cluster bombs as well as one massive 4,000 pound bomb.

Then the order came and the Lancaster's four powerful engines lifted them off the runway. They gained height slowly at first but it wasn't long before the green fields of England were left behind and the outline of the French coast could be seen on the horizon.

As they crossed the Channel, they joined a gaggle of aircraft, some from their own station; many from others so that the sky would very soon literally rain bombs on the city below.

The most dangerous part of the mission, Richard knew, would be when the Lancaster had to fly straight and level until a photograph could be taken of the target after the bombs had been dropped. This was the most nerve-wracking part of the entire operation.

His hands would sweat profusely inside his leather gloves as he fought the urge to turn the aircraft away from its predictable path.

It was while they were still over the target but with only seconds to go before he could alter course that he felt the aircraft shudder and the controls jar in his grip.

'We've been hit,' he yelled. 'We've been hit.'

He knew instantly that anti-aircraft fire had struck the fuselage. He couldn't see the damage but he could feel the impact of it.

He was struggling to control the plane. It fought back like a monster that had turned on him.

Blood poured from his right hand. Shrapnel had pierced his leather gloves and thick leather helmet. The pain in his head felt like a vice being slowly closed around his skull.

Almost all of the cockpit Perspex had been blown out by the impact.

He lapsed into semi consciousness for a brief moment. The plane dipped and began to lose height. It was the rush of cold air through the broken canopy that revived him. His right hand hurt and wouldn't obey his orders—it was almost useless so he fought desperately with his left hand to pull the aircraft up and get it on an even keel.

Still, his first thought was for his crew. He checked on each of his men in turn.

'Rear gunner OK? Mid upper gunner OK? Wireless operator OK? Navigator OK? Flight engineer OK? Bomb aimer OK?'

When each of them responded, he was satisfied.

Then he gave the order they all dreaded.

'Put on parachutes and stand by!'

Just as he thought everything was under control and they would make it back across the Channel in one piece, he felt the aircraft shudder again.

This time he escaped without further injury but the big Lancaster had suffered more hits.

Once again, he did the rounds of his crew only this time there was no answer from his navigator John Bertram.

'Navigator, navigator, do you hear me?'

He repeated the question over and over but still there was no response. Eventually, the wireless operator's voice crackled in his ear.

'He's been hit. John's been hit. Don't know how bad. He's unconscious.'

'Bloody hell,' was all that Richard could think to say.

'I've got to get this bloody crate back to England,' was all he could think of.

His own injuries were almost forgotten. He ignored the blood that dripped from the gaping wound in his right hand. He could feel blood trickling down his face and his head was throbbing. He was fighting hard against the drift into unconsciousness.

Even as they left Germany behind, Richard still feared the German fighter planes that would be on the lookout for returning bombers. He knew that their disabled Lancaster would be an easy target for a Messerschmitt or a Junkers 88. He prayed they would not cross their flight path.

As they flew across the Channel and limped up the coast to Binbrook, he offered each of the crew the chance to bail out before landing but they all declined.

Still there was no word from John Bertram and he dare not ask again. If his friend was already dead, he did not want to know just yet.

Would they make it? He didn't know. He couldn't be sure just how bad the damage was.

Nearing the airfield, he called the control tower for a priority landing, almost shouting into his mouthpiece for a fire engine and ambulance to be standing by.

His right hand was useless. No good fighting it. He'd have to get his flight engineer Fred Summers to operate the throttles and trims under his direction.

Four hours and forty-five minutes after take-off the Lancaster made what looked like a perfect landing. He heaved a sigh of relief as he followed his crew out of the damaged aircraft. He knew just how close they had come to it being their last ever mission.

As he stood on the tarmac, he felt an enormous wave of relief that they had made it back in some sort of state. He saw John Bertram, lying prone on a stretcher, raise his hand in his direction. It was a small gesture. To Richard, it was the best greeting he'd ever had.

He'd begun to walk away from the damaged Lancaster. He could see it would take weeks to repair.

His legs began to buckle underneath him. He could no longer focus. Even as he struggled to stay upright, he knew the struggle was lost.

The world became black as he slipped into unconsciousness.

*

Christmas 1943 came and went for the Bellevilles of Prior Park only this time, it was different for each member of the family, separated as they were for the first time.

December had been hot, as usual, and the grass in the Prior Park paddocks was turning from green to brown as the sun robbed the ground of any remaining moisture.

Francis Belleville fretted around the near empty house, in turn grumbling at the inconvenience of his wife being absent and then muttering vague concerns about his wife when he remembered the official reason for her absence.

Inwardly he worried a great deal about his daughter but he could not share that worry.

He'd only once attempted to discuss Julia's sorry plight with William but his son's lack of sympathy for his sister's situation silenced any further conversation beyond the mutual desire to see both mother and daughter restored to Prior Park and life to resume its regular arrangement.

He longed for news but had to be satisfied with a weekly letter of two pages from his wife. The letters contained little real news and was mainly filled with her complaints of the unruly nature of Melbourne and how all good sense and manners had disappeared from the daily life of the city. Apart from one sentence, repeated each letter, that Julia was well and sent her love, he had no news of the daughter he cared for above all others.

She alone had not come to judge her father harshly, as first his wife and then his sons, in turn, had come to judge him. Julia continued to look to him for her security and for her reassurance.

He felt there had been times when he had let her down but he couldn't escape the feeling that now, having had no say in the arrangements that Elizabeth had contrived, he was letting her down even more, and yet he could not stir himself to defend her. He knew his weakness now. He could give it form. He could understand it and his self loathing grew all the more for the knowledge.

William, on the other hand, was in no mood to forgive his sister or to jolly his father into a better frame of mind.

She had upset his plans. He was meant to be married at Easter and now, with the uncertainty, he and Alice had agreed to postpone their marriage for six months in the expectation that William's mother would return from Melbourne well and cured.

William had weighed up the option of telling Alice the truth but had decided that the charade of his mother's illness must be maintained at all cost. He did not consider this a deception nor a lack of faith in his future wife. It was a decision based purely on his desire to ensure that no scandal should attach itself to the name Belleville, and certainly not the scandal of a baby born to his sister out of wedlock, fathered by a passing American officer of questionable parentage from whom she would never hear another word.

To William, this was an intolerable shame that he alone must shoulder. He did not for a moment stop to consider that the child Julia carried was his niece or nephew. To him it was a bastard child to be spirited out of the family as fast and as quietly as possible.

In Melbourne, Julia and her mother shared a quiet Christmas meal with their hostess Jean Dalrymple, whose endless patience and good sense failed to calm the increasingly agitated Elizabeth Belleville.

With each passing day, Julia was becoming more and more uncomfortable and restless, bored with the small routines that now formed their daily lives and anxious for the birth of her baby to be over.

It was not until several days after Christmas that the letter every family dreaded was delivered to Prior Park. It sat on the hall table for several hours until Francis and William returned from riding out among the cattle in the most distant of the Prior Park paddocks.

As was his habit since his wife's absence, he gathered up the letters that she had normally dealt with and walked to his study, there to sink into his leather chair and first pour himself a generous glass of whisky before dealing with the mail.

The silver letter opener almost slipped from his clasp as he recognised the air force badge on the envelope. His hand shook as he slit open the envelope and unfolded the one page letter.

He read and re-read the three paragraphs and then called for William. He thrust the letter into William's hand and sank back into his chair.

Such news, such dreadful news, how would he ever tell Elizabeth, and at such a time, he lamented.

William, fearing the worst, could not at first focus on the news that was being delivered but eventually understood.

'Father, he isn't dead. You mustn't give up hope. They say here he was badly wounded. That's all. He made it back to England and is now in hospital. Richard's indestructible. He'll survive, you'll see.'

Despite William's optimistic assessment of the situation, Francis could not be easily reassured. He spent the rest of the day in his study, consoled by the whisky he drank until sleep overcame him in the heat of the afternoon.

By the time news reached Prior Park of Richard's injuries, he considered himself, even if the RAF did not, well on the way to recovery.

It had been more than a week after his eventful and unlucky thirteenth mission before he eventually regained full consciousness.

As he emerged from the fog of semi consciousness, he could feel, rather than see, that his right hand, which lay on top of the white cotton sheet, was heavily bandaged. He was relieved that he could feel his fingers.

With his good hand he began to explore the bandages wrapped

around his head but he felt a firm hand gently pressure his arm back down to his side.

To his surprise, he now found himself staring up from his hospital bed at a familiar face.

'Hello, Richard, how are you? You gave us all quite a scare.'

Catherine Cavendish looked quite different in her highly-starched nurse's uniform with her long dark hair swept up under a white nurse's cap.

'I didn't know you were a nurse,' was all he could think to say in return.

'I thought I should do something useful,' she said, 'rather than hanging around at home.'

She smiled at her patient.

'Don't touch your head, by the way. You've had a very bad injury and we want it to heal well.' Her voice was gentle but firm.

It was at this point that the whole mission started to come back to him and his first thought was for John Bertram, Catherine's cousin.

'John .... John, I remember seeing him on a stretcher as I got out. What happened to him?'

Hazy images formed in his mind but he was quickly reassured.

'He's fine. He was pretty much knocked out by a blow to the side of the head, but he's up and about now, just about recovered.'

Richard heaved a sigh of relief.

'Thank God. I thought he was dead as we limped back home.'

'Did all my crew get out?' It was his next anxious question.

'Yes, you did a magnificent job of flying, according to a lot of people I've spoken to. The plane was pretty shot up, they tell me. But right now, all you have to think about is getting better.'

He smiled again and nodded his thanks. Even this small effort at conversation had exhausted him.

She rearranged his pillows and urged him to rest.

In the failing light of the day, he could just make out the row of iron-framed beds on either side of the ward, each bed with its occupant swathed in bandages. Before long he drifted back into a fitful sleep in which his twitching body signalled that his sub-conscious mind was reliving the flight over Germany that had almost cost him his life.

He knew, without being told, that it would be many weeks before he climbed into the cockpit again.

CHAPTER 10: MARCH-MAY 1944

THE TRAIN LURCHED and belched its way across the landscape, heading north away from Melbourne. For Julia and her mother, their destination, the provincial city of Goulburn, was not a matter for interest or anticipation. In the first class compartment they shared, there was little conversation because all that had to be said, had been said months earlier.

Elizabeth Belleville could only bring herself to speak about a future after Julia gave birth to her baby. She could not speak about the baby, about the child her daughter carried. She never acknowledged that the child was her grandchild.

Julia's situation, as she called it, was a problem to be dealt with. She worried less about Julia and more about her elder son of whom there had been no further report, other than the initial report of his injuries. The news of Richard's injuries had reached Elizabeth in a letter from Francis. Was no news good news? This question wasn't often absent from her mind.

The frustration of not knowing how her elder son progressed was worse than she could have imagined but she did not confide this to her daughter, who herself was worried about her brother, but did not in turn confide this to her mother. So a stony silence settled between mother and daughter. It was midday before they reached their destination.

A porter helped the two women off the train and carried their luggage through the station but he went unrewarded for his efforts and walked away grumbling under his breath.

The only taxi in the town took mother and daughter to a private hotel just off the main street. Its black and white marble foyer was surprisingly well kept and the sitting room set aside for their use met with Elizabeth's approval.

At her cousin's suggestion, Elizabeth had written to the private hotel to secure accommodation but she had not expected such an out of the way place to provide any of the comforts to which she was accustomed.

The fact that this obviously wealthy woman was accompanied by her young, probably unmarried, heavily pregnant daughter raised eyebrows but no comment from the proprietor Mrs Jones. She was a small woman, her greying hair swept back from her face to form a small bun at the back of her head. She wore horn-rimmed glasses through which she surveyed everything with great attention but little interest.

Wealthy guests had been scarce during the war and she welcomed Elizabeth Belleville politely, noting the quality of her luggage and of her clothes, which would have immediately raised envy in any other woman, except Mrs Jones, for whom the idea of fashion did not exist.

'I hope this is to your liking, madam. These are our best rooms. There is a fine view of the park. And you will get a pleasant breeze in the afternoon.'

Elizabeth Belleville said nothing in return but a slight nod of her head indicated her approval of the accommodation. She had already taken off her hat and placed it on the table, evidently glad to be at the end of an uncomfortable journey.

Windows were thrust open to let in the promised breeze.

'I'll bring you some tea directly,' and with that Mrs Jones was gone.

Julia sat down in the well padded armchair and sighed.

'God, I wish this baby would come,' she said. 'How I hate it. Hate it all.'

Tears slid down her cheeks, tears of self pity and despair.

She was on the point of hysteria but her mother said nothing to quieten her, except to remind her that tomorrow they had an appointment at the local hospital.

After that, she did not add, I will be calling on St Joseph's Orphanage.

In acknowledging that she could not keep her baby, Julia could not bring herself to ask what arrangements would be made for the child. It was this decision that she left entirely in her mother's hands and it was this, most of all, that she would regret until the end of her days.

It was a mere ten days later that Julia lay in her hospital bed weak and dispirited.

Just an hour earlier, she had cried out in pain as her daughter was lifted from her body. The nurses tried to prevent her from seeing the child but she struggled to sit half upright so she could see the little wrinkled face with a crop of pale damp hair plastered against her fair skin. It was the twenty-second of March, a day Julia would never forget.

'What will happen to her now? Tell me, what will happen to her now.' Her voice was shrill.

When no one answered her, she grew angry and yelled at the staff around her bed.

'There, there, dear, she'll go into the nursery with all the other newborns, for a few days, and then we'll see.'

'She'll get a good home,' she heard someone else say.

They were the only small crumbs of comfort she was offered.

Julia sank back on her bed, exhausted by the effort and by the hours of labour she had endured in the hot stuffy hospital, which no breath of fresh air ever seemed to penetrate.

She could feel her hair saturated with sweat. She wondered where her mother was. There was no sign of her. No doubt having tea somewhere away from the blood and the pain and the suffering she was going through, she thought bitterly.

Tears rolled down her cheeks. She had never felt quite so alone nor quite so helpless nor quite so friendless.

She reached across to the table beside her bed. Her hand closed over the gold locket that Philippe had given her on their last day together. She squeezed it in the palm of her hand as if to summon up the memory. But all that came to her mind now was that their child, their only child, would be raised by strangers. Would they love her? Would they care for her as she and Philippe would have done? There were no answers for Julia in these hopeless questions.

She whispered to the young trainee nurse who was bending over her and taking her temperature.

'What's your name?' Julia could barely get the words out.

'It's Daisy, miss. Now, you must be quiet and rest.'

Daisy's plump hands smoothed the white sheet and expertly tucked the sides underneath the mattress, until she was satisfied with the neatness of the bed.

'Daisy, do you want to earn some money?'

It was a sudden question to the young girl, who leaned back from her task with a look of apprehension on her face. It was clear she did not know what to make of it.

Julia grasped her wrist as she tried to step away from the bed.

Daisy's tone was soothing. It was a tone she adopted with her more difficult patients and it always seemed to work.

'Now, miss, don't be going and getting all het up. You need to rest. You'll be up and about in no time. You just lie quiet now and have a good long sleep.'

Julia's grip on her wrist was surprisingly strong and she found she couldn't free herself without making a commotion.

'I've got five pounds in my purse. It's yours if you do a simple little thing for me. It's just a very small errand I want you to do.'

'Five pounds, miss? I've never seen that much money. And it would be more than my job's worth to do anything I shouldn't.'

Daisy was a simple girl. She liked nursing but she knew that any breach of the rules was serious for someone like her.

'You won't be doing anything you shouldn't Daisy, I promise,' Julia said, a sense of desperation creeping into her voice.

'I just want you to take this little gold locket and make sure it goes with my baby girl, wherever she goes. All you have to do is put it among her clothes so that no one can see it.'

Julia's pleading began to work on Daisy's mind.

'They won't let me see her. All they would say is that she is a fine healthy baby. I'm not married you see. She won't ever know her mother but at least if she has this, she will know I loved her and wanted, with all my heart, to keep her.

'Please, Daisy, do this for me.'

Daisy bent her head closer to Julia's as if to hear her instructions better. The lure of the money was hard to resist.

'Five pounds you say. Show it to me.'

She doubted that anyone would carry five pounds around with them so she thought the offer was just a silly whim.

With difficulty Julia reached into the top drawer of the bedside table. She held out her purse to the reluctant girl.

'Open it up. You'll see the five pounds. Take it, only don't let me down. Make sure that the locket goes with the baby. If anyone asks about a name, tell them her name should be Philippa.'

She rubbed the five pound note between her fingers and then quickly slipped it into the pocket of her uniform along with the locket, for fear of being seen.

'I'll do it miss, you can depend upon it. I'll do it for you.'

'Remember the name: Philippa,' she whispered again.

And with that the girl was gone.

Julia, her energy spent in this one last effort, fell back on her pillow. There wasn't anything more she could do. She sobbed quietly until sleep overcame her.

Elizabeth Belleville had not been idle while her daughter laboured through the day to give birth to her child.

When Julia awoke the following morning, she was relieved rather than pleased to see her mother by her bedside.

Her mother patted her arm in an awkward gesture she had meant to be reassuring but which lacked the motherly warmth that might have made it so.

Elizabeth Belleville's stoic resolve to see her daughter through the past few months had clearly taken their toll on her. Her face was lined and she looked tired.

'It's all over, Julia, we can make plans for the future now. The doctor says you will be well enough to travel in a week, so I have booked the train to Sydney for next Monday.'

Neither of them spoke about the baby, Elizabeth Belleville because she could not bear to speak about the scandalous circumstances of the child's birth and Julia, because she would not bear to hear what arrangements had been made for her child. It was as if the child had never been born. What was left unsaid now between them, could never be said.

Elizabeth Belleville never recounted to her daughter the details of her visit to St Joseph's Orphanage, which had been her destination as soon as she knew that the baby was about to be born.

The orphanage, located just a short walk from the hospital, was housed in what once would have been a large and impressive private home but now it had taken on the less happy task of housing unwanted children.

Her daughter would never know that it had taken all of Elizabeth Belleville's fortitude to proceed with her plans, despite her realisation that there were no alternatives.

She had reasoned that, without a husband, the best she could do for her daughter was to take her out of the community where she was known and spirit her away for the birth. Only then could her daughter return home as if nothing had occurred.

Would Elizabeth Belleville ever recount to anyone how she had noticed immediately that the children she saw at the orphanage were unnaturally subdued?

A small group of children had gathered near the gate as she approached, their wide eyes taking in every detail of her appearance; she guessed that their silence was a signal of their suspicion of unknown visitors mixed with an unspoken fear of what this new visitor might mean in their lives.

The superintendent's greeting had been cheerful enough but even Elizabeth Belleville could not fail to notice the censorious undertone in the woman's brisk manner.

For all her misgivings about Julia's situation, Elizabeth Belleville did not relish the prospect of Julia's child starting life in such a place. She fervently hoped that a young childless couple would come forward to adopt the unwanted child and give it—she could not even come to the notion of referring to the child as him or her—a good home, and this she told the superintendent.

'Well, Mrs Belleville, we'll see when the baby is born, but if it is a fine healthy baby then we have every hope that we will find a good home for it.'

'I hope you will try very hard,' was all Mrs Belleville said in response.

This was not an encounter that Elizabeth Belleville relished. The slight easing in the other woman's stiffness and formality was noticeable when Elizabeth Belleville produced her cheque book.

'I know that places such as this are expensive to run. You'll do your best, won't you? That's all I ask. Try and choose a good family for my daughter's baby. Make sure the baby has what it needs.'

The superintendent's eyes flicked down to the cheque that Elizabeth Belleville had just handed to her. The smile was almost imperceptible yet she said nothing more than a polite 'thank you'.

'I will get the hospital to let you know when the baby is born. I think it best that my daughter does not see the baby.'

There was nothing more to say. The arrangements were in place.

It had taken perhaps fifteen minutes to decide the fate of Julia's unborn child. In all the years that followed, Elizabeth Belleville never spoke about her visit to the orphanage. Mother and daughter never spoke about the baby girl whose life could have been so different. As far as Elizabeth Belleville was concerned, it was now a chapter in their lives that would forever remain closed.

It was to be many years before Richard Belleville came to know what had happened to his sister in March 1944 in an under-staffed provincial hospital in rural Australia.

At the time that Julia was giving birth, he had been much pre-occupied with his return to flying and anxious to regain his wings, so much so that almost all thought of his family was pushed to one side.

If he had any concerns, it was for his mother, whom he thought to be ill, but he had heard nothing more and assumed in his bright optimistic way that no news was good news.

It did not occur to him to question the lack of correspondence from her because he assumed she was being treated for an illness that had no name and no real symptoms, none that anyone had described to him anyway.

Elizabeth Belleville, in turn, not wanting to lie outright to her favourite son had not written, urging Francis to do so instead, providing he maintained the subterfuge.

Richard's recovery had been slower than he excepted, although not slower than his doctors expected. His head wound, now barely visible, continued to cause blurred vision occasionally although that was less and less. The headaches too were declining in intensity and frequency.

If there had been one bright spot at all in his forced and lengthy convalescence it was the attentions of John Bertram's pretty cousin Catherine Cavendish, who spent hours by his bedside, even when she wasn't on duty.

When the time came for his release from hospital, Richard allowed himself to be swept along by Catherine's plans for his convalescence without acknowledging his secret pleasure in the way she decided what must be done and where it must be done and by whom it must be done.

And so he had found himself once again a guest at Haldon Hall only this time the visit was to be for a much longer stay.

Catherine's mother Lady Marina had extended the same cool but polite greeting to her new house guest that Richard had experienced on his first encounter with her.

This time, however, he found himself the subject of an appraising eye that had not bothered with him before.

'Mr Belleville, Catherine told me you had been wounded and that you were quite the hero for bringing your plane and your crew back safely to England. That must have been quite a feat.'

Richard was keen to play down his part in it, saying simply that he thought the story had been exaggerated with each telling.

'Damaged planes and injured crew are a daily occurrence, Lady Marina,' he said, not wanting to assume the status of hero.

'It's the missing planes and missing crews we feel most wretched about. Unfortunately I think victory is still some way off and there will be many more lives lost before this is over. But we will win, make no mistake about that. We will win.'

It was a sobering judgement to which all murmured assent.

It was the longest speech he had made in some time and he was surprised at how the effort tired him. He sank down into an armchair close to the fire and Catherine fussed around him to make him comfortable. His head had begun to ache. He closed his eyes and massaged his right temple trying to get the pain to ease.

It was now two years since he had left Prior Park and set off on what he thought would be the adventure of a lifetime. In many ways it was but all the same the sheer brutality of war and the fear of dying had taken its toll on him and he had only just begun to realise it.

He would carry a small scar on his right temple for the rest of his life to remind him of it all.

'A penny for your thoughts?' Catherine's voice broke into his reverie.

'I was just thinking about all that has happened in the past two years—me leaving home, going to Canada for pilot training, getting posted to the squadron and going on flying missions over Germany. It's not something I could ever have imagined.'

It was the first time he had really spoken about his decision to come to England. Catherine pressed him for more detail.

'I remember you said you'd argued quite harshly with your parents. I take it they were very upset with your decision.'

He smiled, recalling the argument at Prior Park.

'Yes, they were upset all right. My mother is a bit like your mother, used to having everything under control. They don't like surprises do they?'

He thought he could be treading on dangerous ground here because he wasn't really sure of Catherine's relationship with her mother.

'I know what you mean,' she agreed readily and smiled at her own memories.

'When I told her I wanted to go nursing, she was bitterly opposed to it. There is other war work you can do, she said to me, but I'd decided on nursing. I thought it was where I could do the most good.'

Richard smiled up at her.

'Well, I've got to agree with that decision, haven't I?'

It was the first time they had spoken together as true friends rather than patient and nurse and she looked at him to gauge his mood, but just then her mother reappeared in the sitting room.

'Myners is going to bring in the tea tray. I can see you need some looking after, Mr Belleville. I hope you will enjoy our hospitality for as long as you like,' Lady Marina said, noticing for the first time her daughter's friendliness with the young Australian.

It did not occur to Catherine's mother to read any danger signs in the developing friendship, so sure was she that an Australian, even one from a reasonable background, would hold little appeal to her daughter, for whom she had already marked out any number of eligible suitors.

On the other side of the world where the weather was just beginning to cool after a long hot summer, Richard's younger brother William paced the platform at the local railway station, impatient for the train carrying his mother and sister to arrive. It had been a long absence for the pair and he was anxious.

He looked at his watch repeatedly and then compared it with the big railway clock on the platform. Both timepieces told him exactly the same. That only two minutes had passed since he had looked at them previously. He sat down to relax and then was up again in seconds unable to settle.

His mother's letter had arrived two days previously telling them that she and Julia would arrive home on the train on the day after the May day holiday. They had been gone more than six months and in that time, it seemed to William, his life had come to a standstill.

Forced to play his part in the charade that was meant to satisfy the local gossips about his mother's and his sister's long absence, his mood had soured. He, blameless, was caught in the maelstrom, or so he believed and he, more than others, might suffer for it. In this mood of self pity, he spared barely a thought for his sister and her plight. Less still did he spare much thought for his mother whom he blamed for not keeping Julia on a tighter rein. His convenience, it seemed, had never been given much thought but he was determined that this, too, would change.

Somehow, he hoped a new domestic order would emerge from all this wretchedness. Just exactly how the future would unfurl he could not see but almost certainly he wanted to be at the centre of things, not someone swept along on the tide of someone else's misjudgements.

He thought briefly at the satisfaction he had felt in burning the letters that had arrived for Julia in her absence. He could not bring himself to open them and read them. Instead, he had thrown them into the kitchen fire unopened and unseen. He had made very sure that the housekeeper was well out of the way, supervising the cleaning upstairs. He'd watched them crinkle and turn brown before the flames engulfed them. He did it without a tinge of regret, remembering what his mother had said just before she left.

'If Julia receives unwelcome correspondence, you'll know what to do with it, won't you?'

It had been said directly and quietly to him and to no one else, so he had been vigilant in examining the mail every day for the telltale American army envelopes.

Just then, he heard the distant rumble of the train and before long, it was hissing to a stop at the platform.

It took only a few moments to spot his mother and sister. Both looked pale and tired, he noticed as he hurried towards them with a porter in tow.

He kissed them both quickly and awkwardly and then busied himself with stowing their luggage into the car.

'It's good to be home,' his mother said.

Julia said nothing but stared listlessly at the familiar surroundings as William turned the car around and headed in the direction of Prior Park.

CHAPTER 11:

OCTOBER-NOVEMBER 1944

THE WEDDING PEAL rang out from St Paul's Cathedral as a small crowd of onlookers gathered at a respectful distance outside the church to see the bride emerge and judge the success of her dressmaker and, having completed that ritual, comment on the mothers' outfits, before turning their attention to the bridesmaid's dress.

This was regular Saturday afternoon entertainment for Springfield's devoted wedding followers and a local society wedding was certainly not to be missed.

It was a happy day for Alice Fitzroy, now Alice Belleville. Such a nice ring to the name, she thought, as she repeated it silently over and over again and twisted the plain gold band on her ring finger. Alice was not a beauty but as a bride she looked radiant in a long white silk dress which formed a short train in her wake. There was just a hint of tremor in her hands that held a large bouquet of flowers, which were already starting to wilt.

The breeze caught Alice's fine lace veil as she stepped from the shelter of the church door into the late afternoon sunshine. The veil, which had threatened to come adrift, subsided as the breeze dropped and with it the temporary hint of coolness. Her friend and now sister-in-law Julia, quieter and more subdued than usual, adjusted the veil.

Alice turned to her and whispered 'thank you, I thought I was going to lose it'.

Beside Alice, her newly acquired husband William politely accepted the congratulations from first his new mother-in-law and then his father-in-law, both of whom beamed upon the newly-wedded couple.

'We're so pleased to have you as part of the family, William,' Jack Fitzroy said by way of a formal welcome.

'I must say your mother looks well now after being away for treatment. I'm pleased we all agreed to postpone the wedding until she was quite back on her feet. She wouldn't have wanted to miss this,' he said.

William immediately looked for signs that Jack Fitzroy was simply playing along with a story that he, William, knew to be a charade, but he saw no such signs in the older man's face, so he took the words at face value and replied in kind.

'Yes indeed, Jack, my mother is much better, thank you. And you're right, she wouldn't have wanted to miss it.'

Alice felt William's gentle pressure on her hand and answered with a shy smile, but said nothing.

She was determined to enjoy the day. Beyond her own parents, she could see the top of her mother-in-law's hat. She wondered, privately, how she would get along with her mother-in-law under the same roof. It was something that she must face, but not today, she told herself, and banished all thoughts from her mind of what lay ahead in her married life.

For once, Elizabeth Belleville was forced to take a back seat. It was Amelia Fitzroy, as the bride's mother, who had made all the arrangements. It was her day and her daughter's day and Elizabeth Belleville could do nothing but watch and reflect on what lay ahead for her own daughter who had clearly not yet recovered her old spirits despite their best efforts.

After greeting what seemed like a hundred people or more, William and Alice finally settled themselves in the bridal car, her veil forming a flimsy bundle between them on the seat.

'Well, Mrs Belleville, I hope you are happy, darling?'

Apart from when the dean announced them to the congregation, this was the first time she had heard herself referred to as Mrs Belleville. Fitzroy was a name for the past.

'Yes, very happy, William. Everything is just perfect,' she declared with a broad smile.

He leaned across to kiss her but she put her hand up to his chest and pushed him away gently.

'You'll smudge my lipstick, darling. I don't have any make up with me.'

William subsided back on to the seat, not at all worried by the small rebuke, knowing how much it meant to Alice that the whole day go smoothly.

He turned and looked through the back window of the car.

'Here come James and Julia. They're right behind us. Maybe this is a good opportunity for them to get to know one another again.'

'I know James was keen on her last year but ....'

Alice's words tailed off. She didn't want to start talking about Julia's affairs on her wedding day. There would be time enough for that in the future. Today was her day and she was determined that nothing would spoil it.

If Julia had wished that a venue other than the Criterion Hotel had been chosen for the wedding breakfast, she could not say as much. The hotel had returned almost to normal although there was still some army presence.

As the two couples came together at the front entrance of the hotel, Julia felt an overwhelming sense of sadness that she did her best to disguise.

She busied herself straightening Alice's train and rearranging Alice's veil that William had tried and failed to smooth out.

Bridesmaid and best man preceded the bride and groom up the few stairs at the front entrance and past the reception. To Julia's great relief, there was no one on the reception desk. She had dreaded the possibility that the same receptionist that she had encountered on her visit to Philippe might be at her post and recognise her, but she was spared the embarrassment.

It had been almost five months since Julia and her mother had arrived home and in that time she had rarely left the house, except to go riding or to visit Alice, whose preoccupation with the wedding plans had proved a welcome distraction from Julia's misery and despair.

She never confided her secret to Alice and she hoped that if Alice detected a change in her, she would not press her for the reasons. She and Alice had only ever spoken about Philippe obliquely and now, with Philippe gone, the subject remained forbidden between them.

Surmising that Alice was likely to have heard gossip from other sources, Julia was grateful for her friend's reticence on the topic. She did not want to explain or justify her relationship with Philippe, even to Alice. Their relationship had not yet progressed from that of girls to that of women.

It became clear to Julia over the months of the wedding preparations that Alice did not suspect the real reasons for her moodiness or for hers and her mother's absence. Alice understood that she had been jilted by a smooth-talking American and that, as far as Alice was concerned, was all there was to it.

Julia already knew full well that William, for his part, was determined not to share the dreadful secret of his sister's shame, even with his wife. As far as he was concerned, the matter was over with and would never be mentioned again. It never occurred to him that at some future date an explanation would be demanded and his lack of honesty remembered.

He never asked, and wasn't told, if Julia's child had been a boy or a girl. Julia knew that as far as William was concerned, the child had never existed and never would.

But all those revelations were for the future. On this warm late spring day, William and Alice entered the reception room to applause and cheers which was a heartening sound to William.

He felt he had made a good choice in his future wife.

He did not have the easy charm of his brother nor the capricious and headstrong nature of his sister. William was solid, unimaginative and conservative by nature. His decision-making was ruled as much by his head as his heart. Alice would suit him just fine, he had decided, and having made the decision, never once questioned his own judgement or felt the slightest urge to change his mind.

Alice's brother James was, in many respects, his complete opposite. Much more like William's older brother Richard, James could charm and flatter any girl who crossed his path.

Maturity had improved him. He had discovered of late that his dark good looks and easy manners could be a seductive mix which he had turned to his advantage on quite a few occasion. But these encounters were never with girls he would introduce to his mother.

Despite his knowledge of Julia's assignations the previous year, she was no less attractive to him, but he was still determined that any relationship would be on his terms. Deliberately eyeing her up and down, he smiled at her and their eyes met briefly.

'You really look beautiful today, Julia. I hope we see much more of each other, now that we're related.' He smiled, his dark eyes crinkling attractively; his face turned fully towards her.

She wondered how much James knew about her 'fling', as she had overheard someone describe it when they thought she was out of earshot.

She wondered too if he had heard the suggestion that was now widespread, so she believed, that her mother's illness had really been a convenient cover story to get her, Julia, away to help her forget her 'unfortunate infatuation'.

She was relieved at least that no one, it seemed, had reached the right conclusion whether out of fear of being ridiculed as the first one to raise the scandalous spectre of her being an unwed mother or because her secret, guessed at by others outside the immediate family at Prior Park, remained just that—a secret not repeated in an unacknowledged but powerful pact of loyalty.

She knew her mother was pinning all her hopes on it. She too if she was honest was hoping her secret would remain buried. The pain of it she would carry to the end of her days, but it was something she would share with no one.

Above all, she could not understand that Philippe, who had declared his love for her, had turned his back on her. She had not heard one word from him since the day he left.

All she had been through since then she had done so alone, or so it felt to her. She tried not to think of her baby daughter but the tiny face haunted her nights and she woke every morning with tears streaming down her face and sobbing silently into her pillow.

'So how do you think William will cope as a husband?'

James's question broke into her thoughts, which was just as well as she was close to tears and needed desperately to think about something other than her lost baby.

'I'm sure he'll be a very good husband,' she said. 'He loves Alice very much and I think they are very well suited.'

Julia thought the question a little strange but she supposed that James was just making conversation.

'I hope Alice won't be intimidated, living under the same roof as your mother.'

Julia glanced at James to gauge the true meaning of his words and was surprised to see a genuine softness in his expression as he spoke about his sister.

'I suspect there's more steel to Alice than you give her credit for. I think she and my mother will get on just fine. I suppose there will have to be a bit of give and take on both sides, though.'

James smiled and nodded.

'I didn't mean to slight your mother, Julia, but she does have a formidable reputation. My mother is terrified of her, you know,' he admitted.

His smile broadened.

'But then my mother does have a fairly nervous disposition. I think Alice is more like Dad than our mother, which is a good thing.'

He paused, reflectively.

'She might need some help though, Julia. I'm counting on you to be a good friend to her now she's part of your family.'

'I'll always help her, if I can, James, but she will have William too, don't forget,' she said, a little defensively.

But she was surprised at James's response.

'Men can be rather blinkered in these circumstances. No disrespect but I wouldn't place too much faith in William easing the way for Alice, not because he wouldn't want to but he won't see what you see. He won't see the small details or the little putdowns. Or if he does, he'll dismiss them as unimportant.'

Julia turned towards him, trying to gauge the seriousness of his words.

'It will all be fine, James,' she said, surprised at his brotherly concern.

He had displayed a sensitive side to his nature that she had not witnessed before. It was more, much more, than she had expected of him.

His face, she noticed, was more tanned than she remember, probably from the constant exposure to the outdoors but unlike other country fellows, he didn't look out of place in the formal attire of the day. The carefully tailored suit fitted him well. He had a fastidiousness that reminded Julia of her father. He was as comfortable in the formal surroundings of a social engagement as he was on horseback at full gallop after a mob of cattle.

She was aware again of just a small stirring of mutual attraction. She knew that this fledgling attraction might have grown to be something more had not a certain American officer intervened.

He slid into the seat alongside of her but he was careful not to presume that their friendly intimacy of previous times would automatically be reinstated, despite his easy manners and obvious interest.

'I meant what I said before, you know. You do look lovely today. But it is Alice's day so thank you for not taking the limelight away from her, which you could easily have done. She'll never have another day like this, when she is the centre of attention. I want her to enjoy it.'

Julia nodded but did not comment.

She looked along the bridal table at her brother William, who was more animated than she had ever seen him. But for all the animation, he could never be as charming nor as easily mannered as Richard, she thought.

'He's grown up in Richard's shadow, you know,' she found herself saying.

'It's only since Richard left that he's had the chance to assert himself,' she added, as if feeling she had to explain her previous statement.

'Maybe Richard's in for a surprise when he comes home then,' was all James said by way of response.

Not every aspect of William's new-found authority had pleased Julia, although she would not have admitted it publicly.

He had been very cold towards her on her return home in May. She could not understand why but he had grown no warmer towards her over the ensuing months; it was almost as if he wanted to go on punishing her.

She wondered how long she would have to spend making up for her mistakes. It seemed, as far as William was concerned, it could be years.

Further along the table, she could see her mother and father, sitting silently side by side; at the opposite end, Alice's parents were chatting animatedly. She knew it was her father's usual practice to make a speech at such events. She hoped that he had forsaken the whisky decanter and would not slur his words.

Ignoring the ebb and flow of conversation at her table, Jane Warner sat quietly observing the rituals of the wedding breakfast. It was the first occasion she had to observe the Belleville family at close quarters.

Having been surprised when the invitation to the wedding had been received, although it was clearly something that her husband Tom had expected when the news of the engagement had reached them, she found some secret pleasure in the discomfort her presence must have caused the Belleville parents.

It didn't take her long to realise that Elizabeth Belleville could not risk the necessity of an explanation if she had insisted to Amelia Fitzroy that the Warners not be invited. Given the choice, it was clear that Elizabeth Belleville had decided it was better to bear Jane's presence in silence than to have to explain the reason for a deliberate snub to a neighbouring landholder.

In a way Jane was relieved too because Tom had no inkling of her relationship with Richard Belleville. He would have been even more surprised to learn that she had been at the heart of the furious row between Richard and his parents before he left for his air force training, news of which had reached her only after his departure.

In the two and a half years since Richard's departure, she had married and had a child, a boy, which had delighted Tom. The child's future was already mapped out in detail, just as she could see their future together in its monotonous detail.

She watched Alice talking to William. She could see how Alice carefully judged his mood and did her best to please him. It was a pattern that, having established itself early, would not be changed, she suspected.

Further along the table, she couldn't fail to notice Amelia Fitzroy's expression of contentment and achievement.

Jane knew it had been her aim to secure one of the Belleville sons for Alice. With Richard still away and with an uncertain future, she had been heard to say William was by far the better catch of the two. It was a boast she had heard Amelia repeat whenever she got the chance. No one begrudged her the triumph, particularly the other women with daughters of marriageable age. A Belleville son was a prize worth boasting about.

She wondered idly what her wedding day would have been like had she married Richard. The scene, no doubt, would have been similar with many of the same people.

Her reverie was interrupted by the whimpering of her child, until now asleep in his pram just a few yards from her chair. She got up and lifted him into her arms. His tiny fingers grasped hers and a gurgled smile stifled his crying. She cradled him in her left arm and with her free hand wheeled the pram out of the room.

A week after the wedding, Francis Belleville made one of his now regular journeys south to Brisbane, ostensibly to see his solicitor and to see to his business interests.

In reality, although the family did not know it, he made the journey as much to enjoy the comforts of the Queensland Club, an exclusive gentlemen's club, and to escape the constant surveillance of his wife as to attend to business matters.

Francis had established the comfortable habit of staying at the club for it had the singular advantage of occupying a prime location very near to the centre of the city yet close to the riverside gardens which softened the urban environment. In the evenings, he was often to be seen seated at one of the baize-topped card tables enjoying the cheerful bonhomie of the all-male sanctum.

Much to his wife's chagrin, visits to the city had become part of the pattern of Francis's life. It was a pattern he was determined would not be altered by the inconveniences and shortages of war.

In the early days, Elizabeth had accompanied him on his business trips but no longer. As their relationship soured, he had made it clear to her, not in so many words, but by his attitude that he would travel alone. It was an unspoken pact: she would not interfere with his short absences and he, in turn, would not interfere with her domain.

So his wife did not ask how he spent his time on these solitary trips, because in truth she did not want to know the answer. Only the smallest scraps of gossip had filtered through to her over the years and she had ignored them all.

Ignoring them was her only defence because to acknowledge them required action and action required her to face the reality that her marriage had become a sham.

The city, normally much preoccupied with its own affairs and that of the state it governed, was for the first time in its short history, engulfed in world affairs. Its streets resounded to a wide variety of unfamiliar accents all bearing the unmistakable hallmarks of the United States of America.

Everyone agreed that the city had taken on a different character from its sleepy pre-war days. The newest and best located of its buildings were commandeered for military headquarters for the war in the Pacific. General Douglas MacArthur himself had made his headquarters in the newest of the buildings, the AMP Building, which had been meant to house that company's executives.

It was a common sight for the local population to observe General MacArthur on his daily walk from his office to his hotel to lunch with his family, a routine he followed despite the pressures of command.

This heightened activity had little impact on Francis Belleville's visit this time. In fact, he barely remarked it at all, except to notice the uniformed men he passed in the street.

He spent the first morning of his visit with his solicitor, Nathanael Dodds, a tall gloomy man of limited conversation but impeccable reputation. His office was on the first floor of a building that caught neither sunshine nor breeze. It was stuffy and made less attractive by the clutter of legal files of long forgotten cases and long forgotten clients that no one had bothered to file away.

The solicitor's sonorous voice added gravity to his lament at the poor financial returns Francis could expect from what remained of the Belleville investments, which he, Francis, had, he was reminded, been selling off year after year until only the least attractive of the investments remained.

Francis listened to this monologue with his usual impatience. Business bored him and it was clear to his trusted adviser that his client's lack of interest was really at the heart of his poor decision-making.

In truth Nathanael Dodds had always felt that Francis should have turned over the reins of the Belleville business empire to his far more capable wife, except that he could not make the suggestion and the idea had never occurred to a man whose idea of the role of women was firmly fixed in his Edwardian upbringing.

Women were to be admired and courted if the fancy took him; they could bring comfort and order to your domestic arrangements, he would often say, and raise your children; they could entertain your friends and associates; and they could satisfy carnal lusts in the dark and silence of the night, although he never spoke of this aloud; but they could not, he had been heard to say, take control of business matters.

When Dodds had finished his summary of the state of affairs, he was surprised at the next request from his quixotic client.

'I want to make an amendment to my will, Nathanael,' Francis said. 'There is someone I want to make some small provision for. That's all.'

His solicitor remained silent waiting for more information.

'I'm not going to do it now. I'll write you with the details and you can have it drawn up. And I'll sign it next time I'm here. No hurry.'

'Very well, I'll wait for your instructions,' was all Dodds replied.

He was not a curious man and he was inclined to believe that Francis, making such an unexpected announcement, might think twice about the desire to add to a perfectly good and straightforward will and the whole idea would come to nothing.

'Good day, Mr Belleville,' he said, as he ushered his client out of the door.

'I'll wait to hear from you before I do anything further.'

Francis had made the short walk back to his club in time for a leisurely lunch after which, Bill, the ever-alert doorman, was not surprised to see Francis make his way across Alice Street, along the footpath past the giant fig trees that hung over the wrought iron fence towards the gates of the Botanic Gardens.

It was a familiar routine that the doorman had observed Francis take, unknown to Francis himself, on many previous visits.

The doorman, a solidly-built man who walked with the slightest of limps from a war injury from which he would never completely recover, continued to watch as Francis approached the gates, to be greeted by an elegantly-dressed woman walking from the opposite end of the street. She raised her hand in greeting.

It was not a surprise encounter for all the outward signs that proclaimed it to be. The doorman had seen that scene acted out any number of times but it always amused him nevertheless. It was their little game, he supposed, although he had not ascertained the name of the woman Francis met on these occasions.

He watched as they stood together for a moment before she took Francis's arm and together they walked into the gardens. Even from a distance, it was possible to see the mutual pleasure they found in each other's company.

The doorman, satisfied that there was nothing more to see, turned and walked back inside the club to his usual station halfway along the hallway, but still near the door for the comings and goings of the club members.

It was perhaps half an hour later when the faint sound of an ambulance siren penetrated the club's thick walls but it seemed too far away to have any connection with his domain, so the doorman remained at his post, expecting to do nothing more during the afternoon that stretched ahead than greet the gentlemen members and see to their requests.

He knew them all well and some, he declared, he knew too well for his own liking.

But that observation was never uttered except in the absolute privacy of his own modest home a short bus ride from the privileged environs that men such as Francis Belleville took for granted.

Meanwhile, a short distance away, the ambulance men worked frantically on the prostrate figure of a well-dressed man, beside whom a frantic woman sobbed and urged them to greater efforts.

They were later surprised to learn that the woman beside him was not his wife.

CHAPTER 12:
NOVEMBER 1944-MARCH 1945

IT HAD TAKEN HOSPITAL staff a full two days to realise that the woman who had sat hour after hour beside Francis Belleville as he lay motionless in the narrow comfortless bed of the public hospital ward was not his wife.

In the first hour, Muriel McGovern had cried volubly but this had subsided into quiet sobs, her face buried in her hands. Her eyes were red from weeping as she held his hand and urged him to open his eyes and speak to her.

It was between these sobs that the duty sister had attempted to fill in the gaps about their patient, who was clearly not going to recover.

'Now there, dear,' she had said, encouragingly, 'can you give me some details about your husband.'

Muriel McGovern seemed inclined to ignore the request, but she managed to stutter out some words that satisfied the nurse. Muriel, at that point, chose not to correct the assumption all the staff had made that Francis Belleville was her husband.

It was only on the second day, when they asked her to sign the admission form, that she recoiled.

'I can't sign that. I can't sign it. You'll have to get someone else.'

She shook her head slowly from side to side.

Her response was so unexpected that the staff were initially taken aback, thinking that she was overwrought and did not understand what they were asking, so they gently pressed their request, only to be met by the same rebuff.

There was a long pause.

'I'm not his wife. I'm sorry, I don't have any right to be here, but I love him, I have loved him for twelve years or more. His wife doesn't love him, you see. He comes to see me to get away from her. But she's the one with the money, so he can't leave her, don't you see?'

Her words came tumbling out, as if a pent up dam of emotion had been breached.

Her fair hair fell across her face as she bent her head, as if in shame or remorse. She could not look at any of the staff clustered round the end of the bed.

Of all this, Francis was oblivious. During those moments, he had drawn his last breath.

Mrs Duffy, the housekeeper at Prior Park, answered the telephone reluctantly. She had a deep distrust of modern implements but with no one else around, she decided she couldn't just let the instrument ring and ring and fill the house with its shrill and unnatural sound.

Just as she let out a stifled scream of disbelief, Elizabeth Belleville came through the front door, hat in hand, followed by Alice and William.

'What is it, Mrs Duffy?' Elizabeth Belleville demanded. 'What on earth is the matter?'

It was the look on the housekeeper's face that stopped Elizabeth in her tracks.

'Not Richard? Don't tell me it's bad news about Richard?' Elizabeth Belleville demanded.

'No, Mrs Belleville, it's your husband. It's Mr Belleville. He's dead.'

She hadn't quite meant to blurt it out in such a fashion but it was the other woman's mistaken impression that there was bad news about her son that forced her to deliver the terrible news about her husband in such a fashion.

There was a stunned silence in the hallway, broken only by the muted chimes of the clock striking two o'clock.

'Is that the hospital?' Elizabeth Belleville said, motioning to the receiver still clasped tightly in the housekeeper's left hand.

'Yes, .. sorry, madam,' she murmured.

She pushed the receiver towards her mistress, who had quickly regained her composure.

'Hello. Hello,' she demanded into the telephone, 'It's Mrs Francis Belleville speaking. To whom am I speaking?'

There was silence in the Prior Park hallway. No one dared speak as Elizabeth Belleville took in the details of her husband's collapse and admission to hospital.

'And there was nothing you could do? Nothing at all? I see. Thank you.'

She replaced the receiver carefully and turned to face her son William and his wife.

'It seems your father is dead, William. A heart attack, they say, while walking in the Botanic Gardens. I must say that's an unusual place for him to be but perhaps he felt like some fresh air.

'I know it's not very far from his club,' she added, as if compiling her own explanation as to the unlikely location for his collapse.

William was the first to regain his composure.

'Did they tell you anything else? When did it happen? How did he get to the hospital? Where will they take his body now?'

Elizabeth Belleville sighed.

'I don't know. That's all I know. That he is dead. What's to be done?' she said, but she did not wait for a reply.

She embraced her son and then her daughter-in-law and turned towards the stairs.

Almost as an afterthought, she said to William: 'Where is Julia? She must be told at once and I must write to Richard. He must be told too. We can't leave this until he comes back from the war. You must look after the arrangements, William.'

For the first time in his life, William heard confusion and uncertainty in his mother's voice. It troubled him.

'Are you all right, mother?' he said.

But she did not respond.

After the strains of the past year, William and Alice's marriage had marked a new beginning at Prior Park, at least for the three people who had been closely involved in keeping Julia's secret.

Approaching Christmas, which was just weeks away, they had even dared feel a hint of optimism that the war would soon be over and that, by itself, was enough to lighten the mood in the household.

Now this new tragedy threatened to unravel the fragile threads that held the family together.

Within minutes of the news being broken to the household, the usual bustle of the house seemed to stop.

The housekeeper and the two housemaids went about their regular chores in unusual silence, gliding between rooms, as if anxious not to disturb the family.

Charles Brockman, the estate manager, summoned to the back door by the housekeeper, heard the terrible news in a whisper, as if speaking loudly would disturb or trouble the newly dead.

'I can't believe it,' was all he could find to say to the housekeeper whose service to the family spanned almost the same thirty years as the estate manager.

Earlier, William had heard his sister's muffled scream of distress followed by loud gulping sobs.

He knew that, of the three of them, Julia had been their father's favourite, perhaps because, William realised too late, in the eyes of his sons, he could see only contempt. Julia, younger and less attuned to the family's practical concerns, had remained oblivious to the growing rifts between her father and her brothers.

William knew too that only their father had offered any comfort in her recent predicament.

He wasn't surprised that the noise of her sobbing filled the house for hours.

William's distress at the news of his father's death quickly gave way to concern at what the news might mean to the family and particularly what it might mean to Alice and himself.

But even William understood that these questions could not be aired just at that moment. He knew he must be patient.

But he also knew, with Richard away, he must take charge of the family.

He drew Alice to him and she kissed him almost shyly on the cheek.

'I'm so sorry William. I'm so sorry.'

Her eyes filled with tears.

'I liked your father. He was always so nice to me. We'll miss him. We'll miss him so much.'

He looked down at his wife's tear-stained cheeks.

'I know, Alice, I know. But we must figure out what's to be done.'

Alice nodded but remained silent. This was for William to decide, she thought. She could see now he would become far more important to the family but she said nothing. Experience had taught her to proceed carefully.

'I must telephone my mother,' she said. 'They must be told before it gets out.'

With that, she broke away from William's embrace and walked along the hall to the telephone table.

As William headed into his father's study, a room he had only ever entered previously by invitation, he could hear Alice's reassuring voice as she broke the sad news of her father-in-law's death to her parents.

A cold late December wind followed Catherine Cavendish through the door of the Marquis of Granby Pub. Snow flurries piled up against the building and on the window panes.

She pulled off her woollen gloves and unwrapped the long scarf from around her neck. She hurried towards the fire and held her hands out towards the flames.

'It looks cold out there. You look frozen.'

'I am frozen, Richard,' she said. 'It's never usually quite as cold as this so early in the winter. It's usually January or February when we get this really biting wind.'

Teasingly she put her cold hands up to his warm face to prove her point.

He recoiled in mock surprise and then grabbed her hands, until she pulled them away.

'Well, good news, I completed all my retraining today. I've got my wings back,' he said.

She sat down on the bench beside him.

'That's great, although I was much happier when you weren't flying,' she said, in a moment of candour.

'Maybe I could just break your leg or something so that you'll be out of action again for a few months.'

He laughed at this but shook his head. The thought of more injuries was unappealing to the normally athletic Richard.

'No, I'm here to fly not to sit around in your mother's armchairs making a nuisance of myself.'

'Don't be silly. You weren't a nuisance. Mother enjoyed having you stay. She told me herself.'

He raised an eyebrow at this idea but said nothing.

'By the way, I picked up your mail on the way here. It looks like one from home.'

'I'll read it later,' he said, putting the letter into his top pocket.

'Can I get you a drink? I assume you're off duty now?'

'Thank goodness, yes, I'm so tired. The injuries we're seeing are just terrible. Every day there seems to be more and more coming in to the hospital. But let's not talk about that. Let's talk about us.'

It was several hours before Richard remembered the letter in his top pocket. He sat on the edge of his bed and unfolded the fragile paper carefully.

My dear Richard, the letter began, *I don't quite know how to write and tell you this news after such pleasant news of William and Alice's wedding last month.*

There is no way to break this news to you gently, for I fear that you will feel it the most being so far away from us.

How do you write to your son and tell him his father has died? I have no experience of this but this is what I must do.

Your father went to Brisbane after William and Alice's wedding. You know how he always liked to go and talk with his solicitor and stay at his club for a week or so. It had become part of his routine in recent years. He never seemed to want me to go with him, but then, as you know, our relationship had become a bit strained.

It's not the time to go into that now.

I have to tell you that your father had a heart attack while walking in the Botanic Gardens—that seems so unlike him, I feel that information may be wrong—but in any case, he was taken to hospital and never regained consciousness.

I only found out after he had died.

The silly woman who rang me from the hospital apologised that it had taken them nearly two days to get in touch with me. She had some story about mixing up his name or they thought someone else was his wife. A Mrs McGovern, as it turned out. I couldn't make any sense of it, I have to tell you.

So we have only just heard the news.

By the time you read this, the funeral will be over and we will have said 'good-bye' for the final time to your father.

It was a shock, I must tell you, because there were no signs that he was unwell. He did drink a little too much, as you know. But no more than any other men of my acquaintance. He was after all only 57. Not old at all.

I will write more when I can tell you how his affairs are to be settled. I know you didn't always see eye to eye with your father and we know he had his failings, but I will miss him all the same.

He was a part of our lives and now he has gone.

I'm sorry to have to write this news to you but it couldn't wait until you come home, because we don't know yet when that will be.

Your loving mother.

He sat on the edge of his bed for a long time trying to take in the news. Reading and rereading the words his mother had written did not really help, except to reinforce in his mind the news that his father was dead.

Perhaps the hospital made a mistake? Perhaps it wasn't his father after all? Perhaps there is another letter on its way to say she made a terrible mistake and they mixed up his father with another man.

They were comforting thoughts for a few brief seconds. That was all, he decided. The fact remained that he would never see his father again. The memory of their final row was now more painful and more real to him than it had ever been.

A single tear rolled down his cheek unchecked. He lay down on his bed, his energy suddenly gone.

He tossed and turned until sleep eventually overcame the torrent of unanswered questions he turned over and over in his mind. His last thought was one of depressing emptiness and disappointment. Was it disappointment at the loss or something deeper; was it disappointment that the father he hoped he would have could now never be and that the father he had, flawed and weak in character, but his father all the same, was lost to him forever.

It would not have surprised his older brother to learn that William had not wasted any time in taking the reins of the family affairs.

Within twenty-four hours of the news of his father's death, William had settled himself into a first class compartment of the southern-bound mail train, which belched steam as it meandered its way for mile after mile through a landscape of browned grass and scraggly eucalyptus trees.

William's task was a grim one. He would accompany the body of his father back to Prior Park but first he must call on the family's solicitor.

Like his father of a few days before, William wasted no time, on his arrival in Brisbane, in seeking out Nathanael Dodds.

He found the building in Adelaide Street without any trouble and took the stairs to the first floor two at a time, impatient to deal with the legal necessities as quickly as possible.

'Mr Belleville, I am sorry for your loss. I knew your father well.'

William accepted the tall man's extended hand and murmured his thanks.

'It was a shock, Mr Dodds, a terrible shock.'

'Indeed. You know I had just seen your father that very morning he was taken ill.'

'I didn't know that, Mr Dodds. How did he seem to you then?'

It was a natural question that demanded an honest answer but for once Nathanael Dodds hesitated. Should he mention Francis's desire to change his will? He quickly decided that it served no purpose because Francis Belleville had not lived long enough to make the change he said he was going to nor had he confided what that change was.

As in all things, Nathanael Dodds decided that he would stick exactly to the facts as he knew them to be. It was a strategy that had served him well in the past and he expected it to continue.

'You know, I thought your father looked very well when I saw him. Impatient to be away from my office, I can tell you that. He was not a man for business.'

This statement surprised William to whom his father had given all appearance of being in control of the family's business affairs. To hear from the family solicitor that this was not the case was the first of the shocks that William was to endure in the days ahead.

'I've prepared as best I could a summary of how the Belleville investments stand,' the solicitor went on.

'I'm afraid you and your mother may be in for something of a shock.'

'What do you mean, sir, a shock?'

William was alarmed by the gravity with which Nathanael Dodds spoke.

'Let me be plain, Mr Belleville, so you understand me.

'I alluded before to the fact that your father was not a man of business. The fact is that he has been selling off the Belleville investments over the years to meet expenses.

'There is very little left for you and your brother, except Prior Park.'

'How is it left, sir?'

'You and your brother are to inherit Prior Park equally but your mother will have the right to live there throughout her life.

'What about my sister Julia?'

'I think you know that your sister inherits money and investments from the Dalrymple side, money that her maternal grandmother set aside for your mother and for her daughter or daughters. There is a trust; your mother is the trustee but your sister will receive it all when your mother passes on.

'Had there been no female child, it would have been shared between you and your brother. But as there is, you have no claim to it.

'Your father took out a loan against Prior Park some years back. In recent years, I know he struggled to pay it back although I think things are looking up a bit now?'

It was really a question to William but he remained silent. He realised quickly how very little he actually knew about the running of the business side of Prior Park. Rather than betray his ignorance, he said nothing.

'I think you'll find he prevailed upon your mother to lend him some cash.'

There was unusual emphasis on the word *lend*.

'I think she knew the money would never be returned to her

trust,' the solicitor said.

'There are one or two other investments and some bonds that will mature soon, but that is it. Most of the wealth your father inherited has been, I am sad to say, and against my advice, squandered.

'All the property he held in Victoria has been sold.'

The old solicitor was shaking his head in silent disbelief at his client's wasteful ways.

'But there is one investment that may yet yield fruit. Your father invested in clothing factories with a partner. These factories have been built in country towns and are supporting the war effort.

'After the war, he thought they could be put to good use, especially as they are close to sources of wool production. I think there are three factories altogether in which he has a minority interest, but only as a silent partner.

'There are dividends from them every quarter, but that is all I know about them really.'

He looked across at William who was taking all of the information in as best he could.

'Once everything is finalised, these will belong to you and your brother too although I daresay your brother isn't too worried about all this at this stage. Too busy flying in Europe, I understand,' Mr Dodds said, finally.

William sat slumped in the visitor's chair, its brown leather shiny with age and beginning to crack.

The family's holdings had never been discussed with him, or with his older brother, as far as he knew, but there had always been the understanding that the family was rich with almost limitless resources at their disposal.

To discover that his father had squandered and frittered away what his own father had built he could not yet fully comprehend.

Had it been a rare stroke of insight on behalf of his maternal grandmother that had preserved his mother's fortune for her and her daughter? Had she, at closer inspection, decided that Francis Belleville was not to be trusted?

She could hardly deny him a dowry as was his due on his marriage to Elizabeth but Anne Dalrymple, by one simple act, had denied Francis the rest of the fortune which the Dalrymple family had amassed. By a clever and cunning plan to which she knew he could not object, she had preserved the bulk of Elizabeth's inheritance in trust, to be passed from mother to daughter to daughter.

He wondered how his father had responded to the knowledge that his mother-in-law had outsmarted him and he could do nothing about it.

Men, she had been heard to say often, can look after themselves but women need independent means to be truly free. Or a successful and loving husband, she might have added. Guessing that Francis might prove to be neither, she had protected her daughter's future from the grave.

William was almost startled by the solicitor's voice. He had drifted off into his own thoughts.

'You'll still be well off, Mr Belleville, but you and your brother will have to work hard and make some good decisions to regain the family's fortune, I'm afraid. There will be death duties too, which can be postponed, but not indefinitely. Once the funeral is over, it would be a good idea for you to visit me again with your mother. Then we can go over things in greater detail.'

William thanked the solicitor for his information and rose to leave.

'I'd be grateful if you didn't speak directly to my mother, sir, until I have had a chance to prepare her,' William said.

'It will be a shock for her, although she clearly already knows much of it. With my father's death, I don't want to add to her burden just now.'

William then, in a way that was to mark his future dealings, sought to assert his role.

'I should tell you that my mother has asked me to take on a power of attorney role. If you can prepare those papers, she will sign them when she comes to see you some time after the funeral.

'She wants me to look after things now, you know. She won't want to be bothered with all the business stuff.'

Nathanael Dodds nodded his agreement although he felt that Elizabeth Belleville was probably quite capable of managing the business affairs on her own.

Still sizing up the younger Belleville son, he was non committal.

'We'll see, Mr Belleville. Let me talk to your mother about it. Without pressuring her too much, it would be good to see her after Christmas so that we can keep everything going along with property transfers and the like. We will need to submit for probate. But we have time. We do not need to rush.'

The younger man grasped his proffered hand.

'Please pass on my sincere condolences to your mother and your sister. Good day to you now.'

William stood at the entrance to the building for a few minutes, adjusting his eyes to the bright sunshine and trying to understand all that he had heard in the past half hour. Could it possibly be true that most of the Belleville fortune was gone? Could his father have been so reckless? None of it made sense.

He hailed a taxi which pulled in sharply to the kerb.

'Where to, mate?' the driver asked through the open window.

'Royal Brisbane Hospital, thanks.'

'Righto.'

Fifteen minutes later he was being shown into the matron's office. The Royal Brisbane Hospital was set high on a hill with a commanding view from its upper floors. Across the road was the Exhibition Grounds where, once a year, the farmers and graziers came to town to display their best cattle and horses.

Maureen Gray's starched white uniform crackled as she stood to welcome William to her office.

'Mr Belleville, I'm sorry for your loss. We did everything we could to save your father, but it was too late. He had a massive heart attack and there was nothing we could do.'

William nodded but said nothing. Without prompting, Matron Gray went on.

'Mrs McGovern stayed with him day and night and then of course we discovered that she was only a family friend so we contacted your mother, but it was too late by then. He never regained consciousness, I'm afraid. He didn't suffer. He wouldn't have felt a thing.'

She felt she should say more but struggled to find the right words.

'I'm sorry my staff weren't more alert though. We just assumed who Mrs McGovern would be. She was so upset. We didn't really press her for any details, at least until the second day. By that time, it was too late. Too late, Mr Belleville, to get you or your mother to Brisbane. Far too late. All we could do was telephone with the bad news.'

Maureen Gray had barely drawn breath. William noticed an anxious look on her face without really understanding the reason.

She had been expecting Mrs Belleville so William's appearance took her by surprise initially but she was equally well aware that the hospital had made a terrible error, which she was anxious to mitigate.

She had decided that being honest with Francis Belleville's family was all she could do, rather than attempt to cover up their mistake.

William sat quietly for a moment. In the silence, sounds from the hallway outside penetrated the office. A hospital trolley rattled by. He could hear the distinct hiss of the trolley buses outside the window.

'I'm sorry my mother couldn't come, Matron.'

William felt ill at ease. He didn't really know what to say but he knew something was expected of him.

'The journey, you understand. Just too far for her,' he stammered. 'But she wanted me to come and say thank you to the staff who had looked after my father.'

He twirled his hat round and round in his fingers in a nervous fidget.

Maureen Gray offered more words of comfort to the serious young man who sat across the desk from her.

'I understand. It's a shock when a loved one is travelling away from home and you hear such dreadful news.'

William cleared his throat, not quite knowing how to phrase the next question.

'Who is Mrs McGovern? Do you know her? My mother couldn't place her among her friends and acquaintances. But it's quite likely it was someone she's forgotten all about.'

Maureen Gray had guessed that this question was coming and she did her best to answer, without betraying the secrets that the distraught woman had blurted out.

'I can't help you there, Mr Belleville, I'd never seen her before. No one on my staff knows the lady but she was very upset. Very, very upset in fact so we assumed she was a close friend of the family. I have her address here. Maybe you could arrange to call on her.'

As soon as she had made this offer, Maureen Gray regretted it. She knew she had gone too far in her efforts to make amends to the family.

William took the piece of paper and looked down at the address. It didn't mean anything to him but he didn't know Brisbane well. He assumed a taxi driver wouldn't have any problems.

'Thank you, Matron, for your help. We are all grateful.'

He slipped the scrap of paper into his pocket and bade farewell to the matron, who had begun to think through the implications of giving Muriel McGovern's address to the young son of her recently deceased patient.

'Perhaps you should write to Mrs McGovern first seeking an appointment, Mr Belleville,' she suggested.

She said these words to the departing figure of William, as he strode purposefully down the hospital corridor.

He did not hear her. He was already absorbed by this new mystery and was determined to discover exactly who this Muriel McGovern was and what role she had played in his father's life.

Before he had left Prior Park, his mother had reluctantly discussed the fact that another woman had been initially mistaken for his father's wife by the hospital.

He'd accepted this information from his mother with only the obvious question: how could anyone do that?

Solid straightforward William could not imagine any circumstances under which any other woman, other than his own mother, could be presumed to be his father's wife.

This was a mystery that demanded to be unravelled and unravel it he would.

Less than an hour after leaving the hospital, William was preparing to knock at the front door of a modest but well kept house undistinguished from the row of similar houses of which it was the middle house.

There was a small neatly cropped patch of green lawn on either side of the front steps which were framed by tidy shrubs he couldn't identify. The path to the front steps was free of leaves as if it had been swept just that morning. He'd noticed remnants of jacaranda flowers along the footpath but there was no evidence of their intrusion into the neatness that he saw around him.

Just as he raised his clenched fist to knock, the door opened. He knew then that his approach had been observed.

Before he could say a word, Muriel McGovern extended her hand which he took reluctantly.

'Mr Belleville, please come in.'

'How did you know who I was?'

William stammered the words to cover his confusion.

'The matron telephoned me from the hospital. I think she felt

I might need a warning, which was kind of her. But I would have recognised you anyway. You look so like your father.'

This was the first time that William had considered there was any resemblance at all between himself and his father. If there was a resemblance at all, he judged it to be purely physical. Where his father had been charming and feckless, William was as opposite as a man could be.

At twenty-two years old, he was already established in a pattern which marked out his life ahead. He was married and settled in a comfortable routine that a man twenty years his senior might have found boring. Yet, to William, it was reassuring.

The gold signet ring his father had worn would have looked ridiculous on him, he had decided. It nestled in the pocket of his jacket. He hadn't even been tempted to try it on when Nathanael Dodds had handed it over. He was glad it was Richard's. Richard would wear it with the same élan that his father had. He didn't care for such trivial things. Life was a serious matter. And life, with his father's untimely death, had just become so much more serious.

Muriel McGovern stepped to one side to allow William onto the small front porch which led directly to an enclosed sitting room, which he supposed had once been an open veranda.

She motioned him to a cane armchair. Then she sat in the one opposite.

A jug of fresh lemonade sat between them. She offered him a glass which he took without really knowing why although he discovered to his surprise he was thirsty.

He watched as she poured herself a glass of the sweet tangy drink. He was trying to guess her age. Forty, perhaps a little older. Her fair hair was swept up and away from her face. Despite her simple cotton dress, there was an air of elegance in the way she sat and in the way she did the smallest things.

In the normal course of events, these things would have gone unnoticed by William but today he was noticing everything. He wished Alice was here to discuss it all. He had come to rely on Alice's good sense in all things. She would know what to say and what to do.

'Mrs McGovern, I'm not quite sure what to say.'

William was hesitant, hoping that she would fill in the story.

'What do you want me to tell you, Mr Belleville?'

Muriel McGovern's questioning reply gave him no help at all, so he plunged on.

'Mrs McGovern, how did you know my father? How was it that you came to be with him when he had his heart attack?'

She looked down at her lap and then glanced up at him.

'This is not going to be a happy story for you and your family to hear, Mr Belleville. Are you sure you want to? You can go now and we need never see each other again.'

William thought for a moment. Could he take such an offer? Could he walk out of this neat little house and pretend he had never been there? It was a tempting prospect but one that tempted him only for a moment.

To have these nagging questions about his father go unanswered, he decided, would be worse than hearing the truth. The truth after all, he had been taught, was always the best policy.

He sat perfectly still as Muriel McGovern began her story. When it was over, William wondered if he had really known his father at all. How much he would tell the rest of the family was now in his hands.

As he walked away down the street towards the tram stop, he looked back just as a young boy pushed open the front gate of the house from which he had just emerged.

It only occurred to William much later that the boy bore a marked resemblance to the young lad he had once been. That knowledge, he decided, he would certainly keep to himself.

CHAPTER 13: JUNE-OCTOBER 1945

IT WAS MORE THAN eighteen months before Philippe Duval gave up searching through his mail for a letter from Julia. Within days of arriving in Hawaii, he had written to her and had continued to do so almost every week so he found her silence baffling.

He could recall the first letter he had written her almost word for word. In it he had promised to come back for her after the war.

Each time he received mail he flicked through the envelopes quickly, his hopes for a letter from her rising whenever he saw an unusual envelope only to be dashed time and again.

He was not an impatient man but he became a disappointed man as the months stretched by.

He did not understand her silence. He was now as sure as he had been of anything in his life that he loved the young Australian girl and he was sure too that she loved him. He had believed it to be more than just another wartime romance and he had thought she felt the same way too.

Was she already dancing in the arms of another American officer? He hoped not but he feared as much, or had her mother discovered their secret and forbidden her to go out and forbidden her to write to him?

He could only speculate and he found that the endless speculation did him no good at all. Thoughts of Julia tormented his waking hours and his dreams.

He slapped wearily at a mosquito which had landed on his

forearm. Its blood trickled down his arm. He wiped it away, as he had done a thousand times before.

He got up from his desk where he had been updating his medical reports and headed out to the makeshift surgical wards housed in a flimsy prefabricated building that had been hastily constructed following the bombing of the hospital in 1941.

He knew that plans for a new hospital were well advanced but in the meantime, the conditions for the medical staff and patients were difficult. Still there was a sense of satisfaction that he had done his best, as a surgeon, for the wounded men now recovering under his care.

'How are you feeling?' He bent over a young man whose head was swathed in bandages.

'Not bad, sir, not too bad.'

The young man tried to lift his head but Philippe laid a restraining hand on his shoulder.

'Try not to move too much, at least for another day or two. You'll find a day or two will make a big difference.'

'Thank you, sir,' he said, and closed his eyes.

The young nurse alongside Philippe marvelled at his gentle and reassuring manner.

'You're very good with the patients, doctor,' she said. 'They like you and they trust you.' She did not need to add that she liked and trusted him too.

'Thank you, nurse,' he said quietly. 'But they'll soon be someone else's responsibility. I'm being sent home. In fact, back to Washington. The Army has plans for me, it seems, although I'm not sure I have plans for the Army, once this is finished.'

He turned towards her and realised she wasn't one of the regular nurses on his wards.

'You're new here, aren't you?'

'Yes, my name's Rosemary. I've just qualified for the surgical ward,' she volunteered.

'Thank you, Rosemary. Keep a good eye on this patient, but I think he should be fine.'

He smiled at her and walked back to his office.

She watched him until he closed the door.

'Not falling in love with the doctor are you, nurse?'

One of her patients, Jack, well on the road to recovery and bored with the hospital routine, hadn't failed to notice the extra spring in her step and her eagerness to please the young surgeon.

'I bet all the nurses are after him,' he said, when she failed to respond to his question.

'But the rumour is that he fell in love with an Australian girl and hasn't gotten over her yet. She threw him over apparently.'

Rosemary absorbed this new piece of information in silence.

So that's why he hasn't been going out with any of the nurses here, she thought. That explains everything.

With that, she turned her attention to Jack who was eagerly anticipating the attentions of the pretty young brunette.

Morning in London dawned bright with the promise of a fine day. Richard stretched out in the luxury of clean crisp sheets. His injuries had healed. Only the faintest of scars was visible above his right eye and he felt only an occasional twinge in his right hand.

Peace in Europe had been declared although no one was yet counting the cost. The euphoria of victory was real. VE Day might have been a month ago but everyone continued to celebrate. It was as if a heavy veil had been lifted from the country.

Beside him, Catherine slept on, her hair, slightly dishevelled, spread across the white pillow.

He caressed the curve of her right breast lightly. His hand moved down her body slowly and confidently.

She stirred and rolled towards him.

'So, Mr Belleville, this is how you wake a girl in the morning?'

He began to kiss her but she pushed him away teasingly.

'You haven't heard of rationing then, I take it?'

He laughed.

'I see no sign of rationing in this hotel.'

The Dorchester was already stirring to life as it had every day throughout the war, except that now the war was over, there was a sense of relief and a feeling that the world could resume its normal tempo.

'You never did explain how you managed to get this room?'

'Richard, I can do a passable imitation of my mother when it suits me. As far as the hotel is concerned, I am Lady Marina Cavendish. Respectable, middle aged and in London to consult a Harley Street surgeon. A very plausible cover story, don't you think?'

'There's one flaw. You won't pass for middle-aged.'

'Ah … but the hotel is the absolute ultimate in discretion.'

Richard assumed that this fact was known to Catherine by hearsay so he did not pursue it. Instead he rolled out of bed and headed for the bathroom.

'Let's not waste this beautiful day. Let's see the sights of London, or what's left of it.'

He was making a determined effort to banish thoughts of the future, thoughts of home, the loss of his father and the terrible cost of war from his mind. In quiet moments he was haunted by the things he had done, the things he had seen and the friends he had lost.

For the first time in a very long time, he was determined to think only of the day ahead, a rare day of leisure and pleasure.

For some time, they walked almost aimlessly past damaged buildings and gutted houses. He was surprised to see red, white and blue banners running the full length of St Pancras Station, the remnants of the victory celebrations from a month before. He noticed that the shops had begun to remove their blackout precautions. The Union Jack waved from every balustrade.

They walked on until they could see the towering dome of St Paul's Cathedral which had survived the blitz while buildings close by had been reduced to piles of rubble.

They noticed queues of housewives, ration books in hand, desperate for meagre meat rations. Groups of wide-eyed children scuttled past them at regular intervals.

They had walked without speaking for miles, too stunned by what they saw to feel that idle chatter was even appropriate.

As if reminded of something she had read, Catherine broke the silence.

She pointed to a group of children getting off a bus, small suitcases in hand, to be met in eager embraces by parents they hardly now knew.

'I believe all the children are being brought back to their homes now, that is, if their homes are still standing—or their parents are still standing, come to that,' she said. 'They must be the lucky ones.'

'Yes, indeed, the lucky ones,' Richard responded, but he could find nothing else to say.

They stood together watching the touching scene for a few minutes until the bus moved off and the newly-reunited families dispersed.

There were no 'lucky ones' in war, he thought, only survivors, and some of them not so lucky after all.

Richard's early morning exuberance had given way to a sombre reflective mood. The devastation of the city reminded him of the devastation he himself had caused over Germany. They were not pretty thoughts.

The smallest thing would summon up haunting images of bomb damage and each time he fought a losing battle to banish the images from his mind. Each time he resorted to the only sure way, to think of home, to think of Prior Park, to remember the sun and the heat and the trees and the wide open spaces and the blue sky. Especially the blue sky.

In his very being, he yearned for home, and yet he feared a return to his old life.

He had left as a boy; he would return a man, changed forever by his experiences. The old life was gone, he told himself. His father was dead; he and his brother now owned Prior Park. What did it all mean to him now?

After a few more minutes of silence, Catherine ventured again. 'A penny for your thoughts?'

Catherine's instinct was unerring. She had only to look at his face to know when his mind had wandered to another continent, another time, another place.

'This city will take a long time to rebuild. In fact this country will take a long time to rebuild, now that the war is over,' he said, finally.

Everywhere they looked they saw damage: to buildings, to roadways, to people. Broken lives that would never be the same again. Broken people who would never mend. Broken buildings that would demand a reconstruction of the extent that London had never seen before.

Finally he said what she had expected him to say for a month or more.

'I will be going home, darling, you know that. I will be going home in a few months' time, when the squadron is disbanded.'

He put his arm around her shoulders and drew her close.

But he knew it was what he did not say that stood between them. He did not say: 'come with me, be my wife and live in Australia.'

He did not say it because he wasn't sure he wanted it.

While the war continued, they had lived each day as if it were their last. With the war ended, the question mark remained. Was this a war-time romance that would end, just as the war had ended? Was it destined to end on a day of their choosing, perhaps with celebration and a final good-bye? Had he completely forgotten Jane Saville?

She wanted to say 'I'll go with you', but something held her back.

She wanted him to ask. She wanted him to make the offer. She wanted him to offer his whole heart to her.

But was this what she really wanted? Or was it just the euphoria at the end of the bleak years of war that both of them were mistaking for love. She did not know. She did not know if she could give up her life in England for a country across the other side of the world that took weeks to reach by ship.

For his part, he could not picture her at Prior Park. He could not see the fine aristocratic face, whose family connections would gain her entrée to the best of London society, beneath a straw hat in a sun frock on the back veranda at Prior Park, so far from the gaiety and sophistication of the society she knew.

So they continued to walk on, in silence mostly, each lost in their own thoughts, unsure of the future, only sure of their pleasure in each other's arms and of their physical longing for one another.

At Prior Park, Richard's mother was in an altogether different frame of mind from what Richard had imagined.

It had been more than six months since her husband's funeral. As expected the whole district had turned out en masse for the event which took place in the church where Alice and William had married just a month before.

To those around her, Elizabeth Belleville seemed diminished by the event.

She no longer commanded the household with quite the same air of invincible authority. Somehow her authority had been eroded just a little with her husband's untimely death.

At the same time her second son's authority had grown unchecked. With no older brother to restrain him, William was free to do much as he pleased and that situation pleased him enormously.

With the Belleville properties and wealth, what remained of it, to be split between William and his older brother, Elizabeth soon realised that she was powerless to act as a restraining hand on her younger son's plans.

In the end she surrendered meekly to William's urging to hand over full power to run the family's interests, except of course, for her trust fund, over which she would yield not an inch.

She did not know or even suspect that William's account of his visit to Mrs Muriel McGovern was one that he had carefully rehearsed silently over and over. So well rehearsed had his story been that the excellent piece of fiction he eventually relayed to his mother and his sister was accepted without question.

She had expressed only mild surprise that someone her husband had known as an assistant in the office of his club could react in such a heartfelt way to his misfortune. But she did not probe further, for which William was thankful. He was not a natural storyteller and he felt he had reached the limits of his invention with the carefully structured tale.

He murmured something that hardly encouraged her in the idea that she must thank the woman personally for her efforts, but not now.

There's no urgency for that, Mother, he had said. She felt certain anyway that William would have said all that was right and proper in the circumstances.

She sat down at her desk. From the first floor, there was a fine view but it was now a lonely view.

Her growing sense of disappointment and bitterness at her husband's shortcomings was now forgotten, or if not forgotten, set aside, replaced by a new understanding that theirs had been a comfortable relationship, which she now missed. Her world seemed suddenly incomplete. She had not valued him in life but now she found much to value in her dearly departed husband in her widowhood.

She sat at her writing desk for a full half hour without moving, except to slide open the bottom left hand drawer. Beneath an untidy bundle of solicitor's papers, her fingers closed around a pile of letters, tied with kitchen string.

The letters were unopened. The collection of them had represented a successful conspiracy between herself, Francis and William for which she would never admit any shame. William, she knew, had destroyed any that had arrived while she and Julia were absent from Prior Park. They had all agreed that there was nothing to be gained by Julia receiving letters from her American lover.

The fact that she had lied openly and without remorse to her only daughter about the existence of the letters caused her no grief at all. She hardly felt the need to justify her actions to herself, let alone to her daughter. In her mind she was providing the protection her daughter needed and for which she would one day thank her. On that point she would never be moved to change her mind.

She was grateful that the weather was cool enough for a fire to have been lit in her sitting room. Such days were rare so she decided to take advantage of the opportunity it presented.

She got up from the desk and moved to the fire where a very small flame flickered from the dry wood and kindling. One by one she fed the letters into the flames. She watched the paper curl and crackle as each letter burned.

Their vigilance had paid off, she decided. There had been no letters for four months. Maybe he was dead; maybe he'd given up. She didn't know but what did it matter? It was all in the past. It was all forgotten. No one would ever talk about it again. Ever.

She gave a small smile of satisfaction as the last of the letters turned to ash. She stirred it with the brass poker just to be certain, until no evidence remained and the fire subsided.

She then turned back to her writing desk and began the task of writing to Richard. With the war already over in Europe, her hopes were high that he would return home very soon. That, at least, was something to look forward to.

*

In his now more frequent trips to Brisbane, William had quickly become familiar with the short walk from his hotel to the solicitor's office.

On this occasion he had more reason for urgency than usual. In his eagerness to see the solicitor at the appointed hour of ten o'clock, William had left his hotel a full half hour before the appointment so he sat in the visitor's chair in the outer office, impatiently drumming his fingers on the secretary's desk.

In the time since his father's death, he had been frustrated at the slow pace of the legal process that would eventually grant him effective control of the Belleville inheritance but today he carried with him all the documents that had required his mother's signature to grant him sole operating authority. All that remained was for the solicitor to agree that everything was in order and he, William, would be in effective control, pending the return of his brother, at which point they would be in joint control.

In an unexpected provision in his will, Francis Belleville had foreseen the possibility of war and the possibility that one of his sons could be overseas for an extended period. In that instance, he had nominated his wife to act for the absent son. What he had not expected was that his wife would so readily abdicate this responsibility by assigning the power to the remaining son. The fact that she had done so at very little urging from William would have surprised him.

What would not have surprised him was William's persuasive argument to his mother that he would take care of Richard's interests as if they were his own.

Nathanael Dodds had been heard to say to his partners that he was far from happy at the direction the young Mr Belleville was taking but he was powerless to stop him.

'If only Mrs Belleville was prepared to take a greater interest, all would be well,' he lamented a number of times to anyone who would listen.

'But she is happy to trust William to run everything for himself and his brother, so what can I do but advise him, as best I can.

'If only his brother would come home then things could change.'

But far from wishing his brother was back home, William was beginning to understand the advantages of having his brother on the other side of the world.

As far as William was concerned, he was in no hurry to welcome home the prodigal son.

It had been almost three years since Jane Saville had married Tom Warner. In that time she had become a mother and Tom Warner had the son he craved.

Little Tommy, as he was now known, gave every appearance that he would grow up in the image of his father. He was a sturdy child with a strong little body, his face framed with a smattering of light brown hair that already looked more boyish than babyish, as if he was in a hurry to leave his baby looks behind him.

In the time that had elapsed since her marriage, the small circle of people who had known of her previous attachment to Richard Belleville had been reduced by the death of his father. Now there was only herself, Richard and his mother Elizabeth who knew. And with the reducing circle, the fear that her secret would slip out reduced too.

She had been reassured, not so much by words, but by deeds that William Belleville did not know the reason for his parents' violent argument with his older brother, so Jane knew that her secret had been a secret of just four people. And if William did not know, then his new wife, Alice, certainly did not.

So meeting Alice did not hold any fears for Jane. They could meet as friends or neighbours.

Alice had just arrived in town when Jane caught sight of her. Alice had just finished carefully manoeuvring the big black Buick into a parking space along the river bank.

Alice had persuaded William to teach her to drive, so that she could drive herself between Prior Park and her parents' house in town. It was an arrangement that suited William. He had been surprised at how quickly Alice had mastered the gear changing and the management of the big car. She did not tell him that her father had previously given her driving lessons. She did not want to diminish William's pride in her achievement.

It was also an arrangement that suited Alice who, for the first time in her life, had a chance at some independence of action that had previously been denied her.

She had quickly discovered the secret to domestic harmony. She had only to humour William; to agree with his every move and to provide for his every comfort. It was easy for Alice. She did not resent it.

She did not resent the lack of consideration to herself because by not drawing attention to herself, she found she could do very much as she pleased. She had slipped easily into the role. She had observed how her mother had managed her father, a fractious man used to getting his own way, and she had applied these lessons to her own marriage.

She had not expected them to yield such successful results, but they did. William declared himself contented with the arrangement. It came as no surprise to her that he did not ask her about her contentment.

On this particular day, with time to spare, Alice deliberately walked along the street in the direction of Jane and her child, rather than walking in the opposite direction to avoid the meeting, as she might once have done.

'Hello, Jane, it's a long time since I've seen you. How are you? And how is little Tommy?'

The two had never been close friends. It was as neighbours they knew each other. It was as neighbours that Tom and Jane Warner had been invited to Alice and William's wedding the summer before.

Jane returned the greeting, resisting the efforts of little Tommy to keep them moving. He wasn't a child who enjoyed being still, but his mother continued to resist his efforts until he began to complain.

The two women exchanged the usual gossip for the district and spoke of the people they both knew. Both expressed relief that the end to the war in the Pacific could not be but a matter of a month or two away, if the reporting was to be believed.

'And how is Mrs Belleville coping since her bereavement?' Jane asked.

'Well enough, but she was pleased to have William to handle everything for her. He's just back from Brisbane and the solicitors. He has total control over everything, at least until his brother returns. But I suspect Richard will be happy to leave it that way.'

There was an innocence in Alice's statement that surprised Jane but it was the mention of Richard's name that caught her unawares.

Suddenly impatient to be gone, Jane looked at her watch.

'Alice, I must go. I have to meet Tom. It's good to see you. Give my regards to William and Mrs Belleville.'

Hardly waiting for Alice's reply, Jane hoisted Tommy onto her hip, turned and walked away. Within minutes, she was lost to Alice's view.

If their parting seemed abrupt to Alice, she soon dismissed it, reasoning that Jane had not wanted to keep her husband waiting while she engaged in idle gossip on the river bank. To Alice's way of thinking, taking care of your husband was paramount. She did not know if Tom Warner was given to moodiness but she could understand Jane's desire not to provoke a show of ill humour.

Jane was pleased that her hat shaded her face. Ahead of her, about a hundred yards away, she could just make out the figure of her husband waving to her. She slowed her pace.

With her free hand, she fumbled in her handbag for a hand-kerchief. She dabbed at her face and her eyes, her head bent. She took a deep breath to regain her composure. By the time they came together, her breathing had regained its regular rhythm but she was worried that her face might be blotchy.

'Daddy, Daddy, I saw a big bird.'

Tom swung the boy into his arms and hoisted him overhead.

Little Tommy squealed with delight.

'Big bird eh? And what else did you see?'

But the boy was already pestering his father to swing him overhead again.

Jane smiled and relaxed. Tom had not looked at her closely. He had eyes only for his son.

She followed the two of them as they headed in the direction of the main street, the child chattering endlessly and unintelligibly and the father indulgently listening as if he understood every word.

CHAPTER 14:

OCTOBER-DECEMBER 1945

JOHN BERTRAM TRIED unsuccessfully to steady his friend's nerves but as soon as Richard had finished one cigarette he lit another, then continued his pacing back and forth along the stone path to the little church. He paused at the gate only long enough to glance up and down the road, before turning and heading back to the porch where John sat patiently, glancing at his watch surreptitiously so as not to add further to Richard's growing anxiety.

'She's late, isn't she?' Richard said.

'Richard, she's only ten minutes late. Brides are always late. It's women, they're always late.'

'I don't like it.'

'Don't like what, old man?' John answered, not sure what his friend meant.

'I don't like this skulking off.'

'I don't understand it either, but if it is what Catherine wants, you have to do the decent thing, old man.'

'I know. I always would. But I'd rather do it the proper way.'

Just as the words were out of Richard's mouth, a car slowed and then stopped about twenty yards from the front gate. It pulled off the road.

A few minutes later Catherine emerged alone. She wore a pale blue suit with a matching hat. She carried a small posy of flowers but that was all the concession she had made to the special day.

Richard went forward to meet her.

'Are you sure you want to go through with this?'

To Catherine, it was a poor choice of words and she stepped back from him.

Did he mean 'go through with the marriage' or did he mean 'go through with the wedding in a secret way' or 'go through with the pregnancy'?

He noticed her momentary hesitation.

'I only meant that I am prepared to see your parents and do the right thing, in the proper way.'

She shrugged her shoulders.

'It's better this way. They can't interfere. It will be done and then they will have to get used to the idea. We've already been through this.'

John hovered behind the pair, the awkwardness of the meeting not lost on him, but Catherine moved towards him with a smile, pleased to see a familiar friendly face.

'Thank you for being here for us, John, I appreciate it so much.'

Her pleasure at seeing him was genuine and they hugged briefly.

The three of them moved towards the village church where the minister was waiting, along with his wife, who had agreed to act at the second witness.

'Good afternoon, Miss Cavendish, it's nice to see you again. Are we ready then? Shall we proceed?'

It was three o'clock and the weak late autumn sun had already disappeared behind the trees flanking the small church. It was chilly inside. Although the church was small, the four electric lights cast only small pools of light creating odd shadows in the dark corners of the old building.

Catherine clung to Richard's arm as the two of them followed the minister down the aisle towards the altar.

There was no music. Flowers from the previous Sunday's

service had begun to wilt, but no one noticed.

The minister spoke the essential words.

John, his fingers numb with the growing chill, fumbled in his pocket for the plain gold ring which Richard had entrusted to him earlier. Richard slipped the ring onto Catherine's finger and they kissed briefly.

The whole service had taken perhaps fifteen minutes.

John Bertram signed his name beneath theirs, followed by the minister's wife. There were handshakes all round and then the trio left the small church, which was already in darkness by the time they reached the front gate.

Catherine's travelling cases were transferred to Richard's car before John eased into the driver's seat of Catherine's car and gave the pair a final wave as he headed back down the road towards the base.

Richard and Catherine headed in the opposite direction. With a leave pass of five days, they were determined to have a honeymoon knowing that in that time the news would have to be broken to Catherine's family.

Richard could only speculate as to how the news of their sudden marriage and the reason for it would be received by Catherine's mother.

He had long since removed the framed photograph of Jane Saville from his bedside table but he had found he could not bring himself to part with it. The photograph itself remained tucked deep inside his pocket book. He told himself it was a part of his life that was gone forever. She was married with a child; he was married to someone else. But where did his heart belong?

He banished these thoughts from his mind and smiled at Catherine.

'Hello Mrs Belleville,' was all he said.

She smiled and moved closer to him.

Later, on that dark October night in 1945 as an early frost spread outside and they lay together for the first time as man and wife, she no longer felt any uncertainty, at least for herself. She had wanted to marry him. She had not planned to trap him but that was how it had turned out. And he, hearing her news, had not turned his back on her.

If she was less certain about his feelings, it no longer mattered. She was Mrs Belleville and the child she would bear him would cement their relationship forever. Of that she was sure.

The tip of his cigarette glowed in the dark. He turned and stubbed it out in the ashtray.

As she lay in the dark, she felt the baby in her belly move for the very first time but by then Richard was already asleep.

Almost a week passed before John Bertram saw his friend again. He called to him across the tarmac.

'How was the honeymoon, old man?'

'Fine. Just fine.'

'Where's Catherine.'

'She's gone back to her nurse's quarters for now, but we expect to be embarking for home in early November.'

'Did you see her family?'

It was the question John had most wanted to ask and the question Richard was least prepared to answer, but he knew John, of all people, deserved an answer.

'We did. Her mother raised a stink, as you can imagine. Said why was Catherine throwing her life away on some colonial or words to that effect. Said the baby could have been had quietly and no one would have known. As if you can just give a baby away like an unwanted gift or something and not think twice about it. It was pretty bloody awful, to tell you the truth.'

'I feared as much,' John said quietly.

He could not at that moment meet Richard's eye. They were after all his kin too as much as he might have wanted to disown them at that particular moment.

'Me too. I knew they wouldn't think I was quite up to snuff for their daughter. Had some earl or duke in mind for her apparently,' he said.

'But I pointed out they wouldn't have to suffer the social disgrace of having their daughter marry beneath her because we wouldn't be in England much longer. My son—or daughter—will be born in Australia, with my name and with my family.'

John could imagine the heated scene. He was pleased he hadn't been there to witness it. His friend went on, as if finally relieved to tell the whole unhappy story.

'That settled it. There were more tears and recriminations but in the end they seemed to accept it grudgingly. Had no choice really. So Catherine was right; get married and then tell them so they had no choice but to accept it.'

John heard the story in silence. He knew, from experience, how Lady Marina Cavendish could carry a grudge but he did not say so.

His own mother had borne the brunt of her disapproval. Now she had turned the same savage sights on her own daughter and it did not surprise him. He just hoped that Catherine would fare better than his own fragile, beautiful, wilful but ultimately embittered mother.

*

Back at Prior Park, Elizabeth Belleville opened the telegram that had been left lying on the hall table since the morning mail had been delivered. No one had bothered to tell her that a telegram had arrived but there was no one within earshot so she did not bother to complain.

She deftly opened the envelope with the silver letter opener, her fingers shaking. Only bad news was delivered by telegram but with the war in Europe at an end, she had hoped it would be news of Richard's return and not the bearer of bad tidings that she had feared for more than three years.

She read the words and then reread them. The message was short.

'Returning home. Due Brisbane Monday 4 December. Expect us mail train Wednesday. Bringing wife. Love Richard'

'William, William, where are you? Alice, Alice, come quickly. Julia, there's news of Richard.'

Elizabeth's excited voice caught both William's and Alice's attention although Julia was nowhere to be seen. Alice had been cutting flowers in the garden. William had been in the office, which had once been Francis's domain, going over the accounts and discussing his plans with Charles Brockman.

'What is it, mother?'

There was almost a sound of irritation in William's voice, but he quickly suppressed it.

She would not have noticed anything. For the first time in years, her face broke into a broad smile.

'Richard is on his way home. He'll be here in two weeks' time, can you believe it. He'll be home, safe and sound.'

She held the telegram aloft. Alice hugged her and for the first time, Elizabeth responded to her daughter-in-law's display of affection.

'That's wonderful news. We must have a homecoming dinner for him.'

Alice was quick to join the mood of celebration.

William, though, took the time to read the telegram that his mother had dropped on the floor in her excitement.

'Mother, did you read this properly? He says he's bringing a wife. Did you see this? Do you know anything about this?' he demanded, expecting that in some way his mother had received information from Richard that she had withheld from him.

William's brow creased and his face resumed its familiar worried look. For such a young man, the frown lines had grown quickly and burrowed permanently into his forehead.

Elizabeth Belleville waved her hand in a dismissive gesture.

'I think someone got the message wrong. They probably got two telegrams mixed up and that was meant for the next message.

We would know if Richard had got married. He never mentioned anyone special. No, I'm convinced it's just a mistake,' she said dismissively.

Outwardly convinced by the certainty of her explanation, totally wrong as it turned out to be, neither Alice nor William referred to it again, at least within Elizabeth's earshot but later, lying beside Alice, their heads close together on the pillow, William raised the matter again.

'Do you think Mother's right? That part of the message about 'bringing wife' was meant for someone else?'

Alice was always good at sensing William's mood and opinion but this time, she had her own firm opinion, which she had not expressed to her mother-in-law. She rolled over in the bed to face him.

'You know what. I think Richard is about to surprise your mother—and us. I think he is bringing home more than souvenirs from the war in Europe. Let's hope we like her, that's all I can say. We don't even know her name or when they were married or anything.'

William pondered Alice's words for a minute and then decided he agreed with her.

'My dear, I think you're right. I think we are soon to meet the new Mrs Belleville but we won't say anything further on the subject to Mother. Time will prove one of us right and I have a feeling it won't be her.'

Alice slid her arms around his neck. She kissed him shyly for she was still adjusting to the freedom of marriage, the freedom to have a man in her bed and the freedom to seek him whenever she wanted him.

For the first time since their marriage, William turned away from her, his mind preoccupied with the news of his brother.

'Good night, Alice.'

She did not feel slighted. She had learned to live her life to suit William's mood and she knew this latest news had given him much to think about.

Their lives, she knew for certain, were about to change. Just how it would all work out she had no idea but she knew one thing. William would never be happy going back to being the brother in Richard's shadow. She had seen how he had grown used to being the master and she knew he would not relinquish that position now without a fight.

Perhaps Richard would live somewhere else, she mused, as she drifted off to sleep. Perhaps unpleasantness could all be avoided …. perhaps.

'Why do you live such a long way away from England?' Catherine asked, only half jokingly.

It was a statement really, not so much a question, but Richard smiled and retorted.

'Why do you live such a long way from Australia?'

Catherine sat on the hard timber bench on the railway platform at Brisbane's Roma Street railway station and for the first time understood fully the heat of an Australian summer.

She was uncomfortable, whichever way she sat. She used the newspaper as a fan but it didn't stop the sweat trickling down her back and her dress clinging to her legs.

There wasn't much to distinguish this railway station from those in England except that it was much smaller than the main London stations with which she was familiar.

One platform was all that was needed to serve the country trains that took it in turns to depart to all corners of the vast state.

Ahead of them was a twelve hour trip during which the train would stop at what seemed like a hundred places she'd never heard of before finally getting to Springfield.

'There'll be a storm tonight, for sure,' Richard said, as he surveyed the darkening sky from the open platform.

'Usually is a storm when it's as humid as this. There'll probably be hail I'd say, looking at the colour of the sky, but we'll be gone before then I hope.'

Catherine did not find the news of an impending storm reassuring but she guessed he was right.

Anything would be better than the oppressive heat, she thought. Even a hail storm.

He sat down beside her and put his arm around her shoulders.

'As soon as we get home, we'll get you in to see the doctor and book you in to the private hospital. There's a very good local doctor who sees to all the local births. He's been there for years. You'll like him.'

His words were meant to be reassuring but he could see that Catherine was getting tired and irritable.

'Right now, I'd like anyone who would relieve me of this burden.'

She shifted position for the umpteenth time and leant forward to ease her back ache, but it was hard for her to find any relief, so she was pleased when the train drew into the platform and they boarded and settled into their first class compartment.

The leather seats were more comfortable than the wooden bench and she was able to stretch out fully while Richard sat opposite. He had booked the whole compartment, realising that the last thing his wife would want was to make small talk to strangers on the final leg of a 12,000 mile journey.

Now that they were getting close to their final destination, Catherine asked a question that until now had been foremost on her mind, but unspoken.

'What do you think your mother will make of her new daughter-in-law?'

She had already quizzed him about life at Prior Park and about his family but she had found his vague answers lacked the detail she'd hoped to glean

The impending birth of the baby had been their sole focus such that their future as a family seemed to depend upon it, as if it was the bedrock on which all future decisions and plans would be made, but only after the event.

'Well, I think she'll be surprised but I think the imminent arrival of the first grandchild will put everything else into its proper perspective. As far as I know, Alice isn't pregnant yet although it's some months since I had a letter. I have a feeling our baby will be the first,' he said, smilingly broadly at the prospect.

Catherine rubbed her stomach.

'Boy or girl? What do you think?'

'Boy, definitely a boy,' Richard said, without hesitation.

'I think you're right. I don't think a dainty little girl would kick so much.'

'Paul Francis Belleville.'

'I know where the Francis comes from, but Paul?' She looked at him questioningly but even as she did she tested the names.

'Paul for a very good friend who ditched in the channel and was never seen again. I was following him home after I got hit. He knew I was hit and slowed down so I wouldn't lose sight of him, but he copped it. Least I can do in his memory. His name for my first born son.'

Catherine looked up at him, quizzically.

'You never told me about him. How come?'

'It's hard to talk about. I want to put it all behind me and never think about the stinking war again but it's one promise I want to keep.'

'It's a good name. Paul Francis Belleville it will be … or Paula.'

She closed her eyes and relaxed with the gentle rocking of the train as it gathered speed beyond the city limits.

Richard took in the familiar landmarks and revelled in the soothing warmth of the afternoon sun through the carriage window.

He felt relaxed for the first time in years. He was home, or very nearly home, and it felt every bit as good as he expected it to feel. Beyond that he did not venture in his imagination. There were too many unknowns to speculate. Today was a day to be savoured and enjoyed. He was home.

*

William paced up and down the platform, anxiously looking down the line for any sign of the train that was now half an hour overdue.

The station master had assured him that the mail train would be along 'any minute now' but that minute had been and gone and still there was no sign of it.

William, as expected, had been nominated to meet his brother on his return home. That left all the other inhabitants of Prior Park free to indulge in the frenzy of homecoming preparations.

For the first time in a very long time, Julia had been raised from the torpor of the past eighteen months.

In that time, she had endured more than most. The birth of a daughter she could not keep and the loss of a father she loved deeply, for all his faults. Only he had shown any compassion towards her.

Her mother continued to pretend it had never happened and William, worried that Alice would come to know the scandalous truth about his sister, was mute on the subject.

A final whispered conference between William and his mother, just as he departed Prior Park for the hour's drive into town, had laid the groundwork for a conversation with her mother that Julia did not want to hear and did not want to have.

'Richard doesn't know about your 'little trouble' of last year, Julia,' she said, in a voice just loud enough for Julia to hear.

'I never wrote to him about it. I trust you didn't?'

She almost hissed the words at her daughter, for fear that her meaning had not been clear. But to Julia, there was no mistaking her mother's intention.

'Don't worry mother, I won't disgrace you. I won't blurt everything out to Richard or his new wife,' she said curtly.

A nervous tremor snaked through her whole body so she thrust her hands into the pockets of her dress to hide the shiver. She had grown thin and pale but no one had seemed to notice.

She was quietly pleased that her words had found their mark, just as she had intended.

'I don't believe Richard would have got married without telling us so I think it's all a huge mistake,' her mother retorted, dismissing the idea with the same certainty she had previously.

Like her brother William, Julia had decided that Richard's arrival would very quickly reveal who was right and who was wrong. She could see no point in arguing further with her mother, who she noticed had regained her energy at the prospect of her favourite son's return.

Despite herself, Julia was beginning to feel just a small tinge of excitement at her brother's return too. She had just been turning eighteen when he left; she was now twenty-one and no longer the innocent girl of his memory.

It was Richard who spotted his brother first as the belching train slowed to walking pace and then stopped at the platform amid the hissing of brakes and a final explosion of steam. The train had reached the end of the line and so had Richard and Catherine.

In one bound, Richard jumped onto the platform and embraced his younger brother heartily, forgetting, just for a moment, the solitary figure of his young, very pregnant wife immediately behind him.

'William, it's so good to see you. Tell me everything. How's mother? And Julia? How's Prior Park? Is the season any good?'

The words tumbled out. He didn't wait for an answer to any of the questions.

It was a minute or two before he remembered and turned towards Catherine, but William was already raising his hat politely and formally shaking hands.

'William, it's lovely to meet you. I've heard so much about you. And all the family, I feel as if I know you all. It must be such a surprise to hear that your brother was bringing home a wife.'

Catherine's well-bred English voice sounded strange amidst

the cacophony of broad Australian accents that surrounded the trio.

'Welcome, you're very welcome. Mother will be delighted to meet you, I'm sure. And Julia too. And of course my wife Alice.'

William had recovered his composure quickly from the shock of first meeting Catherine, hearing the cultured English voice and then seeing, with his own eyes, the advanced condition of her pregnancy.

The first thoughts through his mind were surprise and delight at the girl Richard had chosen to marry and then a creeping speculation that the marriage might have been a rushed affair. Just what his mother would make of the whole situation he could only guess, but they would all find out very soon.

Before very long, both men were struggling along the platform under the weight of a small mountain of luggage.

Catherine followed behind, carrying her beauty case and taking in her new surroundings. The first thing she noticed was the more intense heat of the tropical climate.

Brisbane had been hot and humid and she had complained about that, but it was nothing compared with the heat that now greeted her. It was bright hot heat that sapped everything of its moisture.

William, noticing Catherine's distress, stopped briefly.

'Are you all right? I know it's hot today and it's hard if you're not used to it, but it will be cooler at home. We have big fans and high ceilings and the back veranda is shaded in the afternoon.'

'The house has had a big spring clean since we heard you were coming too,' he added by way of conversation.

Catherine, unsure how to respond to this small titbit of domestic news, remained silent.

William, unusually tactful, did not mention his mother's opinion that the news of Richard's marriage was not to be trusted, but that, as a precaution, the only other double bedroom at Prior Park had been made ready for possible use.

No one, he thought, had considered the possibility that the room should be equipped with a cot but he conjectured that they would need to do so very, very soon.

With the three of them settled into the car and the boot tied down securely with rope—for there had been no chance that the luggage would fit and the boot close properly—William eased the car out of the station car park and headed away from the city in the direction of the road that would take them directly to Prior Park.

Despite his tiredness from the long journey, Richard was pointing out the landmarks and remarking to his brother on the continuing Army presence in the city.

As their car crossed a long street that led up to the mountain range above the city, Richard pointed and turned to Catherine, who sat in the seat immediately behind him.

'The private hospital is just up there. As soon as we're settled we'll make an appointment for you to see the doctor.'

Catherine's eyes followed his pointing finger but she could see nothing that resembled a hospital. As far as the eye could see, odd little timber houses on stilts seemed to have been jammed side by side facing the street. She had noticed a few houses like them in Brisbane from the train but here there seemed to be streets and streets of them.

'What are those funny looking timber houses?' she asked no one in particular.

Most of the houses had steps leading directly to a front veranda. On some of them the veranda had been enclosed with a crisscrossed pattern of light timber lattice work for extra privacy, she assumed. All of the houses had iron roofs and almost all of them were desperately in need of painting.

Richard laughed.

'They're typical Queensland houses. Built high to catch the breeze and keep the floodwater and the snakes out. Most of them would be fifty to sixty years old now. The better homes are up on the range above the city. I'll show you when we come into town next.'

She could believe his explanation of the floodwater and the need for a breeze but she doubted the snake part of the explanation. She knew that this little teasing comment was likely to be the first of many she would receive in this foreign landscape. Would she get used to it in time?

She sat quietly in the back of the car and wondered what her girlish plans had been for her future. She couldn't remember having ever mapped out a plan for her future at all but somehow she assumed that she too would end up with a husband and a family and a house just like that of her parents.

Then the war had intervened and given her a sense of freedom she never thought she'd experience. Too much freedom, perhaps, as her mother was quick to point out. Was it too much freedom, she wondered, that had resulted in her present circumstances?

Now she was finally beginning to face the prospect of settling in Australia forever with an Australian husband and with an Australian child. Only now did the enormity of it all strike her. In one sense, she told herself, it was a grand adventure but adventures ended and people went home to their established lives. This was a permanent adventure.

She remembered how, just as they were leaving Haldon Hall for the last time before boarding the ship for Australia, her mother had clung to her even as she continued to upbraid her for her foolishness.

What is done cannot be undone, she had said. You must make the best of it now, were her mother's words that Catherine recalled now as she headed for her new home.

Whether she would ever see her mother or father again, she did not know. If she was paying the price for her impetuous ways, they too were paying a price she did not yet understand but they knew only too well.

On a chilly October day, they had farewelled a daughter they knew they might never see again who, on the other side of the world, would bear them a grandchild who might remain forever unknown to them.

In the privacy of her bedroom, away from the curious eyes of the servants, Lady Marina Cavendish had done the unthinkable; she had wept for the loss of her daughter and for the lonely days that lay ahead of her.

The smooth bitumen road soon gave way to a hard gravel surface that made conversation impossible inside the car. Dust swirled and then settled again on the brown landscape. Not much stirred in the heat of the day, just an insect here and there.

'Not far now,' Richard said over his shoulder, turning his head just enough to give her an encouraging smile.

Without being able to see his face fully, she could still sense his growing excitement as he craned his neck to get a good view of the countryside as it passed them by.

Finally, William slowed the car and swung into the tree-lined driveway and within a minute the house came into view and Richard could see his mother, his sister and his sister-in-law all standing at the bottom of the front stairs.

As the car came to a complete stop, Elizabeth Belleville stood back momentarily to let the spiral of dust settle but Richard, impatient to greet his family, flung open the passenger door and bounded from the car to embrace everyone in turn. His mother could not contain her tears.

Behind him, Catherine took her time to get out of the car.

Only to anyone standing next to Elizabeth was the involuntary gasp of surprise audible. Her eyes immediately went from Catherine's attractive but tired face to the roundness of her stomach.

Finally, Richard extricated himself from his sister's embrace and brought Catherine forward.

'Mother, I'd like to introduce my wife, Catherine.'

Catherine extended her hand, which the older woman took

and then, unexpectedly, kissed her on the cheek. Elizabeth recovered her composure with lighting speed. It hadn't been a mistake after all. Richard was married and there was no mistake about the imminent event which none of them had even considered up until this point.

'Welcome, my dear, I fear you've had a long journey and you must be absolutely exhausted. Come inside and rest. The men can deal with the luggage. We must take care of you and you can tell me all about how you and Richard met, because you have sprung quite a surprise on us, I must say.'

With that, Elizabeth put her arm around Catherine and drew her into the house. Julia and Alice followed in silence. Julia had never previously seen her mother display such tenderness. Watching it unfold before her eyes, she felt a wave of sadness envelope her. She could not help but compare her treatment and that of Richard's wife, who, within a minute of their meeting, had been welcomed in the bosom of the family and fussed over.

In that fleeting moment, Alice too was taking stock of the situation. She could bear with equanimity Richard's well-born wife being placed above her, but she could also see how the first born son had a special place in the Belleville family and now he had come home, he expected to resume his birthright without question.

The two brothers walked together into the house. They were laughing and smiling and joking together but all eyes were on Richard as the household staff and Charles Brockman came forward to greet him.

In that moment, Alice could see how William's hard-won position as head of the family in Richard's absence was being taken from him, not by a word or a deed but by custom and by expectation and by the natural order of things.

She observed Richard's easy charm and affable good manners but she saw something else as well: his automatic assumption that he was now the head of the household and his younger brother William would take second place.

William will not like this, thought Alice. He will not say anything for a while, but he will not like it. Not at all.

But there was nothing she could do to influence the events that would unfold. Everything must take its course, she decided to herself, everything must take its course.

CHAPTER 15:
JANUARY-FEBRUARY 1946

IN THE FIRST HEADY weeks of Richard's return from the war and the novelty of his marriage, everything went along smoothly at Prior Park.

William was cordial; Alice was helpful and fussed over Catherine; Elizabeth commanded the redecoration of the nursery, as if it was the most important task she had ever undertaken, and Julia, quieter and more withdrawn than usual, nevertheless responded to her older brother's charm and easy manner.

To Catherine, everything she saw was new and exciting or at the very least amusing in its oddness: the heat in December and January; the traditional English Christmas lunch eaten on an unbearably hot day when an egg would easily fry on the front steps of the house.

She marvelled at the birds and at the wildlife. She grew accustomed to the night sounds of the possums running across the roof. She would occasionally see their large round eyes staring at her out of the darkness as they paused on a tree branch or on a veranda post.

She trembled at the howls of dingoes in the distance. Their eerie high pitched call, for it couldn't really be called a bark, unnerved her at first but after a while she grew accustomed to the nightly chorus.

On one particularly hot afternoon, she lay on the bed, tossing and turning, first hugging a pillow and then trying to reposition it to support her back, which now ached almost continuously.

She fought a losing battle to get comfortable now that she was within weeks of giving birth.

To her surprise, Richard walked quietly into the room and sat on the edge of the bed.

'Are you settling in all right? We've hardly had a chance to talk about things since we arrived home.'

She could see it was a tacit admission on his part that, for him, returning to his home had thrust him back into the life he had left behind.

In that life he had been a young single man without responsibilities. It had been so easy for him to resume the role that he had done it unconsciously, except that now, of course, he began to realise that more was expected of him, or was it?

Catherine pulled herself into a sitting position. She too was becoming uneasy but whether it was natural worry about the impending birth or something much deeper she did not know.

'That's the first time you've thought to ask that question.'

She hadn't meant her words to carry such accusation. His face changed. She could see signs of real concern.

'I know. I'm sorry. It's really just the fact of getting home, then Christmas and then the baby coming. I started to realise how easy it was for me to slot back into my old life but I know it's a new life for you ...'

His words trailed off. He didn't really know what to say. What could he say? In his unbounded enthusiasm to return home, largely unscathed, from the war in Europe, when so many others hadn't, he felt blessed. He did not want to question or complain or seem ungrateful for his luck.

Catherine managed a weak smile but she did not say what she was really thinking. She wanted to blurt out that for her the world was not as rosy. She had been brought to a foreign country as far from her birthplace as she could possibly be because she was paying the price for illicit passion.

For her the adjustment was the greater and it was her first inkling that he saw this fact for himself.

But still, she was surprised at his sudden questioning and she wondered what had precipitated it.

'I sometimes think that our life has been settled without us even discussing our future. It's as if the baby coming has decided everything for us, that there was only one course of action,' she said finally.

She felt a vigorous kick in her belly and lay back, wrung out by the heat and humidity.

'I know we sort of rushed into everything, but you couldn't have the baby and not be married. I couldn't walk away and leave my child.'

'I couldn't leave you and I couldn't stay,' he said finally.

'I know. I know.'

There was a hint of impatience in her voice that he put down to her condition. That excused everything, her moodiness, her fretfulness, in his mind at least.

He got up and smoothed the bed covers.

But he felt still that he had to explain himself and his decisions even though the same conversation had passed between them any number of times.

'I guess I assumed there was only one course of action—for me to come back here to Prior Park and for you to come with me and for us to be a family here,' he said.

'I belong here. This is mine, well half mine.'

Catherine said nothing at all.

For the first time in months he looked at her appraisingly. He noticed the pale skin and the patrician looks. He could hear the cultured voice echoing in his mind.

And for the first time, he began to understand that his wife was as much out of place in Australia as he was in place. What he didn't know was whether that would ever change.

He felt comfortable. He didn't mind the heat. He had returned to the house he'd spent his whole life in. Eventually he would carve out a role for himself. His restlessness he viewed as temporary and understandable.

Her restlessness and ennui he had seen as natural with the restraints the late stages of pregnancy had placed on her activities.

For the first time though he began to see that she might not settle as he had expected and he began to wonder what the future might hold. As quickly as these thoughts took hold of his mind, he dismissed them.

But still he felt that more explanation was demanded of him. He repeated the words much as they had been said before.

'I'd have found it hard to get a job in England, you know. I'd have been just one among thousands of uniformed men on the scrapheap.'

Catherine sighed. When she finally spoke, her voice was quiet and reflective. She ignored his words as if she hadn't heard them.

'I didn't ask myself what it really meant—the two of us coming to Australia, I mean. I didn't really think about it much until now. I guess I always thought I'd be mistress of my own house and of my life, but I see how our lives are now part of other people's lives and we can't have our own life, not in the way I expected we would have our own life. It's hard to explain but I don't feel as though I belong. Not like you do. I feel like a long-staying guest.'

He did his best to hide his concern at this admission.

'And you didn't realise it was so far away,' he said the words for her as if he'd heard the words many times, although she had not said them out loud except when they seemed to add to the adventure of leaving England.

'My ignorance I suppose,' she conceded ungraciously.

He took her in his arms as best he could. It was meant as an act of reassurance but she drew away from him.

'Darling, living here is really the only practical solution at the moment. Perhaps later on we can build our own house but then, this house is half mine.'

She sighed and shifted on the bed.

'Richard, I know, but you do realise it is an unusual way to leave everything. In England it would be the eldest son who inherits.'

He had not realised that she was taking such a different view of how things stood with his family and his inheritance, the extent of which he did not yet fully understand. He could see that she was beginning to wonder why Prior Park was not theirs and theirs alone.

'It's not our way here,' he said, smiling. 'We're much more democratic than your lot.'

'But what about your sister, Julia? She doesn't share in it.'

Their conversation had taken a quite unexpected turn. Here he felt on much firmer ground.

He answered her quickly realising that she now had a right to know how everything stood.

'That's because my sister Julia will inherit the trust fund from mother. My grandmother set it up for her daughter and it continues. It may only pass from daughter to daughter. I don't know what it is worth; only mother knows that but it will all go to Julia. So that is why Julia didn't inherit any of father's estate.'

She shrugged her shoulders.

'I see. Lucky Julia. What happens if there are no daughters?'

It seemed as if money was becoming a preoccupation with Catherine.

'I don't know really but I think, from memory, it would all be wound up and distributed between William and I if Julia hadn't come along. But Julia will have to have a daughter for it to continue.'

Richard knew that he and Catherine had not discussed money at all and it was a topic that he was not keen to discuss now, except to say the obvious.

'You and our child are the most important things to me right now,' he said quietly. 'I will always put your interests first.'

He could see that she was in need of a rest. He tried to calm her mood.

'And when the baby is old enough, we'll take a trip back to England to see your family. I'm sure your mother urges it with every letter.'

He realised he had not said that before. It seemed to reassure her for the moment.

But their discussion had unsettled him and once again his mind turned to the one issue that had begun to occupy most of his waking thoughts: why had his brother stalled him on every question he asked in relation to his father's estate in which he, Richard, now shared on equal terms with an equal right to know everything.

He moved to the window and pulled the curtains together to block out the bright light so she might rest more peacefully.

'Let's talk about it all later, after the baby is born. You'll feel a lot better then. We can make some plans. We can plan that trip to England for when the child is older.'

And with that Catherine had to be content.

The first week of February turned out to be hotter and drier than the previous month, despite daily predictions of rain. The only green grass was that on which water could be lavished by dedicated gardeners, providing the water was available.

There were days when there was absolutely no breeze at all to bring even a modicum of relief. Cloudless blue skies became a monotony.

Around Prior Park there were signs of smoke on the horizon. The fire danger had been declared at extreme levels. The long dry grass would fuel a fire into a frenzy in minutes. Everyone knew that a casual tossing of a cigarette stub or a match could have dire consequences for thousands of acres of grassland.

It was a Tuesday when Catherine woke Richard in the early hours of the morning. Complete darkness still enveloped the landscape outside.

'I think the baby's coming early.'

It was all she could say. She lay on her side and writhed in pain.

Richard was out of bed in seconds and dressing quickly. He knew it was an hour's drive to the hospital.

He tapped on William and Alice's bedroom door. His brother's face appeared through the crack in the door.

'What's up?' he said. He could just make out Richard's face.

'It's Catherine. The baby's coming early. I'm taking her into hospital.'

'Do you want me to do anything?' he whispered.

William was unsure what Richard wanted. He was wrapping a dressing gown over his pyjamas and trying not to wake Alice, who stirred but continued to sleep.

'I just need you to carry her case down to the car. I'll have to carry her. Maybe you could warm up the engine.'

William slipped into the hallway, going quietly so he did not wake the rest of the household.

Richard handed him Catherine's case while he went back to their bedroom.

By the time Richard appeared at the front door with Catherine in his arms, William had started the engine of the trusty Buick. William had bought another car, a big black Ford, but the Buick was always the preferred one.

It was just coming light as they reached the outskirts of the town. Fifteen minutes later, Catherine was being admitted to the maternity ward.

For several hours, Richard sat beside her bed offering what little comfort her could. At regular intervals, she would cry out in pain and grip the side of the bed to haul herself into a sitting position in the hope that it would bring her relief. The palms of her hands were covered with sweat. She could feel a sticky dampness between her engorged breasts.

Richard put his arm behind her shoulders to support her: 'It's all right. It will all be over very soon.'

Her response was almost angry.

'How dare you say that. You know this will take a long time.'

Her face was contorted. He had never heard her speak like that before. He mumbled something she couldn't hear but he continued to support her weight with his left arm while he used a damp face cloth to wipe the trickles of sweat from the side of her face.

The bedclothes were becoming damp. Her nightgown clung to her like a wet rag.

He was glad when a few minutes later a tall imposing figure appeared in the doorway, motioning him to leave.

'They want me to go, darling, it must be close now.'

Catherine clung to him for a few moments until she sunk back on the pillow, already exhausted, yet with the main effort still to come. He kissed her damp forehead and wished he could somehow relieve her pain.

'Mr Belleville, please leave now.'

There was a distinct note of urgency in the matron's voice so he merely nodded and left the room, glad to be away from it all. It wasn't the place for a man and he felt embarrassed to be there. He welcomed the command to leave Catherine's side although he would never have admitted it.

The crying of newly born babies followed him down the hallway towards the hospital entrance but the sounds barely penetrated his consciousness.

Eight months ago he had been a carefree bachelor enjoying the end of the war in Europe and his unexpected survival. His overwhelming emotion had been one of relief mixed with the pleasure of returning home.

Then events had overtaken him.

Four months ago he had stood before the altar of a village church in England and promised to love, honour and cherish the woman who was now bearing his child. There had been no wedding reception and no happy families blessing their union. The blessings had come later and reluctantly at that.

Less than two months had passed since he and Catherine had arrived home and then all their thoughts had been focused on the imminent birth.

He walked outside and lit a cigarette. Is this what the fathers did when they were awaiting news of the birth? He didn't know. He paced up and down the hospital veranda for perhaps twenty minutes before impatiently heading off down the hill towards the town.

He was glad of the activity. The sun was now high in the sky.

He walked without clear direction and with no particular aim in mind but he knew the town layout well. After half an hour he found himself on the steps of the Criterion Hotel, now returned to its pre-war civilian use and quieter since the departure of the American officers.

He did not know anyone in the bar so he sat by himself at a table near the doorway. The first glass of cold beer he drank quickly and a refill arrived at his elbow almost before he had ordered it.

This time, he sipped at the cold liquid and savoured the pleasure of sitting in the cool lounge. A large fan rattled overhead. It stirred the warm air languidly which mixed with a breeze coming off the river to relieve the heat.

'We do lunch very shortly, sir, would you like to see the menu?'

He was momentarily startled by the question because he had not heard the waitress approach. He looked at his watch, not realising that the morning was nearly over. He looked up at the waitress and nodded his assent.

'Thank you, yes, I'd like to see the menu. That sounds like a good idea. I didn't realise it was lunchtime. And I haven't had any breakfast today.'

Richard's eyes had quickly scanned the waitress and he noticed first the dyed red hair and the heavily painted lips, which somehow seemed out of place, as if her attempts at glamour belonged else-where. But she had a good face, he decided, even if it was a bit over-painted and she seemed friendly.

He smiled at her and held her attention for a few moments.

'I was told that this hotel was used by American officers during the war. It must be a lot quieter for you now,' he said, by way of conversation.

She paused and lent on the back of a nearby chair, as if ready for a chat.

'You're right. It is quiet, quieter than usual anyway. But we're seeing some old faces back again. Men who've been away to the war. We're getting some regulars back and some of the country families are able to come and stay with us again.

'Some of the men we won't see again of course,' she sighed, as if remembering one or two special customers who were now lost to them forever.

'What about you, sir, were you overseas?'

She had guessed at the truth, because he was a new young face. Probably not old enough to come into the bar before he left, she thought.

To his surprise, he did not mind the question. He had vowed not to speak about the war, but her question was so artless and sincere that he found he did not mind it.

'Yes, I was in England for several years, in Bomber Command. Terrible stuff. I don't really want to remember it. We lost a lot of men. I was lucky. Only a minor injury.'

He pointed to the fading scar on his face.

'Sorry, sir, I didn't mean to bring back bad memories. There are lots of men with bad memories. We see them every day. They're worse, a lot of them, when they've had a drink or two. But I expect it's good to be home. Do you live in town, sir, or out of town?'

'Out of town. Prior Park, about an hour's drive out of town.'

The waitress was silent for a moment, deep in thought, as if struggling to recall a half-forgotten memory.

'Then you'd likely be the brother to William whose wedding reception we had here—must be eighteen months ago now—or maybe not quite as long as that. I don't suppose you were at the wedding?'

'No unfortunately, I wasn't. You miss things like that when you're away.'

She nodded thoughtfully.

'And didn't Mr Belleville senior die in Brisbane not long after the wedding, so that means you lost your father while you were overseas too. I'm so sorry, I shouldn't have blurted it out like that.'

She busied herself setting the tables, to cover her confusion. She realised she shouldn't have let her tongue run away with her, but it was clear that not much of importance happened locally that she did not know about.

'Yes, my father passed away unexpectedly,' Richard said.

He did not offer up any details, quickly realising that he did not want to add further to her store of gossip.

He said nothing more, hoping that the waitress now would be called to another table. He did not really want the conversation to continue but nor did he want to offend the woman. But she was capable of more insight than he gave her credit for.

'I'm so sorry. I just burble on sometimes without thinking. So it would have been your sister maybe who was bridesmaid at your brother's wedding here?'

He was happy to change tack to William and Alice's wedding, what little he knew of it.

'Yes, I think so. I remember my mother writing to me about it. I'm sure Julia was the bridesmaid – slim blonde girl. She would have been twenty at the time. My brother married Alice Fitzroy. The Fitzroys have the neighbouring property to Prior Park.'

It was, Richard thought, a pretty good summary that dealt only with the facts of the matter.

The waitress stopped polishing the nearby table which was cleaner than it had ever been.

'Ah, yes, now I place her. It's been bugging me for ages. I was sure I'd seen the bridesmaid before somewhere but I just couldn't remember.'

Richard said nothing, offering no encouragement, but she continued.

'I don't think she saw me on the day. I was helping in the kitchen because it was a big wedding and we were short-staffed. I noticed her at the bridal table. I said to myself: it'll come to me one of these days. I knew I'd seen her somewhere before.'

All this was no more than a distraction for Richard at the time. He had suddenly realised how hungry he was so his attention was more squarely focused on the choice of meals than on the waitress's chatter.

'Well, I expect you might have seen her around town with my mother.'

Now he was anxious to order and end the conversation.

'I'll have the roast beef, thank you.'

He handed the closed menu back to the waitress and she wrote his order carefully on her order pad, before turning back towards the kitchen.

He thought no more about their conversation but instead turned his attention to the view of the riverbank beyond the window. There was very little movement in the street but just as he was about to turn his attention elsewhere he noticed a small boy running ahead of his mother.

The small boy he did not recognise but the mother's tall slim figure and distinctive bearing he recognised in an instant.

He did not rise from his seat to walk the few yards out of the hotel to greet Jane Warner.

Instead, he sat there not moving a muscle. Not even daring to breathe for fear of attracting her attention.

It had been less than two months since his return and on

every one of those days he had dreaded the prospect of seeing her.

He felt their first meeting must come at some time but the longer he could postpone it, the easier it was to pretend that she no longer meant anything at all to him.

Seeing her now, from the safe vantage point of the hotel, he knew he could no longer deny to himself that the woman he had pledged to marry on his return still attracted him. It was an unwelcome feeling.

He sat lost in thought for a full five minutes, quite unaware of his surroundings, thinking only of the past and how the future he had planned then was so much different now.

He was brought back to the present as the waitress placed his meal in front of him but she had noticed him looking out of the window. Nothing much escaped Violet's notice.

'I see you noticed Mrs Warner across the road. She lives out your way, doesn't she? She used to be the governess but then married the son. And that was her little boy with her. Spitting image of the father. I heard some gossip though—they say she looks less than happy a lot of the time.'

Again, she received no encouragement but she went on anyway.

'My flatmate says she's a very cultured woman but you wouldn't say that Tom Warner is a very cultured man—just turning out like his father. Loves the bush and the work on the land. His idea of a day out is to go to the cattle sale at Gracemere and then a few beers with the blokes.'

Richard heard all this in silence. He had not encouraged the woman to gossip but had not discouraged her either. She was naturally talkative and her quick summary of Jane's life accorded with what he had already heard from other sources.

'I'll let you get on with your meal then. Let me know if you want anything else, sir.'

With that, Violet turned to go, but she paused, and then turned back towards his table. The lounge had filled with more patrons but she ignored them for the moment.

'I remember now where I saw your sister. It just came to me. She came here to visit one of the American officers. What was his name? He was a captain but a medical man too. Philippe, that was it. I don't remember the last name. I wonder if she still hears from him? She seemed very much in love with him.'

With that, she was gone.

Richard digested this information in silence. He did not know if the gossip from Violet was intentionally malicious. He could not judge that at all but he was sure that he had not heard any news of his sister's liaison with an American officer.

He tried to remember what his mother had written about in her letters but he was certain there had been no mention of Julia's involvement with an American officer.

He ate the remainder of his meal quickly then paid his bill. He was unsettled by the sight of Jane Warner and Violet's gossip about her. He was uneasy too about the gossip about his sister. He did not know how he would broach the subject at home, or even if he should.

These thoughts had temporarily banished the impending birth of the baby from his mind but as he headed back up towards the hospital, his spirits rose for no accountable reason except the feeling that he had now become a father.

By the time he reached the hospital, Paul Francis Belleville was lying contentedly in his mother's arms. Catherine herself, although exhausted, smiled serenely at the beautiful baby whose little fingers curled around hers.

The gossip he had heard about Julia and about Jane was banished from his thoughts in the excitement of sharing the news about his son.

For Richard, the birth of his son brought the future into sharp relief and he knew he could no longer drift along, letting William control everything. It was time to take a stand and assert his authority.

If Paul's birth had acted as a watershed moment for Richard, for Catherine, it became a watershed moment of quite a different kind. She saw the future laid out before her more clearly than at any other time and it troubled her, even as she murmured endearments to the tiny child that lay asleep contentedly in her arms.

CHAPTER 16: JULY-OCTOBER 1946

PHILIPPE DUVAL'S SAD TASK was nearly finished. In the Sag Harbor cottage he had shared with his mother throughout his childhood, all that remained of their connected lives was packed in several large boxes which had already been stacked neatly for collection by the removalists.

He thought it didn't seem much for a life of 54 years, but then, he knew that anything she had managed to scrimp and save had been spent on his education and his future. She had spared so little for herself. He could see that now. He felt in turn grateful for her commitment to him and guilty for the sacrifices she'd had to make.

It was his last link with a childhood that had left its indelible mark on him.

He paused in his final look around the tiny house remembering her determination that he would not suffer the poverty and deprivation she had suffered. He had rarely seen her give way to emotion in their years together but he had always understood that she had spent her every effort in compensating him for the lack of a father.

She had never spoken about his father, or rarely at least. She had said he had promised to marry her, but it didn't come to pass. His family, she had reluctantly volunteered, had not considered her a good match for their only son. He was weak, she said, and wouldn't go against them. She would never speak his name and he did not press her for details. He could see how much it hurt her to speak of it. He understood, even without being told, that his father's rich and socially ambitious family would not countenance the marriage of their only son with the daughter of their gardener.

That was all there was to say. He knew his father's name. In a brash moment he had challenged her to confirm it and her eyes could not lie but even then, on that one occasion, he could not bring himself to ask her for more details. Whenever he raised the question of his father, she had put a finger up to her tightly-pressed lips in a gesture of secrecy.

"We'll never speak of him again," he remembered her saying. And now she would never speak of that or any other subject again, and he would never know the full details.

Were they young lovers who met in a secret place? Did he really love her or did he just use her? Was he weak like she said and wouldn't stand up to his parents? Or did he just abandon his pregnant young lover to her fate callously and coldly?

In his private thoughts, he could not imagine it but in the cold light of day, he realised that his father had lacked the one essential ingredient he valued the most—moral courage.

Faced with the same choice, he pondered what his own response might be but he did not let his mind wander back too far. As far as he was concerned, he would only look forward from now on. There was no yesterday; there was only tomorrow.

Surveying his mother's meagre possessions, he was angry that she had died just as he was on the point of real success and could have offered her an easier and more comfortable life. She had deserved that, at the very least, but even that was denied her.

On that hot July day, he had greeted solemnly the handful of neighbours who had attended her funeral and he listened to their kind words quietly, as if to speak aloud might disturb his mother. He knew that they had came out of respect for her, not for him, whom they did not know, except through her proud boasts of his college education, which none of them had ever dreamed of achieving for themselves or their own children.

But now it was all over. There was no link for him with the past or with the small community where he had grown up or with the neighbours who had hugged him and spoken such words of kindness.

He had kept back from the packing of her few belongings a battered tin that seemed likely to hold his mother's most treasured items. She had nothing of any material value to pass on, he knew that.

On first inspection, it was much as he had expected: small trinkets from a long-forgotten girlhood; a faded photograph of a man in his late twenties whom he could not identify and, tied with string, the letters he had written his mother from college and later from the army.

He was just about to close the lid when his eye caught a separate envelope. It caught his attention because the envelope was not of the type he would have ever used and yet it looked quite recent.

He put the tin down on the table and examined the envelope closely. He moved towards the window so he could see more clearly.

The letter was postmarked Springfield, Queensland, and addressed to him, not to his mother.

He recognised the girlish handwriting almost at once. His hands trembled as he fingered the envelope, turning it over and back again as if the envelope itself would give up the letter's secrets without the need to open it.

Why did my mother not send this to me? was his immediate thought. He shook his head in disbelief.

He held the envelope up for closer inspection. He could just make out the postmark date of 4 October 1943.

'My God, that's nearly three years ago' he said out loud, although there was no one to hear. 'Three years ago,' he muttered again.

He took the letter outside and sat on the front steps of the porch. The timber was splintered in parts and the paint was peeling. The daylight was fading but there was still enough light to read by. His hands trembled as he tore at the envelope. It was clear his mother had never opened the letter yet she must have known that, one day, he would find it.

Had she seen the act as a final protective act? He would never know.

He recalled writing to her while he was stationed in Springfield. He remembered writing about the city, about its fine river that sometimes destroyed all in its path and about the camps that had been built in the virgin bush. He had written about the local people and the countryside that he had photographed. And he had written about Julia Belleville.

Had she, with a mother's care and caution, tried to protect him from the demands of a wilful girl half a world away? Is that why she kept the letter from him, he wondered?

Had she, knowing the folly of young love and the tragedy of it, wanted to protect him from the same trap into which she had fallen.

All these thoughts ran through his head but he could make no sense of it at all.

His hands were shaking so violently he could barely keep the thin pages still long enough to read. His eyes quickly skimmed the girlish handwriting before he began to read what she had written.

My dear Philippe

Since you left in July, I have had no way of contacting you, and I have not heard from you, and this distresses me more than I can say, more so now.

So I am writing care of your mother in the hope that she will pass this along. You remember you gave me a photograph of yourself with your mother, and it had her address on the back. I am sure you can't forget that.

What I have to say is both distressing and frightening and there is no way to break this news gently. I am carrying your child.

With this news, you will also realise that with no way of contacting you, I have had to confide in my mother. She guessed my condition because the morning sickness was really bad for a while, and she had suffered the same apparently.

I won't bore you with the details, but there was a great scene. I had not seen my mother like that before. You'll know she can be quite stern but also quite caring. I had to endure her cutting remarks which I won't repeat.

I found it hard to listen to them and to listen to how she condemned you as a vile seducer, which isn't true, but she would not let me say a single word in your defence.

My father knows too and William of course but that is all. My father has been surprisingly supportive but Mother, as you know, takes charge of everything.

I am to travel with Mother south to Melbourne to stay with her cousin and then we will go to some provincial town where I will have the baby, possibly Goulburn.

Wherever Mother decides, it will be well away from here and all the people we know. Mother has concocted a story that she is ill and needs treatment that can only be obtained down south and I must go with her to help her, but I don't know who will believe such a story. Still, she has too much influence here to be openly questioned.

She says I must go away, have the baby, come back and hold my head up as if nothing has happened and we will not speak of it ever again.

I don't know what lies ahead really. I am frightened. I don't know how I shall bear it all. I wish you were here.

The chance that we would be married was very remote. I know my parents would not have countenanced it with you being American and I know we didn't speak of it, with the war dominating everything.

But I do believe, in my heart, that you would have wanted to do the right thing by me, if only you knew about my situation, but war separates us and plays havoc with our happiness.

I feel I will have a daughter but who can say for sure. The baby is due in March and she will pay the price for our folly, more so than even you and I.

If you have written to me at my home, it is likely that Mother has intercepted your letters, although I asked her and she denied it.

As I write this, I do not know if you are alive or dead. We fear for my brother Richard who is with the RAF in England now flying Lancaster bombers. So far, he has come to no harm, or none that we know of. Mother says she will not tell him about 'my situation', as she calls it, and that I must not either.

I must sign off now as we are leaving tomorrow. I will post this when I get a chance. I cannot let Mother know that I have written to you. She would be furious and I cannot stand any more arguments.

In March, we will be parents. My grief is that our child will never know us. Will she ever forgive us?

I hope one day you read this. I hope you spare a thought for me but especially for our child.

Love always

Julia

Philippe clutched the letter tightly in his hands. Tears streamed down his face. Great sobs rose unchecked from deep within his chest. He did not try to stem the flow. He hid his face in his hands. He had never cried like this before.

He sat for a long time on his mother's front porch; how long he did not know. The street lights cast a feeble glow in the encroaching darkness. The occasional passerby looked at him but did not speak. They assumed the tears were for his dead mother.

So much to take in and yet there was so much he did not know. When was the baby born? Did they both survive the birth? What happened to the baby? Was it a boy or a girl? What happened to Julia?

His tormented mind held a million questions and no answers at all.

The questions went round and round in his head until eventually he folded the letter and put it in his pocket. Finally, he locked the door of his mother's home for the last time. He left the key in the letterbox. He did not look back. He could not look back.

He drove a short way to the water's edge and sat and stared at it without any idea what he would do next.

All he knew was that he had likely fathered a child who was at least two years old. He could not bear the next thought. He could not bear even for a moment the idea that his baby son or baby daughter was being brought up in some charitable institution or worse still even by someone else. Everything else, every other part of life ceased to exist in his mind. He could only think about the news contained in the out-of-date letter he might never have seen.

Where was Julia? And where was the child? What should he do now? Should he write to her? Should he return to Australia? What if he found the child, what would he do then? What if Julia had married someone else in the meantime?

Questions were all he could come up with. There were just no answers at all. He slid behind the steering wheel of his car and sat motionless for a long while before finally heading west back along the island towards the beckoning lights of Manhattan.

The inhabitants of Prior Park were meanwhile settling into life together.

Richard had quite forgotten the titbit of gossip about his sister that the hotel waitress had volunteered on the day of his son's birth, but it came back to him for no particular reason as they all sat drinking tea on the back veranda at Prior Park one languid Sunday afternoon.

To an outsider it gave all the appearance of a scene of domestic bliss but there was no outsider present to pass such a judgement.

William fussed over Alice who was now beginning to show the signs of her coming baby. Elizabeth fussed over baby Paul who rewarded her with a big smile that only meant she fussed more, at which Catherine smiled serenely, content to let her child be the focus of attention.

Conversation was desultory, as if they had little to say to one another that hadn't already been said.

In the lull of chatter, Richard turned to Julia.

'I meant to mention to you, Julia, and I clean forgot,' he began.

'The waitress who served me lunch at the Criterion Hotel the day Paul was born said she thought she remembered you going to the hotel to visit an American officer. She saw you later when you were bridesmaid for William and Alice, that's how she knew who you were, she said.'

Julia's face was blank; her response an apparently disinterested shrug of the shoulders but out of sight, under the folds of her skirt, her hands gripped the edge of her chair in an effort to still her mounting panic.

Richard plunged on unaware of his sister's growing unease.

'She told me she'd felt certain she'd seen you before. I said I hadn't been at the wedding but I was sure that you had been the bridesmaid. She's probably wrong and mistook you for someone else. No one mentioned that you'd been going out with an American.'

He looked at her directly as if waiting expectantly for an answer. She looked up but she could not meet his eyes at first. Her face flushed momentarily but then she replied defiantly. She shrugged her shoulders with practised nonchalance.

'She's wrong,' she said emphatically.

'I had a dance with one or two Americans but that was all. There was no one special. Most of them were loud mouths and very rough.'

With a very deliberate movement, she picked up her cup and saucer from the side table and put it back on the tea table. It was a deliberate act to distract attention from her answer.

Her mother said nothing but concentrated harder on playing with baby Paul.

William, the other keeper of the secret, frowned but did not utter a word for fear he would say too much and betray the secret.

Alice, roused from her near slumber, was about to remind Julia of the American doctor but thought better of it when she caught William's stern eye. She said nothing, except to offer her opinion that it was a relief that all the Americans had gone home now and left them in peace.

'I guess she made a mistake,' Richard said.

But it was clear that he remained unconvinced by his sister's explanation.

Still, he thought, if there was anything back then, she's got over it. He thought that maybe his mother and sister had disagreed about the appropriateness of a relationship, so he didn't pursue it. He didn't want to provoke a family row.

He relaxed back into his chair and marvelled at just how quickly baby Paul was growing.

There was no more talk of Julia and American army officers. William's shoulders relaxed a little. Julia, thankful to escape her brother's searching questions, began to stack the teacups and saucers on the tray.

Baby Paul let out a frustrated cry when he discovered his favourite toy was out of reach and he soon became the centre of attention again, much to Julia's relief.

To outward appearances, Julia, though more mature, was the same Julia that Richard remembered.

But outward appearances were deceptive. There was no day that she did not think about her baby daughter. There was no day she did not weep for what she had lost, but her weeping and her sorrow were private, locked deep within her soul. It was a sorrow she felt powerless to overcome.

'William, it's time for us to talk properly.'

Richard lounged in the chair opposite his father's old desk, while William sat behind it, ledgers opened in front of him, like a clerk, thought Richard, although he did not say so.

'What do you mean? Talk properly?'

William said the words very evenly but even so he found it hard not to lapse into defensiveness, as if he was about to justify all his actions to his older brother.

'I've been back more than six months now and we've never had a meaningful conversation about how Prior Park is run or how the other business interests are run, or the money situation or anything.'

William looked intently at his brother, attempting to gauge his mood.

'You know that Mother gave me the power to run everything while you were away and that's exactly what I've been doing,' William said.

Richard could sense William's rising anxiety at his questioning.

'I know, William, and I'm grateful that you stepped into the breach, but I'm home now. I'm ready to take the reins.'

He noticed the look of concern on William's face.

'Alongside you, of course, alongside you,' he added quickly. 'I didn't mean to say that you shouldn't have a say. I'm sorry if it sounded like that.'

But William was already bristling.

'You know there's debt on Prior Park. I told you that. I told you too that Mother had put some money in just recently, but it's unlikely we'll be able to pay that back to her trust fund any time soon. There's going to be death duties too.'

William seemed ready to rattle off a list of problems to discourage his brother's questions, but Richard intercepted him.

'How much do you think they'll be?'

Richard was always quick to go to the heart of the matter.

'I don't know. We expect to hear any day now. Here's the latest letter from the solicitor in Brisbane, setting everything out.'

William handed a four-page letter to his brother.

'You didn't think to show this to me when it arrived?' Richard asked.

It was an obvious question to which William really had no answer but he mumbled an apology.

'Yes, I'm sorry, I should have shown it to you. It was wrong of me.'

Richard scanned the letter trying to take in all the details.

'It says here that there is an investment in the Goulburn Woollen Mills. I'd never heard about this?'

'Neither had I,' William admitted.

'Father didn't talk about any of the inter-state business interests with us at all, which is a pity. I had to find out about it all from the solicitor.'

'Wasn't there a piece in yesterday's paper about the government offering a subsidy to mills to buy wool for Australian manufacture?'

Richard asked the question but he was already well on the way to discovering the answer for himself.

He was searching through the newspaper, which had been discarded on the table next to his chair.

'Yes, I thought so. There it is.'

He stretched over and handed the newspaper to William, who scanned the article.

'How much ownership do we have? Do we have a seat on the board?'

Richard realised as soon as he uttered the questions that the answers lay not with William but with the letter from the solicitors.

'We own forty-five per cent of it and a seat on the board,' he said, thrusting the letter back towards his brother.

'And the same percentage of two other woollen mills.'

William perused the letter more carefully.

'Look, there are dividends listed here in the accounts. Quite good ones really.'

He continued to peruse the details the solicitor had set out for him.

'But we may still have to sell off quite a lot to settle the death duties,' William cautioned.

'I assume we'll sell cattle to settle that? Not shares in the woollen mills?'

William nodded.

'I've ridden around with Charles since I've been home quite a few times,' Richard said.

'Will that drop our cattle numbers too low?'

For the first time, William gave a firm response to his brother's question, for he had obviously considered the same problem.

'Charles says it will take two to three years to breed up the numbers again, that's if we don't sell too many stock in that time, although we'd sell off the steers of course. We're going to introduce new blood lines too. Father was far too conservative in that aspect. Even Charles admitted that and he worked alongside Father for years. We need stock better able to cope with the heat.'

His voice was animated and he spoke passionately. He was surprised that Richard digested the information in silence so he prompted his older brother for a reply.

'What do you think? Do you think we should be improving the breeding?'

Richard shrugged his shoulders.

'Probably, but this is far more your area of interest than mine. Why don't we agree, here and now, that you run Prior Park without interference from me and I'll run the other business interests, without interference from you?'

William lent forward in his chair. This was an extraordinary offer from his brother.

'You're happy for me to run Prior Park as I want to?'

William's voice betrayed his incredulity. He had half expected to have to fight his brother every inch of the way but now Richard was offering him what he had been manoeuvring for months to gain by stealth.

'Yes, I'm happy for you to run Prior Park as you want to. As long as you are happy for me to run the other business interests as I want to.'

For fear that his brother would change his mind, William stuck out his hand.

'Let's shake on it, then.'

William gripped Richard's hand firmly and the brothers agreed. What animosity had begun to take root between them seemed to evaporate.

'I think the next thing for me to do is take a trip to Goulburn,' Richard said. 'I think I need to see the woollen mills for myself and Goulburn is the biggest of them.'

'Will you take Catherine with you? And baby Paul?' William asked.

'I'll take Catherine. She wants to go to Sydney anyway to meet up with a friend who's coming out from England. It may be better to leave Paul here with the nurse. I'm sure between Julia and Mother, he'll get plenty of attention. We'll only be gone a month at most,' he said.

The two brothers walked out of the office together. In the hallway, Julia was just about to head upstairs to her room but she paused.

'You two have been in deep conversation by the look of it,' she said to neither of them in particular.

'Yes, we have. William's going to look after things here. I'm off to Goulburn to look at the woollen mill that Father invested in, to see how things are going.'

Fortunately, Richard did not wait for his sister's response but went instead in search of Catherine.

All colour had drained from her face. She looked at William, who frowned, but said nothing. He heard the door of her bedroom slam shut but by then Richard was already through the house and out the back door to the garden, where Catherine was playing with Paul. The little boy squealed with delight as his father hoisted him overhead.

CHAPTER 17:
OCTOBER-NOVEMBER 1946

PHILIPPE DUVAL CLOSED the lid of his suitcase and snapped the two metal locks firmly shut. On the bed beside the suitcase, he had carefully assembled his passport and his ticket. The small Manhattan apartment where he lived alone already looked lifeless. He barely glanced back as he closed the door behind him.

Since the discovery of Julia's letter among his mother's possessions, he had found it impossible to settle back into the routine of life as a surgeon at St Luke's. Every waking moment had been consumed by the knowledge that Julia had borne his child and he had not been there for her.

The doorman to his apartment block raised a hand to his cap in a half-salute.

'You going away, Dr Duval?'

The doorman nodded towards the suitcase but received no immediate reply.

'Are you going for long?'

The doorman persisted with his questions. He liked to know the comings and goings of his residents.

Philippe paused, uncertain what to say, not wanting to say too much, yet feeling that some explanation was needed.

'I don't know. I don't really know. Here's my key.'

He thrust the key towards the older man, who took it and hung it on the appropriate peg.

Almost as an after-thought, Philippe said quietly.

'I'm going to Australia. I don't know when I'll be back.'

He was already half way out the door before the doorman could ask why.

He was grateful for that. He did not want to have to explain. Explanations had been difficult enough at the hospital when he had asked for three months' leave. The fewer times he had to explain the story he had concocted the better, he thought.

A yellow cab eased into the sidewalk and Philippe tossed his suitcase along the back seat. The cab ride to Union Station would the shortest part of the journey. Ahead of him lay weeks of idleness, first from east coast to west coast and then on the vast ocean that separates the west coast of the United States and Australia. His destination, Sydney. Beyond that he had no plans.

While Philippe was contemplating the long journey ahead of him, Richard Belleville was making plans of his own that would see their paths cross in a most unexpected way. It had not been possible for Richard to travel south immediately and he was irked by the delay.

He prowled around the house at Prior Park seeking meaningful employment and found none to his liking, apart from amusing his small son.

Left to himself, William was enjoying the freedom to run Prior Park just as he chose but the decision that Richard had intended would ease the growing tensions in the household had entirely the opposite effect.

Alice, further emboldened by the brothers' agreement and by William's elevation to master, gradually took over the role that Elizabeth Belleville had once regarded as entirely hers. Where once the housekeeper looked only to Elizabeth for instruction, now Alice stepped into the breech and decided on their menus for the week. And so gradually, bit by bit, the control of the household became Alice's and no one, except Catherine, demurred.

'So that's the way it's to be, is it?' she asked Richard as they lay side by side, with barely a breeze to give them any relief from the heat of the room.

'So, what's the way it's to be?' Richard was bemused. 'I don't know what you mean?'

He sounded genuinely perplexed although she could not see his face in the pale sliver of light from the fading moon.

'Alice.'

She almost spat out the name.

'Alice has taken over everything. It makes me feel more and more like a visitor here. In your home. In our home. You don't exert yourself at all to have any authority here.'

He sensed her bitterness but refused to acknowledge any truth in her words.

'Well, William is much better at running the country property than I am. To tell you the truth, it doesn't interest me all that much, although I love living here. You know he's going to let me look after the other interests.'

'I know. You told me. How interesting for you.'

Her words were sharp but he did not respond, instead he drew her in a close embrace, but she pushed him away.

'Not tonight. It's too hot. I feel like a wet rag.'

He let her go, reluctantly.

'Well I don't want you to feel that you don't belong. You're my wife, for heaven's sake, of course you belong,' he said, his voice rising just a bit.

'You said you are going to come with me when I go to Goulburn to see the woollen mills; you will have to leave Paul behind though; he's too small for such a tiring journey. When he's older it will be fine for him to travel with us, but not yet.'

She said nothing. She rolled onto her side away from him.

'Let's talk about it tomorrow. I promise you, if things go well, perhaps we will build ourselves a house, just for us. I'm sure William would agree to a block being cut off for us.'

With this, she had to be content. The future stretched out in front of her. The boring future, with a husband either too disinterested to assert his natural authority or too loyal to his family to risk an upset.

For his part, Richard began to see there was a yawning chasm between the kind of world Catherine wanted to live in and the world they did live in. What he feared most of all was the growing gulf that was beginning to separate them. He could see clearly that it would threaten the very fabric of their life together yet he felt powerless to stop it.

'I've asked James to come to dinner,' Alice said, addressing no one in particular but all of them in general, although she cast a sidelong glance at her mother-in-law.

Elizabeth looked up from her lunch plate and nodded.

'Your brother is always welcome, Alice. It's quite a while since we've seen him.'

It was the first time that Alice had really tested her authority and she was surprised at how little comment there had been at her announcement. She was quietly satisfied but careful to hide any appearance of triumph.

Here she was, married to the second son, with her mother-in-law still at the head of the table and Richard's wife alongside her, and yet the household was beginning to revolve around her decision-making and her wishes.

She was quietly and triumphantly pleased when the housekeeper referred to her as Mrs William, when she had once been plain Alice to all the staff.

So the announcement that her brother would dine with them raised no comment at all. Julia, she noticed, seemed entirely unaffected by the prospect. Alice, determined not to give up, continued to harbour ambitions for her brother in that direction.

She dreamed of walking behind Julia as her matron of honour and beaming at the congregation, all the while knowing that in marrying Julia to her brother, she had removed one more obstacle to her ambition to exercise complete authority at Prior Park.

Julia, she thought, hardly seemed to notice what went on in the household anyway. Once or twice she had caught her looking longingly at baby Paul, but it would be years before Alice came to understand that her interpretation of Julia's interest was entirely wrong.

It was just growing dark as James pulled up in front of Prior Park. He took the shallow front steps two at a time and hammered unnecessarily loudly on the front door, which had been closed against the wind that threatened to cover the carefully polished floor in a fine sandy dust.

Alice greeted her brother with a quick peck on the cheek and a hug.

'How are things here? A bit livelier since Richard came home, I bet? You look well. Not long now.' He smiled as he surveyed her swelling figure.

It had been some months since the two of them had met and then the main topic of conversation had been their father's failing health and her happy news.

'Yes, well, it has been busy since Richard got home.'

That was all that Alice had the opportunity to say as first Richard then William greeted James and Alice was all but forgotten as the men made their way into the dining room.

'Richard, aren't you going to introduce me?'

Catherine's words halted the conversation mid-sentence.

'I'm sorry, Catherine, I'd forgotten you hadn't yet met James, Alice's brother. James, this is my wife, Catherine.'

James stood up and extended his hand. She took it briefly, then moved to the seat beside her husband.

The conversation resumed, animated and loud, but James's eyes followed Catherine as she sat down.

He noticed her fine looks and graceful body. He noticed too

how her eyes held his for just a moment longer than necessary, before she looked away.

Beside him, a chair remained vacant.

'Where is Julia?' asked Alice.

'I don't know,' was the general reply.

Just then, Julia appeared in the doorway and Alice motioned her to the vacant seat beside her brother.

It was all too contrived but Julia could do nothing but slide into the seat beside him and murmur 'hello'.

Unbidden, long forgotten images of Julia locked in another man's embrace flooded into James's mind. It was just for a few seconds and then he regained control of his thoughts. He didn't think she had noticed any change in his outward countenance at all.

His quick 'hello' somehow sounded inadequate and banal. He turned towards her, his eyes quickly scanning her maturing figure.

'It's good to see you. I haven't seen you very much lately,' he said in an undertone.

She relaxed just a little. A faint smile played on her lips. Despite everything, she was pleased at his attentiveness and that surprised her.

'Well, we've been busy with Richard and Catherine arriving and then the birth of their baby. There's been a lot to do. And of course before that I was away with mother and then there was William and Alice's wedding shortly after we got back.'

She didn't add, although she wanted to, that I lost my beloved father too. It seemed unnecessary somehow.

The lie to cover her long absence from Prior Park came easy to her now. She had repeated it so often that even to her own ears it sounded like the truth if the truth could be established simply through the retelling over and over again of a convenient and plausible lie.

'Your mother looks well, considering everything that's happened,' James said, without wanting to dwell on the sad details either.

Was he just playing along? Or was he really accepting the story at face value? She couldn't tell. She couldn't tell if he had heard the neighbourhood gossip at the time or if he was simply being polite.

'Mother has been given a new lease of life, I think, since baby Paul arrived and of course Alice, as you can see, has really taken over the running of the house.'

James looked down the long table towards his sister, who was efficiently directing the clearing of soup plates.

'She looks happy and in control, if I may say so,' he said, as if surprised.

'I think she is happy,' Julia said. 'And what is even better is that mother is happy to gradually pass over the running of the household to Alice.'

She was going to add but decided against it that she hadn't thought that Alice was capable of it but she kept the remark to herself. It sounded needlessly critical of her friend and now sister-in-law.

'I wonder how Richard's wife feels about Alice running every-thing?' James asked thoughtfully.

Trust James to get to the heart of the matter, thought Julia, but she was reluctant to concede that he had a point.

'I think she's happy with it. She's been recovering from the birth and enjoying motherhood I think.'

Julia had not, in truth, thought much about Catherine's view of the arrangements.

'I'd seen her about but not to be introduced to,' James said.

She felt some explanation was demanded for their absence from local events.

'Well, Richard and William have been busy with father's affairs and setting up a new structure for the business, I believe, so that's not surprising. We haven't been going around very much.'

He smiled encouragingly at her, enjoying the intimacy of their conversation.

'Your new sister-in-law seems very elegant,' he said, as if to encourage Julia to tell him more.

Julia's eyes followed his to rest on Catherine, her long fingers clasped tightly around the stem of her wine glass, her face set in a polite almost frozen smile as she paid attention to the conversation around her.

'You're wondering if she will settle here, aren't you?' Julia whispered.

He shrugged.

'Well, it's a fair question, I think, don't you? I believe she has aristocratic blood coursing through her veins. She's probably used to a far more sophisticated society than she'll find here.'

Julia nodded in agreement.

'Yes I expect so, although I've hardly heard her mention it, to be fair to her,' she said.

'Rushed marriage was it?'

'You can do the sums,' she retorted, 'as well as I can.'

The hint of a smile crossed his face.

'Ah, yes, I can do the sums all right,' he said.

Julia blushed and fumbled her fork so that she was forced to retrieve it from the floor.

James meanwhile resumed his silent appraisal of Catherine, who suddenly became aware that she was being observed. His gaze did not falter. Just the faintest colour rose in her cheeks before she looked away.

The city of Sydney was an entirely new experience for Philippe Duval. His wartime service had taken him much further north in Australia than the south eastern capital so the size and beauty of the country's largest city might have come as a pleasant surprise to him had he been visiting for any other purpose than his single-minded pursuit of Julia and the fate of her baby.

As his ship sailed through the heads, he was seeing one of the finest harbours in the world for the very first time, but the sparkling blue water hardly registered in his mind.

He did note the grey monotone of the now idle warships at anchor at the navy base as they passed it but beyond that, the city's natural appeal was almost entirely lost to him. His mind was filled only with his plans to see Julia again, to find out any information he could about the baby and to decide what to do for the future—for the future of them both. Did it involve him? There were still as many questions to answer as there had been on the day of his mother's funeral. The questions had tortured his mind every waking hour. He would have no peace of mind, he had decided, until the questions were answered.

As the big ship was nudged into its berth by the attendant tug boats, Philippe gathered together his possessions and prepared to disembark. Exactly where he was going he did not know.

He knew that Goulburn, where Julia's baby might have been born, was just several hours by train from Sydney. That perhaps was the easier part.

He was familiar with hospitals. He could easily find some reason to engage the staff and to ask some questions. That he thought would be a starting point. He had taken the precaution of asking St Luke's senior registrar to write him a letter of introduction, although for what purpose he could not foresee.

The other prospect, of heading north to Springfield, he was less certain about.

Apart from the one letter, he knew nothing at all about Julia's life since he had left more than three years ago. Had the ruse succeeded? Perhaps she had had the baby and then gone back to her life, protected by her mother from gossip and resumed her life. Perhaps she was married? Perhaps she had already started another family?

The most difficult question he refused to even think: would she want to see him again? There were many questions and no answers yet.

In this state of mind, he asked the taxi driver to take him to a good hotel. The driver, having made a quick appraisal of his passenger, deposited Philippe at the entrance to the Australia Hotel. Philippe hardly noticed the marble steps but his attention was immediately caught by a name. Just as he was about to enter the foyer, he heard the porter utter a familiar name but the man was gone before he could catch a glimpse of him.

'Did you say that was Mr Belleville?' he asked the young porter who had ushered the unknown gentleman into a waiting taxi.

'Yes, sir, that was Mr Belleville. He's just left the hotel, sir. I believe he is on his way to Goulburn.'

'Was that Mr Richard Belleville, by any chance?' he ventured.

It was a stab in the dark that was to be rewarded.

'Yes, sir, Mr Richard Belleville. I believe he comes from Queensland, but he has business down this way,' he said.

'Thank you very much. That's most helpful,' Philippe said.

It was a very small snippet of information. Why would Richard Belleville be going to Goulburn, he wondered? More questions to which there were no immediate answers but it decided his plans. He would go to Goulburn too as soon as he could.

A gaggle of small children clung to the iron fence and silently watched the tall man stride past. The youngest of them was not yet three, but already she was wary and watchful. Her blonde hair was untidy. A hastily tied ribbon had unravelled so that the ends of it straggled down the side of her head. There was a smudge of dirt on her cheek that no one had bothered to wipe. Her shabby little dress had been worn many times before and by many little girls before her. Beside her, two boys, stronger and rougher, pushed her aside.

Richard Belleville hardly seemed to give the children a glance, such was the purposeful nature of his mission. He was already a few minutes late for the ten o'clock board meeting at the Goulburn Woollen Mills.

When the secretary announced his name, there was an audible murmur among the five men seated around the table. The chairman, a portly man unused to anything interrupting the routine of his meetings, rose to his feet and was about to demand an explanation.

Richard, prepared for such an eventuality, interrupted him.

'Good morning, gentlemen. I'm Richard Belleville representing the Belleville interests which are now owned by myself and my brother William.'

He did not add, for he presumed they already knew the Belleville interests, which had previously been silent, represented nearly half of the voting stock. The fact that his father had chosen not to attend any board meetings was irrelevant as far as he was concerned.

'Mr Belleville, we did not expect you,' the chairman said, 'but you are most welcome.'

Was he welcome, Richard wondered? To him, it looked like a cosy club that did not welcome outsiders. An extra chair was hastily arranged and the board settled down to the business of the day.

Two hours later, Richard shook hands with each of the men in turn, carefully noting their names.

His sudden appearance had been but a temporary distraction to the chairman who controlled the meeting with almost military precision.

'Mr Foster, I'd like to have a tour of the mill tomorrow, if I may,' he said, almost as an after thought.

It was less a request and more a demand and the chairman was inclined to demur at first but Richard persisted.

'It's my first visit here and I really need to understand what work goes on here. Wasn't there a problem with cloth quality at one stage?'

Richard's knowledge took the older man by surprise.

'Mr Belleville, that was a long time ago. Much has changed since then and certainly the quality has improved immeasurably.'

Richard nodded an acknowledgement.

'I'm not saying it hasn't, Mr Foster, but nevertheless, I would like to see for myself. After all, my family owns a substantial portion of the mill, but I don't have to remind you of that, do I?'

'No, Mr Belleville, you don't have to remind me. I'm very aware of it.'

It was clear the chairman was less than happy about the sudden appearance of such a substantial shareholder who had previously allowed the mill to be run without interference.

'Shall we say 10 o'clock, Mr Belleville. I will arrange for Mr Chambers, the manager, to take you around.'

'Thank you. That will be fine,' Richard said as he collected his hat and walked out the door.

He strode back along the street but this time with less purpose. He was in no particular hurry to get back to the hotel. He was at a loose end as to how to fill in the afternoon that stretched ahead of him.

He noticed that the children he had seen on his walk to the woollen mill were no longer huddled in a small group in the grounds of the orphanage. Probably having their lunch, he thought, poor little blighters.

His aimless walk eventually led him back to the hotel for want of another purpose.

'Mr Belleville, we are still serving lunch. Would you care for a table in the dining room?'

'Thank you, Mrs Jones, that would be good.'

He wasn't particularly hungry but he felt it would pass the time. As he entered the dining room, his ear caught the unmistakeable sound of an American accent.

'You have American visitors, Mrs Jones?' Richard asked, simply to make conversation.

'Yes, an American gentleman, Dr Duval,' she replied, without further explanation.

'I wonder what brings him to Goulburn?' he said, without

really expecting a reply.

'I've no idea, Mr Belleville. I don't ask my guests personal questions,' she said pointedly.

Had Julia or her mother been present, they would have been relieved by the woman's insistence on the privacy of her guests.

It had taken Mrs Jones only a few minutes to connect Richard Belleville of Prior Park with Mrs Elizabeth Belleville of Prior Park, for she never forgot a name, but she had remained silent about the earlier visit, for there had been no doubt in her mind about the purpose of the earlier visit. She was not about to betray a young girl's secret.

At the mention of Richard Belleville's name, Philippe Duval immediately began to doubt the wisdom of introducing himself to Julia's brother but he had come this far, he argued with himself, there was no going back but he decided to proceed cautiously.

He recalled, word for word, Julia's only letter and in particular the fact that Richard had not been told of the impending birth of her baby. If he had been told since his return home, it was possible that the existence of Julia's child was the reason for this visit to Goulburn or was it something else altogether? He did not yet know but he did not want to be the one to betray her. Of that fact alone, he was certain.

Finally, Philippe Duval picked up his coffee cup and walked the few yards to where Richard sat alone.

'Mr Belleville is it?' he said.

Richard looked up at the American.

'Yes,' he said, in reply. 'Have we met before?'

'No, Mr Belleville, we haven't but I have met your family I believe. I overheard your name.'

Richard's interest was immediately piqued.

'Really? When was that?' he asked.

'During the war. I was stationed near Springfield. I used to visit the American camp near Prior Park. I'm a doctor. I was in the medical unit there until I was posted to Hawaii.'

It was a short statement of the bare facts yet it omitted so much.

'Please, pull up a seat. It's good to have some company,' Richard said, happy to have the interruption.

For some minutes they chatted about the war. Richard, who had missed much of what had happened locally during his air force service, was eager for details.

Eventually, he remembered some long forgotten details but fortunately not the one detail that would have connected the American doctor now sitting at his table and his sister in an altogether more intimate context.

'I remember. You were probably the American doctor who helped my sister when an American army truck ran my brother's car off the road and Julia got a broken arm as a result.'

Philippe smiled, remembering the incident but knowing too that he was moving on to dangerous ground yet he could not resist the next question.

'It could have been a lot worse. Your brother was quick to react. How is your sister, by the way. None the worse for that accident, I hope?'

He had tried to sound nonchalant but he could feel his body tense. He hoped his voice did not betray his intense interest in the answer. The casual conversation had been easy to sustain but this new direction required all of his self control not to blurt out the true reason for his return to Australia.

Richard for his part viewed the question as nothing more than polite interest.

'Julia's fine. We're hoping to announce her engagement to our next door neighbour James Fitzroy very soon,' he said, anticipating an event that was yet far from certain.

Before Philippe could reply, he added, chatting happily now as if Philippe was an old friend of the family.

'And both William and I are married. William married Alice, James's sister. I have a son, Paul, and William and Alice are soon to have their first baby.

'My father, sadly, died while I was overseas,' he added.

Philippe, stunned by the sudden mention of Julia's name and her likely impending betrothal, was grateful that, at that particular moment, the waitress interrupted them to refill their coffee cups. He reached for the sugar and absent-mindedly ladled spoonful after spoonful into the black liquid.

'Like your sugar, I see,' said Richard, nodding towards the now overflowing cup.

Philippe shook his head and grimaced.

'A bad habit,' he murmured. 'I think I'm still trying to stay awake for long hours on the ward.'

'I thought as much,' Richard said, mistaking his companion's nervousness for the aftermath of stress from the war.

'You must have seen some horrific injuries,' Richard said.

Philippe nodded, happy to be on safer ground.

'I did. It was terrible. Such a waste of young lives. I did what I could but it wasn't enough many times.'

Their conversation was now in familiar less personal territory.

'Were you injured, Mr Belleville?'

Richard pushed his chair back and stretched out his long legs.

'Yes, on a mission over Germany. I made it back to England but I had a long convalescence. No lasting effects, though, except a small scar,' he said, pointing to the side of his head.

'You were lucky,' Philippe said. 'Very lucky.'

Richard turned the conversation back to the present, wanting desperately to do anything but revive his still painful memories of war.

'So what brings you to Goulburn?'

Philippe lied convincingly.

'I'm on a three month study tour of Australia, but I decided to break my journey between Sydney and Melbourne. I felt I needed a rest for a few days.'

It sounded lame but Richard had already presumed the nervous

American was desperately in need of some well-earned rest and he said as much.

Philippe smiled an acknowledgement.

'And what brings you here, Mr Belleville, you're a long way from home.'

Given the tone of their conversation, Philippe did not imagine that it was in any way connected with Julia and so he was proven correct.

'My family has interests in woollen mills. In fact a substantial interest in the Goulburn Woollen Mill,' Richard said.

'I've been at the board meeting today. With my father gone, William and I have control of the family affairs, so I thought I would come down for the board meeting. My father never attended the meetings as far as I know.'

'Yes, you said about your father passing away. I'm sorry to hear it. Was it sudden?'

'Yes, a heart attack not long after William and Alice were married in '44,' he replied.

'That would have been hard for you,' Philippe said.

'Yes, I got the news while I was serving overseas. It hit me very hard, I have to say.'

Philippe suddenly stood up from the table and offered his hand to Richard.

'Well, it was good to meet you, Mr Belleville. Please pass my best regards to your family,' he said.

He was suddenly desperately anxious to end their conversation. Richard shook the American's hand warmly.

'I'm sorry, I didn't get your name?'

Philippe hesitated.

'Dr Philippe Duval.'

CHAPTER 18:
NOVEMBER-DECEMBER 1946

PHILIPPE WAS DETERMINED to avoid Richard Belleville for the remainder of his stay in Goulburn. After the conversation with Richard, he had gone almost immediately in search of alternative accommodation so that when Richard enquired for him the following day, he was told that the American had checked out of the hotel quite suddenly. In fact, Philippe had moved to new lodgings only a mile away but he was careful to ensure their paths did not cross again.

With so little information to go on, Philippe had decided to present his credentials at the local hospital without really knowing for what purpose or how he could possibly obtain information about children born out of wedlock during the war, which was his ultimate objective. He wasn't even sure that Julia had, in the end, come to Goulburn. When she had written, he knew it had been no more than half a plan which could have changed a dozen times.

As he walked towards the hospital, at first he hardly noticed the large Victorian building that lay on his route between the town and the hospital. He was almost past the building when, for some reason, he glanced back at the plaque attached to the wall. The words proclaimed it to be St Joseph's Orphanage.

On impulse he turned and headed back towards the front steps. He pressed the doorbell hard. He could hear the harsh sound of the bell echoing through the building. After what seemed an interminable time, he heard footsteps and then the door being opened with some effort. A middle-aged woman, clearly suspicious of all callers, greeted him cautiously.

'Yes? Can I help you?'.

It wasn't a friendly greeting.

'I'd like to see the person in charge please,' was all Philippe could think to say.

'My name is Dr Duval,' he added quickly.

He hoped his medical standing would gain him entrée without further questions.

'Are you expected, Dr Duval?'

It was the next obvious question. He hesitated to lie outright.

'Not exactly,' he said, 'but I am here on a study tour in Australia. I'm studying the impact of war deprivation on young children.'

It was the explanation he had rehearsed privately but not previously used. It sounded vaguely plausible, he thought.

'Come in and wait in the hallway and I'll see if the superintendent can see you.'

With that, he was ushered in just a few yards. The woman pointed to a chair, one of several lined up against the wall. He noticed the faded wallpaper and the almost threadbare carpet.

'Wait here,' was her abrupt command.

He sat down and began to take in his surroundings. He noticed how the tread on each of the dark timbered steps heading to the upper floors was worn and scuffed. Two tall windows allowed in a small sliver of natural light that failed to illuminate the dark corners of the hallway.

He sat in anxious silence for some minutes until the woman returned.

'The superintendent will see you for a few minutes. She is very busy, you understand.'

She spoke sharply as if to remind him that there was much more important work to be doing than talking to him. He simply murmured his thanks and followed her to the superintendent's office. The superintendent rose and extended her hand as he entered her office. He had half expected to meet a nun but instead he found himself sitting opposite a woman clearly in command of her surroundings. He guessed she might have medical qualifications although he did not ask.

He introduced himself and sat down. He could not know that he sat in the exact same chair that Elizabeth Belleville had occupied some years before when she came to arrange the fate of Julia's unwanted baby.

'I was on my way to call on the hospital,' Philippe explained, 'when I noticed the plaque on the door and called in, merely by chance. I'm looking at the impact of war on children and I thought perhaps an orphanage might be one place to gain a real insight into this problem.'

Ada Collins listened politely to this short speech before replying.

'Yes, Dr Duval, war has had a major impact on children. Many children here have lost one parent; some have lost both and of course there has been what we might call a sad moral decline with so many young women giving birth to babies out of wedlock.'

He did not challenge her assessment of the moral decline. He detected clear and unambiguous disapproval in her tone. He was simply relieved she seemed to accept his pretext for asking questions but concerned all the same that the questions he asked would lead to any real information in satisfying his ultimate quest.

They spoke generally for some minutes, he trying to imply some authority on the topic he was supposedly researching while the superintendent pressed on, happy to have an audience for her opinions on the plight of the children in her care.

'I assume that quite a number of the children coming through here move on to adoption. Have you had much success in placing many children?' he asked eventually, trying to steer the questions in a more specific direction.

He was really stumbling in the dark, more in hope than in real expectation that anything useful could be gleaned from the superintendent.

'Yes, where we are able to although some children are simply placed with us, as I said earlier, until parents get on their feet again and then they come back for them. Others are not so lucky. I have some statistics here that might interest you.'

She handed him a sheet of paper. He saw that it was carefully compiled in a neat hand with meticulous columns of figures that, at first glance, he could make no sense of at all, but he thanked her all the same.

'We've had hundreds of children through here over the past few years,' she said, emphasising the scope of the problem.

Philippe nodded encouragement.

'Some are lucky. We had one young girl obviously of good family but no husband who gave birth to a baby girl some years back. The baby was very pretty. She was adopted out very quickly to a local couple who couldn't have a family of their own. I mention her because I see her from time to time in the town with her mother.'

Philippe was silent for a few moments, devouring this piece of information, trying to decide if this was important or merely a coincidence.

'So, a happy ending, do you think? But what about the young woman who had to give up her baby?'

He was desperately trying to keep his voice in check. He was taking care not to betray anything but the most casual interest in this particular case.

But he was fortunate. Ada Collins was not an overly perceptive woman.

'Well, I didn't meet the young mother but I met her mother. Quite a formidable woman. She arranged everything and was generous in her donation to the Orphanage. I remember the cheque she gave me was drawn on a Queensland bank so I assume they were going back to Queensland. She'd obviously brought her daughter south where she would not be known to have the baby.'

Philippe was beginning to shake just slightly. He gripped the edge of the chair to steady himself.

'A local family, you say? That was fortunate.'

To his own ears, the words sounded strange, his voice unnatural.

'Yes, the local family has big wool-growing interests. I think they supply a lot of wool to the local woollen mills. They had tried for years to have a family with no luck. The husband wouldn't hear of adopting a boy—son and heir and all that but he relented and agreed to adopt a daughter.'

She barely paused for breath before continuing.

'They called the little girl Pippa. Apparently there was a message from the baby's mother to say she wanted the baby called Philippa but Mr and Mrs Jensen didn't like the name, but they wanted to honour the young mother's request, so they called her Pippa.'

She had warmed to her subject.

'I remember too she had this lovely gold locket hidden among the baby clothes. Normally we wouldn't leave anything like that with the baby to identify her natural mother but on this occasion I relented. There's not much chance she'll ever meet her mother.'

Ada Collins shifted uncomfortably in her chair, realising that she had said far too much to the polite, soft-spoken American doctor sitting across from her.

'This is all very confidential information, you understand. I shouldn't have spoken quite so freely. I got a bit carried away remembering that particular case so please keep all that I am telling you confidential.'

Philippe opened his mouth to speak but words came with great difficulty. He struggled for breath even as he rose from his chair, apologising as he did so.

'I'm sorry, Mrs Collins, I have to get some air. Of course I will respect the information you have given me. Thank you for seeing me. I have some troubles still from the war,' he said vaguely, in an effort to explain his sudden near collapse.

She nodded.

'I understand,' she said. "I've seen many men in the town badly affected by the war. Terrible it is, just terrible.'

He thanked her for her time, declining her offer of help as he headed as fast as decency would allow to the front door.

Outside the building, he stopped and lent against the solid stonework for support.

In a few minutes, he had learned the fate of his daughter, for he was in no doubt that the baby whose story he had just heard was the daughter that Julia had given birth to.

He could not bear to think how different it could have been for her, for the baby and for him, had he known about it.

He walked, head down, directionless until he found a park. Out of sight, beneath a large tree that afforded protection from the sun and out of sight of the passing traffic, he sat huddled on a low wooden seat. For the first time in his life he did not know what to do.

He did not know how long he sat there. It was the desperate need for a cup of coffee that eventually forced him to move. Even then he could not decide what to do next once he had consumed the weak brown liquid that passed for coffee in the local cafe. The vital information about his baby daughter had come to him too easily, too quickly, he hadn't been ready for such revelations. He had prepared himself for the likelihood that he would never know her fate. Instead he now knew too much, far too much.

There was no longer any doubt. What started as a quest for answers he thought he would never find, instead had become a new burden to bear.

He now knew that his baby daughter and Julia herself had survived and the baby had been given up for adoption. His child was now someone else's daughter, by law, and he might never know her. He wondered how Julia could bear that knowledge for he found he could not.

At the same time Philippe Duval was at St Joseph's Orphanage, Alan Chambers was greeting Richard Belleville warmly and beginning an extended tour of the woollen mill. Richard, for his part, was encouraged by the older man's enthusiasm and his genuine pride in the woollen mill, which until now, had simply been a footnote to the Belleville family's financial interests.

'It's a complicated process, Mr Chambers, and a labour-intensive one,' Richard said, as they moved through the mill, observing the complexity of the process that turned raw fleece into attractive woollen cloth ready for the tailor or great skeins of yarn for the knitter.

He noticed some of the girls casting sideways glances as him as he walked alongside the manager. A stranger in their midst, particularly a young handsome stranger, was fertile grounds for gossip, but the supervisor was quick with a sharp word to get them to pay attention to their work and not mind what the manager was doing.

'Well, Mr Belleville, that is about as much as I can show you today,' the manager said.

'I'm due to meet with one of the big woolgrowers this afternoon to discuss the next clip and there are some things that I must do before I can get away.'

Richard nodded, knowing that the manager would have a busy day, particularly the day after a board meeting.

'I completely understand, Mr Chambers. And thank you for your time. By the way I did read in the newspaper recently that the government is offering subsidies to mills to buy wool for Australian manufacture. Are we taking advantage of that subsidy?' Richard asked, keen to demonstrate his knowledge of the industry.

'Yes, we are indeed, Mr Belleville. It is a great idea, I can tell you.'

Richard smiled and nodded his agreement.

'Yes, government help is always welcome in this business, I imagine.'

Alan Chambers relaxed a little. He had been concerned that this unknown director, representing a major shareholding in the mill, might be a difficult man to deal with but he was relieved to find that Richard Belleville was proving to be entirely the opposite. It was this knowledge that encouraged him to issue an unexpected invitation.

'I'm due to meet Harry Jensen this afternoon at his main property Essex Downs. Would you like to come along? I'm sure he won't mind.'

The offer was too good to refuse so Richard readily agreed.

'That's settled then. I'll pick you up at your hotel at half past two. It's only a twenty minute drive. You'll get to see some of the countryside too.'

The two men shook hands at the door.

'Until 2.30 then,' Alan Chambers said.

Richard deep in thought about the woollen mill he had just visited headed back to his hotel. He did not notice the hunched figure under the large tree in the park. Philippe, for his part, did not know how close he came to encountering Richard Belleville again, an encounter he was desperate to avoid.

Catherine Belleville had chosen not to travel to Goulburn, rightly assuming that the attractions of Sydney would prove to be more interesting than the provincial town over a hundred miles away that was Richard's ultimate destination.

So she had remained at The Australia hotel where the refined atmosphere reminded her of the classic London hotels she was beginning to discover how much she missed.

'A penny for your thoughts.'

It was a familiar voice that broke her reverie as she sat in the foyer of the hotel the day after Richard had left for Goulburn.

She turned her head searching for the source of the voice but it was not immediately apparent.

She stood up and it was then she saw the familiar face of John Bertram, whose broad grin was the most welcome sight she had seen for a very long time.

'John, I didn't know you were coming to Sydney,' she chided him gently. 'How did you know I was here?'

'I didn't,' he conceded, 'not for sure, but Richard wrote to me and said he was planning on coming to Sydney and then going to Goulburn and that he hoped we would have a chance to meet.'

Catherine smiled and relaxed, delighted to see her cousin again.

'So here I am, at your service, madam,' he said, bending at the waist in an exaggerated bow.

'It seems so long since I've seen you,' she said, her mood improving immediately and the brightness in her voice returning.

'Too long,' he said, 'but you live up there in the wilderness and it's a long way to travel. I take it Richard is in Goulburn?'

Catherine nodded in reply.

'Yes, I'm not sure when he will be back. In a day or two I guess. He was attending a board meeting at the woollen mill.'

John made no comment but stood back from her a little.

'You look well. Motherhood suits you. How is baby Paul? You didn't bring him with you, did you?'

She smiled at the mention of her baby son.

'He's very well; he's growing very sturdy and strong. Richard decided it was better to leave him in the nursery than bring him on a long trip. But next time, when he is older, he will come with us.'

'I imagine your mother is very keen to see him.'

John was always one to go straight to the heart of the matter. Catherine smiled ruefully.

'Yes, she is. We write often and send photographs but I never thought my mother would be so keen on being a grandmamma,'

Catherine said, failing to conjure an image of her mother in the role of doting grandmother.

'Well, distance probably adds something there,' John said.

'I suppose so,' conceded Catherine.

'I take it the rift about your marriage to Richard has been healed then?'

'Yes, of course. More so of course when they found out I was pregnant.'

John laughed and grimaced.

'Yes, that would have come as a shock,' he said.

'Indeed, a quick inhalation of the breath, followed by a few sounds of disapproval and an even quicker change of subject.'

She laughed at the memory now but it had been a tense discussion with her mother following their quick and unannounced wedding.

'So this trip is by way of an anniversary present, is it?' John asked.

'You could say that,' she said.

'And how do you find life in the deep north?'

'Deep north?'

She was perplexed by the question.

'The opposite of the deep south in America, my dear,' he said, explaining the use of the term.

'We southerners see it as a conservative state where new ideas are slow to take root.'

She pulled a face.

'Well, that's not far off the mark. It is, shall we say, very provincial. Richard loves it of course but his younger brother is running the property and he is running the other interests, so perhaps in time I can get him to move south.'

It was the first time she had speculated that their future together might not include Prior Park but she had never said as much to Richard. She was, however, willing to say it to John.

'A word of caution. He'll take some moving from Prior Park, I think, Catherine,' he said gently.

'He will be suffering the after-effects of the war. It was terrible stuff we had to do so don't push him. He may seem all right but underneath, he's probably suffering, just like I am.'

For the first time, she looked closely at her cousin and saw the lines in his face and the few strands of grey hair that made him look older than his years. It was the honesty of his words that struck her most.

'Thanks for the warning. It's hard to remember that terrible stuff when we are so far away from it here in Australia.'

He noticed her mood becoming quieter so he pulled her arm through his and guided her towards the door.

'Let's put all thought of war and terrible things out of our minds. It's a lovely day. Let me show you Sydney. Let's just enjoy the day. We'll head down to the harbour for a cruise.'

She smiled and nodded, matching his upbeat mood.

'I'm in your hands, Mr Bertram. Lead the way.'

With Richard and Catherine away and Alice absent awaiting the birth of her baby, Julia found herself in a house unusually quiet except for the routines of the nursery which seemed rigid and strict to her but which appeared to suit baby Paul extremely well. His grandmother spent much of each afternoon with her grandson watching his futile attempts to stand and smoothing over his frustration at not achieving it.

Left to her own devices again, Julia rode out most days, enjoying the freedom of the countryside, no longer worried by strangers in the district. The American soldiers were long gone and the bush had begun the task of reclaiming the cleared sites such that in a few years there would be little evidence of their presence.

Her life had reached a plateau. She no longer cried daily for her lost daughter but the ache in her heart remained. Slowly as the memory receded she began to look to her future.

On her frequent rides, she tried to avoid the spots she had visited with Philippe for the memory was too painful and the hurt of his rejection of her, because that is how she saw it, too deep. Instead she sought out new paths on her faithful mare.

On this particular day she took a path that led into Mayfield Downs so she was not surprised to be find James Fitzroy alongside her before she had gone very far at all.

He smiled a greeting and raised his hat with a flourish.

'Have you come to see how we're doing over this way?' he said by way of an opening gambit.

'I just felt like a ride and decided on a new path. I didn't think you'd mind me trespassing just a little,' she replied.

'You may trespass all you like, Julia. I'm just surprised to see you. Any word from Alice?'

He knew his sister was already in town awaiting the birth of her baby but he was clearly keen not to miss out on any news.

'Nothing so far,' she said.

'William will go into town tomorrow I think to see her, but she isn't due for another week or two,' she reminded him.

It was becoming a difficult conversation for Julia so she changed the subject.

'Richard and Catherine are in Sydney, or at least Catherine is. Richard's gone on to Goulburn. He didn't know that Father had invested in woollen mills—one of them is in Goulburn—so he decided to check it out for himself,' she said.

Even the mention of Goulburn was painful for her but out in the glare of the sun it was a simple task to put her hand up to her face to shield her eyes so that James did not notice the tears that threatened to engulf her.

'That sounds like a smart move on your father's part,' he said. 'I'm going to be looking to diversify too. My father was really stuck in a rut but he's said he will let me make all the decisions in the future. I didn't expect it to be so easy a transition.'

This was the first time they had really spoken as adults on

adult matters. Julia looked at him critically. He was suntanned from many days spent in the saddle but his looks had matured. Gone were the boyish cheeks and the schoolboy grin; in their place was a strong fine face and dark eyes that spoke of Spanish blood long buried in his ancestry.

'I was going to call over and ask if you would like to go to the Christmas Ball with me. It's the Cattlemen's Union annual function. It's usually a good night.'

She did not reply immediately.

'I'm sure Mother would be delighted for you to stay with us in town,' he added, certain that his mother would welcome Julia for her hopes of having Julia as a daughter-in-law had never dimmed.

'Very well, I accept. Thank you. You'll have to let me know the date,' she said a little ungraciously.

'In time for you to get a new dress?' he said, smiling.

'Of course. I can't go in something I've worn before,' she said, with a logic that he failed to fathom but did not question.

With that, she urged her mare into a trot and waved back at him.

He raised his hand in return and then turned his horse in the opposite direction. She did not see his small smile of triumph. It was not only his mother who had not given up hope, it seemed.

Alice Belleville had only just settled into her parents' house in town and resumed the old familiar routines of her single life when her baby made an early but welcome appearance into the world. She had expected to enjoy the pleasure of being pampered by her mother for at least another two weeks but it was not to be.

Unlike Catherine who had struggled for hours to give birth to baby Paul, Marianne Alice Belleville saved her young mother a lot of pain and trouble by arriving within two hours of her mother's admission to the same room that Catherine had occupied earlier in the year.

The baby's brown hair crowned a face so like her mother's that in years to come there would be no mistaking their close relationship.

Alice was already happily cradling Marianne in her arms by the time William arrived at the hospital, his usually calm and unexcitable demeanour replaced by an agitated and anxious face that was immediately wreathed in smiles at the sight of his baby daughter, contented and asleep, and his wife, tired and happy.

They had settled on Marianne, his mother's second name, or rather he had suggested it and Alice had agreed, for a girl, although William had confidently expected to father a son the first time around, like Richard had. The next William Belleville, for he had a mind to repeat the name in the family line, would have to keep until next time, he decided.

After a few minutes of fussing around Alice and a quick nurse of the new baby, which seemed like such a fragile little thing, William was keen to let Alice know some of the latest news he had received from Richard but by no means all of it. He was grateful that Alice did not ask to see the letter.

'Richard says the woollen mill in Goulburn is run very well,' he told Alice, who barely registered the information.

'He and Catherine are staying in Sydney for a week or two before returning home. They should be home a week before Christmas,' he said quickly, for he could see that Alice was in desperate need of rest.

'I'll tell you more tomorrow,' he said, as he kissed her gently and smiled at the small bundle which lay in her arms.

As he turned to leave, he met Alice's parents at the door to her room. Their delight at the arrival of their first grandchild was obvious to all.

His mother-in-law kissed him enthusiastically and his father-in-law pumped his hand with a surprisingly strong handshake for an ailing man.

'We should wet the baby's head,' he said. 'I'll see you at the Criterion later.'

It was a command rather than an invitation so he could not refuse it, as much as he wanted to get home to Prior Park to be the first to convey the news of his baby daughter to his mother but there was an even more important mission that he felt could not wait.

There was much in Richard's letter he had not told Alice. There was much he never could. He patted the inside of his jacket to make sure the envelope and its contents remained intact.

He congratulated himself for the good sense in having stopped the mail van at the gates to Prior Park on his way to see Alice. There was only one person he could discuss the letter with in detail and that was his mother. And the sooner the better, he thought, for any day now Richard and Catherine would be home and at all costs certain information must be suppressed. Just how that could be achieved he did not know but he felt sure that his mother would have the answer.

CHAPTER 19: DECEMBER 1946

IT WAS SOME HOURS before William was able to excuse himself from the gaggle of men gathered at the bar of the Criterion Hotel on the invitation of his father-in-law to celebrate the birth of the baby girl.

By then, they had all but forgotten the reason they were there in the first place so he finally slipped away almost unnoticed. Unlike most of the men present, he was careful about the amount he drank so he was completely sober when he headed the trusty Buick onto the road out of town towards Prior Park.

The house seemed quiet as he approached the front door but on entering he was immediately surrounded by his mother, by the housekeeper Mrs Duffy and by Charles Brockman, all of whom were keen for news of Alice and the baby. He did not notice that Julia was slow to join the group.

'Alice and I are the proud parents of a baby girl, Marianne Alice,' he said.

'Both Alice and the baby are well,' he added as an after thought.

His mother was the first to ask the obvious question.

'So who does the baby look like?'

At this, William was perplexed. To him, she looked like a baby but he decided against saying so. Instead he asserted that the baby was the spitting image of her mother, which on his part was an inspired guess. As to the baby's weight, there was exasperation among the women who could not believe he had forgotten to ask such an important detail.

She's a regular size was all he could think to say for he had no idea at all what weight a baby should be so he could not even make an educated guess.

'I shall come with you to see her tomorrow,' his mother said. 'That is barely a report at all and no doubt, knowing Jack Fitzroy, you've already been at the Criterion wetting the baby's head.'

He smiled at this and nodded.

'Yes, I couldn't get out of that obligation, I'm afraid. James was there too. By the way, he tells me he is taking you to the Christmas Ball, Julia,' he said, turning towards his sister who by now was on the fringes of the group.

Before Julia could answer, her mother intervened, nervous that William might say the wrong thing.

'Yes, your sister is going with James and we are shopping for a new frock for Julia to wear.'

William heard the warning note in his mother's voice so he said no more on the topic, knowing only that Julia would be wearing the most expensive and the most stylish dress of any woman at the ball if his mother had anything to do with it. It was clear she still had hopes for Julia in that direction and he was not about to upset his mother's renewed plans.

Dinner had been delayed awaiting his return so he and his mother and Julia headed towards the dining room. Charles Brock-man had been invited to join them but he declined, preferring not to be the odd one out at such a small family table so it was just the three of them who sat down together.

It was his mother who spoke first.

'Thank you for naming your daughter after me, William, I'm touched,' she said.

'It's just your second name, Mother,' he said, a little defensively. 'I couldn't imagine another Elizabeth Belleville, but Marianne is a nice name and Alice liked it too.'

'Yes, it was my maternal grandmother's name, so it is nice to see it continued. How long do you expect Alice to be in hospital?'

Again, it was a question he hadn't really asked.

'I'm not sure, ten days perhaps. I think her mother wants her to go to them for a few days before she comes home to Prior Park.'

For once, Elizabeth Belleville did not mind the proposed arrangement.

'I thought she would go to them,' she said. 'It's probably easiest for her to remain in town until she has her first check up.'

'They'll certainly be home here for Christmas,' he added.

'Perhaps we should invite the Fitzroys to come to us for Christmas,' his mother said unexpectedly.

William had not considered this idea but on reflection he found much to agree with in his mother's proposal, knowing that Alice's parents would want to spend the first Christmas with their granddaughter.

Through all of the conversation about his new baby daughter, the contents of Richard's letter, which still remained in his pocket, were never far from his thoughts but he dare not mention the letter at all in Julia's presence.

It was only after dinner that an opportunity presented itself to draw his mother to one side with the urgent news that they must discuss a letter he had received from Richard that morning.

Taking his cue, Elizabeth Belleville followed her son into the study that had once been the sole preserve of her husband. The room still looked much the same but the level of whisky in the decanter now barely moved from one week to the next. She was grateful her sons had not developed the same liking for the drink that her husband had.

'What's this about a letter from Richard? When did you get it?' his mother demanded.

'I intercepted the mail van this morning on my way into town. Just as well as it turned out,' William replied.

'Why what news does he have that we can't share with everyone?'

Elizabeth Belleville was clearly perplexed by William's secretiveness.

'In a nutshell, Mother,' he said, 'he met Philippe Duval in Goulburn and Philippe Duval asked to be remembered to us.'

The colour drained from Elizabeth Belleville's face.

'He met Philippe Duval in Goulburn? There must be some mistake. This doesn't make any sense at all. Not at all.'

Her voice was shrill. William remained silent as she stood up and started to pace the room.

'What does he say? How? How could this be? Show me the letter.'

She held out her hand and William reluctantly handed over the letter.

Richard was not a great letter writer so it wasn't a long letter. She read it through quickly, merely scanning the business matters.

It was the second last paragraph that concerned them both.

He wrote:

I ran into an American doctor at my hotel in Goulburn. He's out here for a few months on a study tour. What a coincidence though. He was the American doctor who treated Julia when you were forced off the road by the American Army truck. I remember Mother writing about it. He asked to be remembered to everyone. His name is Dr Philippe Duval. He's left the Army I understand and is now practising neurosurgery in a New York hospital. He seemed to be suffering a bit as a result of the war. He said he was on his way to Melbourne from Sydney and decided to stop off in Goulburn for a few days rest. He certainly seemed to need it. Remind me to tell Julia about it. I wonder if she remembers him?

Elizabeth Belleville considered this entirely unexpected news for a few minutes before she spoke again.

'Do you think there is time to write a letter to Richard in Sydney saying that he left Julia broken-hearted and it's best not to mention his name in her presence?'

The idea had come to her as the only possible solution. William shrugged.

'I'm not sure. This letter has taken almost a week to get here. We could send a telegram but that would seem odd to him. He'd suspect the matter was much more important than we're claiming. You don't propose to tell him the truth, do you?'

This idea had not occurred to Elizabeth Belleville and she said as much to her younger son.

'Of course I'm not going to tell him the truth. There are only three people who know about this here and I don't plan for anyone else to find out. Can you imagine what it would do to Julia if she found out that Philippe Duval was back in Australia? She thinks he deserted her and I want her to go on thinking that. Hopefully, she'll be married to James Fitzroy before very long and have another baby. I never thought we'd have to talk about this matter again.'

Her voice was hardening and with it her resolve to keep the unfortunate matter, as she was inclined to describe it, from being talked about again.

William now was not so sure that everything would turn out quite as well and as neatly as his mother planned but he knew better than to say so.

'It's the only option,' she said, with a note of absolute finality.

'You must write a short note to Richard, explaining that Julia had a crush on the American doctor and that he let her down and it took her a long time to get over it so it's best not to mention his name in the household.'

William murmured his agreement with his mother's plan.

'Anyway,' she continued, 'you'll pick them up at the railway station so you'll have to make sure and ask him if he got the letter. You can write under the pretext of announcing the news of your daughter's birth. That way it won't seem unusual that you've written to him when he's due home so soon. Do it now and it can be posted tomorrow when we go and see Alice.'

With that his mother was gone and he was left to take up his pen and write to his brother. He agreed with her that, at all costs,

Philippe Duval's name must never be mentioned in Julia's presence.

William did not speculate further about the meeting but Elizabeth Belleville was struck by the coincidence that Philippe Duval should be in Goulburn. Why Goulburn?

It was a question she repeated to herself again and again but it was one to which she could find no satisfactory answer, yet her instinct told her that the explanation he had given Richard was a long way from the truth. By some means did he come to know about Julia's pregnancy? Did he come to know of their plans for the secret birth?

It was to be a sleepless night for Elizabeth Belleville as she pondered these unanswerable questions long into the night.

It had taken Philippe Duval the best part of two days to decide what his next course of action would be. In that time he had walked the streets of the town barely noticing the hum of daily activity around him except that he found himself staring at every golden haired little girl wondering if she was his daughter.

It had not taken long for him to discover where the Jensen family lived for they were well known locally. His pretext for seeking information had changed. He invented a cousin of the family he had met in Queensland during his war service. His questions seemed so natural that the hotel receptionist gave him far more information than he expected. He found it had taken just a little encouragement of the young woman whose natural inclination was to gossip about everyone she knew and some she didn't to get the information he needed to confirm what he already knew.

In the privacy of his room, he sat down to write the most difficult letter he had ever written. He had torn up many attempts before he was finally satisfied.

Dear Mr Jensen

This is the most difficult letter I have ever had to write, and most likely will ever write.

Through my enquiries, I have to come to the certain knowledge that the daughter you adopted is my natural daughter.

I was in love with a young woman up in Queensland during my war service but I was posted suddenly and I know she subsequently found herself to be pregnant. I know this because she wrote to me care of my mother, a letter I only found when my mother died recently. It was among her possessions. My mother chose not pass it on to me unfortunately.

I believe the young lady in question was prevented from receiving my letters by her family. I would certainly have married her before I went had I known about the child. I had plans to come back for her after the war, but, apart from the letter sent via my mother, I never heard from her, obviously because she never received my letters telling her where I was. I naturally assumed she had lost interest in me, until I found the letter among my late mother's possessions. The young lady, sadly, assumed I had abandoned her.

What a terrible web we weave.

It pains me to acknowledge that I can have no part in my daughter's life because you have legally adopted her.

I know from my enquiries that your family is prosperous and able to give my daughter all the advantages in life that I would have given her myself.

I would, however, ask this one thing of you. I will not seek to disrupt your life, or that of your wife, or your daughter, but I would ask you to keep this letter until she turns 18 and then, once she knows she is adopted, to share it with her.

I would like her to know that she wasn't abandoned. I will not name her mother to you, but she is of a good family and it must have cost her dearly to give her daughter up. That I do know.

I understand that her name is Pippa and that pleases me.

I will shortly return to New York. I practice at St Luke's Hospital, should you ever wish to find me, or you may write to me at my home address, which I have set out below.

I am sure a time will come when Pippa will be curious about her natural parents. I hope you won't deny her the opportunity to find out more, if she wants to.

In the meantime, I trust you will provide a safe, loving and happy home for my daughter, whose loss is almost more than I can bear, but I must bear it and return to my life in New York.

I believe the child's natural mother is likely to marry another soon so I do not plan to disturb her life afresh.

I understand that this letter may cause you consternation. You may not wish to share it with your wife who, I am told, has formed a warm and loving bond with the child.

I do not wish to upset your life. I write to you only so that you will have the information about Pippa's natural parents in the event that she should ask, when she is older. I have enclosed, in a sealed envelope that I ask you not to open but to give to Pippa when the time is right, the details of her natural parents and how it is that she was given up for adoption.

All this I entrust to you, having learnt that you are a man of honour and much respected in your local community.

He signed his name, folded the letter with its precious enclosure and addressed the envelope. He walked two blocks along the street to the post office, which was just about to close. He was determined not to change his mind so within ten minutes of finishing the letter, he had mailed it and was walking back towards his hotel.

He felt an immense sense of relief. He knew there was nothing further he could do now.

He had discovered the awful truth: that the daughter he had fathered with Julia had been put up for adoption. The rest he could piece together. He was now sure that his letters had been intercepted. He was certain too that her mother had never considered it possible for Julia to keep the baby she bore out of wedlock.

For a few moments, he sat with his head in his hands. He was tortured by the knowledge that, had his posting come through a month later, he was sure she would have known by then of her pregnancy and they could have married quickly. But it was not to be.

It had been the chance meeting with Richard Belleville that had finally helped him decide to return to New York. He could not see that anything was to be gained by seeing Julia again. He did not want to disrupt her life. After so many years, he did not know how she would feel about him. Could they resurrect what they had shared together? In his heart he doubted it.

Now that he knew their baby daughter had been adopted by another family, he could not see how they could make a life together. He had tried to imagine how their relationship would ever survive the knowledge that their child had been given away and he could not.

Slowly, he began to pack. Tomorrow he would return to Sydney and within days he would board a ship to return to New York. He doubted he would ever return.

The next morning, as he boarded the train, it took all of his strength to turn his back on the town where he knew his daughter would grow up. It took all of his strength not to stay and search for her among the young children he had seen on the streets.

All that remained for him now were his precious memories of a beautiful young Australian girl whom he had loved and whom he still loved. But now he knew for certain they had no future together. For her sake, he knew he must let her go and live another life, with another man, and he must live another life.

Yet he knew they would be bound together unknowingly by an invisible thread. It was a bond of love that would never be entirely severed.

As the train pulled away from the platform, he glimpsed a golden haired child, her right arm raised in an uncertain wave, her left hand holding tightly to the skirt of the well-dressed woman beside her.

They waved together at the train as it gathered pace. He did not know who was the intended recipient of their farewell. He only knew that his heart broke anew because he saw, just for a fleeting moment, a gold locket around the child's neck.

Could it be? Could it possibly be? He did not know for certain. He watched until he could no longer see the mother and daughter standing on the platform. Only then did he sink back into the worn leather seat and begin to imagine, once again, a different life, a life where he was father to his own daughter and husband to Julia.

It was now a shattered dream, a dream that lay in tatters around him and his life with it.

William Belleville felt a very strong sense of déjà vu as he paced the railway platform waiting for the train that would return Richard and Catherine home after their trip south.

In his mind, he had rehearsed a hundred times what he would say to his brother to prevent him mentioning Philippe Duval's name in the household. The explanation sounded lame to him and he thought for sure it would sound lame to Richard, but proceed with it he must.

At last, the train pulled in, hissing and wheezing amidst vast belches of steam as it shuddered to a stop.

Richard was the first out of the door of the carriage, turning to offer his hand to his wife who in reality hardly needed to be helped down to the platform at all. She sprung down lightly, looking little the worse for the twelve-hour train journey.

As William approached them, he was unprepared for the warmth of their greeting as they hugged him in turn to congratulate him on the birth of his daughter, and demanded to know how both mother and baby were faring.

He did not mention that Alice and the baby continued to stay in town with her parents, a fact that was beginning to irk him although he never said as much. The nursery at Prior Park, increased to accommodate the new arrival, was yet to receive its new tenant. The pretty pink and white cot was empty and baby Paul continued unchallenged as the little king of the infants' domain.

Desperate to get Richard to one side for a few moments, William settled Catherine into the back seat, but put a restraining hand on Richard's shoulder as he was about to get in to the front passenger seat.

'There's something I need to have a quiet word with you about,' William said, his voice just above a whisper.

Richard, his mood buoyant with the expectation of seeing his baby son again soon after a long absence, simply raised his eyebrows.

William lent in closer to him to ensure he could not be overhead. It was difficult for him because Richard was the taller of the two.

'I just wanted to remind you about the other news in my letter, which you obviously got. You wrote in your letter to me about a Philippe Duval you met in Goulburn. Mother says to remind you not to mention the name in the house, or to Julia. Julia was very keen on him but he let her down, so we don't want to remind Julia of him.'

There, it had been said. He had delivered the message just as his mother had instructed.

'What's that? Yes, I remember,' he said before William could say anything further.

'You said that Julia was infatuated with him, if I understood you correctly?'

William nodded.

'That's right. And he went off and she took a long time to get over it, so we don't want to remind her of it, so don't say anything. That's Mother's instruction, by the way.'

He added the emphasis so that he could be sure Richard would be in no doubt as to where the instruction was coming from.

'Ok, I won't say anything. But we will have to remind Catherine because I told her about it when I got back to Sydney and then she read your letter too.'

William hadn't anticipated this but he could see then that it was most likely Richard would share all the news of his trip to Goulburn with his wife and that she would read the letter he had written to Richard too.

Catherine, on being told, simply nodded and instead demanded to know just how much baby Paul had grown in their absence.

William, completely at sea in the conversation, said he thought he had grown a lot and was looking more and more like Richard every day.

The long tiring journey could not dampen the young mother's anticipated pleasure at being reunited with her baby son. That delightful prospect had pushed all other considerations out of her mind as they drew closer to Prior Park.

It was a mere two days later that Richard and William were to be found deep in conversation in what had been their father's study. Used to the steady flow of letters from their Brisbane solicitor, they had not hurried to open the latest envelope expecting it to contain more of the same legal papers as the many previous letters.

So it was with some surprise and consternation that William, first to peruse the letter, sought to discuss it with his brother, who could make no sense of it at all.

'Do you remember when Mother wrote to you about Father's death?' he said.

'I'm sure she would have told you there had been a mix up at the hospital and that there was a lady with him they thought was his wife?'

Richard, sitting in the armchair his father had often occupied, threw back his head as if trying to remember, but clearly failing to do so.

'I'm sure she did, my dear brother, but I was too stunned by the news to take in much detail and too preoccupied with our missions to reflect on it too much to be honest,' he replied.

'Well, it doesn't matter now, does it? It's all a bit irrelevant.'

William pursed his lips. It was a habit that made him look very much like his father.

'Indeed you could say that, since this lady, as you call her, but perhaps there's another name for her, wants some money,' Richard said.

He eased his tall frame out of the armchair and walked to the window. He stared at the view for a while before turning back towards his brother.

'Do you think it is likely that our father had a mistress for more than a decade and none of us knew about it?'

William was flustered by the question when it was put so bluntly.

'I don't know. We were just children. You know Mother and Father didn't get on very well in the last few years. She was disappointed in him. In his own way I think he was disappointed in her.'

Richard hadn't expected William to rise to their father's defence or to reveal such an insight into their parents' relationship. He had always imagined that William would take his mother's side in all things. He had witnessed his father's failings at close hand and had struggled to hide his disappointment as he grew older. He had not known that William, younger than him by more than two years, had come independently to the same conclusion.

'So she has a son that she says is our father's, which I guess makes him our half brother,' Richard said, perusing the letter again, hoping he had misunderstood the details.

'You know I've met her. I saw the boy too although I wasn't meant to,' William admitted finally.

'When did you see her?' Richard demanded. 'You never said anything.'

'I didn't want to talk about it in front of Mother. I've kept it to myself. I didn't tell Alice, I didn't tell the solicitor. I didn't tell anyone,' he said.

'I got her details from the hospital and went to see her that same day. I was curious.'

Richard was silent, waiting for him to continue.

'She lives in a very neat house, small but neat. She's quite attractive. Very elegant actually. I suspect our father bought her the house,' he said, pleased to have finally shared the information that had troubled him for some time.

'So do you think she has a legitimate claim for the boy?' Richard asked, sensing that he already knew the answer but he wanted William to spell it out for him.

William was silent for a few moments, remembering the house and the street and the boy he glimpsed walking through the gate. In the boy, he had seen himself and it had shocked him.

'Do you think she has a claim for support of the boy?'

Richard repeated his question, the concern in his voice rising as if to provoke an answer from his brother.

'Yes, I think she has a very good case. There is no doubt the boy is a Belleville. He looked like me. He looked exactly like me,' William said finally.

Richard looked up sharply, staring at his brother, a hint of anger in his voice.

'You never thought you should tell me this? You never thought I should know about this? What else have you been keeping from me? Any other dark family secrets that it's better that I don't know about?'

There was more than a hint of bitterness in Richard's voice but in reality it wasn't directed at William, it was directed at the war that had kept him away for so long.

He had failed to notice the sweat breaking out on William's forehead and the paleness of his face as he sank into the seat behind the desk. To cover his confusion William began searching for fresh writing paper, pulling out drawers at random and then ramming them back in.

Finally, William spoke.

'I don't think so, but we must be sure that Mother never finds out about Muriel McGovern. She must never know. Promise?'

It sounded to William like he was back in the schoolyard extracting promises from a reluctant school friend. He looked up at his older brother expectantly.

'I agree. There's no reason for Mother to know. Or for Julia to know for that matter. I suggest you write to the solicitor asking advice as to what settlement she would be prepared to take.'

William nodded. He was on familiar ground now. Richard had left it to him to be the main correspondent with the family solicitor and he was happy with the arrangement.

'I'll write this afternoon,' he said. 'Hopefully this woman will be reasonable.'

Richard shrugged.

'I hope so. Let's wait and see what Nathanial Dodds recommends.'

With that he was gone and William was left alone to reflect on their conversation.

In the course of their short tense discussion about Muriel McGovern, it had begun to dawn on William the enormity of their deceit in not telling Richard about Julia.

It also began to dawn on him he had missed the one opportunity he might ever have to tell Richard the whole story about Philippe Duval and Julia without further repercussions.

Yet his courage had failed him. He could not bring himself to launch into the sad humiliating story of their sister's unwanted baby. Was it only his mother's determination that the secret be kept among the three of them that stopped him? Or was there a deeper fear within him of damage to the family's reputation?

He did not know. Yet he had come to realise in those few minutes at some point in the future there would be a day of reckoning when all the secrets they held would be exposed. On that day he knew for certain none of their lives would ever be quite the same again. He knew that relationships would be fractured and the family tested as never before.

But today was not that day. Yet he knew it would come. He knew that much for certain. It would come. It would eventually come and they would all look back and consider how different their lives could have been, but for the secrets they could not share.

CHAPTER 20: DECEMBER 1946

FOR SOME DAYS after his return Harry Jensen had ignored the letters that had accumulated during his absence from Essex Downs. In his experience the letters contained nothing exceptional, mostly statements of bales of wool sold or saleyard notices. Before his regular trips to town, it was his habit to gather up the envelopes and deposit them, generally unopened, with his accountant whose job it was to keep his accounts in order and give him a summary of his affairs every quarter.

He was not a man who enjoyed dealing with the banal details of his life; instead he preferred to focus on his big vision of land ownership and growing the size of the sheep flock. He sought to influence local affairs only in his own interests. He did not do what he dismissively described as the work of clerks.

His regret, if he had any, was the lack of an heir, but he had finally become reconciled to the decision, for it was the only sensible one, to leave his growing empire to his brother's son Andrew, who he thought was beginning to show promise. He never for a moment considered the possibility of bestowing such an honour on his adopted daughter.

So it was, as he sat flicking casually through the accumulated envelopes, that one caught his attention. He did not recognise the handwriting although he recognised the name of the local hotel.

He slit the envelope open with the seldom-used letter opener that lay half buried by the clutter on his desk.

He smoothed out the letter and scanned it. His first instinct was to crumple it up and discard it, but something stopped him. Instead he read it again, this time taking in every sentence and every scrap of information.

When he had finished reading, he placed the letter on his desk. He sat for some time staring through the doorway at nothing in particular. In fact it had stunned him to learn that the tiny child now fully accepted in his household was half-American. He remembered the reassurance from the orphanage superintendent that the child came from a good family where the daughter had suffered a 'sad lapse' in morals. He remembered those words because he had noticed particularly how his wife Anne had reacted to the description, as if the woman was condemning the child as much as the mother.

He noticed how his wife had bitten her lip in an attempt to restrain the instinct already taking hold in her to defend her new daughter from any slight, real or imagined. He knew his gentle, softly-spoken wife would love this tiny abandoned child with every fibre of her being. Could he love the child? Perhaps but it was not the same as your own flesh and blood. He had agreed to the adoption for his wife's sake, not for his own.

So the information about the child's parents that had come to him unbidden was disturbing. He could find no reassurance in it. Should he keep the letter to show the girl later on? He could not yet come to the idea of calling her 'his daughter'. One thing was for certain, he would not show Anne, for she would, he knew, feel only greater distress at the child's abandonment. It was better to leave things as they stood. The household was happy; his wife contented; the child no trouble to him.

He opened the big heavy safe in the corner of his office. Within the safe lay a worn leather satchel containing his most important documents. He pushed the envelope and its contents into the satchel, replaced the satchel on the middle shelf and slammed the door of the safe.

With that the matter had been decided for now. It would he

hoped be many years before the letter was read again, if it was ever read again.

He walked through the door of his office on to the wide verandah that encircled the house. Across the lawn his wife sat on a blanket. Beside her little Pippa sat pulling the petals from a white daisy. The little girl was laughing happily, her fair hair turning golden in the sunlight. Her mother smiled broadly. She now had everything she had longed for. She was alive again. She had a daughter. A beautiful child whom she could indulge and shower with love and attention. She no longer thought of Pippa as an abandoned child. The child was now absolutely secure because Anne loved her as she would have loved her own child.

Harry Jensen waved a hand in greeting but he did not join them. Instead he picked up his hat and headed in the opposite direction, away from the house towards the shearing shed. This was his territory. Here he was boss with no questions asked. Here there no uncertainty. This was the world he knew. A world of men, of sheep, of shearing, of cursing and swearing, of heat and sweat. Here he could push all uncertainties to the back of his mind. This was where he belonged. This was where his longed-for son would have belonged.

But he did not dwell on this regret. He kicked at some fleece on the floor and yelled to the rouseabout to do his bloody job or he'd be out on his arse. The fleece was quickly gathered as he continued his inspection of the shearing shed.

It was mid December and pre-Christmas festivities were in full swing in Springfield. With the war now well behind them, the ranks of revellers had been swelled by the men returning from the alien world of war to the familiar world of home and everyday life. It was late in the evening when Richard Belleville sought a temporary haven away from the noise of the over-crowded ballroom.

Around the corner of the building and well away from the

entrance to the building, he leant against the wall and lit a cigarette. Smoking was a habit that had stayed with him from his air force days when all the men smoked to calm their nerves and to pass the time as they sat around waiting for their orders.

He stood by himself for a few minutes listening to the muted sound from within the ballroom. He knew he would have to return before too long even though the crush of people and the noise was beginning to get on his nerves.

He drew deeply on his cigarette until the tip of it glowed bright red in the darkness.

'All alone I see.'

He recognised James Fitzroy's voice although he could barely make out his face in the shadows.

'Yes, just enjoying a breath of fresh air. It's pretty hot and steamy inside,' he said.

'It is, isn't it. But not unusual for this time of year,' James replied.

'I see you and Julia seem to be getting along all right.'

It was less of a statement and more of a question really.

'I'd like to think so,' James said. 'I'd like to think so. In fact I wanted to have a word with you about Julia. I assume you stand in loco parentis as it were now that your father has passed on?'

Richard smiled at the idea that anyone had much control over his sister's life or that she would look upon him as a father figure.

'I don't feel like a father to her, if that's what you mean. In fact, I've hardly had a serious conversation with her since I returned from Europe.'

It was James's turn to smile.

'Well, that's young women for you nowadays, I guess. You have to admit your sister is quite privileged. She doesn't have to do much work at home I imagine. She probably doesn't have much to occupy her.'

'No she doesn't. That's true,' Richard said.

He crushed his cigarette butt under his shoe and seemed ready to walk back into the ball.

'I am in love with her you know,' James said suddenly.

Richard glanced at him but it was hard to judge, in the poor light, if this was a sudden whim or a genuine declaration.

'So, if you're in love with her, what are your plans?' Richard asked, uncertain as to why James would be talking to him in this way but feeling in some way that he should protect his sister's interests.

'To be honest, I hope to pop the question very soon, perhaps on Christmas Day even, if everything goes well,' he said.

The two of them had moved back towards the doorway into the ballroom.

'Yes, I'd quite forgotten. You and your parents are coming to Prior Park for Christmas dinner. We look forward to it,' Richard said.

'Do you think Julia will accept me if I ask her to marry me?'

It was the first time Richard had sensed any uncertainty in James Fitzroy.

'I don't know, to be honest. I did hear of a wartime romance with an American that she took a while to get over and no one is allowed to mention it at home,' Richard said, not knowing that James was fully aware of Julia's earlier entanglement and still bitter that a rival had thwarted his early plans.

James hardly knew how to respond.

'Well, what can I say. I knew about it of course but he left rather suddenly. Posted overseas I think or back to the States. I don't know really. Good riddance I say.'

Richard chuckled at the vehemence of James's response.

'A bit jealous, were we?' he said.

'You might say that,' James conceded. 'There were lots of American soldiers here. You missed it all. Many of the girls were very taken with them.'

'I hear the occasional American accent in town now and then. It seems as if a few of them might have been induced to stay,' Richard said.

'Yes, I think a few of them did stay and marry local girls. Some local girls went over to the States too as war brides. But thankfully not your sister.'

Richard was on the very point of mentioning to James that he had met Philippe Duval in Goulburn but in the end he decided against it. He did not want to create any obstacle to the match for Julia that they all hoped would come to pass.

'Well, if you've come to ask my blessing for the match, you have it. And the rest of the family too. It would be good to see Julia settled. But I can't vouch for the reply she will give you. That is something you will have to find out for yourself.'

It was little enough encouragement but James smiled to himself, knowing that with her family's approval, he was just that little bit closer to claiming the prize he at one time thought could elude him.

With that thought, he walked swiftly back into the ballroom to claim another dance with her. He was now more confident his patience was about to be rewarded and she would agree to become his wife.

Richard was about to follow him but just at that moment he sensed a movement in the shadows. He paused momentarily and looked around. At that very moment, Jane Warner looked up towards the door. She had been standing only a short distance away and had been on the point of returning to the ballroom when she had seen Richard and James deep in conversation. Not wanting to be seen she had remained in the shadows, long enough she hoped to avoid an encounter.

But Richard had not immediately followed James back into the ballroom. She could see now that a meeting with him was impossible to avoid, unless she chose not to return to the ballroom at all, in which case her husband Tom would no doubt come in search of her.

Seeing her a short distance away, Richard stood his ground, as if forcing her to make a decision. This was the first time he had seen her face to face since his return a year ago. He had not sought her out and she had not sought him out. They were married, both of them, to other people. What had been between them years before had become a secret each of them harboured and never shared.

Now, face to face, Richard would not step back. He was married to a beautiful woman. He had a son. But still deep within him he could not quite discard his first love. To him it remained something that was unresolved. To him her reasons were unfathomable. Only now, seeing her, did he remember how much she had hurt him.

'Hello, Jane,' he said.

He was surprised his voice sounded normal.

She whispered a response and then moved to walk past him back into the crowded ballroom.

He could not let the moment pass. There might never be another such as this.

Without thinking, he grabbed her arm and she stopped.

'So that's all you have to say. Nothing else? No explanation. Not even 'I'm sorry, Richard'.

She was startled by his manner and by the strength of his grip on her arm. She tried to free herself.

'It's all in the past, don't you think?'

He did not immediately relax his grip on her arm.

'It may be in the past, but I'd still like to know why you married Tom Warner so soon after I left.'

She began to back away from him.

'Let go of me,' she cried out.

She could see his face now, close to hers. His anger was rising and there was bitterness too. She had not expected to ever have to answer his questions, now that they were both married. She had deliberately avoided him. He had not, until now, gone out of his way to meet her.

'I'll let you go when you tell me why?'

His voice was quieter now, as if he had begun to realise he had acted on an impulse he now regretted. Was it just his pride that was hurt? Did he still feel something for her after all this time? To him they had been, until now, unanswered questions.

'Because I fell in love with someone else.' Her voice was just a whisper but he heard her all the same.

Suddenly he let go of her and she stumbled back and almost fell.

'Just like that. You fell in love with someone else. I hope you're very happy.'

The anger had drained from him completely but there was a hardness in his tone. He was shaking slightly as if the intensity of his response to seeing her again had surprised him and he did not know how to deal with it.

'Richard, it's true,' she said. 'Or at least it was true at the time.'

It was the first hint she had given him that her decision might have been one she later regretted. Did she still regret it?

He said nothing. He hadn't expected her to make such an admission. He was unprepared for it. Their conversation was venturing on to dangerous ground and they both knew it.

They stood silently together for a few moments before she moved past him towards the door. He did not try to stop her. She dare not look at him.

After a few moments, he followed her. He could see her searching the crowded room for her husband. He likewise scanned the crowd for his wife but he could not see her.

He continued to watch until he lost sight of Jane in the crowd of dancers. What option did he have now but to pretend their brief conversation had never happened? But he found he could not. Her words echoed through his memory for days afterwards such that there were times he wished he had never to spoken to her, that she had remained a ghost from his past.

Instead she was very much alive to him. He did not know how to deal with this sudden, unexpected emotion. He did not know how it might threaten the pattern of his life. He only knew that he wished he had never spoken to her.

The days leading up to Christmas Day were a hive of activity at Prior Park. One or two of the unused rooms in the west wing of the house had been hastily cleaned out and refurbished in preparation for the extra guests. The housekeeper had put forward her niece to help out with the extra work but even so tempers were beginning to fray among the staff.

It seemed for a while that the household lacked a guiding hand. Alice, unused to managing a large household staff and still recovering from the birth of Marianne, turned all her energies towards her new role as a mother. Elizabeth Belleville, who had in recent months allowed Alice to oversee the day to day running of the household, was inclined to dismiss the housekeeper's complaints with a wave of the hand. More than once, she was heard to say 'I'm sure you'll sort everything out, Mrs Duffy'.

Catherine observed this without comment for several days until she could no longer stand the chaos that threatened to engulf them.

On the last of the occasions when Mrs Duffy left Elizabeth Belleville's sitting room having failed to gain a decision about the menus for the festive days, Catherine intercepted her.

'Mrs Duffy, can I help? What is it that you need a decision on? I think my mother-in-law is a little low in spirits just at present.'

The housekeeper looked at her, as if assessing her for the first time. She was reluctant to say outright that these decisions could only be made by Mrs Belleville senior. It had become an awkward household to negotiate with so many Mrs Bellevilles in residence she had told Charles Brockman on more than one occasion. He had lent a sympathetic ear but could offer no solution to this particular dilemma.

Catherine sensed the other woman's reluctance to go into any details but she persevered.

'Let's go down to the kitchen and sit down with a cup of tea and see what needs to be done,' Catherine suggested, her tone conciliatory.

Mrs Duffy could hardly refuse. She had drawn the line at calling Catherine Mrs Richard. Alice they had all known since childhood so to call her Mrs William was quite comfortable but Catherine was still a relative stranger in their midst and the staff eyed her warily.

To them she would always be Mrs Belleville; Mrs Belleville the younger if they needed to make a distinction, but they did not warm to her refined English manners and her upper class English accent that made their own voices sound so harsh and uncultured.

As they entered the kitchen, it was the scene of much activity but for quite another purpose. It was these extra interruptions too that irritated Mrs Duffy for the staff from the nursery made much of the importance of their frequent need to prepare bottles for their tiny but important charges. She had joined the household when Elizabeth Belleville's children were already in school so she had not encountered the demands of the nursery until now and she could not hide her irritation at the many interruptions to the kitchen routine.

To her surprise the younger Mrs Belleville breezed through the decision making with an ease that suggested she had done this many times before. Mrs Duffy did not know for certain but she had heard that Catherine Belleville had been raised in a grand English country house with many servants. Catherine herself did not know how it was that she fell naturally into the role but she had often been at her mother's side when she heard her mother giving orders to the cook or to the butler.

Alice, who was inclined to spend each afternoon sleeping, was unaware that her role as the de facto mistress of the house was being usurped by Catherine.

Catherine, for her part, was amused at the turn of events and she took the opportunity to impose her ideas on the household for the first time.

It was to be the first Christmas that French wine was served at the Belleville table. She had also insisted too on replacing some of the heavy puddings with something lighter. To this idea Mrs Duffy simply raised an eyebrow but said nothing for there was nothing she could say.

Among the last of the preparations was the installation of a large Christmas tree in the drawing room. To Catherine the powerful and unfamiliar smell of the she-oak with its spindly leaves was no match at all for the luxuriantly green Christmas trees of her memory.

'It looks very pretty.'

She turned towards the door where Richard stood surveying the tree. Baby Paul was happily ensconced in his father's arms, one small hand exploring Richard's necktie.

Catherine stood back and surveyed the tree.

'Well, it does look pretty.' She paused. 'But it's not a fir tree.'

'And there's no snow,' Richard added.

'It wouldn't last long in this heat would it?'

Outside summer was well and truly established. The days were hot, with a brightness of light that could be overwhelming.

'Do I detect some homesickness?'

Richard said it brightly but underneath he was concerned for her answer.

'Just a little,' she admitted. 'Just a little. I think it's only natural at this time of the year.'

At that point baby Paul had decided it was time his mother paid attention to him so he began to give voice to this idea. She reached out and he slid into her arms with a delighted shriek.

'I have a surprise for you,' Richard said.

He held aloft an envelope.

'Are you going to tell me what's in the envelope or do I have to guess?'

'Tickets,' he said without elaboration.

'Tickets to where?' she said, playing along.

'Tickets to England.'

He was being deliberately vague.

'When are we going?'

Her voice was already betraying her excitement at going back home.

'I'm sure your parents would be delighted to have their grandson celebrate his first birthday with them.'

He could see Catherine mentally calculating the travel time.

'So we must be leaving very soon after Christmas?'

He smiled.

'Well not quite. But in January certainly.'

She frowned at him.

'But that wouldn't give us enough time to sail half way across the world. His birthday is on the 2nd of February, you know.'

Again, Richard smiled, enjoying his gentle teasing of her.

'We're not sailing, my dear. We are flying. In a Constellation. It will still take us more than a week, but imagine the thrill of it.'

She was speechless for a few moments.

'Flying. You can't be serious. Flying all that way. Are you sure it's safe?'

He ignored this question.

'You'll love it,' he declared. 'We leave on the 15th of January.'

Catherine pulled a face, not certain that she agreed with him.

'How did you get the tickets? I didn't know the service was fully operational?'

Richard smiled.

'John Bertram got them for me. He knows the pilots. It's a test flight, but they're happy to take paying passengers to offset the cost.'

'Good old John,' Catherine said, with some uncertainty in her voice.

'It will be fine,' Richard said. 'It will just make it so much quicker.'

Catherine could do nothing but agree. Her fear of the prospect of flying all that way was quickly replaced by the knowledge she would see her family again very soon.

For Richard it was a desperately needed distraction from the memory of his conversation with Jane Warner. Above everything, he knew he wanted his marriage to work. He did not want it tested by old loyalties.

For Catherine, all thoughts of Christmas were now forgotten. Her mood brightened. In a month's time she would take her baby son to meet his grandparents.

Suddenly, Prior Park didn't seem like home anymore. She was going home to a place she felt she belonged. She began to hum a bright tune as her thoughts turned to the preparations needed to leave the hot summer of Queensland for the cold English winter.

CHAPTER 21: DECEMBER 1946

A QUIETNESS HAD settled over Prior Park and its inhabitants following a lengthy Christmas lunch that had threatened to drag on into the mid afternoon until Elizabeth Belleville stood up abruptly from the table and announced she was going to take a nap.

With the hostess's sudden departure, the rest of the party took their cue and left the table so it was a quiet scene that greeted Julia as she stood at the doorway to the living room a short time later. It seemed to her that the heat of the summer day had added another layer of drowsiness to the already drowsy inhabitants of Prior Park. No one appeared to move.

She noticed Alice sitting quietly cooing to baby Marianne who lay nestled in her arms. Alice's mother was never far from her side, ready at any opportunity to relieve Alice of her tiny burden. Alice's father Jack had been fussed over all day as if he was one of the babies and had been urged to rest, rather than empty the rum decanter so conveniently placed alongside him.

She almost turned to leave in search of more stimulating company when she saw Catherine motioning to the empty seat alongside her.

'You must be excited going back home to England?' she said to Catherine in a low voice so as not to disturb the dozing guests.

'Very much. Very much indeed.' Catherine smiled at the prospect.

She and Julia had not spoken together very often and when

they did, it had been about day to day events. For Catherine's part, she had found Julia withdrawn and at times petulant. For Julia's part, she had seen in Catherine the more polished and elegant version of what she might have become had the war, and other things, not intervened. Therein lay the gulf between them that could not easily be bridged.

For the first time, Julia pressed her sister-in-law for details of her English family and her life before she met Richard. Julia's approach lacked subtlety but Catherine could see that the girl was genuine in her enquiry.

'You've never told us much about your family or your home in England,' she said, as if she was almost accusing Catherine of hiding family secrets from them.

Catherine smiled and wanted to say 'you've never asked' but decided instead to answer Julia's question.

'Well, my family have been at Haldon Hall for several generations now. It isn't a vast house, by English country house standards, but it is beautiful. My father inherited it when he was only twenty-five so I spent all my life there, apart from going away to school. I never thought to bring any photos with me when I came out here but I will take some when we are over there.'

'So what would Christmas Day be like back in England at your home?'

For a moment, Catherine felt an immense wistfulness, thinking, not for the first time, what she was missing and what she might never again experience.

'On Christmas morning we always attended church. The whole family would walk in slow procession along the village streets between our house and the parish church. Our family has attended the church for generations so it is an accepted ritual from which no one is excused, except my mother who is usually driven to the church.'

Too far from any convenient church, it was hard for Julia to imagine this ritual taking place at Prior Park.

'Wouldn't it have been very cold to walk?'

Catherine smiled at the memory.

'Yes, it is always cold. And often there is snow. I remember I would bury my hands deep in my fur muff. But we were always frozen by the time we got to the church, even though it only took about fifteen minutes to get there.'

'You said 'family' but I thought you were an only child?'

Catherine nodded.

'Yes, I am an only child, but my father's sister and her family always come for Christmas, plus one of his aunts so it wasn't just the three of us.'

Julia looked carefully at Catherine trying to judge her mood. She noticed, for the first time, a fleeting look of resignation, as if the enormity of the change that marriage had brought was not altogether to her liking.

'Do you find life here intolerably dull after your life in England?'

It was a blunt question that startled Catherine and she did not know quite how to respond. She was cautious for fear her answer would be repeated to Richard. She did not think Julia would do it to spite her but an unguarded comment could be just as devastating.

'Perhaps,' she said guardedly, 'but I haven't had much time to think about it really, with Paul's birth and our trip south. I'm hoping we can get away more often though with Richard managing the other businesses.'

Julia pondered this for a few moments.

'Have you talked to Richard about it? Getting away more often I mean. He seems very settled here even though he lets William run the place.'

Catherine paused briefly before replying.

'I haven't talked to him about it. I was waiting for the right moment, and now of course we're going to England, I don't really want to raise it. I loved Sydney when I was there. It's a pity it's so far away. My cousin John Bertram took me to see all the sights while Richard was in Goulburn. Maybe I could buy a house in Sydney.'

As soon as she said it, she regretted sharing her secret plans which had begun to take shape in her mind since their return from the south.

'Wouldn't that be expensive?' Julia asked, dismissing all the other more obvious obstacles that might be presented to the plan.

'I haven't told Richard yet but I came into some money when I turned twenty-five. My maternal grandfather had set up a trust fund for me but I couldn't access the money until recently.'

Julia smiled at this.

'Lucky you. Fancy having your own money. How wonderful,' she said, with just a hint of envy in her voice.

'But you will too, one day,' Catherine replied unthinkingly.

'Me? I don't think so. Richard and William shared father's estate. I expect they will make some settlement when I marry,' she said, accepting without question that her brothers were the lucky ones and that she had been left out because she was a daughter.

'But your mother's trust fund? That comes to you, surely, when she dies?'

As soon as she had spoken, Catherine wished she hadn't. Even as she said the words, it began to dawn on her that no one had told Julia about the Dalrymple legacy she was bound to inherit.

'What trust fund? No one talks to me about money or business. They ignore me. Generally Mother gives me some money when I ask for it or she pays the bills.'

Catherine could see that Julia's surprise was genuine. Even so it was not her place to explain further.

'I suggest you ask your mother about it, Julia. You're not a child anymore. You've got to stop letting them treat you as a child.'

'You're right, Catherine. It's time I made my own decisions. In fact I should have made my own decisions much much sooner.'

Catherine looked directly at her young sister-in-law, trying to gauge the impact of her well-meant but casually given advice. Above all else, she did not want to be the cause of a family row. She was an outsider and she knew full well that she must tread carefully.

'Well, don't do anything rash,' Catherine cautioned but Julia was already up and heading out of the room in search of her mother.

William, entering the room just as Julia walked out, said nothing but he could not fail to notice the determined look on his sister's face and he worried immediately just what that might mean.

Elizabeth Belleville was just beginning to stir from her after lunch nap as her daughter burst into her bedroom. The girl hardly seemed to notice her mother's drowsiness, instead launching headlong into a flurry of accusations.

It took Elizabeth Belleville only a moment or two to grasp the essential points of her daughter's emotional outburst. It was as if every bottled up emotion was spilling out of the girl who until now had been largely compliant with her family's wishes.

As Julia paused for breath, her mother seized the slim chance to gain control of the situation.

'What's all this about, Julia? What are you saying? What do you want to know?'

It was her mother's calm and authoritative voice that eventually quietened the tirade.

Elizabeth Belleville had, by this time, risen from her bed and walked to the door, closing it firmly so that the conversation would not be overheard.

With the same air of calm deliberation she led her daughter towards a chair. The girl did not resist.

'Now, what has Catherine been saying to you?'

It was a simple question to which she waited silently for the answer.

Julia, more coherent now, relayed the gist of the conversation about the trust fund.

Faced now with the full details, Elizabeth Belleville took a deep breath before replying.

'Yes, that is true. You will inherit the Dalrymple trust fund from me when I pass. I hadn't told you before this because I felt I would keep this information until such time as you were about to marry. Only Richard and William know.'

She paused slightly, trying to judge the effect of the revelation on Julia before she went on.

'Obviously Richard told Catherine. Perhaps she asked why you didn't inherit anything from your father. I don't know but I suspect that might be the case. I should have told you when your father died but with Richard away and William handling everything, it just never occurred to me.'

Julia remained silent as if the information was too much for her to take in.

'Julia, I didn't try and hide anything from you. I just didn't want to make it public knowledge because we would then have had every fortune hunter claiming their undying love for you. It was for your protection really.'

The final part of the explanation sounded false even to Elizabeth Belleville and she knew she had gone too far, in a desperate attempt to avoid the next inevitable question. It was the question she feared most. It was the question she had foreseen all along. It was, she knew deep down, the real reason she had failed to tell her daughter about her future inheritance.

'So this trust fund is passed down the female line; that's what Catherine told me and that's what you're telling me?'

She looked towards her mother now for confirmation.

Elizabeth Belleville nodded. She replied, choosing her words carefully.

'That's right. The inheritance goes down the female line.'

She did not say 'it goes to your daughter or daughters' but Julia was already filling in the blank spaces that her mother would not.

'So you are telling me that my daughter, the child I gave birth to and gave away, is actually heir to the trust fund after me?'

There was now a hint of rising hysteria in her voice. She was trembling. Tears were starting to slide unchecked down her face. Elizabeth Belleville, for her part, had almost reached the limits of her patience.

'Well, she won't inherit it will she? She isn't legitimate. She isn't part of this family.'

She was relieved that Julia did not notice the deliberate choice of words for she had been careful not to say that Julia's illegitimate daughter couldn't inherit it only that she wouldn't.

Above all else, Elizabeth Belleville did not want to revisit the events of March 1944. She did not want this discussion to go any further for she knew it could only end in a series of recriminations, for there was no way now to offer any different outcome.

She waited for her daughter to respond but Julia said nothing. Instead, she continued to sit with her face buried in her hands, her blonde hair spilling over her fingers unchecked.

In a steady voice, she tried to soothe the girl.

'Julia, you must put that event behind you. You must think no more about it. You must get on with your life. I think James Fitzroy is on the point of proposing to you; you would do well to accept him.'

Julia was calmer now, her emotions spent. She shrugged.

'So that's it. You think the best thing is for me to be married off? You want to get rid of me as if I'm some problem that you have to solve.'

'We do not see you as a problem to be solved but I do think marriage would be good for you, Julia, we all do. Your brothers and I, that is. And hopefully you will soon have another baby on the way. This time, a legitimate baby.'

She looked up, surprised that her mother would be so heartless.

'If I get married, will you stop treating me like a child? Catherine says you all treat me like a child.'

If Elizabeth Belleville was annoyed at Catherine's suggestion, she did not show it.

'We don't treat you like a child, but a married woman has much more, shall we say, status. You will run your own home and be mistress of that home.'

Julia was much calmer now, as if the emotional outburst of the past few minutes had somehow made everything much clearer to her.

'So you want me to marry James Fitzroy?' she asked finally.

'Are you considering it? He's a good catch.'

'He hasn't asked me yet.'

'He will. He's spoken to Richard already.'

'About me?'

'Yes, about you. I think he assumed it was right to speak to Richard first because your father has passed on.'

She thought for a moment.

'Well, it seems settled then. I'm to be married off to James Fitzroy.'

Before her mother could reply, she went on.

'But I want you to know, for sure, as I go up the aisle on Richard's arm to marry James Fitzroy that there will only ever be one man for me. I will never speak of it again but I will love Philippe until the day I die.'

Elizabeth Belleville tried to silence her daughter but she was determined to say, in the privacy of her mother's bedroom, what she felt she would never again have the chance to say.

She had become agitated again, pacing the room and resisting her mother's efforts to silence her.

'I still love Philippe. I still love him. He would have married me if he had known I was pregnant. He must have been killed in the war. That's the only reason why he didn't ever write to me. I know that for sure.'

She was done now. All emotion spent. But she had forced her mother to share the knowledge that she would never love James

Fitzroy the way she had loved Philippe.

She did not notice how her mother turned away to avoid her gaze. What she took to be callousness was her mother's desperate attempt to avoid looking directly at her daughter.

For a few moments, Elizabeth Belleville searched noisily among her lipsticks for the right colour. She needed something, anything, to occupy her for a few moments while she regained her composure.

She knew she had to say something. She knew she had to go on with the lie. It was too late now, far too late to do anything else.

How could she now tell her daughter how they had conspired to prevent Philippe's letters reaching her? How could she ever tell her that her own brother had met Philippe as little as a month ago?

Fully composed now, Elizabeth Belleville's voice betrayed nothing of her inner turmoil.

'We'll probably never know, Julia, what happened to him. That's what war is like. People lose the ones they love.'

Julia never suspected for one moment that her mother was lying. There was no sign of emotion in her voice, nothing to betray the lie.

'So what about James? I know what you said but do you think you could make a go of marriage with him?'

Elizabeth Belleville waited patiently for her daughter to answer. She did not say 'do you love him?' for Julia had already made her feelings plain.

Julia shrugged her shoulders in a non-committal way, as if resigned to the inevitable.

'I guess so. I admit he's very attractive. I've seen quite a bit of him lately. He's been the perfect gentleman though.'

'I'm pleased to hear it.'

Elizabeth wanted to say that one unplanned pregnancy was enough but decided against it. She was instead pleased to see signs of recovery in her daughter and wanted to say as much, but there was still one piece of advice she could not resist.

'You must never tell him about having borne a child out of wedlock. I don't think he is the kind of man to understand.'

Julia stopped, more horrified by the prospect than her mother.

'Don't worry, Mother, I'm not that stupid. He will never know as far as I am concerned. I certainly won't tell him.'

Elizabeth nodded, satisfied with her response. She was now anxious to bring their tense conversation to a close.

'I'm pleased we've had this chat, Julia. Now go and wash your face and comb your hair before we join everyone for tea.'

She gave her daughter a quick hug. It was a small sign of affection that Elizabeth Belleville rarely bestowed on anyone except her grandson.

Alone in her room, she continued to sit at her dressing table for a few minutes, the conversation with her daughter constantly replaying in her mind. She felt no remorse at the lie she had been forced to repeat. From the very first time she had intercepted his letters to Julia, she had vowed to prevent Philippe Duval from ever seeing or contacting her daughter again. There was nothing that would ever change her mind. There was nothing that would ever make her admit she was wrong.

She closed her eyes and whispered a silent prayer of thanks that all their secrets were safely held. She could not know then that secrets are never safe. They may lay hidden from view and not spoken about but they are never safe. She did not know that there was a time, in the future, when the family's secrets would be exposed and her lies and her deception would be remembered. Above all else, it was her actions that would lie at the heart of it all. Actions for which she would never be forgiven.

On the other side of the world, the man Julia presumed to be dead was very much alive. Like many New Yorkers he was drawn to the Christmas sights of the city that had quickly shrugged off the shadows of war.

Crowds were six and seven deep in front of Macy's window

display on Christmas Eve as Philippe Duval struggled to make his way along the sidewalk. Like everyone on the street, he was rugged up against the biting cold of the wintery day. Still there was a cheerful mood amongst the crowd who jostled to get a better view of the extravagantly decorated shop windows.

For Philippe, Christmas was anything but a time of cheer. He had been back at the hospital only a short time after his trip to Australia so it had been easy enough for him to bury himself in his work. It was the hours he spent alone that troubled him.

As he walked along 34th Street among the last minute Christmas shoppers, he could not help himself. He could think of nothing but his little daughter, now approaching her third Christmas. What would he be buying her, he pondered. A doll probably? Certainly the prettiest doll in the store. A party dress perhaps? He did not know for sure but he hoped that her Christmas would not lack for gifts. His heart ached for the loss of her, and for the loss of her mother.

The crowd in front of Macy's window parted momentarily. It allowed him a good view of the window display and the colourful array of toys on offer. For just a few seconds, he was tempted to walk into the store and buy a present for Pippa. But the urge passed almost as quickly as it came. What would he do with it? Would he send it to the family? How could he possibly do that? Would he year after year buy presents that were never sent? To his rational mind, the idea sounded bizarre.

He turned away knowing then that he would never buy his daughter a Christmas gift or a birthday gift. The sudden knowledge, that he had known all along, came to him with a clarity he had not known before. It was then, at that very moment, he made a silent pact to get on with the rest of his life. He could not, he knew then, continue to mourn the past or mourn for a life he never had. All chance of that was now gone. He had done what he could and now he must move on. It was a silent pledge he made there and then that no one would ever know he had fathered a child in Australia. The war and all that it had done to him was now locked away, never to be discussed.

He hunched his shoulders against the biting cold and headed along the street. As he moved away from Macy's building, the crowd thinned so he walked faster, grateful for the physical effort it demanded of him. By the time he reached his apartment, he was almost running, as if a sudden urgency had come upon him.

But there was no urgency. Just a need to be alone, to sit quietly for a last few moments of reflection on what might have been.

As he sat in the growing darkness, he could see clearly now what was in the past must stay in the past. He was certain the past would never intersect with the future. To him they were separate and there was now no point at which they would ever meet. He saw the future as fresh and unsullied.

Only he would know about his past and he would never share it. He would keep the secrets of his past until the grave.

But he could not know then there would be a day when his secrets would be exposed and his life shattered afresh. He would wonder then if he had chosen the right path but by then it was too late; too late for all of them.

Chapter 22: January 1947

ELIZABETH BELLEVILLE WAS completely unconcerned by any talk that surrounded the hasty announcement of her daughter's engagement immediately after Christmas and the equally hasty decision on the wedding date in the coming winter.

Having discovered that Julia had no strong feelings against marrying James Fitzroy, her mother had taken every opportunity to throw the young couple together, such that even James had noticed the deliberate ploy. But for once he did not mind.

As the old year ended and the new one began, Julia faced the year knowing that it would bring big changes in her life.

Occasionally she glanced surreptitiously at the sparkling diamonds on her left ring finger. The ring felt strange and foreign and cold to the touch.

She had nevertheless admired it from many angles. She could not help but ponder what Philippe would have chosen for her. Something simpler, she thought. Something less ostentatious but for all her misgivings she was swept up by the moment and the attention.

'It's a beautiful ring,' Alice said. 'I didn't know my brother had such good taste.'

There was no hint of envy in Alice's voice. She considered the blue sapphire and diamond ring she proudly wore to be incomparable.

'Yes, it is beautiful, but it takes some time to get used to wearing it,' Julia replied.

'I know James is delighted you accepted his proposal. I've never seen him look so happy.'

At this point in the conversation, Alice replayed in her mind the warnings from William not to mention the war, the American or anything else that would upset Julia so she stood beside her sister-in-law silently, not quite knowing what to say next for fear that she would say the wrong thing and the happy moment would be spoiled.

For the first time, Julia sensed Alice's reticence and was quick to reassure her.

'I've put everything behind me, you know, Alice.'

She was deliberately vague, testing now to see just how much Alice knew, despite her mother's reassurance that only she and William in the household knew her deepest secret.

'I'm pleased about that. So many girls had wartime romances that ended badly,' Alice said, adding without any artifice, 'A lot of girls I heard about ended up in trouble and no chance of marriage.'

The slight rise in colour in Julia's cheeks went unnoticed. She spoke quickly moving the conversation on to safer ground.

'You will be my matron of honour won't you, Alice?'

Alice's smile was one of relief and sincere pleasure.

'Of course I will. I'd love to be your matron of honour. Unfortunately Marianne is too small yet to be a flower girl.'

They laughed together at the prospect for she was indeed far too small and would hopefully sleep peacefully through the entire proceedings.

While the two young women chatted together, Elizabeth Belleville was already busy writing invitations to a hastily arranged engagement party. It had taken only one reminder from her daughter to avoid the usual venue. She did not know the details of her daughter's intimacy with the American doctor but she did know that the Criterion Hotel had been the base for American Army officers. Nothing would be left to chance, as far as Elizabeth

Belleville was concerned so another venue was chosen. She did not have to give a reason. If asked, she would have said it was simply a desire to do something different for Julia, but in the event she wasn't asked.

Richard and Catherine's imminent departure for England provided the perfect excuse for the party to be held quickly, and so it was.

For Elizabeth Belleville, only one hurdle remained and she could see no obstacle now to achieving her ambition of having Julia safely and suitably married. The next few months would be a hive of activity of wedding plans for which no effort would be spared.

Richard Belleville had been slightly too bold in his prediction that they would reach England in plenty of time for Paul's first birthday. As it transpired, it was with only two days to spare that they knocked on the big oak door of Haldon Hall as flurries of light snow swirled around them, causing baby Paul to shriek delightedly. Myners, older now and slightly bent, was slow to open the door so it was some minutes before they could retreat from the cold outside.

Richard was struck immediately by the stark contrast between their welcome now and their departure fifteen months previously. No one, least of all him, was going to revisit the harsh words of that visit. Instead baby Paul was being wrapped in the embrace of a doting grandmother while Sir Anthony looked on, slightly bemused by the whole scene.

'You made it at last. I was so worried by your telegram from Singapore that the whole trip would have to be cancelled,' Lady Marina said.

Richard could sense that she was about to add that she didn't think flying was a suitable method of travel for her daughter or her grandson so he cut in quickly.

'I knew there might be delays in the trip,' he admitted. 'It was a test flight after all and we were lucky to get on it. The regular service won't begin until later this year. It will only take four days, they reckon, with a total of six stops. Flying is definitely the way of the future.'

She smiled at him indulgently. In the end, it did not matter to her how they had travelled only that they were here and she was seeing her daughter again and her grandson for the first time.

Later, alone in their room, it was Catherine who was first to comment on the change in her mother.

'I can't believe it. I can't believe my own eyes. My mother, who never showed much affection towards me or my father, is so warm and loving towards Paul. It's as if she was completely besotted by him the moment she set eyes on him.'

Richard was sitting on the bed, rubbing his still cold hands together in a futile attempt to warm them.

'Yes, it's a lot warmer reception than we got last time as I recall.'

Catherine smiled at this, acknowledging the truth of what he said.

'Well, that's all clearly in the past and best forgotten, it seems.'

'So it seems. I see your mother thought of everything, even hiring a nursemaid for Paul. That's very helpful.'

'Yes, I expected her to do that,' Catherine said. 'I did tell her we were travelling alone, so she took the hint.'

'Good planning I must say. Did she say what she has in mind for his birthday?'

Catherine, whose full attention was now directed on what she should wear for her first dinner back at her old home, said nothing.

'I hope she doesn't go over the top. He's only one and he won't remember a thing about it.'

But Catherine's look said it all. She suspected that Master Paul Belleville was about to be given a first birthday party that, even if he would never remember it, everyone else would.

After the initial pleasure of seeing his wife so animated and happy back in her home country with her family, the bleak English weather and the lack of occupation began to turn Richard's mood from his normally easy going and charming self to a more moody and difficult man. It became clear too to Catherine and to her parents that there was something troubling him but they did not pry. Instead they accommodated his occasional moodiness and said nothing. Above all else, Catherine did not want to bring their visit to a premature close. Suddenly and clearly she was beginning to understand the extent of her social isolation in what she thought of as the wilds of Australia. Richard was seeing it too but what he also saw was a growing gulf between them.

On this particular morning, he was standing at the library window, looking out at the drifts of snow and then to the sky which promised only more of the same. After his cursory observations of the heavy snow that enveloped the countryside, he walked restlessly around the room, admiring the leather bound volumes on the shelves and the untidy stack of newly arrived editions from Hatchards. As soon as he picked up a book, he almost at once discarded it, unable to sustain his interest in any topic.

He turned as Catherine entered the room.

'A penny for your thoughts,' she said flippantly.

'I wish Paul had been born in the English summer,' he answered, nodding towards to landscape that now made travel beyond the house almost impossible.

She slid her arm through his in a gesture of affection to which he hardly responded.

'You won't believe me when I tell you that it isn't normally like this. We've just chosen a very bad winter to decide to come home.'

Even as the words were out of her mouth, she regretted her choice of them. It would have been far better to say 'to decide to visit my parents' but she hadn't and she hoped that he would let it go as a slip of the tongue. But he did not.

'Yes, it is home for you, isn't it?'

He did not say it with any rancour. There was too much honesty in his words for her to deny his statement.

'Yes, it will take me a while to adjust to Australia as home. I'll admit that much.'

She smiled as she said it but behind the smile there was a small seed of doubt. Doubt that she would adjust to the country life with its limitations of society and its sometimes monotonous seasonal rituals.

'Would having your own home help you settle do you think?'

It seemed as if the lack of occupation had given Richard time to think about their situation.

Catherine moved away from him, not knowing exactly where the conversation would lead and trying to judge his mood before replying.

'Perhaps. Yes, in fact, I believe it would,' she said eventually, deciding there and then to pursue a conversation that had started months earlier.

Richard merely nodded as if knowing the answer and that asking the question had simply been his way of confirming what he already knew.

Once again, the discussion was curtailed, this time by Myners shuffling in through the door, the small silver salver he held trembling noticeably.

'A telegram for you, Mr Belleville. I hope it's not bad news.'

Richard ripped open the envelope. Considering the state of the weather, he knew someone had gone to a great deal of trouble to deliver the message.

Catherine held her breath, fearing the worst.

'It's OK. No one's dead,' he said bluntly.

'It's from William. There's concern at the woollen mill in Goulburn that our main supplier Harry Jensen might sell his wool to Japan. The Prime Minister has announced plans for Australia to supply 120,000 bales of wool to Japan this year.'

'So why send you a telegram? What does he want you to do?'
It was an obvious question.

'I think he wants me to cut my visit short and come home to deal with it. I went out to Harry Jensen's property when I went to Goulburn last year. We got on very well. I think William thinks I'll be more influential than the mill manager.'

'What do you think? Should you go home and deal with this? Or is William over-stating the case?'

Richard shrugged, torn now between his desire to please Catherine and stay the allotted two months in England and his restlessness, which had been exacerbated by the bad weather which had kept them indoors.

Before he could give Catherine a definite answer, for he was still mulling over the necessity of an early return, the door to the library opened, this time to admit an unexpected and entirely welcome visitor.

'G'day, mate,' was John Bertram's exaggeratedly accented greeting to his friend.

Catherine was the first to hug the newcomer in an enthusiastic embrace. Richard clasped his hand in a firm handshake and all thoughts of an early return to Australia were immediately sidelined as the three of them sat together talking excitedly over each other, such was the powerful effect of his presence on the two people he had often declared himself to be most fond of, if you excluded his mother.

'I'm sorry I'm too late for the famous one-year-old's celebrations,' he said. 'Where is he, by the way?'

'Afternoon nap, but he'll be awake soon and the nurse will bring him down,' Catherine said.

John noted how easily Catherine had reverted to the nursery routines of an upper class English household to which she had been born and bred but he did not voice these thoughts.

She chided John for not mentioning his plans to visit England.

'Well, it was a bit of a last minute thing. I haven't been able to settle since we demobbed—and my cousin is far better at managing the family's country properties than I'll ever be. I decided to try my luck with the new industry that's starting up—aviation.'

Suddenly, he was animated and enthusiastic, regaling them with talk of the first American commercial Pacific flight from San Francisco to Sydney by Pan-American World Airways.

'In fact the flight should have landed in Sydney by now,' he said. 'How was your flight coming over here?'

At the mention of it, Catherine pulled a face.

'It was very trying with a small child,' she said. 'It was noisy, and smelly, and rough at times. And we didn't think we'd get past Singapore.'

'Engine trouble, I suppose?' John asked, looking at Richard.

'Yes, engine trouble, but they managed to fix it eventually. I did warn everyone that it was a test flight so it wasn't surprising really that we had some trouble on the way, but it certainly beats being cooped up on a ship for six weeks.'

'So how are you going home?'

There was a silence that followed the question and John immediately perceived that this was a matter of disagreement between them.

'Since the news of the French Dakota crash with fifteen people dead, there hasn't been much enthusiasm in this house for flying,' Catherine said pointedly.

It was at this pivotal point in the discussion that Lady Marina Cavendish swept into the room. She greeted her nephew with unaccustomed warmth and immediately picked up the thread of the conversation.

'If it is considered safer for the Royal Family, who have just embarked on a trip to South Africa, to travel by ship, then my grandson and daughter must travel by ship. It's far safer. Much, much more comfortable in a first class cabin.'

Richard and John exchanged glances. It was an almost but not quite inaudible aside from John that threatened to set off an unseemly fit of laughter in both Richard and Catherine.

'Hasn't she heard of the Titanic then?'

'What was that, John? I didn't hear what you said.'

'Nothing of consequence, my dear aunt, nothing at all. I'm sure there will be a suitable vessel departing Southampton docks in the near future to take Catherine and Richard home to Australia.'

She seemed vaguely satisfied with his answer.

'So what are you going to be doing with yourself, John. I didn't expect to see you back in England quite so soon. I thought you would have had enough of the place during the war. How did you get to England so quickly anyway?' she asked, casting a critical eye over her latest visitor.

'Well, I got on a test flight up to Singapore and then a flight across to Bombay. And then the next leg and so on. As you know, I was a navigator during the war so I was able to work my passage so to speak. And with the new airlines starting up, I thought I'd come across and see what was happening here. I might be able to get a job flying the London to Sydney route because they'll be looking for crew. One of the blokes I know from the squadron is already involved in a syndicate.'

Lady Marina shook her head.

'It will be a flash in the pan, John. No one will fly that distance regularly. It's far too dangerous. It's a shame you weren't in the navy.'

John stood his ground, diplomatically.

'My dear aunt, one day the skies will resound to the throb of aeroplane engines, one after the other, landing in England from all corners of the globe and taking off to all corners of the globe. It is the future,' he said, determinedly, but she remained unconvinced.

'Well, I certainly won't be flying off to all corners of the globe, you can depend on that,' she said, sipping delicately at the gin and tonic the butler had placed alongside her.

Both Richard and John were relieved at not being required to sip indifferent sherry. Instead they gratefully received their glasses of whisky and soda and were soon motioning quietly to Myners for a refill.

John turned to Richard, lowering his voice.

'When I came in I heard the tail end of your conversation with Catherine about needing to go home early. Am I right?'

'William sent me a telegram about a business matter that really needs my intervention. I'm in two minds. It's hard being stuck here in this weather. I'm surprised you got through.'

'Yes, it's pretty bad out there. I managed to find a way via train and bus, but I wouldn't recommend it just at present unless you really had to venture out. It's bloody cold and you could get stuck. Not the weather for sightseeing.'

'That's part of the problem,' Richard said. 'There's nothing to do in this weather.'

Just then the door opened and a determined Paul Belleville made his first faltering steps, watched over by his nurse. He shrieked happily at the sight of his mother but was then suddenly overawed by the new experience of walking. Within seconds of his first steps, he was scooped up in his mother's arms and introduced to John Bertram.

'You know, I'll be going home in a couple of weeks' time on another test flight. I'm sure they could find a seat for you, if you really need to get home early,' John said.

Richard looked doubtful.

'I'm not sure Catherine will agree with the plan.'

'She'll be fine, old man. You need to give her a bit of time here. Heaven's knows when she'll see her parents again.'

Richard smiled at his friend.

'I know. I'm just worried the longer she stays the more accustomed she'll become to her old life again and not settle down when she gets back to Australia.'

John nodded thoughtfully.

'Yes, there is that. I agree. Have you ever thought of getting a place in Sydney? She liked Sydney when I took her around to see the sights.'

'We haven't spoken about that possibility but we did talk about having our own house. I know she doesn't feel entirely comfortable at Prior Park. She feels that she's an outsider,' Richard said.

There was no chance for further discussion as Sir Anthony entered the room. He gave his grandson a quick pat on the head before greeting John and then Richard with a pessimistic summary of the fourth cricket test in Adelaide, forgetting for a moment that both men were Australians and delighted at the Australian team's dominance of the old enemy.

*

Back at Prior Park, William had quickly assumed his father's habit of spending time each day in the study that was now largely his domain. He found it peaceful and he was grateful for the separation it gave him from the minor irritations of the domestic life that went on daily around him. He did not however adopt his father's other habit of drinking whisky at all times of the day and night. He had little taste for it. He was a man of temperate habits. He liked an occasional beer when it was hot and could be tempted by a good port after dinner, but that was all. With Richard away, he enjoyed not having to share the space nor having to talk about the business matters that frequently came from the solicitors with his brother. Richard, he had learned, was much less interested in details anyway such that, in the end, it was only on major questions of investment that he consulted his brother.

So it was that it was only William who knew the terms Muriel McGovern had set down in accepting their modest offer of assistance. William reread the letter from Nathaniel Dodds indicating that Mrs McGovern had accepted the offer with the provision that her son could choose to meet the family if he wanted to when he turned eighteen. William smoothed the letter out carefully and then placed it in a folder, along with the earlier letter. This he locked in the bottom drawer of the desk.

Five years is a long time, he thought, a lot can happen in five years. Besides the boy might not want to meet us. He dismissed the matter from his mind, satisfied that his mother had been spared a painful and unnecessary revelation about her husband. She must never know, he muttered to himself. Above all, she must never know about this betrayal.

It was beyond William's imagination that he could betray Alice in such a way. He did not understand at all how his father had maintained the charade of the husband and father they knew while having a separate life that none of them knew anything about and yet he had done it for years.

William sighed and got up from his desk. He simply did not understand it and he never would. But he now understood, finally, how his father, through his self indulgence, had betrayed them all.

There seemed no reason at all to William that this sordid secret should become public knowledge. When the time came, if the boy did want a meeting, he would refuse. There was no way, no way at all, as far as William was concerned, that a bastard son of his father would share the standing of himself or his brother. That, as far as William was concerned, would never happen and he would see to it that it never did.

In the hallway, he paused to look at the family photographs on the wall. There were wedding photographs, to which his own had been added. He regretted that there was no photograph of Richard's wedding. Instead there was a photograph from Paul's christening.

He stared for a long time at the photograph of his parents, trying to understand the character of the man whom he thought he had known, only to discover, too late, it was all just a mirage. There had been no substance to the man, he now understood all too well. He was, just for moment, tempted to smash the frame, but the moment passed and he walked on in search of Alice and Marianne, who made him feel safe and contented.

CHAPTER 23: JUNE 1947

AS JULIA'S WEDDING DAY approached, Elizabeth Belleville began to reflect on everything that had happened since her daughter's eighteenth birthday, five years earlier. She could not help but wonder if her daughter had simply yielded to her pressure and agreed to marry James Fitzroy, not out of love but out of a sense of resignation that her dreams of marrying Philippe Duval were never to be realised. Was that the foundation for a happy marriage, Elizabeth wondered? What was the foundation for a happy marriage? She did not know herself so she could hardly offer her daughter any meaningful advice. She was honest enough to acknowledge this, but only to herself.

It was in this frame of mind that Elizabeth took up her pen to write a long delayed letter to her cousin, Jean Dalrymple.

My dear Jean

You have been much on my mind of late. It's more than three years since we trespassed so heavily on your hospitality and so much has happened since then, but I'm pleased to say that Julia's little secret remains just that—a secret.

I know you'll forgive me for not inviting you to her wedding this week. Yes, that's right, she is getting married to James Fitzroy, a match I once thought was only passable but now I think is ideal. His father is unable to manage the property so it is all now with James. Of course his sister Alice is William's wife.

The Fitzroys provided a settlement for Alice when she married which I expected but was more generous than we thought it would be. She is proving to be a fine wife for William. She understands him well and their daughter—little Marianne—is very sweet.

Richard and William have divided the responsibilities of managing the Belleville interests between them, having arrived at this arrangement without too much rancour. William manages the rural property while Richard looks after the other interests. He seems particularly interested in the investments Francis made in woollen mills, one of the few decisions that seems to have gone Francis's way, God rest his soul. I do miss him. He would have enjoyed having a grandson around—a granddaughter too, no doubt.

Paul is sixteen months old now. He spent his first birthday in England with Catherine's parents. Can you believe that Richard and Catherine flew to England, only taking a week? Richard's friend got them tickets on a test flight. It sounded very dangerous to me. Then Richard came home early to attend to business. Catherine arrived home three months later, by ship I might add—her parents insisted—so we really noticed the change in little Paul. He was walking quite well by the time he got home.

Julia will be moving to Mayfield Downs when she gets married. There is already work under way on the house to redecorate it. James is certainly letting her have her own way in that department. His mother Amelia Fitzroy must feel very triumphant with her offspring married off so well. Julia says she isn't at all worried seeing her former home gutted by workmen, with new curtains and furniture and all the rooms being painted. The older Fitzroys of course have a house in town that overlooks the river so she is very comfortable and contented and happy for Julia to do whatever she wants with the house. It's not as grand as Prior Park, but then it is less to worry about, I say.

You'll know why I didn't invite you to the wedding and I know you will understand entirely. I could not risk Julia being reminded of her time in Melbourne. It was a risk I just wasn't prepared to take, and besides it is such a long journey, I thought you would be relieved not to have to make it. I do, though, promise to visit you after the wedding. I shall be pleased to get away. Richard says I should fly between Brisbane and Melbourne. I said I would think about it. It seems such an unnatural method of transport, as if we were birds, but of course, he, being a pilot, sees it very differently. He says it is the way of the future.

I think the war, though, has really affected Richard. There are times when he seems very edgy. I wonder if there is something else troubling him. He says not, but since Catherine returned, there has been a tension in the household. I cannot say what it is because I do not know, but I did say to him it was only natural that Catherine would feel a little unsettled after returning from England. Who knows? She may never see her parents again. I think they are somewhat older you know, already in their sixties. That is the impression I got. I said to her recently we cannot tell what is in the future. I, most of all, feel that with Francis gone so suddenly. She merely nodded so I am not sure if that is at the heart of her apparent anxiety.

Actually Richard startled me the other day by mentioning a little girl he came across in Goulburn, the small daughter of a wool grower. Apparently he was visiting this fellow—the name was Harry Jensen I think—to talk him out of switching the sale of his annual woolclip to export away from the woollen mill. Anyway Richard said the little girl was the spitting image of Julia. I didn't know what to say for Richard does not know about the baby. Would a well-to-do couple like that be adopting a baby? It hardly seems likely. I let the comment go. I can't even warn him against saying it to Julia. I can't warn William to tell him not to say it either. I must just hope and pray he forgets about it. A careless word could do so much damage at this critical time.

You'll think me heartless. I know you and I disagreed about what should have been done about Julia but I could not risk her future. Do you think James Fitzroy would have looked at her if he had known? I don't think so.

I must close now. I am due for a final fitting for my dress. My hat should arrive today. Julia's dress has already arrived. It has come direct from Sydney. It is beautiful, very elegant and fashionable, all lace and taffeta, but she hardly seems to have taken much notice of it since it arrived. I can't tell you the number of times she has said 'don't fuss' or 'I don't want a fuss'. Alice is to be the matron of honour. She is due for a fitting today too so we are going together, as Alice can drive. It's so nice not to have to bother the men to drive us to such appointments. Julia has been learning too, but she isn't as competent as Alice. I feel quite safe with Alice. Catherine can drive too of course but I always feel more comfortable with Alice. She is very thoughtful.

So spare a thought for me on 7th June. Richard will walk Julia down the aisle but I will miss Francis. I'm still not quite used to being a widow. After all I have only just turned 50. I did not expect to be a widow just yet, even though Francis was so much older than me.

I never quite understood what went wrong with our marriage. But there it is I cannot turn back the clock. I can only look to the future and I will be much more settled in my mind when Julia is married.

I will write again to let you know when I plan to travel down to visit you. I promise it will be soon.

Your affectionate cousin

Elizabeth

The morning cloud, which early on looked to threaten rain, cleared quickly on the seventh of June. By ten o'clock the sky was an uninterrupted blue from horizon to horizon.

Yet when Julia woke in the bedroom of her childhood for the very last time, she did not bother to look out of the window to check the weather. Instead she lay for a long time in the single bed that had been her comfort for all that time. Under the window, a neat collection of dolls was almost all that remained to remind her of her childhood, apart from a small shelf of books that she treasured. The contents of her dressing table had changed, over the years, from a clutter of childish hairpins and ribbons to the powders and perfumes of a young woman.

From her bed, she could see the small powder compact which Catherine had chosen for her as a gift on her wedding day. The stylish black enamel case was crisscrossed with fine lines of red and gold. The loose pink powder was held in place by a small piece of rigid net. On top of that sat a delicate powder puff. A small mirror was fixed inside the lid. Catherine's choice of gift had, as always, been impeccable.

A jewellery box, as yet unopened, sat waiting for the moment she would finish dressing for the church. It contained a gift from her mother. Would she wear it? Or would she spurn this final act of conciliation?

She turned her head to look at her dress and veil. She noticed how the cowl neckline hung quite limply and the taffeta of the wide overskirt that formed her train was beginning to show signs of crushing. She had chosen a short veil, cut down from her mother's wedding veil, to complete her dress.

So that was the 'something old', she insisted, when other items were pressed on her. Something new, of course, was the dress; something borrowed was the bracelet that William had given Alice on their first wedding anniversary; something blue? There had been an argument about this, but finally some tiny blue flowers were to be added to her bouquet.

Just as she was about to get out of bed, her mother knocked and entered the room in what seemed like one continuous movement. As she sat on the bed, Julia remembered an entirely different occasion when her mother had barged straight into her room. She tried to shake the memory, but for a few moments it stayed lodged firmly in her mind. It was an unbidden memory, buried in the deep recesses of her mind; a memory that on this day, of all days, Julia did not want to recall.

'You look pale, Julia, are you all right?'

There was a look of genuine concern on Elizabeth Belleville's face for just a moment, but she did not wait for her daughter's reply.

'You'll have to get up soon. The kitchen is preparing a tray for you. You must eat something. The hairdresser will be here in an hour. She is bringing your bouquet with her.'

Her mother paused, as if mentally ticking off the things that still had to be done.

'I still think it would have been easier to stay in town,' she said. She shrugged her shoulders knowing that battle had already been fought and lost.

'I wanted to spend my last night as a single woman, here, at home, at Prior Park,' Julia said quietly.

'Well, we need to make sure we leave in plenty of time, that's all I can say.'

'I know, Mother, I know.'

There was a small hint of exasperation in Julia's voice. How could I not know, she thought, how could I not know that it will take an hour to drive to the church? But she did not say it.

'I've arranged for Alice to get dressed early and then she will help you with your dress.'

Julia merely nodded. It had all been said before, endlessly. She hated the fuss.

Catherine and Richard stood together in the hallway, waiting patiently for Julia and Alice to emerge from Julia's bedroom.

'Do you wish our wedding had been more like this?'

She took his meaning. The household had been a hive of activity for days.

'Perhaps, it would have been nice,' she said, somewhat dismissively. What was the point in looking back. There was no way to change the past now.

'I think there will certainly be a lot of people at the wedding I don't know,' she said.

'That doesn't matter. I don't know that many of them would be of interest to you anyway,' he said.

'Of interest? What do you mean?' She was puzzled by his statement.

'Well, they'll be country folk of limited horizons and equally limited imaginations,' he said, by way of an inadequate explanation.

'Actually, I don't think you are altogether right there. Alice introduced me to Jane Warner the other day. She seems a very cultured woman, although a frustrated one. I imagine she'll be there.'

Richard could not resist asking the obvious question.

'Frustrated you say. Why do you think that?'

Catherine shrugged her shoulders.

'Oh, it was something that Alice said, about how she thought that Jane had hoped to broaden her husband's interests but she's met with little success apparently. According to Alice, it was a rushed marriage because she thought she was pregnant but it turned out she wasn't. She has had a baby subsequently though as you no doubt know.'

This was new and startling information to Richard and he could not resist the urge to delve further.

'How does Alice know all this? I didn't know Alice was particularly friendly with her.'

Catherine smiled, as if Richard should have known the question was completely unnecessary.

'You must know Alice is one of those people that everyone confides in eventually. She's nice, she's reliable, and she isn't competitive. Heaven's she doesn't need to be. After all, with the exception of you, she has made the best marriage in the whole district in marrying your brother. She has status and is sought after.'

This was all news to Richard, who had seen his brother's wife as a compliant and undemanding woman with whom he almost never had a conversation except about the minor issues of everyday life in the household. If there was something not quite right about the domestic arrangements, he had learned quickly to mention it to Alice and it would be fixed without fuss. He appreciated this part of her character, but he did not bother to consider how she was received in the world beyond Prior Park.

'You know she has taken the role at Prior Park that should be yours?' he said.

'I know, Richard. I did take everything in hand at Christmas time when she was still recovering from the birth of her baby but now she's in full command again. I can't be bothered disputing the ground with her. Let her do it.'

It seemed an odd time to have the conversation they had both been avoiding since Catherine returned from England.

'You're not really settling here are you?' Richard asked finally, but in a low voice so that no one would overhear.

She did not answer him directly but instead posed her own question.

'I could ask you the same. Are you settled here? Wouldn't you like to get away and live somewhere else? You're travelling more now for business than ever. Wouldn't it make sense to move south?'

'Do we have to have this conversation now? Prior Park is my birthright as much as it is William's. I can't just walk out on it.'

Catherine persisted.

'I'm not asking you to walk out on it. Just to consider it a place you visit from time to time, rather than live in.'

He did not answer. Just then, Julia appeared at the top of the stairs, with Alice fussing over her train.

'We'll talk about it later, I promise,' he said, grateful for the appearance of the bride.

'We will indeed,' Catherine said. 'We will indeed.'

Now the time Julia dreaded most had come. With some difficulty, for her dress made movement awkward, Julia turned towards James.

The cathedral was silent. She could hear his voice clearly, saying the familiar words:

I, James Stewart Fitzroy, take thee, Julia Elizabeth Belleville, for my lawfully wedded wife. To have and to hold from this day forward; for better, for worse, for richer, for poorer, in sickness and in health, to love and to cherish, till death us do part; according to God's holy law .....

She felt a wave of panic rising in her. She knew it would be her turn soon. Could she take James's hand as he had taken hers, and say those words and mean them? She held her breath, desperate to calm herself. Up until this very moment, it had all seemed possible. Her hands began to shake almost uncontrollably such that his grip became stronger. He smiled at her encouragingly, mistaking her panic for the natural nervousness of a bride.

Then it was her turn. Her words were barely audible. Her mouth was dry. She murmured the words unconvincingly but no one told her to speak up. Alice put a comforting hand on her back.

Then James was holding the ring above the fourth finger of her left hand. His words echoed in her mind.

With this ring, I thee wed; with my body I thee worship and with all my worldly goods I thee endow ....

Suddenly, a small nervous shiver swept through her body. How can I get through this? How can I get through this? It was the one thought that began to go through her mind on what seemed like a continuous loop. How can I share this man's bed, knowing my heart belongs, forever, to someone else?

Now she heard the Minister say the final words ... *bless, preserve and keep you*. Was it almost over? She tried to bring her mind back to the present, to concentrate. But all she could see was Philippe's face in her mind. All she could feel was the agony of her daughter being taken from her.

She felt a slight but insistent pressure on her elbow. It was time to sign the register, James whispered. She nodded vaguely and tried to smile but her lips refused to form the required shape.

It was Alice's arm around her waist that finally brought her back to the present.

'Are you all right, Julia, you look very pale?' she whispered.

She was grateful for Alice's intervention. It had come just in time.

'I'm all right, thank you. It's just a bit hot in here,' she replied, by way of explanation.

For the last time, she signed her name Julia Belleville. James signed his name with a flourish. William and Alice added their names as witnesses.

In a loud authoritative voice, the Minister commanded the congregation to rise and greet Mr and Mrs James Fitzroy.

As they reached the end of the aisle, the cathedral bells began to peal loudly, as if proclaiming an important event.

For James Fitzroy, it was the achievement of an ambition that he had thought would elude him. Now, smiling broadly, he was keen to share his pride in his beautiful wife. He slipped his arm around her waist and kissed her lightly on the lips, which drew a ripple of applause and approving murmurs from the crowd gathered around them.

Now she knew she could not back away from him. This was his right as her husband. He owned her, body and soul. At least that is what it seemed like to her.

Just for a moment she closed her eyes, as if on opening them again, she would be waking from a dream, and she would find that, after all, she was still Julia Belleville.

Instead, she saw the smiling crowd around them and beside her, Alice, and beside James, William, both looking happy and contented. Her mother, as she expected, was taking control of everyone.

In that moment, she resolved to put the past behind her, finally. Would she succeed in that resolve? She did not know. It seemed possible then, she was to remember. On that bright sunny winter's day, it seemed possible.

It was only later, as they lay together for the first time as husband and wife, that she understood the depth of her despair. James was now her husband and her lover but he was not the lover she yearned for with every fibre of her being. But he did not know this.

He revelled in the conquest of her beautiful body. For him there was no disappointment, only triumph. He had won her and that was all that mattered. Julia Belleville was now his wife and would bear his children. She was his, and his alone. For him, victory was sweet and complete.

In the darkness as he lay sleeping she turned her head away from him. A single tear trickled down her cheek. Then she felt him stir as his arms reach out for her again. She closed her eyes. She felt his lips on the back of her neck, his hands roaming at will over her body.

'I love you,' he said.

'I love you too,' she replied, but she knew, within the deepest part of her soul, she had lied to him and she would go on lying to him for the rest of her life.

To be continued ...

The Belleville family series

BOOK 2
To Love, Honour & Betray (2017)

BOOK 3
Return to Prior Park (2019)

BOOK 4
Heirs and Successors (2023)

For more information, go to
www.jmarymasters.com

JULIA'S STORY